Carmen Reid is the bestselling author of, most recently, *The Personal Shopper* and *Late Night Shopping*, also starring Annie Valentine.

She has worked as a newspaper journalist and columnist, but now writes fiction full-time. Carmen also writes a series for teen readers, *Secrets at St Judes*. She lives in Glasgow, Scotland with her husband and two children.

For more information on Carmen Reid and her books visit her website at www.carmenreid.com

HOW NOT TO SHOP

Carmen Reid

CORGI BOOKS

TRANSWORLD PUBLISHERS
61–63 Uxbridge Road, London W5 5SA
A Random House Group Company
www.rbooks.co.uk

HOW NOT TO SHOP
A CORGI BOOK: 9780552158855

First publication in Great Britain
Corgi edition published 2009

Addresses for Random House Group Ltd companies outside the UK
can be found at: www.randomhouse.co.uk
The Random House Group Ltd Reg. No. 954009

The Random House Group Limited supports The Forest Stewardship
Council (FSC), the leading international forest certification organisation.
All our titles that are printed on Greenpeace approved FSC certified paper
carry the FSC logo. Our paper procurement policy can
be found at www.rbooks.co.uk/environment

Typeset in 11/14pt Palatino by
Kestrel Data, Exeter, Devon.
Printed in the UK by
Cox & Wyman, Reading, RG1 8EX.

2 4 6 8 10 9 7 5 3 1

HOW NOT TO SHOP

Chapter One

Dr Yasmin 'cosmetologist' at work:

White cotton coat (medical suppliers)
White gauze mask (same)
Black and pink silk high-collared dress
(Alexander McQueen)
Pink peep-toe slingback heels (Christian Louboutin)
Total est. cost: £960

'And how does that feel now?'

'Just hold nice and still, this is going to be a little uncomfortable.'

Annie's heart began to pound. When a straight-backed professional in a pristine white coat, paper mask and latex gloves, carrying a syringe, tells you something's going to be 'a little uncomfortable', you know it's going to hurt like . . .

'Nice and still,' the outrageously expensive Harley Street 'cosmetologist' repeated as Annie instinctively nudged her face away from the tip of the needle.

Then *yow!!* the point was in and she could feel her first ever hit of Botox coursing coolly into the offending frown lines between her eyebrows.

Ouch! Ouch! Ouch! It hurt. Why had she not been told how much it hurt? And the 'Doctor', though really she was probably just a souped-up dental nurse with a very snazzy client list, was going to do her brow lines next. There was even less skin up there on her forehead. That would really sting.

Dr Yasmin's assistant pressed a tissue to the side of Annie's face to catch the tears of pain slipping silently from her eyes.

To take her mind from this horror, Annie let her eyes roll towards the corner of the room, where four large shopping bags were stacked in a fat heap against a chair.

She hadn't wanted to let those bags out of her sight and now, just stealing a quick glance at them helped to soothe her. Those four bulging carriers represented something very important. Crucial. Fundamental. Those four glossy bags symbolized the end of her old career and the beginning of a whole shiny, brand new phase.

A veteran of self-improvement, Annie Valentine was about to move on and up in the biggest way imaginable. She had worked in London's most glamorous, most high-end fashion emporium, The Store, for nine whole years and now she was leaving.

She had been The Store's top, best known and most trusted personal shopper. She had shopped for, styled and made over women from every walk of life. In short, there was nothing about fashion or buying clothes that Annie didn't know. In several swift minutes, Annie could size you up from head to toe and teach you more about what shapes, sizes, colours and styles you should be wearing than all that time spent schlepping hopelessly in and out of changing rooms could possibly have done.

Working for The Store had transformed her over the years too. The hair in her tight, high ponytail had become increasingly blonde. The slightly too short and slightly too curvy figure had been lifted and lengthened with expensive high heels, ramrod posture and a hefty dose of Lycra in all the right places. Now that she was in her . . . erm . . . late-thirties, she was at Dr Yasmin's because she wasn't going to let some pesky little frown lines give the game away.

Annie knew she was leaving more than just a job. Over those nine years, The Store had become her second home. When she'd lost her husband, she'd been able to lose herself in The Store; when she'd struggled to meet the school fees for her two children, her clients from The Store had rallied round to give her extra out-of-hours work. Even the new man in her life, Ed, though he understood not one shred about fashion, understood completely the importance of The Store in Annie's life.

But she was about to leave! Leave her job and her monthly commission (not to mention her regular bonuses for best saleswoman) and her hugely tempting staff discount (the kind of discount which meant there were labels she could previously only have dreamed about hanging in her wardrobe) and the staff who had become best friends.

Annie was about to walk away from it all because she had been offered the perhaps once in a lifetime chance to become a real, live TV STAR. Oh yes! She still had to pinch herself to believe it.

After two auditions and a screen test, finally, the call had come. Now Annie and her ridiculously wealthy client-turned-friend, Svetlana Wisneski, were going to be the makeover gurus on a new Channel Five show, *Wonder Women*.

Well, OK, to be honest, Annie wasn't wildly enthusiastic about the series name either, but maybe there was still time for a rethink.

The shopping bags in the corner of Dr Yasmin's office contained the framework of the TV presenter wardrobe Annie had bought for herself today in a six-hour non-stop retail session.

Inside the bags – two from The Store, one from Prada and one from H&M – was the culmination of nine years of shopping expertise.

In expectation of the money she was about to earn, Annie had allowed herself to buy several amazing treasures, like the complicated ankle boots from the best shoemaker in London and the jewelled leather long-lace sandals by inimitable Miu Miu.

Then there were slightly more practical items: scoop-necked tops, beads and bracelets from H&M, a pair of vibrant, stretchy dresses by her favourite American designer and two architectural, nipped-in (whisper it, *Westwood*) jackets.

She'd also chosen sling-backed, red patent pumps for walking briskly from shop to shop with the women she'd be making over, and an extravagant bright blue, creamily soft, Chloé silk shirt.

But the most wonderful purchase of all was the Prada skirt wrapped up in layers of tissue paper as carefully as a museum exhibit. The kind of skirt that you didn't get your hands on just by turning up at the Prada shop and hoping for the best. No way. She'd been on the waiting list for that pleated, crinkled, dip-dyed fashion masterpiece for seven weeks, knowing full well it would fly out of the doors without ever hitting a hanger.

Everything she'd bought was vibrant and colourful because she knew television drank in colour and she suspected that the women she'd be making over would be dressed in the dowdy, sludgy colours of the unconfident or fashion-inexperienced.

The shopping trip had cost . . . well . . . including the Jimmy Choo ankle boots . . . Oh. My. Lord. Just over £4,000. Then the Botox with snazzy Dr Yaz, another £600. Ouch.

Ed had warned her. He'd told her not to get too carried away with the TV presenter preparations until she knew *exactly* how much money she was going to be paid and *exactly* how long the job would go on for. But it had been hard not to get very, very excited. Channel Five! And had the producer, Donnie ('call me Finn') Finnigan, not told her over and over again how much 'potential' he could 'sense' in *Wonder Women*? Had he not bandied about phrases like 'bigger than Trinny and Susannah' and 'Look out, Gok Wan'?

Filming was due to start in just a few weeks, so really she had to have something to wear! Finn was just waiting to 'hear the final details' of 'the commission' and he'd promised to get back to Svetlana and Annie this afternoon. So, just as soon as Dr Yaz had finished with her instruments of torture, Annie was going to meet Svetlana, so that they could be together when the news arrived.

'Come to my house,' Svetlana had drawled on the

phone in her rich and melodious Ukraine-beauty-meets-serious-Mayfair-millions accent.

'Your house?' Annie had echoed with surprise. Although Svetlana had rarely bought so much as a belt without Annie's advice for about six years, this was Annie's first ever invitation to Svetlana's four-storey, prime Belgravia Divorce Settlement.

But they would be working together now. Annie was no longer a member of Svetlana's service personnel: she was on the verge of becoming her colleague, her slightly more equal – her friend, even? It was interesting new territory. At least in the old roles, they'd both known exactly where they were: Svetlana, the ex-wife of two multimillionaires and one billionaire, and Annie her trusted personal shopper . . . in London. Obviously there was another personal shopper in Paris, one in New York and one a little under-used in Moscow. ('Just for fur, she know nothing, bumpkin from Siberia.')

'And how does that feel now?' Dr Yasmin asked cheerfully.

Although the real answer was: Like you're sticking a long, sharp needle into my forehead! Annie managed a more polite, 'Just fine,' as the assistant continued to dab at her trickling tears.

Ed would never approve of what she was doing here. Very sweetly, he always told her he loved her just the way she was. Although, honestly he had no idea. She shuddered to think what she would really look like if she stopped waxing, plucking, highlighting, manicuring, applying make-up and dressing with care and concentration.

If he ever found out about the Botox and the shopping spree, he'd have one of his rare, but nevertheless unpleasant, freak-outs. But there was no need for him to find out, was there? She kept her own severely tested credit cards well away from his gaze and stored the bills carefully on-line. Plus, apparently men never, ever noticed when you'd had Botox. This was something she was doing, on Svetlana's recommendation, for the searching gaze of the small screen.

At last, the syringeing was over and Annie was allowed to sit up and survey the results in the mirror.

'Now, it may look a little puffy or bruised over the next few days and I always warn my clients . . .' the doctor began.

Oh no, she was going to do the warning bit again and Annie had tried so hard to blank it out the first time: partial paralysis, cardiac arrest, stroke, blah, blah . . .

But no, the doctor had new information. 'It may be hard to express anger, shock or intense emotion. You may have to tell people how you are feeling,' she said.

'Right.' Annie nodded, looking fixedly at her forehead. The lines had gone! Totally gone! Erased! This was amazing! She was coming back here every three months just as soon as her TV salary was hot in her hands. The doctor had performed nothing short of a miracle.

'That is brilliant, thank you!' she exclaimed, trying to give the doctor a delighted smile, but feeling a dull tug from the top of her head as her forehead tried, but failed, to move with her expression.

'That feels strange,' she added.

'Yes, it takes a little time, but you get used to it.'

Dr Yasmin removed her paper mask and gave a careful, lower face only smile which Annie at once understood.

When she was back in reception paying her hefty bill,

Annie's mobile began to buzz. She checked the screen as she picked it up, wondering if it was her daughter Lana, 16, making an after-school phone call because she'd run out of pocket money, or her son, Owen, 12, making an after-school phone call because he'd run out of food.

No. It was Ed.

Annie answered, then wished she hadn't, slightly panicked that somehow he would be able to tell over the phone that she'd spent close to five grand on her ever-expanding wardrobe and her newly flattened face.

'Annie?' Ed asked.

'Hello, babes!' she replied. 'Good day at school?'

Ed taught at her children's school. Despite her previous conviction that she would never, ever find another good man no matter where in the world she looked, as it happened, she'd not had to look far. She'd just had to look closely, many, many times, before she'd finally spotted him.

'Fine,' he replied.

Before he could say anything else, she rattled off: 'Did you get the dry cleaning?'

'Yes.'

'And the cat food? And post the parcel for me?'

'Yup to both.'

'And write out the cheque for Lana's tennis thing?'

'Yes, ma'am,' he joked.

'Thank you, you're very good.'

'Very, very good,' he reminded her. 'Bet you've not done anything about the Jeep windscreen, have you?'

Oh brother.

The large, ramshackle black Jeep in which she still bowled around London had a serious windscreen chip.

14

Her name was on the insurance policy, so she was supposed to have phoned to sort this out.

'Sorry, I'll try and remember that,' she told him.

'Where are you anyway?' he asked. 'When are you coming home? And what would you like to eat?'

'Whatever you're making,' she suggested. 'It's always good. I'm going to be out a bit longer, Svetlana wants to see me at her house, in Mayfair! And we're expecting the call, you know, from the TV producer.'

'Ooh! The money call?'

'Here's hoping.'

'I have my early retirement plans all worked out,' Ed teased.

'Am I in them?'

'Oh yeah, don't worry, you'll be invited onto the yacht for a little cruise once in a while. When you can take time out from your hectic TV schedule.'

'That's big of you! And you all bronzed and buff, sailing your boat about all year long . . .'

'Yup, a total Annie magnet.'

'Nice . . .' Annie thought about that for a little moment, but then had to leave the yacht and return to reality. 'And how is everyone else?' she asked.

'They're fine,' Ed replied. 'Lana's still at school, working on something until six, then she's here for something to eat, then she's going to Greta's to talk about their project, allegedly. Owen's practising his violin for a bit then I'm taking him to Scouts.'

Family life was relentless. 'Are you OK doing all that?' She felt guilty now. 'I thought there was something you wanted to go and see?'

Ed was a music teacher, a musician and an avid

concert-goer. For Ed, going to a concert, gig or general thrash about with instruments was his relaxation time; if he didn't do it several times a week, he got grumpy.

'No, no I'm fine,' he insisted, 'honestly. Head off to Mayfair. Go meet The Ukrainian.'

Outside Dr Yasmin's surgery, Annie flagged down a cab. Extravagant, but she couldn't take the bus, could she? Not with a Prada shopping bag and a face full of Botox.

Plus, if she saved some time with a cab now, she might make it home while Ed was still out dropping Owen at Scouts. That way, Annie would be able to haul her four carrier bags' worth of booty upstairs and into her office without having to answer any awkward questions.

She glanced at her watch . . . yes, but she would have to hurry. At the thought of what Finn was going to tell them within the hour, her stomach gave a lurch.

Chapter Two

White Lycra catsuit (Move Dancewear)
Gold and diamond watch (Cartier)
One-carat diamond earrings (second husband)
Three-carat diamond and ruby ring (third husband)
Total est. cost £197,600

'Maybe you have to come train with me . . .'

From Harley Street to Mayfair was a twenty-minute taxi journey through some of the very smartest streets in London. Past the flagship stores of Oxford Street, down by the swanky car showrooms of Park Lane and into streets of the finest, most fabulous red-brick houses London had to offer.

Quiet streets where the black railings were polished to a shine, where front doors were as dark and glossy as patent leather and even the plants and flowers in the window-boxes looked manicured.

Then there were the pedestrians. Were security guards

posted on the edge of Mayfair to stop people from coming in unless they'd styled and highlighted their hair, changed into one of this season's designer outfits and bought a very, very expensive bag?

The cab driver pulled up in front of a house so impressive that Annie double-checked she had the right number before she dared to ring the bell.

Yes, it was definitely number 7, according to the piece of paper she'd tucked into the back of her big leather Filofax. Oh good grief, she was going to have to update, she really would have to put away the leather and paper organizer and make another foray into the world of digital data. Surely she could handle a BlackBerry now, couldn't she? They even came in pink and she would back everything up straight away, so there wouldn't be another total wipeout trauma like back in the days of her early Palm Pilot.

When the shiny black door opened, a *maid*, a real, live maid – small and dainty, possibly Filipino – in a black dress with a white apron on top, greeted her.

'Ms Valentine?' the maid asked with a smile, 'Ms Wisneski is expecting you. Please to come in and be comfortable with us.'

'Thank you,' Annie said and gave the maid as much of a smile as the fresh Botox would allow.

Still weighed down with her four bulging bags, Annie bustled into the hallway where she had to stop and gawp.

Walls had obviously been removed and skylights inserted. Clever, very expensive architects had been at work. Although Annie had stepped in through the door of a Victorian red-brick house, she was now standing in a dazzling white, modernist creation. And the paintings!

They looked familiar, as in possibly-seen-on-the-walls-of-a-gallery-before familiar.

Svetlana – tall, lusciously beauty-queen-gorgeous and only admitting to 'thirty-something' – had been married three times so far, to increasingly wealthy men who had either died, or left her for increasingly younger and more beautiful women. At the end of her third marriage, she'd hired her own barrister and been to the divorce courts to claim an eight-figure settlement which the *Daily Mail* had headlined: 'Guzzling ex-wife taps gas baron's fortune.' It had earned her an at-home photo shoot in *OK!* magazine and plenty of press coverage ever since.

After all, she was still the mother of Igor Wisneski's two sons. And the little boys (aged nine and seven) were the only direct heirs to a staggering fortune.

Svetlana's divorce court battle had brought about another happy result. She was now engaged to Harry Roscoff, the recently divorced (entirely Svetlana's fault) QC who had taken on her case and fought it so successfully. Fourth time around, Svetlana's marriage was going to be very different. Harry had already insisted she take independent legal advice to ensure that no matter how this relationship turned out, she would keep all her hard-won assets and never be a penniless ex-wife again.

'Not that I am ever going to leave you, my darling,' he'd insisted. 'But if you leave me, you can take the lot. My life won't be worth living anyway.'

This time, despite the impending wedding, Svetlana wasn't moving and she definitely wasn't selling. Her Mayfair home was her security. Harry was coming to live with her.

'You think I go through all that marrying for nothing?' she'd asked Annie.

'Why get married again?' Annie had wanted to know. 'If Harry's your husband, then one day he can claim against your estate.'

'No. We have contract,' she'd insisted, before adding with her most charming smile, 'I love veddings! I love to be bride!'

Just like its owner, the Divorce Settlement house was drop dead beautiful, extremely high maintenance and flawlessly tasteful . . . if a touch extravagant. Annie's eye travelled to the staircase where the original wooden steps and banisters had been replaced with a wrought iron and marble installation.

'Ms Wisneski is upstairs with her trainer,' the maid explained.

'Oh, right,' Annie tried out another smile. 'Shall I wait somewhere until she's finished?'

'No, no,' the maid insisted, 'she say to come up and visit her.'

So Annie began to follow the little woman up the stairs, their footsteps ringing out against the polished grey marble.

The maid opened a door on the first floor and announced Annie's presence. 'Miss Valentine to be visiting with you Miss Wisneski.'

As Annie took in the huge white room, decked out with mats, mirrors and an elaborate metal weights machine which looked like a torture rack, Svetlana gushed 'Annnnnnah!' enthusiastically. She didn't come over to make her usual greeting of a rapid fire of Ukrainian kisses, but then, she was bent over backwards in the crab position with her head hanging upside down.

'Hello my love,' was Annie's cheerful greeting, 'how's it going?'

'Good!' Svetlana insisted, with some effort. 'Lisa is just vorking on my abs. I pay her to keep them as strong as a dancer's.' She slapped her stomach, which was so flat and so firm it sounded as if she'd smacked her hand against the wall.

'And twenty-six . . . twenty-eight . . . thirty and up,' Lisa barked. She was a tiny blonde with the kind of taut physique only seen on dedicated fitness fanatics like Madonna or Paula Radcliffe.

Svetlana, dressed in a shiny white catsuit, which displayed every single one of the ripples, nipples and breathtaking curves that had turned her into Miss Ukraine and many other Mrs since then, bounced up onto her feet.

'And plié,' Lisa instructed.

Obediently, Svetlana placed her heels together, toes turned out and began bending and straightening her legs elegantly. Only when she'd done about forty or so did there seem to be even the tiniest display of effort.

Annie watched in open admiration. She knew perfectly well she'd struggle to do even one of these pliés, let alone be counting towards one hundred.

'You've been shopping!' Svetlana pointed at Annie's bags, without breaking the rhythm of her bends.

'Yeah!' Annie set the carriers down and began to pull things out eagerly. There was a real possibility she was going to look like a blimp on TV next to Svetlana, but at least she'd be an incredibly well-dressed blimp.

'Yes! Oh yes! I love it,' Svetlana enthused as Annie showed her a dress, then the boots and finally the skirt.

Meanwhile, Lisa kept up her flow of strict instructions and Svetlana began to lift dinky dumb-bells in hundreds of different directions to give her arms and back the seriously sexy definition that Annie had in the past urged her to show off with strapless Valentino and backless Armani dresses.

'And my head,' Annie pointed to her frozen forehead: 'have you noticed?'

'I see now,' Svetlana said, looking closely. 'You are going to be vonderful on screen – ' she gave a little clap of excitement – 'but maybe you have to come train with me and Lisa, I heard the camera puts on ten pounds.'

'Oh,' Annie said, a little taken aback. Secretly, she'd been hoping her brand new pair of extra-firm Magic Knickers would see to the meaty little spare tyre which was firmly welded to her middle.

'Lisa not mind, as long as I make sure her Christmas bonus is good. Very good,' Svetlana added, shooting Lisa a wink.

Lisa turned to Annie and looked her up and down in an entirely uncomplimentary way. The idea of an extra client tagging along on training sessions was clearly not to her liking.

'Well, I'd have to assess her,' Lisa said, 'and do a physical, first. That would be extra.'

'Oh Lisa!' Svetlana exclaimed. 'With Lisa everything is extra.'

'I've got a long waiting list,' Lisa said and then, giving Annie another hyper-critical look, added: 'and I only work with the dedicated.'

They were spared any further investigation of the Annie working out with Svetlana nightmare scenario by the loud bleeping of Svetlana's phone.

Well, at least, Annie assumed that's what the tiny sparkling piece of chrome technology was that Svetlana swept up and clamped quickly to her ear.

'Hello, Svetlana speaking . . . oh Finn! How vonderful to hear from you. Yes, Annie is right here.'

At the flick of a switch, Annie could now hear Finn too.

All of a sudden, she didn't seem to be able to breathe. This was too big. It felt as if too much depended on this one phone call.

'Great news, girls!' he began in his tone of non-stop positivity. 'The deals have finally been signed. Phew! We're all set. We're definitely going ahead with a six-part series of *Wonder Women*. It's going to air first on the Home Sweet Home channel.'

Svetlana and Annie glanced at each other in surprise. Home Sweet Home? Neither of them had even heard of it before.

'Vhat's this?' Svetlana interrupted. 'Zis not Channel Five.'

'Erm . . . no, I know,' Finn had to admit, 'it's one of the smaller digitals. But it's very up and coming and I think it has just the right following for this show,' he sounded all brimful of enthusiasm again. 'We are so confident this will be bought up by one of the big channels. Home Sweet Home is just the start! So very, very good news, girls. Congratulations. Woohoo!' he added.

Annie and Svetlana couldn't help smiling at each other.

'Now, just one little thing . . .' Finn continued. 'They weren't happy with us using total unknowns, so we do have to bring in a slightly bigger name to co-present.'

Annie could feel the panicky beat of her heart. Was that good? Was that bad? She had no idea. So, it wouldn't be just her and Svetlana, then . . . there would be someone else.

'Do you know Miss Marlise?' Finn asked.

While Svetlana shook her head, an image of a domineering, bossy, sourpuss popped into Annie's mind. Miss Marlise? Hadn't she been in some programme that the children . . . ?

'From *The Apprentice*?' Finn prompted.

Oh good grief! Annie remembered her. She'd been awful. A total witch.

'Well, she's on board,' Finn continued, 'so it's all systems go, we just need you to sign up for your deals and we can start researching, then shooting, ASAP.'

'So vhat are you going to pay us?' Svetlana asked bluntly, although she'd already told Annie she would do this for free because she had always, always, ever since she'd crossed the Miss World podium in a silver spangled bikini, wanted to be on television.

'Well . . . erm . . . obviously Miss Marlise is a name and has sucked up a big chunk of our presenters budget,' Finn began, slightly hesitantly now, 'and it's only on Home Sweet Home channel at the moment. But stick with me, girls, because when it's bought up by a bigger channel there will be much more money in the kitty for all of us.'

Annie realized her nails were digging into her palms. This did not sound good. This was not going to be the big pay cheque she was expecting, was it? Never mind, she told herself, it was a start; sometimes you had to step back to step up.

'So,' Finn paused for breath, 'right. OK, for the first six episodes, which will take about three months to complete, we're going to pay you £1,200, per episode . . .'

Annie was doing the maths. Six times £1,200, was only £7,200! That was terrible: that was much, much worse than she'd expected. It was about a quarter of what she'd expected. And she'd given notice on her job!

'Split between you,' Finn added.

Split between us? How could she do three months of work for just £3,600? Annie looked down at her bags. She'd just spent £1,000 more than that.

Despite the paralysed facial muscles and the doctor's warning, Annie managed to roar, 'WHAT?' in a way that perfectly expressed her anger, shock *and* intense emotion.

Chapter Three

Annie's farewell outfit:

*Slinky red knit dress with fabulous neckline and long
sleeves (Vivienne Westwood, with store discount)
Purple patent T-bar heels (Timi Woo, direct from China)
Chunky purple beads (Topshop)
Tiny diamond stud earrings (Tiffany's via Ed)
Sheer red seamed stockings (Topshop)
Total est. cost: £580*

'The show must go on!'

It was two minutes to 9 p.m. and Annie was fiddling. She
was fiddling with the rows of champagne glasses laid out
on the trestle table in the personal shopping suite. She
was twitching the pink tablecloth to make sure it was
hanging perfectly. She was making tiny alterations to the
way the champagne bottles were facing.

This was it. This was definitely it.

After nine years, she was about to leave The Store
for good. The glossy and glamorous, luxuriously high

fashion department store in London's Knightsbridge that she had been lucky enough to call her workplace for all this time. Well, yes, OK, she had left it once before, but that had been an unfair dismissal and she'd come back within months.

This was *really* leaving. This was exiting in a blaze of glory. For good. For ever.

She cast her eyes about the richly carpeted suite with its pink velvet curtains and bright pink sofas. There would be no more hanging out here with her clients, old and new. No more gazing critically into those full length mirrors with them, no more delving through the racks of wonderful, wonderful clothes brought up from the glittering white and glass floors of dazzling fashion.

There was no doubt in Annie's mind that almost as much as the people here, she was going to miss the clothes. Not to mention the staff discount which had let her build a vividly colourful and totally eclectic wardrobe. From Prada to Primark, from Alexander McQueen to Zara, her wardrobe (now stretched across *three* wardrobes, plus all the boxes and bags in the spare room) covered the entire spectrum.

Over in one corner of the suite was the little cubicle which had served her as an office for all this time. She'd already unplugged her laptop and packed it away in its case. She'd taken down the family snaps from her walls, heaved a huge collection of fashion magazines into the recycling bin and packed up all the assorted belongings that had accumulated in her desk drawers over the years: lost buttons, snagged stockings, pins, pens, badges, Polaroids of customers, thank-you letters from delighted clients.

It had taken nearly an hour, and plenty of quiet tears, to get through it all. Now, at 9 p.m. exactly, The Store was shutting its doors for the night and the staff, along with Annie's family and friends, were coming up to the suite to drink her health and wish her well.

'You all right there, my love?' Paula, her beautiful, lean, black, soon to be ex-assistant, called out as she sped into the room on teetering heels with an enormous platter of canapés in her arms.

'Yeah, definitely!' Annie tried to chirp back brightly, but it didn't sound quite convincing.

Paula set down the canapés, then swooped over and treated Annie to a long-limbed hug.

'I'm gutted that you're leaving us,' Paula told her. 'I'd be insulted if you weren't upset, girl. But it's *so* great for you. You're going to be on the telly. You're going to be a star! From now on the Annie Valentine touch isn't just for the ladies who can afford to shop here, it's for everyone!'

Well, everyone who watches the Home Sweet Home Channel, which, by the way, I hadn't even heard of until yesterday, Annie thought.

With a lump building in her throat, she told Paula, 'That is so sweet, babes, that is just so sweet,' and hugged her tight.

'Let's take a look at you,' Paula said, stepping back to scrutinize the woman who had been her mentor.

Annie's hair was tied up in its trademark high ponytail. Her lightly tanned face with hazel eyes, small features and ready smile looked bright and alert. Paula thought this had everything to do with Annie's session down on the cosmetics floor with the very talented girl at the Bobbi Brown counter. She didn't know about the Botox.

'You look gorgeous,' Paula was quick to compliment her. 'You're rockin' the Westwood. On fire.'

The red dress, which pulled and nipped, plumped and tucked in all the right places on Annie's bosomy curves, wasn't new. It was a tried and trusted favourite which she knew wouldn't let her down.

As she'd always tell her clients, 'Big, nerve-racking events are not the best time to try out new outfits. You're safer wearing something that you've worn before and can rely on. Why do you think brides are always so anxious?'

'God save the Queen!' Annie joked, which was her and Paula's code for Westwood. ('God save the Queens' meant Dolce and Gabbana.)

'Long live the Queen,' Paula added.

'I'm really, *really* going to miss my staff discount,' Annie admitted with a sigh.

'Annie Valentine, I bet you are,' Nadine, one of the shop assistants, who was just entering the suite, had to agree.

She was leading in a posse of about ten others, so the party was definitely about to start.

'She won't need a staff discount,' Dale from Menswear countered, 'will you my love?' He came and wrapped his arms round Annie's waist. 'She's going to TV, she's going to be rich! We'll be reading about her in *heat* magazine and buying her books at Christmas, won't we, doll?'

Annie felt a lurching, sick feeling in the pit of her stomach. If only they knew how much she was giving up. She felt she was risking everything for just the vaguest chance at small screen glory.

To excited whoops, a cork flew from a champagne

bottle. Glasses were passed around, filled and clinked together.

Annie could see Geoff and the two ladies from Accounts coming in; they'd been in the pub already, waiting for kick-off. Now there was Dinah, Annie's sister, hesitantly entering the room.

But still no sign of Ed and her children, or her best friend Connor, or her boss, Helena Montserrat.

Dinah, Annie's younger sister – she also had an older one, Nic – was a very important person in her life. She lived close by in north London, with her husband Bryan and daughter Billie. She was a more anxious and less impulsive person than Annie, who kindly did a lot of Annie's worrying for her, but she was a close confidante and supporter in every twist and turn of Annie's life.

'Hey you!' Dinah called out and gave a little wave. A much more arty and experimental dresser than her big sis, she was wearing something vibrantly lilac and blue-green from the latest Warehouse collection. Whereas Annie liked labels and long-lasting 'key pieces', Dinah liked cheap, chain store or, even better, second-hand fashion.

'Dinah!' Annie said, and wrapped her arms round her sister, 'I'm so glad you could come!'

'Wouldn't have missed it for anything,' Dinah assured her. 'Ed and the kids here yet?'

'No, but I'm sure they're on their way.'

'What about the Mung Bean?' This was their current nickname for Connor, their actor friend. Connor had recently moved to LA, because according to his new US agent he was 'totally hot, right here, right now' and he had to capitalize on it. According to Connor's reports, living in LA had not allowed him to carry on the easygoing, boozy lifestyle he'd enjoyed as an actor in London. No. Living in LA seemed to involve endless meetings, eating only tofu and mung beans and sweating it out with a personal trainer for five hours a day, which was all so vain and ridiculous that Annie and Dinah saw it as their duty to tease him at every possible opportunity. As Connor was in London for four days – for an audition, not just Annie's party – now was their chance.

'So is the whole contract thing sorted out then?' Dinah asked her sister in a low voice, but meeting her eyes.

'Oh!' Annie exclaimed, not wanting to talk about it here.

'The deal?' Dinah pressed: 'did you get what you were looking for?'

'Babes, I got enough to keep a squirrel in nuts and that's all I'm saying about it,' came Annie's fierce reply.

'Oh no!' Dinah whispered, 'is it bad?'

'It's the worst,' Annie whispered back.

'What are you going to do?'

But it was too late, Annie was being swooped on from all sides. So many people to talk to. Annie felt as if she was being passed from group to group like the parcel at a children's party.

She caught sight of Ed and her children in a far corner, talking to Dinah and Paula, but it was a few minutes before she could break away from the group she was with and get over to them.

'You all look gorgeous!' she cried. 'You've made such a fantastic effort for me.'

Owen, who had adopted the internationally accepted 'smart' outfit of a 12-year-old – ironed shirt, ironed chinos, passably clean Converses – was the first to get a hug. He accepted it without complaint, even though his mum had ruffled the hair he'd carefully smoothed over to one side.

Lana was kissed on the cheek, then Annie took a moment to admire her new blue dress. Although it was worn with a self-conscious teenage slouch and some badly applied eyeliner, to Annie, Lana still looked beautiful.

Ed had made a huge effort. Somehow, he'd brought his unruly mop of hair under control and he'd replaced his usual baggy, tweedy, woolly look with the stylish jacket, shirt and tie that Annie had picked out for him long before she'd even known she was in love with him.

'Hey you,' she said softly, brushing his lips for hello, 'you look seriously cute.'

He smelled good too.

'Aha,' he agreed, 'I had to live up to your dress.' He ran a hand down her back.

'Total Annie magnet. It's OK, go out there and mingle. We'll be fine. We know we get you back at the end of the evening.'

'Have you seen the snacks?' Owen pointed to the trestle table, which was now covered with food. 'Awesome!'

Suddenly Annie's face – Bobbi Brown, Botox and all – was buried in the amply warm and friendly bosom of Delia, the second floor's cleaning lady.

'Annie Valentine,' she boomed in English accented with deepest Jamaican, 'what's I goin' to do witout choo? If you be needing any cleaning on them fancy TV places, you let Delia know right away, you hear? I don't think Mr Geoff here is goin to mind me saying that, are you?' Delia gestured to the head of personnel. 'If there was a job for him on TV, he'd be the first to go, wouldn't choo Mr Geoff?'

Geoff obliged with a loud laugh.

Annie felt the lurch of unease again. This was supposed to be her big, big moment. The sort of exit from the everyday that everyone dreamed of making. All these people that she'd worked with for so long were so excited for her, so pleased for her and really, she was walking off into nothing. Into £3,600 for a digital channel. Some show no-one would ever hear about. She felt as if she should press pause on this party or at least put out the word that she might be coming back. *Think of this as temporary,* she wanted to go around the room saying: *it might not work out!*

'Oooooh!' one of the floor assistants exclaimed with excitement, 'isn't that Connor McCabe over there?'

Annie turned to catch her first glimpse of Connor for several months. It was enough to make the sick feeling recede slightly. Whatever her problems were, Connor usually had a way of cheering her up.

She scrambled through the crowd towards him, but he was already surrounded by a group of fans, shaking hands, or just staring at him with intent, excited looks on their faces. He was a big TV star now and had recently done a movie, so he was really well known. He'd just featured in a double-page spread in *Hello!* for goodness sake!

'Connor!' Annie greeted him, 'you came.'

'Oh yeah, at the sight of you,' he joked, treating her to a bear hug.

'You look fabulous,' she told him, and it was true. Bronzed, buff, dark hair, twinkly movie star eyes and big broad shoulders, teeny tiny waist. He was gorgeousness personified. But oh, so tragically, for the women anyway, he was gay.

'Can I just speak to you for a micro-moment?' Annie asked, holding her thumb and forefinger millimetres apart.

'Yup, where can I put my bag anyway?'

She ushered him slightly away from the buzz of the party and into her tiny office.

'This is so great,' he told her as they crammed into the bare white space together, 'I am so proud of you. A major new development!'

'OK, a little less Hollywood please,' she warned, 'this is me you're talking to now. Not some snazzy producer.' She scanned his face.

'How are you?'

'I'm fine,' he said, smiling reassuringly.

'And Hector?'

'Great,' Connor answered for the partner he'd taken out to LA with him: 'getting even buffer and browner than me.'

'It's fantastic to see you,' Annie couldn't help telling him. 'I miss you. Spend every free minute you have over the next few days at my house. OK?'

Connor nodded his agreement.

'But there is a problem,' Annie went on immediately, knowing she only had a few moments this evening with the one person in her life who knew all about TV. 'It's airing on a tiny digital channel and they've brought in a third presenter. She's a name, so they have to pay her properly and I'm supposed to do this series, the whole series, for £3,600.'

34

Connor's face didn't change. She'd expected him to gasp with astonishment, or at the very least shoot up an eyebrow or two.

'Is there a lot less money in television than I thought?' Annie asked: 'is this something you've not told me? Is working on TV something that only people with a private income can do?'

'No! Don't be silly,' Connor replied, 'but starting salaries are low. Everyone puts up with them because they want their shot at the big time. And that's what you've got to do.' He took hold of her ponytail and ran it smoothly through his hand.

'OK,' he went on, 'have you and Ed got enough to live on for the next few months if you take this job?'

'Ha! I've been trying to work out how we can scrape through . . . maybe just. But *only just.*'

'OK. Scrape,' Connor told her. 'Scrape and work your butt off for the TV company. Something else will come of this. I promise. If the show is great, someone big will buy it. If you're fantastic, someone else will hire you. What's the worst that can happen?'

Annie noticed the transatlantic twang, not to mention vocabulary he was developing.

'The worst that can happen? Let's see,' Annie began in exasperation, 'my children can't go to St Vincent's any more, because I can't afford the fees, I lose our house because I can't afford my share of the mortgage and The Store doesn't take me back, so I'm unemployed.'

'Well . . . yes, that's all quite bad,' Connor admitted, 'but what are you honestly going to do? Give up now,' he challenged, 'before you've even started?'

'No,' Annie said, with a hint of a smile.

35

'No way!' Connor confirmed. 'So, I have two things to say to you: get out there with a big, successful smile on your face, because the show must go on. And never, ever make another deal without my agent.'

Helena's speech was very kind. Although Annie's boss had only been in the job for five months or so, she let everyone know what a valuable member of staff she was losing. She finished by assuring Annie that if it didn't work out in front of the camera, she'd be welcomed straight back behind the velvet curtains, and this stiffened Annie's resolve to leave. She was going to go forward now. She couldn't come back. Even if she wasn't going to work in TV beyond her three-month contract, she couldn't come straight back to this same job. It was definitely time to move on.

Annie's eyes met Paula's and suddenly her vision blurred. Then she was blubbing hopelessly into a cocktail napkin and hoping that Trish, the make-up artist, had thought to use waterproof mascara.

The goodbyes took too long and felt too sad and final. What had begun all fizz and nerves, like a wedding, was ending with weeping and hugs like a funeral. Until finally, Annie was outside on the pavement with her family around her for comfort.

Both Ed and Owen had their arms around her waist as they walked away from The Store, while Lana kept up a cheerful commentary on her impressions of the evening.

'How are you doing?' Ed wanted to know.

'I'm OK,' Annie tried not to sniffle, 'I'll be fine . . .'

'You were great,' he reminded her. 'What did Helena call you again? Annie V, queen bee of shoppers. Here – '

he held out a crumpled, but clean, man-sized tissue fished from his trouser pocket, 'I came prepared.'

'Thank you.' Annie pressed it to her eyes.

'So, TV star, are we going home by taxi or by limousine?' Ed joked.

'Oh look!' Annie began to break into a jog, 'there's the bus!'

Chapter Four

Ed's school uniform:

Tweed jacket (can't remember)
Thin silk tie (Cancer Research)
Checked shirt (Hackett's via Annie)
Chinos (Gap)
Battered briefcase (his mum)
Total est. cost: no idea

'It's my turn to bring in the biscuits.'

'So when you say you don't know what to wear, what do you mean exactly?'

Ed was still lying in bed, although the alarm clock had gone off exactly seven minutes ago.

Annie was already up. She'd slept restlessly and woken early. She'd spent a whole forty minutes in the bathroom, twiddling with make-up and tweezers and re-doing her ponytail about twenty-seven times until it was satisfactory.

Because today was the first day of her new life.

Today, at 9 a.m. sharp, a car was arriving to whisk her off to the studio where she would meet the rest of the production team and make the very first steps towards filming.

The night before, Annie had thought it was all sorted, her crucially important first outfit of the first day. She'd laid it out so carefully: the new Chloé blouse, a tight red skirt, purple tights and the black patent shoe-boots which had looked just so sexy, so slinky and so perfect then. But now, as she held the boots and the skirt up in front of the full-length bedroom mirror, she wasn't so sure. Was this outfit not a bit over the top? A bit too much for day one? There wasn't going to be any actual filming today, it was 'team talk' and 'getting to know each other' sort of stuff. That's what Finn had told her.

'You're not wavering, are you?' Ed asked, propping himself up on his elbow to get a better look at her, 'You've spent hours and hours over the past few days organizing your TV wardrobe haven't you? And weren't some very expensive purchases involved?'

'I'll be taking some of those back,' she reminded him.

'Yeah . . . might be an idea,' he agreed.

The night she'd returned from Svetlana's house with news about the TV deal and her slim salary, she'd needed to pour them both a generous glass of wine.

At first Ed had been even more shocked and disappointed than she had.

'Do you still want to do this?' he'd asked, but then answered the question himself: 'Of course you do. You've left The Store and it's a great chance for you.'

'Can we manage?' she'd wondered. 'It's just three months and I'll try and sell some stuff on eBay . . . at least

39

make a few pounds that way. But we still have the mort-gage and school fees and . . .'

'You have to give TV a try. We'll manage,' he'd assured her. 'I've got some savings that will help tide us over.'

'You have savings?' she was astonished.

As a woman who lived on the very extreme edges of her budget, whose credit card bills were a source of monthly concern, the idea of savings was just so alien. But then this was Ed, a different kind of person altogether.

'Why do I know nothing about your savings?' she'd asked.

'I wonder!' he'd answered with a smile. 'Maybe because I don't want my savings to be translated into "really great investments" like Miu Miu shoes or Hermès handbags.'

'Oh Hermès!' she'd informed him, 'Hermès is so over, only corporate lawyers carry those things.'

Facing the mirror now, with her tight orangey-red skirt in one hand and her ankle boots in the other, Annie had to confess, 'I'm having a last-minute panic. It's not so unusual, you know.'

'No,' Ed agreed. He pushed back the duvet, and went through his endearing morning ritual of yawning, stretching his arms up, then running a hand through his tangled mop of brown, curly hair before coming over to stand naked behind her.

He put his arms around her waist, kissed her neck, then they looked at each other via the mirror in front of them.

'Please stop fussing,' he told her, 'you're going to look great, because you always look great.'

'But that's because I fuss!' she told him.

'Well, I know, but try not to worry. You're going to be

brilliant at this. I just know it,' he assured her, 'you're really, really good with people and you'll be a natural on TV.'

With Ed's warm hands on her stomach, Annie's churning nerves calmed. With Ed's warm hands holding her, she could almost believe his soothing words. With Ed's support, she sometimes felt she could do just about anything.

'You're great,' she told him, putting her hands over his, 'I really don't know what I would do without you.'

'You'd be just as fantastic,' he insisted.

'No, I definitely wouldn't!' she objected. 'And you need to know that.'

She held his hands tightly in hers for a few moments. 'Thank you for having so much faith in me,' she told him: 'it helps. It definitely helps.'

'Wear the boots,' he urged, 'and I love you in that skirt, it makes your bum look like a ripe . . .' he pinched her buttock to make the point.

But that was it: she dropped the skirt on the floor in horror. If the camera was going to add ten pounds to her already quite ripe enough behind, the skirt would be staying here.

'Let's just try not to burn too big a hole into my savings over the next few months,' Ed warned as he watched the skirt being tossed aside.

'No! Definitely not, I'm going to be working so hard,' she said, 'I won't have the chance to go shopping or spend anything.'

At this, Ed's eyebrows shot up and a broad smile broke over his face. 'Right well . . . this will be very interesting,' he said, certain that just because Annie didn't work in a

41

shop any more, that was hardly going to stop her being seduced by beautiful things.

'And no cheating with your credit cards,' he warned. 'You're on a tiny budget!'

With a parting kiss, he went to take a shower, leaving Annie, still in a frenzy of indecision, in front of the mirror.

'KIDS!' she directed a loud shout at the ceiling, because Owen and Lana had attic bedrooms directly above, 'GET UP!'

It was ten past eight when Ed, Lana and Owen were finally dressed, breakfasted and ready to walk to school. Annie stood at the front door to kiss each of them goodbye.

Ed was first in his music teacher uniform of tweedy jacket, thin silk tie, slightly too baggy chinos, holding a battered brown briefcase. His hair was still all over the place because he liked it that way but Annie made him stand still so she could take off his little gold-rimmed glasses and clean them for him.

'C'mon,' he hurried her, 'I have to get to the staffroom early today . . .'

'Ooooh, the headmaster's handing out big new promotions,' she winked at him.

'No, it's my turn to bring in the biscuits.'

'Ah.'

'High powered, eh?' He put his arms round her waist and kissed her firmly on the mouth.

'Good luck, you're going to be great.'

Then it was Lana's turn.

'Bye-bye, babes,' Annie told her, kissing her on the cheek. She was very proud of her daughter right now.

The sulky, Gothy, irritating phase seemed to be over and in its place Annie had a model teenage daughter. Maybe this was a phase too. But, please, please, let this phase last for ever.

Lana's long, dyed black locks had been replaced with a natural brown choppy bob, her uniform was neat and ironed and her skirt was respectably within sight of her knee. Plus, she was working impressively hard for her exams. She'd even gone straight to her room to do homework as soon as they'd come in from the party the other night.

Annie knew who she had to thank for this improvement. Lana had had this charming boyfriend Andrei (yes, yes, Annie perhaps hadn't appreciated his charms as much as she should have done when Andrei was around) but although Lana and Andrei had called it a day, his swotty, sporty influence seemed to have had a very good effect on Lana.

Owen, now 12 was maybe in need of a good influence of his own. As she bent down to kiss him, she couldn't help noticing his overgrown, unbrushed shock of hair and his anorak, half on, half off with the hood twisted inside the collar. Even his bags were in a muddle; his rucksack and his swimming bag had got tangled up together in the journey to his shoulders. On his feet were shoes as scuffed and muddied as they'd been yesterday morning when she'd decided to give them a good clean. And they were still fastened with Velcro because Owen coping with laces in the rush to get to school had tipped everyone close to the edge.

'Lunches!' Annie remembered and ran back to the kitchen to get the three lunchboxes.

They were easily capable of making their own packed lunches, but this was Annie's thing. Usually, she wasn't home in time to make dinner, plus Ed enjoyed doing dinner, so Annie's love and nurturing were channelled into the lunchboxes. Every day there was a freshly made sandwich and a yoghurt, then a selection of extras: fresh fruit, berries or raw vegetables sliced up in little Tupperware boxes. Or nuts, dried fruit, cartons of juice and always a little something. A wrapped sweetie, a square of chocolate, a tangerine with a love heart carved on the side, a row of kisses drawn on a napkin. She wanted them to know that, although she was busy, she didn't stop thinking about them.

Handing Owen his lunchbox, Annie had to ask her son, 'Why are you carrying a placard?' even though Ed was holding the front door open and it really was time to go.

'Raffle tickets,' Owen answered.

'Yeah, I noticed that,' Annie informed him, because the words RAFFLE TICKETS had been drawn across the placard in large capitals then coloured in orange, red and yellow, 'but tickets for what?'

'I'm in the eco-committee,' Owen said breezily.

'Are you?'

This was the first Annie had heard of it.

'Yeah!' Ed confirmed, 'hasn't he told you? He's really chuffed, they're having a big sale—'

'To raise money for the WWF,' Owen confirmed.

When Annie looked at him questioningly, Lana filled her in with an exasperated sigh: 'The World Wide Fund for Nature, Mum.'

'We really have to go,' Ed reminded them.

'Well that's great,' Annie said proudly, 'but why am I always the last to know these things?'

Ed gave her a reassuring wink. He didn't like her to beat herself up. She was a good mother, just a bit busy — like almost every other mother he knew.

'Your mum will buy ten quids' worth of tickets tonight,' Ed promised Owen as he ushered him out of the door.

'Hey, I thought I was on a budget!' Annie warned them.

'Will you go and get dressed?!' Ed ordered, pointing at his watch.

As soon as her family had gone for the day, Annie fled back upstairs to the bedroom. A frenzied burst of wardrobe ransacking followed in which at least twenty different outfits were chosen, put together, even tried on in some cases, and then discarded.

This was the curse of being a personal shopper and wardrobe adviser: there was too much pressure on Annie to wear the perfect outfit.

The problem was, she felt totally unsure about today. This was her first meeting with everyone . . . was she supposed to dress up? Dress down? Look authoritative? Or friendly? One of the gang? Or the star? It was enough to make her scream.

Carefully, she studied her latest outfit in the mirror and wondered if it was right. Having tried on five different dresses and several skirts, she was now in trousers, which was highly unusual. She was a dedicated dress wearer. But the wide-legged grey trousers with heels, a waistcoat and this funky pink blouse looked pretty good, and she'd add a long trailing scarf plus necklaces. Would that be TV-ish? A little bit creative? Arty?

Maybe not.

No.

She'd change – try something else.

The loud honk of a car horn blasted through her thoughts.

They were here! This was her car! It was now or never, she had to get her bag and go. She looked in the mirror and hated the trousers. Hated them. This was all a terrible mistake. Nevertheless, she grabbed her favourite, most luxurious handbag, threw in her purse, and headed out of the front door.

At the side of the road, waiting for her was a rather beaten-up looking estate car. The man in the driver's seat was waving to her cheerily. As she approached, he slid the window down and called out, 'Hello glamour puss, you must be Annie Valentine then?'

'Hello,' she replied, 'Are you taking me to the studios?'

'Yup, Bob Barratt, *Wonder Women* cameraman at your service,' he gave a jokey salute and leaned across the front seat to open the front passenger's door for her.

'Come sit up front with me, it's nice and friendly and that way you won't get tangled up in all the clobber on the back seat.'

Annie jumped in and shook Bob's hand enthusiastically. Glancing over her shoulder, she saw that the entire back seat and boot of the car was filled with equipment: cameras, camera bags, tripods, cables, lights and a selection of jackets – waterproof, waxy, down, plus a pile of baseball caps.

'I like to travel light,' Bob joked as he fired up the engine, 'so . . . it's a forty-minute journey. Time for us to get acquainted.' He turned to shoot her a cheery smile and pushed up the brim of today's baseball cap to get a better look at her. 'You were sort of on my way, so Finn suggested I pick you up. Saves him a taxi fare, I suppose. I think saving will be the name of the game on this show. Mind you, it's like this all over TV now . . . I've been in the business for twenty-eight years and I've never seen anything like it.'

'Twenty-eight years? You don't look nearly old enough,' Annie was quick to tell him.

'Aha!' Bob laughed the compliment away.

If he'd started at 18, that would make him about 46, she guessed. He was a fit-looking 46, carrying his slim jeans and rugged brown leather jacket well. Gunmetal grey hair curled out from beneath his cap, and laughter lines were deep set into his darkly tanned face. He either went on holiday a lot, or he was a very outdoorsy, weather-beaten kind of guy. He seemed relaxed, quick to smile and joke, so Annie tried to relax too.

'So you're new to TV?' Bob asked as the car pulled out into the stream of traffic.

'Yeah, first day,' she confided.

'Well, the number one rule is to be very, very nice to the cameraman,' he joked. 'I'm the one who picks which angle to shoot you from, Missus. I can make you look like Marilyn Monroe or Marilyn Manson. So be nice.'

'OK,' she agreed, 'now if you could just tell me everything else that I need to know . . .'

It took a full fifty minutes to get to the studios. The traffic was bad, plus Bob insisted on pulling over at a drive-thru to get them both cups of coffee and a breakfast bun: 'You

47

never know when you'll eat next. Have to have a good breakfast,' he insisted.

Finally, the car was parked up and Bob unloaded the heavy camera bags and tripod.

'Follow me,' he said. 'Time to go in and meet the family.'

As they were signed in at the reception area, Annie realized that she was growing clammy with nerves. Along several narrow corridors they went, until Bob opened the door on a small room already busy with people.

Annie was relieved to see that Svetlana was there. Perched elegantly on a chair, she was sipping tea from a china teacup, wearing a drop-dead glamorous cream dress. Svetlana liked to emphasize her blondeness, her immaculate complexion and her perfect curves in all the shades of pale.

Before Annie had even managed to utter a hello, a thin girl in a tight grey jacket and skinny leather trousers stepped in front of her, looked her up and down critically and barked out, 'Trousers? I thought we'd all agreed that on this show, *I* wear the trousers.'

Chapter Five

Finn tries to stay hip:

Leather jacket (AllSaints)
Skinny jeans (Nudie)
T-shirt (Cult)
Converse boots (Office)
Total est. cost: £470

'Woohoo!'

'Woohoo, here comes Annie! Hello!' Finn bounded up to Annie as she stood dumbstruck, and kissed her flamboyantly on both cheeks. He was a forty-something doing his best to look younger and cooler. Both probably essential qualities in the TV world. He wore his skinny jeans with red Converse boots and a scuffed leather jacket and his greying at the temples hair was cut into a youthful Caesar crop. In Finn-speak, everything was 'groovy', 'crucial', 'woohoo' or 'sooo happening'.

'Welcome, come in, hello Bob . . . time to meet everyone.' Finn took Annie by the arm and, although the room was compact, led her round to introduce her to the surprisingly small team of people who would be putting the show together. Finn was producer and director, he explained quickly. Then there was Nikki, his assistant and 'right hand girl'. Thankfully, Nikki was good at make-up too. Bob was in charge of 'lights, camera and action'.

'So there's no sound guy, then?' Bob asked a little bluntly.

'Erm . . . I'm hoping you'll be able to manage,' Finn admitted sheepishly; 'the budget just keeps getting tighter . . . Annie, you know Svetlana of course.'

Svetlana stood up and treated Annie to the multiple-cheeked Ukrainian kissing ritual, then Finn steered her in the direction of the terrifying girl in the trousers: 'Meet Miss Marlise.'

Annie guessed the 'Miss' was because of the strict, teacher-ish persona she had styled for her television self. She didn't look much older than 25 but with her short ebony black bob, pale face, red lipstick and severe clothes, she certainly looked as if she'd like to crack a whip at someone.

Marlise extended a hand and gave a small smile: 'A pleasure to meet you,' she said in very clipped tones.

'Hi,' Annie smiled at her as they shook hands, 'I've heard lots of good things about you,' which wasn't exactly true. In fact, in the car, Bob had rolled his eyes at the mention of Miss Marlise and declared, 'As far as I've heard, she's trouble.' But here on day one of her TV career, Annie wanted only to be a ray of sunshine.

'Sorry about the trousers,' she added, 'nobody told me . . .'

Marlise's tense smile remained and she gave a little nod.

'Right!' Finn opened a large black file, 'we've got lots to get through. I'll tell you about the format for each thirty-minute programme, then we'll work out our shooting schedule. Talent on my left please, girls,' he gestured, 'crew on my right.'

There was a shuffling of chairs and people, then at speed he began to tell them about the format of the show.

'Miss Marlise will be our introducer: our compere, if you will,' Finn began. 'She may be young and gorgeous, but she's already a veteran. She's presented two solo shows already and of course, made her first TV appearance on *The Apprentice.*'

Miss Marlise gave the room a practised smile.

'She's going to guide us through the home of each of the victims, tell us a little bit about their life, give us a tantalizing peek into their bedroom, and their wardrobe, then finally we will meet our subject. And the fun will begin.'

'*Victim?*' Annie was used to thinking of her dressing-room subjects as clients. She really wasn't sure about the word victim. Did Finn mean it as a joke?

'Think of Marlise as a life coach. She's here to tell these women how to get up and get going again. They're down, they're in a rut and we're here to make them feel better,' Finn went on.

'Does our fabulous Svetlana need an introduction? I don't think so!' Finn gushed. 'She's made headlines, she's made *OK!* magazine, she's the gas-guzzling divorcee who walked away with the biggest settlement of them all.'

'No, no, Heather McCartney get more,' Svetlana joked.

'Svetlana has had three amazingly wealthy husbands and will soon be married to her fourth. Go, girl! She is obviously our dating coach. She will teach us all her secrets for snagging and bagging a real winner.'

Svetlana let one of her dazzling smiles break through and beamed it out across the room.

'Annie Valentine comes to us from The Store . . .'

Now that Finn was focusing on her, Annie could feel the heat rising in her cheeks. She wasn't exactly used to people giving talks about her.

'So what Annie doesn't know about shopping, looking gorgeous and stylish isn't worth knowing. I'm sorry you didn't know about the trousers, love,' he added, 'but we want Marlise in the leather jeans barking instructions and we were thinking of a softer, more dressy look for you.'

'No problem,' Annie agreed quickly, wishing Finn had chosen a slightly more private moment for this. Both Nikki and Marlise seemed to be glaring at her. She wondered if they thought she was pretty or stylish enough for this job. Nikki, with her titian red ringlets and urban chic outfit, was too cool to be true. Was she looking at Annie and thinking, 'Ha! I could do your job so much better!'?

Annie brushed the thought away and tightened her grip on her comforting piece of Miu Miu hand luggage.

'Now, Miss Marlise and I have had a bit of a practice at one of her intros, so just to give you all a bit of a flavour . . . take it away, girl.'

Miss Marlise walked slowly and carefully into the middle of the room. She took up a pose, legs planted on the floor, hands on hips and leaning forwards slightly as if she was about to confide.

'Here I am in a quiet street in Hackney, north London,' Marlise began. 'Look at this horrible little house behind me. There are net curtains and toy dolls at the windows. Even a gnome or two on the lawn.' She paused theatrically. 'Now we're in the bedroom. There hasn't been any romance in here for months, can't you tell? Flowery wallpaper, flowery bedclothes, two cuddly toys and fussy little doilies all over the place.

'I don't like the look of these clothes either.' Here Marlise pretended to open a wardrobe door and gingerly pick something out with her fingertips. 'Look at this! Just horrible! I think we can all agree that whoever lives here needs help.'

Now Marlise grew animated: she waved one hand about and gyrated on her hip. 'Help is on its way. Christine Thayer, this is your very, very lucky day because you're about to meet – The Wonder Women!'

'Woohoo!' Finn shouted, as everyone applauded heartily.

Annie clapped too, although she was feeling a bit taken aback. Was Miss Marlise really going to be so nasty?

'Brilliant, Marlise, really excellent! Wicked, girl,' Finn added. 'Now just you wait, girls, until you see some of the porkers and sad cases we've got lined up for you. Boy, you are going to have a wicked challenge on your hands!'

Porkers and sad cases? Annie stole a look at Svetlana and tried to gauge what she was thinking. The inscrutable Ukrainian face remained blank and Svetlana didn't meet her eye.

Annie was feeling slightly shocked. Years of dressing

women had taught her that people got into ruts, that they didn't make the most of their appearance for complex reasons and had to be coaxed back into life with the most tender of care. She sometimes felt she was a sartorial psychiatrist, unveiling layer after layer of body issues and personal problems before she could finally see the root of the problem and help women slowly rebuild both their wardrobes and their confidence.

But then this was TV, she reminded herself. Each woman would be dealt with in a thirty-minute episode, so what had she honestly expected? Long, loving chat sessions, bringing the women slowly forward over week after week?

Now Finn was telling them how he wanted each programme to go: insecure, bedraggled, single women from who-knows-where were to be – bish bosh bing! – transformed in the blink of an eye.

'We cheer them up, we dress them up, then the idea is we take them out to a party to meet some men,' he informed them.

Good grief! He didn't want a makeover, he wanted a fairy godmother to wave a magic wand. Annie took a long gulp of the black coffee which had been placed in her hand. *C'mon!* she rallied herself. She was up for this, wasn't she? If she backed out now, there would be any number of other shopping experts who would rush to fill her shoes, who would probably do the job for free. Who would probably even pay Finn to use them. This was TV! Hundreds of thousands of people were going to see her at work . . . Surely it would lead to something incredible. She had to seize the chance and make the most of it. And she really did believe that there wasn't a single, badly turned out woman in the world who wouldn't be at least a little bit better off after a session with her.

But still . . . taking them out to meet dates? What if the women didn't want dates? What if there weren't any good men at the parties? What if the men didn't like them? As Annie recalled from her days as a single mother-of-two, dating was a minefield.

'As you all know, the budget is small,' Finn was telling them. With a glance in Annie's direction, he added, 'for outfits and hair . . . we're looking at two hundred pounds, maybe two-fifty.' When Annie's eyebrows shot up, he said quickly, 'I'm hoping you'll be able to persuade them to buy a few things for themselves, to help us out a little.'

Two hundred and fifty pounds! In a job where she had been surrounded daily by designer labels, Annie had got used to thinking that £250 was *almost* enough for a nice pair of shoes!

Svetlana looked in her direction, and now she too had a shocked expression on her face.

Nevertheless, Finn carried on. 'The women you will be making over . . . I'm sure you can't wait to find out who these lovely girls are and where we've found them? Well, we ran a radio competition, asking people to nominate themselves or a friend. And we have got some corkers, I assure you.'

He pulled a brown envelope from his file and took out a set of large glossy photographs.

'These lovely ladies are from up and down the country. So some travel will be involved, to capture them in their natural surroundings. Maybe we'll rig up a *Wonder Women* bus, create a little excitement.'

Again Annie winced. 'Capture them in their natural surroundings'? Finn was comparing the women to wild-life!

He held up the photos so everyone could take a look. The pictures were full length and not exactly flattering. Annie took in the bad haircuts, black trousers, lumpy vest tops and meaty arms. Eughhh, huge dangly ear-rings, badly dyed hair, sandals with thick tights. All of the worst fashion crimes seemed to have been committed by this group. Still, Annie couldn't help making mental notes: something a little longer on that body, a brighter colour for her, a fitted dress there, because those arms are actually good . . .

Suddenly, she was beginning to feel better than she had done all day, because she knew she was going to be fine. Even though it was telly and not real life, and she would have to do her job in about one tenth of the time that it usually took, and with a fraction of the budget, she would still be doing the job she loved. And something big was going to follow. She just knew it!

Just then Miss Marlise turned to her and asked in a low, clear voice, loud enough for everyone in the room to hear: 'You're not a presenter though are you, Annie? You're the wardrobe lady. Shouldn't you be over there with the crew?'

Chapter Six

Owen chills after school:

Hoody sweatshirt (H&M)
White shirt (school uniform)
Jeans, outgrown to ankle-length (Gap)
Grey socks (school uniform)
Slippers (Santa)
Total est. cost: £60

*'We've identified you as the
number one household polluter.'*

'That's a very nice place you've got there,' Bob the cameraman commented when he pulled up outside Annie's home at the end of the day. 'Your old man works in the City, does he?'

Yes, she was lucky to live in such a lovely old house in Highgate, one of the nicest parts of north London. But it certainly wasn't because she'd married some wealthy old banker.

'Ha!' Annie laughed, 'you're totally wrong there, mate. For a start my old man is younger than me.'

'Nice one.'

'This was his mum's house,' Annie explained as she gathered up her handbag and the sheaf of shooting schedule papers she'd acquired during the day. 'We mortgaged ourselves to the hilt to buy out his sister's share.'

'Very nice.'

'Yeah, lovely, until I realized what was wrong with it and how much more money we were going to need to put it right,' Annie confided.

'Looks all right now though.' Bob took a closer look at the pretty white house with its blue pots of flowers lining the path to the welcoming blue front door.

'It's not bad,' Annie said, out of the car now and ready to close the door. For a moment she almost considered asking him in, but she was too tired. It had been a long, long day and she knew there would be domestic chaos indoors.

'So what does the old man do then?' Bob asked, with what Annie considered an unreasonable amount of curiosity.

'He's a music teacher,' she answered, then in case he found that disappointing after assuming she was married to a banker, she added, 'and he makes the best dinners I've ever eaten . . . and he's very sexy.'

'Lucky girl!'

'I know!' Annie pushed the car door shut, and Bob wound down the window.

'Don't pay any attention to that Miss Marlise madam. From what I heard, she'll climb over anyone on her rise to the top. You just stand and fight your corner.' With that he put his car into gear, gave her a wave and drove off.

Now that she'd been reminded of the horrible 'wardrobe lady' moment Annie could feel her shoulders sag. But as Bob said, she just had to stand up to that cow. At least Finn had rushed in and quickly explained that no, Annie was definitely to be counted as a presenter.

Pushing open the front door of the house, she announced to the warm fug of sizzling onions, blaring Radio Four, animated boy-chat and all the other familiar smells and sounds, 'Hello, I'm home!'

'The TV star returns!' Ed shouted from the kitchen and there followed the mini thunder of boys' footsteps coming down the stairs.

'Muuum!' Owen was the first to make it down to the hall, closely followed by his friend Milo.

'Hello!' Annie greeted them.

'How was it?' Owen was desperate to know.

Annie wrapped him in as much of a hug as he would allow, then ushered them into the kitchen where she could tell them and Ed all about it.

'So what is this exactly?' Ed asked as Owen and Milo came into the room carrying a long sheet of paper.

The meal was over, homework and music practice had been done, Lana had retreated to her bedroom for more swotting, and Annie and Ed were still at the table, debating whether or not to pour another glass of wine.

'I'm on TV now,' Annie had warned Ed, 'I can't be chubby. According to Connor, I'll have to get a personal trainer and a nutritionist . . .'

'Not on your salary, honey,' Ed had reminded her.

'Are you sure you're OK about the money?' she'd had to ask.

'Yes,' Ed had agreed and topped up her glass, 'To you,' he'd added, raising his glass: 'To you and your fantastic new career. And I mean it.'

'Me and Milo have drawn up a list for you,' Owen began. He stretched himself up to his full height, which was tall for 12. He was so skinny, his head looked too big and he loomed forward slightly like an overgrown sunflower bending on its stem. Milo was much the same, his shaggy mop of dirty blond hair maybe making him look even more fragile.

'Are you sure you two don't want something else to eat?' Annie asked, instinctively. 'A yoghurt? Some bread? There's plenty more crumble left.'

'No, no, we're fine,' Owen insisted and brought his paper higher up so he could read it aloud.

Some time in the last year, Owen, who'd been one of the shyest children ever, had discovered that he liked performing to an audience, even without his violin in his hand.

'OK,' he began, 'here are the suggestions compiled by Owen and Milo.'

'Suggestions for what?' Annie asked, as Owen gave a theatrical pause.

'Shhh!' Ed told her off, 'I think this is to do with the eco-committee.'

'Oh.'

'OK. The two most important things are to turn down the heating and to use the car less. Especially as it's such a big, gas-guzzling car, Mum,' Owen said, and gave Annie a pointed look.

'Sorry,' Annie felt she had to reply.

'Then we've made up a list of smaller, but nonetheless important actions,' Owen went on. 'Always turn everything off properly, don't leave it on stand-by. Fit low-energy light bulbs everywhere. Recycle much more. Give old things to charity. Then everything else relates to Mum.'

'Does it?' Annie asked in surprise.

'Yes, we've identified you as the number one household polluter,' Owen told her solemnly.

'Me?' Annie sat up in her chair, while Ed gave a chuckle at her expense.

'Yup,' Milo came in on Owen's side, 'there's a list of things just for you.'

'Mum to spend much less time in the power shower,' Owen read out, 'Mum not to go by taxi so much, Mum to use her mobile less, Mum not to buy so many new things, Mum not to drink so much water out of plastic bottles. Mum to give more things away to charity—'

'All right!' Annie broke in, 'I think that's about enough lecturing for one night, isn't it? Why don't I make up for my terrible, terrible crimes by buying some raffle tickets from you?'

'Excellent!' Owen had to agree.

'Too tired for fun then?' Ed asked quietly, letting his finger trace gently down Annie's side as they lay together in bed.

She pulled his arm until it was warm and tight around her, then moved her back so it was snugly fitted against his fuzzy chest.

'Too tired,' she confirmed.

'Alas,' he said with a sigh.

'A lass?' she teased, 'which lass? Is this something I should know about?'

'Don't be silly,' he said into the hairs on the back of her neck, 'you're the only lass for me.'

This caused a shiver to travel down her spine which made her wonder for a moment if she really was too tired. She wriggled her buttocks against his warm, naked body and felt him stir slightly against her. But then came the question which made her change her mind completely.

'I know you're very busy and this is a big new thing you're taking on . . .' Ed began gingerly, 'but have you at least given just a little thought to my question from the other night?'

There was silence. A big, deafening silence between them. The last thing Annie wanted to do right now was have this conversation.

'It's OK,' Ed was the first to speak. 'It's OK. You don't have to give me any sort of answer now. I don't even know if I want an answer now, I just want to know that you're thinking about it.'

'Ed . . .' Annie began. She turned over so that she was facing him but still in his arms.

His eyes were on hers. Light blue eyes searching her face very seriously. She pulled him close, so that her mouth was against his soft, pale shoulder and she didn't have to feel the eyes on her face. Then, in a quiet voice, she told him: 'You know how I feel about this. I haven't changed my mind and I really, really don't think I'm ever going to change my mind. I've got a fantastic girl and a brilliant boy, and we are so lucky to have you. That's my family, Ed.'

Taking a deep breath, knowing how much disappointment she risked causing him, she added, 'I don't want to have another baby.'

Chapter Seven

Svetlana on the small screen:

White and blue plunging day dress (Issa)
Purple leather and python bag (Francesco Biasia)
Blue suede heeled sandals (Jimmy Choo)
Two-carat sapphire ring (third husband)
Total est. cost: £86,400

'Bin bag!'

'Cath? Cath, vhat is dis?!' Svetlana, looking too impossibly sexy and glamorous for this neat beige bedroom in one of the pleasantly green corners of south-west London, had opened a cupboard drawer.

She was not at all happy with what she had found in there.

With a flick of her manicured fingers, Svetlana hoisted out a large, saggy pair of beige underpants. Next a worn-out bra, its straps curled up into spirals, dangled helplessly from Svetlana's long, pink fingernail.

The 52-year-old woman who owned the shapeless

underwear did not look happy either. She crossed her arms over the also saggy and also beige polo neck she'd decided to wear for her first appointment with the Wonder Women and replied matter-of-factly, 'That's my underwear.' She didn't seem unduly embarrassed about the state of her smalls.

'Cath, you have been alone for too long and if you vear undervear like this, you stay single for ever. Bin bag!' Svetlana commanded and flicked the offending items straight into the rubbish. After a brief inspection, the rest of the contents of the drawer followed.

'Wait!' Cath protested, an astonished look on her face, 'those are all very comfortable . . . I only bought the bras a few months ago!' She jumped forward, got hold of the bin bag and for a moment there was a mini tussle between the two women. Bob gripped his camera tightly, knowing that if he missed one second of this he would be in trouble.

'No,' Svetlana insisted, pulling the bin bag back. 'Hideous, ugly underwear! You are a good-looking voman under all this comfortable beige. Ve buy you all new!'

Which was all very well for Svetlana to promise, Annie couldn't help thinking; she wasn't the one who was going to have to make a budget of £250 stretch to buy an entirely new wardrobe.

Annie's eyes travelled to Cath's face. The ever so slightly stern features were deeply troubled. In fact, the troubled look had barely left Cath's face since the entire *Wonder Women* TV crew descended on her flat at 8.45 this morning. In truly insincere TV fashion, everyone had kissed and hugged and gushed over Cath, and had then proceeded to tear her life apart.

Miss Marlise had already done her piece to camera from both inside and outside Cath's home. Cath had listened to the commentary with her cheeks burning and then with her mouth open in horror. Miss Marlise had not thought for one moment to spare the feelings of this rather plain looking, middle-aged accountant.

'Cath lives here in this boring, beige flat all on her own,' Marlise had begun. 'Now that her son has left home, she's busy, busy, busy with her job and her gardening club and her friends, but to be honest, she's got a bit boring and a bit beige herself.

'Cath got divorced five years ago and since then, there hasn't been any fun in her life . . .'

'There wasn't a lot of fun before, believe me,' Cath had said under her breath, and Annie had caught the comment.

Miss Marlise had rattled on, 'No new dresses and no new men. Cath's social life consists of gardening club meetings and going out with her *married* friends once a fortnight. You aren't going to meet a new Mr Right like that, are you, Cath?'

Then leaning chummily into the camera, Miss Marlise had made wide, enthusiastic eyes and gushed: 'But oh, so luckily for you, the Wonder Women are here to sort you out!'

'Woohoo!' had been Finn's inevitable response to Marlise's intro. But Annie had seen Cath wipe at the corner of her eye and had instinctively put an arm round her.

'I'm sure they'll cut that right down,' she had told her quietly, as they walked into the flat together. 'What made you decide to be on the show, Cath?'

'My friends all got together and decided to enter me. I didn't know anything about it until I got a phone call.'

'But you must have quite liked the idea of a makeover?' Annie had asked.

'Erm, yes . . . a new hairstyle, a new outfit. Yes,' Cath had admitted hesitantly, 'but I didn't know it was going to involve delving into my underwear drawer and a blind date.'

'Not a date! Just a party where you'll be introduced to lots of people and we'll be right beside you holding your hand. Honestly,' Annie had tried to assure her, 'some really good things are going to come out of this, I promise.' Annie was still convinced that this was true.

But now, in the bedroom, watching Svetlana at work, Annie wasn't quite so sure.

'OK, I get out my list.' Svetlana reached onto the bed for her luxurious leather and python handbag. The bag, like Svetlana, looked totally out of place in this room, as if they'd been beamed here by mistake direct from an outrageously expensive lunch in Knightsbridge.

The camera was rolling and Svetlana was clearly relishing every moment. Without even thinking about it, her crossed legs and devastating cleavage were pointing camerawards at the most flattering angle. Propped up on her elbow, she lay across the bed, flipping through a notebook. She began to ask Cath questions while she took notes with a little silver pen.

'No boyfriends since your divorce?'

Cath confirmed this with a shake of her head. Annie could see on the monitor that the camera was zooming in close on her worried face.

'Where could you go to meet some interesting men?' Svetlana wondered.

Cath shrugged her shoulders helplessly, then ventured, 'Through work? I mean, not that there's anyone at work that I'm interested in . . . I mean they're all lovely, charming . . . but really, I'm happy on my own.'

The roll of Svetlana's eyes made it clear that this wasn't a good enough answer.

'Vot are your interests? Vot hobbies?' she asked.

Cath looked back at Svetlana. 'I love to garden and visit other gardens . . . and I love to go out with my son.'

'Vhat you like to do before married, before have your boy?' Svetlana asked, with all the subtlety of a police interrogator.

'Ermmmm . . .' The camera zoomed in on Cath's face again. Annie saw how anxious the woman looked. She didn't need this; she should be treated gently, coaxed out of the beige and into the party. But Annie was going to have to wait her turn. The nervousness she'd thought she'd feel at facing her first moment on screen had evaporated, she just wanted to rush in right now and help Cath out.

Because Annie had been inside the wardrobes and most private confidences of people just like Cath so many times. It was all about breaking through the defences and rebuilding confidence, taking things one step at a time and making the customer feel good, rather than humiliated.

There was a hint of sweat on Cath's face. If she was pushed any further, she'd probably refuse to do the show altogether.

'I used to like drawing,' she squeezed out finally, then quickly added, 'but I wasn't very good at it.'

'Drawing,' Svetlana repeated and wrote it down in her notebook with a flourish, 'and?'

'I like to read—'

'Book group? I've heard of dis . . .' Svetlana broke in and wrote this idea down in her notebook too.

'Well . . .' Cath sounded very unsure.

'Anything else? Anything you vant to do? Something new?'

'Ermm . . . I'd like to get a bit fitter.'

'Excellent!' Svetlana's face brightened. 'You join gym and running club. Meet many, many fit men!'

Cath seemed to cross her arms even more tightly at the prospect.

'And cut!' Finn snapped the clapperboard in front of the camera, 'Tea break, everyone. Then it's on to Annie Valentine, mistress of the wardrobe.'

Taking another look at the slightly traumatized Cath, Annie had an idea. 'Why don't I take a quick look through Cath's wardrobe with her, before we film it?' she asked. 'I'll find some interesting things to talk about on camera. It might save us a bit of time.'

'Fine,' Finn agreed, as she'd suspected he might. Anything to save time, save money and come in under budget.

Turning to Nikki, Finn's assistant, with her most charming smile, Annie asked, 'Will you be a total love and bring us both a tea?'

As soon as the crew was out of the bedroom, Annie steered Cath to her bed and made her sit down. 'Good grief!' she exclaimed. 'Well, they were a bit rough on you, babes, weren't they?'

At those words, Cath threatened to crumple. She shook

her head. 'I don't know if I can do this. People I know will watch it! The people I work with! I think everyone should just go away and leave me alone. I really don't think I want to go on.'

For a moment or two, Annie just patted her back soothingly. Then came a tap at the door and Nikki arrived with two mugs of tea. As Annie took them, she gave a smile of thanks but shut the door firmly in the curious assistant's face.

'OK,' Annie began gently, sitting back down, 'what did your friends think about you doing this programme? And what about your son?'

Cath clutched the mug and took a sip. 'Everyone was really excited for me,' she confided, 'I think they all wanted to see me dressed up and looking special. It's been a while since I've made a big effort. I don't really do dressing up . . . or parties . . .' Her voice tailed off.

'Well, that's what your friends and your boy are going to see,' Annie told her: 'their special friend and very special mum, looking gorgeous, just for them. Forget about everyone else and just do it for them, because they'll be so excited for you! Come on,' she encouraged her. 'Get that tea down you. I'd doctor it with something stronger, but that might get me thrown off the show.'

Cath looked up and gave just the slightest hint of a smile: 'I've never been on TV before,' she said timidly.

'Well, that makes two of us. But, as they say in showbiz, chin up – the show must go on!'

'So how bad is it in here?' Annie asked with a wink, as she walked towards Cath's wardrobe and opened the plain white double doors. Cath had obviously tidied up before the arrival of the cameras. Everything was neatly folded or hanging up. Annie was about to change all that. Grabbing two hefty handfuls of clothes, she pulled them out and flung them onto the bed.

It was as she'd expected: lots of well worn, comfortable, baggy clothes. Heavy on the beige, greige and pastel blue. There were a few unexpected outbursts of colour madness, but none had been very successful. Annie held up a pair of wide-legged, three-quarter-length trousers with some sort of graffiti print all over them. Terrible cut, terrible colours for Cath, but still, unexpectedly zany.

'These are just a little crazy,' Annie said, 'I think you have a hidden wild side we've just not seen yet.'

'Oh no!' Cath protested. 'They were just cheap, I bought them for a holiday.'

'They're very interesting.' Annie smiled and put the trousers down on the bed.

It didn't take her long to sort through the rest of Cath's wardrobe. Everything so worn out and saggy it couldn't even be given away went onto one pile. Things which Annie hoped she might be able to breathe new life into went into another. But so many cotton turtlenecks, she noticed dispiritedly. Why not scoop necks and lovely shirts to show off a little skin and a nice necklace?

There was still space on the bed for the gems that Annie was hoping to unearth in the back of the cupboard. Maybe she would find a dress or two, a special blouse or skirt . . . things which would just need a little alteration or a new accessory to turn them into new outfits. Although Annie looked hard and combed once again through the tangle of clothes, she could find only casual, functional, practical clothes.

The tea break was over and the camera crew began to shuffle back into the bedroom. Lights were moved, and Nikki freshened up Annie and Cath's face powder and lipgloss.

Finn discussed the angles he wanted to see, the direction of the dialogue between Annie and Cath, then finally declared: 'And action!'

Annie felt hot and slightly flustered now that the camera was pointing directly at her. But she tried to control the nerves. More than anything else, she just wanted to be herself. Unlike Miss Marlise she didn't want to create a whole larger than life TV personality. She'd understood long ago that it was best to just be fully yourself and if other people didn't like it, too bad.

'Right, my darlin',' she said as she bustled busily through Cath's clothes, scattered across the bed: 'I've seen the sweatshirts, the old T-shirts, the polo necks, the fleeces, the baggy trousers and the long, dark skirts. But what I'm asking myself is: where are your special clothes? Where are your dresses and your shiny things? What do you wear when you've got a wedding to go to? Or a party? Or a night out?'

Cath looked straight up at Annie and replied, 'Oh, I've nothing to wear, so I don't go.'

'Oh babes,' Annie looked back at Cath and forgot about the camera completely, 'that is the saddest, saddest thing I've heard in a long time. But what about when it's your birthday? Everyone's got to have something lovely to wear on their birthday.'

At this, Cath's lower lip trembled slightly and out came the revelation she'd had absolutely no intention of making on TV: 'My husband left me on my birthday,' she blurted out. She didn't need to say anything else. Now everyone understood why there were no party clothes in Cath's wardrobe.

Finn caught the eye of his assistant and mouthed the word: *'Woohoo!'*

Chapter Eight

Connor on his bike:

Tiny black shorts (Nike)
Tiny black bike shoes (Adidas)
Bluetooth wireless headset (Motorola)
Total est. cost: £120

'I can talk and burn, baby.'

Connor McCabe, star of ITV's top-rated Sunday teatime show, *The Manor*, co-star in the box office hit *Never Sleep* by director Sam Knight, was on an exercise bike out on his balcony in the Californian sunshine.

No British actor transplanted from London to LA can ever quite get used to the fact that the sun really does shine here almost every single day. Well, OK, there was a little bit of smog, cloud cover and drizzle now and then, but really, he thought as he adjusted his shades, stretched out his arms, then put them back on the handlebars, it was not a bad life. Not a bad life at all.

It was late afternoon. He'd spent his obligatory two

hours in the gym first thing this morning. Every single actor out here spent two hours in the gym every single day. There was no get-out clause. It was mandatory. Like brushing your teeth. Otherwise some much fitter, leaner, more muscular piece of beefcake would Get Your Part. No matter how well you'd played Prince Hal at Stratford-upon-Avon two years ago, if a centimetre of waist flab poked over the edge of your trousers, it was over.

He'd been on the phone to his agent for half an hour, he'd gone for a meeting with a producer and now he was going to burn some more calories and catch a few rays before going out tonight with Hector, his boyfriend of . . . well . . . erm . . . Connor wasn't quite sure exactly, because there had been a break, but that was all over now. Long forgotten. They were totally together and committed now.

The phone in a holster round his waist began to ring and when he picked it up he was pleasantly surprised to see the words 'Annie babes' on caller display.

'Annie, babes!' he said with pleasure.

'Connor! Can you talk? You're not about to shoot off to a high-powered meeting, or rustle up a bean sprout salad or something?'

'I'm on my bike, I can talk and burn, baby, burn.'

'On your bike? In LA? What about the traffic . . . or getting mugged?'

'On my bike on my terrace in the sunshine. Don't worry, I'm not going anywhere.'

'Oh.' Annie tried to understand. But really, it was too strange. She still thought of Connor as a charming, but quite lazy actor who had sort of stumbled on success somewhere between the pub and his latest bedroom conquest. She couldn't get her head around this all-new Californian fitness- and career-focused star. She didn't want to think of him like that, because then she couldn't think of him as her best friend any more. And he was definitely, despite the eight-hour time difference and the vast Atlantic Ocean now between them, still her best friend.

'I've been thinking about you,' he said, only slightly out of breath from the cycling.

'Oh really,' she teased, 'and it's making you pant.'

'Absolutely. How is stardom suiting you? How are you looking on the small screen? Any hot men tried to bed you yet? I know all about the aphrodisiac of fame . . .'

'Oh yeah, I'm beating them off with a stick baby, beating them off with a stick,' she joked thinking of her daily ride home in Bob's estate car. The aphrodisiac of fame!

'TV is . . .' she began. TV was what? Not exactly as she'd expected? Much more extreme? Much more low budget? Much less glamorous?

'. . . not quite as easy as it looks,' she decided.

'Damn right!' Connor was delighted to agree. He'd lost count of the number of jumped-up actors who asked him why he did something as 'easy' as *The Manor* when he could be doing something much more 'serious' instead.

'I can't believe how long the details take. Doing every shot, every bit of voiceover from sixteen different angles. It makes me want to scream. But the hard stuff,' Annie added, 'the transforming shy wallflower into belle of the ball, they expect that in fifteen seconds!'

'Well, baby, you are at the very tough and gritty end

of reality TV,' Connor sympathized, 'The cliff face, you could say. Who knows what's going to happen next? You could hang in there and be elevated to the TV hall of presenter/personality fame . . . or you could cut loose and fall away into the sea of failed wannabees, never to be heard of again. Still,' his tone perked up cheerily, 'you've gotta be in it to win it.'

'So it's not a career path, it's a lottery?'

'Exactly.'

'Why did I give up my nice, glamorous, staff-discounted day job?' Annie had to ask. 'Please remind me.'

'Because like the rest of us glory-hunters, you wanted your shot at the big one.'

Annie considered the day she'd had today and the day she faced tomorrow: six hours in a shopping mall trying to transform Cath with £250. And Cath wasn't even sure if she wanted to be transformed!

Even when filming was over, there was still so much work to be done: the debriefings with Finn, then all the additional little camera shots that Bob would insist on. Annie smiling, Annie nodding, Annie shaking her head and looking troubled. 'We might need these shots in the edit,' he'd explained. 'It's always good to have plenty of spare bits and pieces.'

'Connor, if this is what it's like making cheap TV, what the hell is it like to make films?' she wondered.

'Oh the agony,' Connor agreed, 'and yet the ecstasy!'

'Have you heard about that big thing you were up for?' Annie asked.

'Which one?' Connor said, but more anxiously than boastfully. 'I'm up for about eight, but I'll probably be lucky if even one of them is made. I think that's the strike rate for films in development right now. Only one in ten ever sees the light of day.'

'Are you worried?' she asked with some concern.

'Not yet,' he told her. 'I can always fall back on the other great LA industry.'

'Drugs?!'

'No, porn. No-one ever tells you this, but LA is only 15 per cent movies and then 85 per cent porn. That's why everyone's so buff. To make sure they can play the part of Miguel the devastatingly attractive pizza delivery boy, if the rent's overdue.'

'You worry me,' Annie told him. 'You can come back to London, you know. There's a new series of *The Manor*, isn't there? And what about the West End?'

'Yes . . . but coming back with my tail between my legs isn't really what I'd planned to do.'

Me neither. Annie couldn't help thinking; once again she was determined that she wouldn't be going back to The Store.

'However you come back, Connor, you'll be welcomed with open arms, by all of us,' she reassured him.

'You are a very lovely woman.'

'I know. How are your food intolerances?' She tried to sound as if she meant this, but it didn't come out right.

'Take that smirk off your face,' Connor commanded. 'Ever since I stopped eating grains, I am *struggling* to keep the weight on.'

'Maybe I should try it . . .'

'I don't know, are you an O type? Maybe you should call my dietician. I'm sure he could give you some guidelines over the phone.'

78

'*Maybe you should call my dietician?*' she repeated incredulously. 'These are words I never thought I would hear you say. But isn't booze a grain?'

'I'm allowed champagne and vodka,' Connor told her, 'because they're pure. Vodka with soda water is the only drink you can buy round here anyway,' he added; 'vodka with soda water means you can get drunk but with hardly any calories or toxins, plus you are rehydrating while you're dehydrating.'

'What do they call a vodka-soda then? The Hollywood Hellraiser?' Annie teased, 'Oh you crazy people! So you can have a big night out and still be up for spin class at six the next morning.'

'Spin class? Soooo over,' Connor said. 'It's all yoga kick boxing now.'

'But I thought yogis were pacifists. Do they just box away their negative vibes?' Annie teased.

'Yeah, you're laughing, but you're a TV presenter now. You are just inches away from behaving like this,' he warned.

'Am not.'

'Are so.'

'Not!'

'Totally.'

'How's your lover?' Annie asked to bring the play-fight to a close.

'He's great,' came the reply. 'He doesn't have a work visa, so he's busy being my companion. He plans my wardrobe, organizes my diary, books all my sessions, makes sure I don't miss a meeting, or a manicure.'

. *Manicure?* Over the phone Annie couldn't tell whether Connor was serious or pulling her leg. Surely even

Californian Connor wouldn't go for a manicure. Would he?

'He's finding out about our baby options over here,' Connor dropped in without the slightest warning: 'there's adoption or there's surrogacy.'

'Hello?!' Annie pounced, 'Your *baby* options?! You two want to have a baby? And you've not even breathed one word to me about this?'

There was a pause. Then Connor felt he had to apologize. 'I'm sorry. We've not even been talking about it that long. It's a very new idea,' he added, 'but it's a fantastic one!'

Annie said the only thing she felt that she could say: 'Well, that's incredibly exciting, babes.'

But really, she thought it was too strange, that the two men she was closest to, Ed and Connor, both wanted babies. All of a sudden. Out of the blue.

'Ed wants to have a baby too,' she risked.

'No! That will be so amazing, Annie! Congratulations,' he added; a little prematurely, to say the least.

'No, Connor. There's a bit of a difference. Ed wants to have a baby, but I don't.'

Chapter Nine

Annie's on-screen outfit:

Bright blue blouse (Chloé)
Purple and blue skirt (Whistles sale)
Purple platform pumps (Miu Miu, Store discount days)
Thick blue tights (John Lewis)
Total est. cost: £470

'Oh practical schmactical!'

Annie walked briskly, three-inch heels clacking, arm in arm with Cath through the shopping mall. Permission to film in the mall and in most of the shops inside it had only just been granted twenty minutes ago after frantic phone calls to and from the director's assistant.

Annie had a tight grip on Cath because she felt that the poor woman was going to need real physical, as well as mental, support to get through this shopping ordeal. Hard enough to go shopping for yourself for the first time in years . . . but to have a camera crew watching your every move when you finally get out there? That was almost too much for any woman to bear.

Five years! Cath couldn't remember hitting the shops for herself once since her son's 16th birthday. It wasn't that she didn't have any money; Cath just felt she should be saving it rather than spending it on herself. Plus, she seemed to have a wardrobe full of things passed on from her friends, or worse, her son.

'I know you love him dearly,' Annie had told Cath, 'but do you not think wearing his old sweatshirts might be taking things a bit too far?

'But they're so practical,' Cath objected.

'Oh practical shmactical! If I hear the p word again I'm going to have to smack you. There are so many lovely, comfortable and cosy ways of getting dressed without baggy sweatshirts and anoraks!'

Cath had an assortment of anoraks in, yes, beige and pastel colours, that wouldn't have looked out of place on a mountain. In fact, if she had been a mountaineer they would have been fine, but for everyday London life they were . . . wrong!

'Look around you, try and enjoy the experience. This is called shopping,' Annie was playfully encouraging her. 'If you see a window display you like the look of, let me know, we'll stop and we'll explore. There is no panic, we've got the whole day,' she soothed. 'And a whole day to buy one outfit is a luxury, believe me.

'The only rule,' Annie went on, 'the one thing I'm insisting on, Cath, is that you buy only things that you love. *I quite like it, this will do, this is so practical* . . . no, no, we're not having any of that. If you don't love it . . . if it doesn't make your heart beat faster, then we're not going to bother. OK?'

'How's your son?' she asked, hoping a little bit of cheer-ful chat would put Cath more at ease.

'Fine. He keeps asking me when I'm going to get my party dress, as if I'm Cinderella or something . . .' There was note of despondency to this which Annie wanted to nip in the bud.

'You are!' Annie insisted, 'and I'm your fairy godmother, so you better start believing in me or I'm going to disappear.'

Spotting one of the funky shoe shops she knew Lana shopped in regularly, Annie steered Cath towards the front door: 'Now,' she began, 'every Cinderella has to have a wonderful shoe.' Annie knew that shoes didn't let you down the way clothes did. You never changed shoe size; shoes never made you look fat. They were a great place for insecure novice shoppers to start.

Cath was sent to look around the shop as both the camera and Annie studied her closely for her reactions.

'Just don't get so in her face!' Annie hissed at Bob. 'How is she ever going to relax and get into this if you're shadowing her every move?'

'I don't want to miss anything,' Bob defended him-self.

'You won't. And if you do, I will personally bribe her to re-stage it,' came Annie's reply.

'Ah, can't do that!' Bob wagged a finger at her. 'It's never as convincing as the first time.'

'Oh rubbish,' she argued, 'I bet you do it all the time.'

Annie turned her attention back to Cath. She was wandering through the shop, looking at the shoes in confusion. There were all sorts of new colours, shapes, heels and designs here. Everything was obviously so different from the last time Cath had gone shoe shopping with nothing but price and practicality on her mind.

'Keep looking,' Annie urged, 'there will be something you like here. Really, just let me know if *anything* catches your eye, because then we can get a clue as to what kind of things you're into. Your love muscle,' she added with a cheeky wink, 'it's all about building up your love muscle. It's obviously not had nearly enough exercise lately.'

Even Cath had to giggle at this.

Three-quarters of the way through Cath's third tour of the shop and Annie saw it – Cath reached up and from a display high above the shop floor she brought down a pair of cherry red, patent leather loafers.

She watched Cath turn the loafers over in her hands, with a pleased fascination on her face.

Quickly Annie turned to the shop assistant hovering by her side, eager to appear on television. 'OK, I need the red loafers in a size six and everything else you've got in red patent in that size.'

After only a little arm-twisting, Annie had Cath striding up and down the shop in the loafers, a look of obvious satisfaction on her face.

'OK, we're taking them,' Annie told her.

'No!' Cath protested, 'I've got nothing to wear with them.'

'We'll go and find you a snazzy little red jacket and maybe a red bag. Maybe a shiny red, waterproof, non-anorak coat. Don't you *love* them?' Annie had to ask.

'Yes,' Cath confessed shyly.

'Well then. You're having them. That's final.' Annie had long ago forgotten all about the camera pointing in their faces. 'Anyway, they're a whole lot nicer than those – ' she pointed down at the sorry, bashed-up black slip-ons Cath had worn for the shopping session. Imitating Svetlana's rich accent, she intoned: 'Bin bag!'

'Now my darlin', you obviously have an unexpressed urge for shiny red, so what do we think of these?'

Annie carefully opened the lid and unwrapped the tissue paper from a gorgeous little pair of patent red Mary Janes. She knew there would be no persuading comfortable Cath into a pair of mincey high heels, but she hoped that this dressy little pair might stand something of a chance.

'Oh! Well . . .' Cath looked at the shoes with surprise as if she couldn't possibly consider something so pretty.

'Just try,' Annie wheedled.

And before Cath could protest, her black socks were off, pop socks were on and she was showing off her tiny white ankles in the dainty shoes.

'Walk,' Annie commanded.

Bob knelt down at the side of the shop to capture Cath's uncertain steps.

'Don't even try and tell me you don't like them,' Annie said. Cath was walking, pausing and taking long looks in the mirror.

'How do they fit?'

'Really well.'

'They will go with trousers, jeans, skirts, dresses,' Annie wheedled, 'and they're on us, remember. You don't need to think about how you could be saving the money instead.'

Cath looked at her feet in the mirror for a good long minute.

'Repeat after me,' Annie began, '*I love them.*'

Bob's camera zoomed in on Cath's face, but she still managed to repeat shyly: 'I love them.'

'And once again, with feeling,' Annie teased.

'I love them!' Cath said, shooting Annie a smile, then colouring up.

'Stop feeling so guilty! Everyone has to wear shoes,' Annie reminded her. 'Might as well wear nice ones and, babes – they only cost forty-five pounds!'

Annie did find this sobering. She'd stopped buying shoes on the high street about a year ago and had to confess, 'Do you have any idea how much I blew on these?' She pointed down at her lavish boots: 'a large chunk of my kids' inheritance.'

The red loafers and the shiny shoes were wrapped and rung up, Annie paying from the envelope with the £250 in cash she'd been given by Finn this morning.

'No company credit card?' she'd asked in surprise.

'You think I'd let you loose with a company credit card?' he'd replied. 'We're still paying off the bill my wife racked up when she came to visit you in The Store.'

'Ah yes.' Annie remembered very well the day when Kelly-Anne had put herself in the hands of the personal shopping suite and come out several thousand pounds lighter. And then there was her hair. There had been a sort of hair accident and Kelly-Anne had ended up having to cut her hair . . . by two whole feet.

Shopping for Cath's dress was never going to be easy. Annie was at the mercy of the high street with an insecure, size 16, highly body conscious client and a grand budget now down to £155. If she'd been back at The Store and had limitless money to spend, she would have known exactly how to solve this problem: with the

Italian labels which swathed the more curvaceous mama in carefully cut taffeta with boning, structure and cleverly chosen colours.

After the shoe success, there followed a very dispiriting session in the Wallis changing room. Cath, in front of the mirror, was mentally listing her defects, Annie could tell. She had seen that look on so many faces before. It began at the top with: 'I hate my hair, I hate my saggy eyes, I hate my neck, shoulders and cleavage,' and it carried all the way down to: 'I hate my knobbly knees, ankles and hideous toes.'

In John Lewis it was worse, and Annie could see Bob deleting their footage. His brief was: happy woman, made-over, breathless with astonishment at how amazing she now looks.

Then Finn phoned.

'Hi, how's it going?' he asked Annie. 'Have you turned our pumpkin into a princess yet?'

Annie frowned at the casual cruelty of the remark before answering, 'Well . . . yes, I think we're getting there,' as cheerfully as she could, while she watched Cath turn about in front of the mirror in a totally hopeless dress which really would be put to better use sheltering the homeless or something.

'I can't wait to see what you've come up with!' Finn said excitedly. 'OK, we'll meet you in the Starbucks on the lower mall at 3 p.m. for a catch-up and a quick look through the footage.'

'I thought we had all day,' Annie said, glancing at her watch and seeing it was already 1.50 p.m.

'All day *filming*,' Finn told her, 'not all day shopping.

There's a bit of a difference, Annie!'

As soon as she'd shut her mobile, Annie knew she would have to take action fast. 'OK, Cath, out of that,' she commanded briskly. 'Don't blame yourself, love, blame that sorry sack of a dress. I need to do some research. And quickly.'

A moment later and Annie was texting Paula, her ex-assistant. Yes, Paula was six-foot-something and built like a pole vaulter on a diet, but she had a sister, Jamilia. As curvaceous as she was vivacious, Jamilia was also a very fashionable woman on a small budget.

It took only a few more minutes for Jamilia herself to text back the reply to Annie's frantic question: 'Where buy hot dresses sz 16 on hi street?'

Here on her phone screen were the magical words: 'Coast, Dthy Prkns.'

'All right, we're off,' Annie instructed and tucked Cath's arm firmly under hers once again.

Cath wasn't allowed to wander round Dorothy Perkins, because time was now seriously limited. Instead, she was planted in the changing room with the curtains pulled firmly shut against the camera lenses.

Then Annie scoured the shop floor: every rack and every dress, like the true professional she was.

Finally, she pulled out something with serious potential. It was structured and black with three-quarter-length lace sleeves, so Cath wouldn't feel too exposed.

Annie didn't personally like black. Black was boring. Black was just so black. But Cath wore so much pastel, wishy-washy and beige, that Annie couldn't help feeling black would be a dramatic change. Plus, black was good with red patent.

'OK girl, I think we could have a serious contender here,' Annie said passing the dress into the cubicle. 'Put it on while I go in search of accessories.'

'Oh!' was the surprised comment from the other side of the curtain. But Annie didn't stop to listen, just buzzed over to the accessories section.

The glitzy, the chunky, the unusual – all the necklaces she could have wanted were out here at just the sort of money she was looking to spend.

She headed back to the changing room with a selection of beads, bags and bracelets, eager to see how the dress was working.

'C'mon,' she said to Bob, 'fire up! I have a good feeling about this one.'

'Are you ready?' Annie asked from outside the changing-room curtain.

'Yes . . I think so,' came the reply.

At that Annie pulled aside the curtain with Bob right beside her, already filming.

'Oh yes!' she declared immediately. 'Yes, yes, yes!! Put on the shoes, we have to have the full effect.'

For a few moments Annie helped to make adjustments. The red patent Mary-Janes went on, then a necklace of silver and black leaves and finally Annie popped a glittery silver clutch into Cath's hand.

'Well?' she asked as Cath turned this way and that, coyly looking at her reflection.

The dress fitted well; Annie just pulled in the back a little with her hand to show Cath how a minor alteration would make it perfect. Cath herself looked different. Finally they had found a dress that seemed to pull her up, lift and lengthen her. Her shoulders were back for the first time today, her head was up, she already looked inches slimmer. The lace brought all the focus to her soft, white throat and cleavage, her dainty hands and wrists. This was just as Annie had planned. The draped skirt quietened down the troublesome tum, bum and hams.

'What I want to do . . .' Annie began, coming up behind her so they could look in the mirror together, 'is put you in the hands of a very nice hairdresser I know who will straighten, lengthen and darken your hair.'

She pulled one of Cath's dull blonde-grey curls out, revealing several inches of length. 'Time to bring you bang up to date and bring out your inner artist,' Annie added with a smile. 'Darker hair with your pale skin . . . And you know, I don't like this bag, or the necklace,' Annie decided, taking both of them from Cath, who didn't protest.

'You know what I love with red? Violet . . . Stay right there, take a long look at your lovely, luscious self and I will be right back with violet.'

Clipping on vibrant violet beads, which made the blue in Cath's eyes sparkle, and pressing a sassy little violet bag into her hand, Annie couldn't help uttering a 'da-nah!' of triumph. 'What do you think?' she asked Cath, meeting her eyes eagerly.

'I think . . . I think the dress is really pretty,' Cath confided. There was a smile threatening to break across her face. 'But I don't feel at home in it.'

She wriggled her shoulders uncomfortably and smoothed the dress with her hands.

'At home? No!' Annie said with a hint of exasperation, 'you are not supposed to feel at home in it. Is this a sweat-shirt and a pair of jogging trousers? No, it is not! I don't want you to feel at home. I don't want you to *be* at home!

You are one hot, juicy mama and we are taking you out to shake your booty.'

'But I don't want to go out,' Cath whined.

'Oh dear, oh dear,' Annie began, 'you've lost a lot, babes. You've lost your man, your boy's growing up, your baby blonde hair's gone, and probably your old waistline too. If you sit around at home and wait, you'll probably lose lots more: your relatives, your friends and finally everything else. Depressed yet?' she winked: 'you should be! There's only one cure for this – you have to get out there and get some new things to replace the old. New friends, new lovers, new hobbies, new interests, new people and yes, for pete's sake, some new clothes!

'Now at least if you're invited to a party, you can say yes . . . because you've got something to wear,' Annie exclaimed.

The dress, the bag and the necklace were bought. Grand total: £102.97. Annie was now itching to take Cath off to buy a nice red jacket and maybe some lipgloss or red nail varnish with the remaining money. But it was time to meet up with the rest of the team in Starbucks. Cath still had a sit-down dating lesson with Svetlana ahead of her and a career advice session with Marlise. Annie had no idea how Cath was going to come through those ordeals.

But just as Starbucks came into view, with Bob ahead of them and his cameras most definitely off, Cath clung to Annie's arm and let out a wounded wail. 'I don't want to wear the dress, Annie! I don't want to go to a singles party! They can't make me. Not on *television*. What will people think?! I'm sorry, I can't go.'

91

Chapter Ten

Lana at home:

Baggy blue tunic (H&M)
Skinny jeans (Gap)
Silver ballet shoes (Topshop)
Lip salve (Nivea)
Silver nail polish (Rimmel)
Total est. cost: £75

'I'd love to go to a party in disguise.'

'Where is Lana, anyway?' Annie wondered out loud.

Her welcome back into the bosom of her family hadn't gone quite so smoothly today, as she'd committed the sin of arriving back with a little Dorothy Perkins treat she'd bought for herself in her hands.

Before she'd been able to stash it safely behind the rack of coats in the hallway, Owen had accosted her with the words, 'You've got a plastic bag! Muuuuuum!! How many times have I told you about this? You've got to carry a re-usable shopping bag with you at all times.'

'Yes Owen, I know,' she'd soothed, managing only a glancing kiss on the top of his head, before he'd ducked away. 'I'm sorry. It won't happen again, OK.'

But too late, Ed had heard, and then he was in the hallway asking, 'Shopping bag? Surely you've not been shopping, on your budget of 28p a day or whatever it is?'

'An incredibly, incredibly cheap mini-handbag from a chain store, seriously!' she'd defended herself.

'Show!' he'd insisted, while moving in for a proper hug and kiss.

She'd opened the carrier and shown him the bracelet, bag and . . . er . . . necklace she'd picked up in the shop. But a big part of her resented having to do this. She may have been relying on Ed's savings to get them through the next few months, but she certainly didn't want to be interrogated about every single little thing she might happen to pick up for herself.

'Watch it,' she warned him, 'I might get snappy.'

'OK,' he backed off with a smile. 'They look very nice.'

That's when she'd decided to go and see Lana. At least she would understand and appreciate a bargain accessory. 'Lana's in her room,' Ed told her, 'she's never out of her room. She's become the most studious person I know.'

'Must be your good influence,' Annie said with a wink. 'OK, well, I think I'll go and say hello. Then come back to my boys in a little bit.'

'I hope you mean us and not the cats,' Ed replied, watching as his two saggy old house cats, Hoover and Dyson, wound their way, purring like engines, around Annie's legs.

It was three short flights of stairs to the attic level where

Owen and Lana each had a little bedroom. Annie tapped on Lana's door.

There was a frantic blast of keyboard tapping and then Lana's voice asked, 'Is that you, Mum?'

'Yeah,' Annie said, stepping into the room. 'Is it all right to come in or am I disturbing the next Einstein?'

'Oh very funny.' Lana swivelled her chair away from her desk and turned to smile at her mum. 'How was your day?' she asked.

'A bit stressful in parts,' Annie told her. 'How about yours?'

'Oh, I'll get over it,' Lana joked.

'Me too . . . I think,' Annie said, then she took a seat on the edge of the very crowded bed. A huge assortment of Lana's clothes, bags, books and belongings had been scattered about here.

'Planning your weekend wardrobe?' Annie asked with a smile.

'Ermm . . . something like that,' Lana replied.

'It's only Tuesday,' Annie reminded her.

'Just as well. Nothing's come together yet.'

'Something big happening at the weekend?'

'Well . . . Daisy's having a birthday party. At her home,' Lana added quickly: 'parents around, nothing too wild.'

'Sounds fine,' Annie responded, 'but you know I trust you. You're older and so much more sensible. I hate you getting older, but I like the sensible bit,' she admitted. 'Maybe it's my compensation.'

She took a long look at her daughter, with her pretty, pale, sweetheart face and dark hair. The older she got, the more she looked like her very handsome actor dad. Annie allowed the thought to cross her mind.

94

There were only a few moments in the day when she let herself think about the late Roddy Valentine, whom she had been married to for six years. Very happily married to, until a small, completely unlucky and unnecessary accident had taken him away from them all.

As she occasionally explained to people who asked: no, you didn't 'get over it', not a loss like that. You eventually just had to pick yourself up and somehow 'get on with it'. Especially for the children's sake. Somewhere along the way, along the years, she'd let go of the fury raging inside her head and made some sort of 'peace' with the situation.

Losing Roddy had become a part of who they all were: Annie, Lana, Owen, Dinah, Connor, even Ed.

The only thing that still broke her heart, whenever she allowed herself to dwell on it, was how proud, how fiercely, fiercely proud Roddy would have been of his children. But they were never going to hear that from him.

So she had to over-compensate. 'You're looking really nice,' she told Lana, 'I like your hair like that.'

'Oh, thanks,' her daughter smiled and pulled her locks over her shoulder a little shyly.

'I'm glad it's not so black any more. I mean, it was fine,' Annie corrected herself, 'but it made you look a little deathly.'

'Yeah, bit too Gothy. I'm over that,' Lana agreed. 'So what happened on the shoot today?' she asked, not able to hide the excited smile that the thought of her mum working on TV conjured up.

'Oh babes, I have no idea what is going to happen next,' Annie blurted out. 'The woman I'm supposed to be transforming from top to toe and sending to the ball to meet Prince Charming doesn't want to go. I've got her the dress, the bag and the shoes, but I can't get inside her head. Well, not in the five minutes I'm allowed to spend with her in front of the cameras, anyway. I've no idea what's going to happen now.'

Annie lay back on the sprawl of teenage clothes on the bed. It took Lana hours to get ready to go out at the weekend. Sometimes it would take her two whole hours just to get to the point of going out, then she'd still have to rush upstairs and make another complete outfit change at the very last minute. She was almost as insecure about going to parties as Cath was proving to be – a thought which inspired Annie to ask her next question.

'How do I turn ordinary, plain Jane Cath into Cinderella for the cameras, baby? How am I going to do that? She hasn't been to a party for years. She's too self-conscious. But this is the happy ending that the producer wants. He needs Cath to look gorgeous and beam happiness and confidence at every handsome stranger she meets at the ball. I mean, good grief! Impossible or what! He doesn't just want a makeover, he wants a personality transplant!'

'Cinderella only knows three other people at the ball and they don't even recognize her,' Lana said thoughtfully. 'It's much easier to pretend to be someone else if you don't know anyone there and if you're in disguise. I'd love to go to a party in disguise. No-one would recognize me and I could just be a fly on the wall. A mysterious guest!'

'Yes?' Annie was trying to understand what her daughter meant. 'So I should put her in disguise?!'

'But she's going somewhere where she won't know anyone, isn't she?' Lana asked.

'Yes . . . I think so. I mean, it's not a family party or anything. She's supposed to be taken to some sort of party. I don't know what yet.'

'So why don't you take her to a masked ball or something like that?' Lana asked enthusiastically, 'Somewhere she won't know anyone and she won't be known. Somewhere where she can hide all her awkwardness behind a mask?'

'You know, babes,' Annie said, feeling a sense of lightness and relief, 'that is a very, very good idea. That is such an amazingly good idea I might have to speak to someone about it right now!'

Lana shot her mum a smile but then her attention seemed to be caught by her computer screen again.

'You're working so hard,' Annie told her, 'I'm so proud of you.'

'Thanks,' Lana replied, but then glanced down at her feet as if almost embarrassed by the praise.

'You are going to do really well in your exams, aren't you?' her mother asked.

'I hope so,' Lana said, a little shyly.

'I'm very proud of you,' Annie repeated.

'Would it matter if I didn't do well in my exams?' Lana asked.

'For goodness sake!' Annie shooed the comment away, 'you're up here slaving away every night. You're going to do brilliantly!'

Chapter Eleven

Miss Marlise on set:

Tight black jacket (Helmut Lang)
White shirt (M&S)
Tight leather leggings (Les Chiffoniers)
Black shoe boots (LK Bennett)
Bright red lipstick (Clinique)
Total est. cost: £940

'Ha!'

'A masked ball?!'

Finn, clipboard in hand, Bluetooth round his ear, was looking at Annie in obvious astonishment.

'Just where the heck are we supposed to find a masked ball?' he asked her. 'And won't our ladies have to wear ball dresses, which we can't afford to buy? And anyway, if everyone's wearing masks, just how will we keep track of them? We'll end up filming the wrong women for half the evening.'

Miss Marlise gave a derisive little giggle and roll of her

eyes, as if to let Finn know that this was all you could expect if you let the 'wardrobe lady' come up with ideas.

Annie could also feel the weight of Bob and Nikki's eyes upon her in this claustrophobic little room. *OK*, she felt like shouting out, *it was just a suggestion.*

Instead, in her defence, she said, 'Cath may seem really cool and collected, but she doesn't do parties. I really don't know if she's going to cope. No-one seems to have mentioned the whole dating party thing to her when she agreed to come onto the programme . . . somehow.' Annie didn't want to point any fingers, but she suspected this might have something to do with either Nikki or Finn.

'I think she might have a panic attack, lock herself in the Ladies for the evening or something like that, unless we really help her out,' Annie added.

'Oh for God's sake!' Finn said with exasperation, 'there's no way we can drop her now! We've spent far too much time and money filming her already. Plus, we'd have a job getting her to part with her shiny new things now, wouldn't we?' He shot Annie a glare, as if this was somehow all her fault. None of it was her fault! She'd done everything he'd asked her to do. She could make Cath over, but she couldn't change her into a different person.

Just then Svetlana swept into the room. She'd always had a loose grasp on the concept of punctuality and appearing on TV wasn't about to change that, despite Finn and Nikki's carefully detailed schedules. So she wasn't just a minute or two late for this briefing, she was a full and glorious twenty-five minutes late.

Still, when she entered, blonde hair tumbling over a white fur coat, no-one complained; there was just a collective intake of breath. Although Annie noticed Miss Marlise raise her eyebrows and take a look at her watch. That Miss Marlise was jealous of Svetlana and all the attention Svetlana seemed to inspire had been clear from day one. Instinctively, Annie felt that both she and Svetlana should watch out for that woman. Hadn't Bob said that she would claw her way over anyone in her quest for the top?

'Svetlana, hi,' Finn smiled welcomingly. 'Don't suppose you've got any spare invitations to a masked ball lying around your Mayfair pad, do you?'

This was obviously a flippant little joke. But Svetlana, settling down in the one empty chair in the room, elegantly shrugged off her fur and in her richly accented voice, replied casually, 'Yes, but of courrrrrrse.'

Which shot a fresh surge of energy into the room.

'Really?' Finn asked.

'Of courrse,' Svetlana gave a little shrug of her shoulders. 'At the Tate Modern next Friday there is big Art Ball. You can wear masks, you can wear costumes, armour, dresses, overalls . . . whatever you like. It's artistic . . . for charity . . . people always do vhat they like.'

'Would they let us film there?' Finn asked, sounding quite breathless with excitement. A wear what you like, major glamorous event, being staged at no cost to him whatsoever. He would just need to turn up with a camera.

'Ya. I'm on committee, I tell them you film or I don't pay my big cheque,' Svetlana added.

'OK, this is great. Great! Svetlana, I don't know what we would do without you!' Finn gushed.

Miss Marlise moved her hands to her slim hips and

rolled her eyes once again. 'Ha!' she couldn't help exclaiming.

The clipboard was out and Finn was both scribbling notes and leafing through notes he'd already made.

'Today, we start with Annie's shopping session. All right, Bob? Sorry love,' he offered in Annie's direction, 'you'll have to meet the next girl in the shopping centre and take it from there. We're doing the "at home" tomorrow morning. That's the way it's going to have to work. So if you can just pretend that you've already met her, looked through her wardrobe and got to know her a bit, that would be great.'

He flicked through his pages and read out: 'Jody Wilson, same shopping centre, permission hopefully still applies. Nikki if you could ring and check . . .'

Annie felt taken aback by this set of instructions. She'd not even met Jody and now she was going to be sent straight to the changing rooms with her.

Of course, at The Store, she'd done this many, many times before: met women, put them in a changing room, then heard most of their recent life history and seen them in their pants before twenty minutes was up. But on camera? On TV? It felt as if she was stepping out on stage without any lines or a single rehearsal

'Oh and if we could keep the budget down below £200 this time, Annie, I'd be more than grateful,' was Finn's parting shot as Annie and Bob headed for the door.

Bob and Annie met Jody Wilson in a café in the shopping centre. As they said their hellos and Bob explained the filming schedule, Annie carefully sized up this petite new makeover client.

101

In her very safe, almost expressionless outfit of black suit and black boots, it was hard to get much of a clue about Jody. Annie guessed she was in her late twenties and wondered if she had volunteered herself or been volunteered by friends for the *Wonder Women* treatment.

'What made you contact us?' Annie asked.

'My mum,' Jody replied with a wary smile. 'She heard the ad on the radio and put me forward. I think she's hoping you can wave a magic wand and suddenly I'll be walking down the aisle.'

'Ah . . .' Annie understood: 'the "why isn't my daughter settled down yet?" obsession.'

Jody nodded.

'But you're here,' Annie went on, then added carefully, 'I take it you'd like to meet someone . . .'

'Special?' Jody suggested. 'I would love to meet someone special. But I'm not sure there's anyone special left. The good ones go early and everyone left is fatally flawed,' she said gloomily.

'Ah well, we're all fatally flawed,' was Annie's verdict.

As they set off from the café, Annie wanted to make sure that Jody knew the makeover was leading to a party.

'Have you heard where you're being taken to, once we've found you the outfit?' she ventured.

Jody shook her short, neat bob as a no.

'This amazing Art Ball at the Tate Modern. It's a big event, packed . . . definitely a few famous faces . . .'

She looked over at Jody, who wasn't smiling. *Careful*, Annie told herself, she didn't want to intimidate a second client.

'Oh, but it's not grand and glam,' she added quickly.

'Apparently people turn up in whatever they want. You could wear a ball dress or a pair of ripped jeans covered in graffiti . . . or both! It's all about expressing yourself, Jody.'

'Right.' Jody didn't sound very certain.

As Annie installed Jody in a River Island changing room, Bob set up his camera.

'I know it's hard,' were Annie's words of encouragement to Jody, when she began to stare at the camera with anxiety, 'but you've got to pretend that he isn't there. Think of this as just about us. Focus on me and my face,' Annie went on. 'I'll focus on you and we'll just try and let Bob do his own thing in the background.'

'OK, hang up your jacket,' Annie instructed her, 'turn around, let me see what I've got to work with here and tell me something really important. Who do you want to look like? Who's your fashion heroine? Whose wardrobe would you love to steal?'

'Whose wardrobe would I love to steal?' Jody repeated.

'Yes,' Annie replied, 'that's the best help of all for me. I can easily run round here and bring in a whole bundle of clothes that would suit your figure. But what I really need to know is what will suit your head.'

'If you love bright blue hats and funky jodhpurs,' Annie went on, 'then we have to go out there and find some! Just please don't tell me that all you really want to wear is plain black suits and nothing else, because it doesn't say enough about you. It doesn't give anyone meeting you for the first time nearly enough clues, and clues are vital. How is anyone going to chat you up if they haven't the slightest clue about you?'

'I love Audrey Hepburn,' Jody said thoughtfully. 'Hers is the wardrobe I'd most like to steal.'

'Oh, Audrey Hepburn,' Annie said with a touch of exasperation, 'so elegant but so . . . chilly. I mean, do you really believe that she and Gregory Peck got hot and sweaty and down to it at the end of *Roman Holiday*? No. She was definitely the kind of girl who would have had a headache. What about Amélie?' Annie suggested. 'Did you ever see that French film? The quirky girl with the chic little bob just like yours and cute dresses and little hats.'

'Amélie?' Jody sounded surprised, 'I loved Amélie, but I don't want to seem weird.'

'Why not?' Annie shrugged. 'Maybe your inner weird and wonderful will attract someone else's weird and wonderful.'

Jody looked unconvinced.

'I've been dressing women for ten years now,' Annie told her with a confident smile. 'I think you're just going to have to trust me here. OK?'

Slowly, Jody nodded.

Chapter Twelve

Harry on parade:

Bespoke dinner suit (Daks)
White bespoke shirt (Thomas Pink)
Navy-blue tie with small white spot (Gieves & Hawkes)
High polished black shoes (Church's)
Total est. cost: £1,750

'This is absolutely marvellous!'

The Tate Modern's vast Turbine Hall made a stunning party venue. Huge sculptures rose up from the bare concrete floor, dwarfing the swarm of guests. There was something amazing to look at on every wall, in front of every window.

Although billed as an 'Art Ball', it was obvious there wasn't going to be any dancing round the priceless modern art treasures. This party was all about sipping at the champagne cocktails, chit-chatting with the other glamorous guests and posing in your fabulously creative outfit.

When Svetlana had promised that guests could wear whatever they liked, she certainly hadn't been exaggerating. In her first quick sweep of the room, Annie could see ageing aristocratic ladies in full-on taffeta gowns, leggy London girls in cocktail dresses in all the colours of the rainbow and all sorts of mismatched, carefully thought out combos in between. No forgetting the self-styled artists in head-to-toe black or ultra-fashionable jeans spattered with oil paint.

Annie had taken one of her cherished slinky Valentino gowns out of the wardrobe tonight, but carefully dressed it down with a denim jacket, a shell and leather necklace and high-heeled sandals with a chunky wooden heel. She hoped she struck just the right note of dressed up nonchalance which she thought the event would need.

On her arm was Cath, who carried a small black sequined mask on a stick.

'Just as soon as you feel nervous, you hold the mask in front of your face and you disappear, it's just like wearing big sunglasses,' Annie had told her.

Cath was surprisingly taken with the idea. Although she'd been sweaty with nerves as she was helped into her slinky black dress and her make-up, the addition of the mask had allowed her to relax a little.

'No-one would recognize you anyway!' Annie had told her, beaming with pleasure at the finished result. 'Look at that fabulous hair.'

An entire afternoon at the hairdresser's had transformed Cath's stiff, frumpy pudding bowl into something darker, more wispy and modern.

'I'll need a lesson in how to handle a pair of straighteners,' she'd told Annie.

'Happy to oblige,' Annie had assured her.

Once they'd been handed their first cocktails, Bob came up and insisted on taking Cath away from Annie.

'Don't you worry, I'll look after her,' he promised. 'I've got my camera all set up and I want her to do some shots for me before she's had too many cocktails and can't walk in a straight line any more. And by the way,' he said, offering Cath his arm, 'you look fantastic.'

For a moment, Annie was alone. But she didn't mind at all. She just lifted her glass slowly to her lips and drank in not just a mouthful of fizz but the amazing scene all around her. She wished Ed was here; she'd struggle to tell him just how over-the-top and wonderful this event was.

So far, she'd only caught a glimpse of Finn, who was charging about issuing instructions to Bob via his Bluetooth, acutely anxious not to miss any shots.

'I want celebrities,' Finn had barked. 'If you see someone, anyone you recognize, stick your camera in their face. Our girls look wicked, so make sure you capture every single good angle. And if they're chatting to anyone, get in there!'

'Annah!'

Annie could hear the raised voice rushing towards her and knew she was about to be pressed to a generous, only slightly surgically enhanced, Ukrainian bosom.

'Here she is!' Svetlana boomed. 'This is Annah Valentine, I so vant you to meet her.'

Then Annie was face to face not just with Svetlana, but with a dapper, dinner-suited man she immediately understood to be Svetlana's husband in waiting.

A big smile broke across Svetlana's high-cheekboned

face: 'Harry! This is Annah,' she repeated. 'Annah, Harry!'

Harry's beaming face, almost as shiny as his dressy black patent shoes, was split with a generous smile and as he smoothed down his remaining hair with one hand, he extended his other to Annie.

'Annie Valentine, hello, how absolutely scrumptious to meet you,' he gushed in the kind of terribly, terribly posh English which would, once upon a time, have made Annie feel nervous and unsure of herself. Now she took it in her stride. If anything, it made her ramp up her broad, Londoner vowels.

'Annah gave me your phone number, remember, back at the beginning when ve meet,' Svetlana offered generously, anointing Annie as the matchmaker who had brought about this happy union.

'No, well . . .' Annie pointed out quickly, 'another client of mine recommended you, Harry. I was just the go-between.'

'This is absolutely marvellous!' Harry's eyebrows shot up and his grin seemed to grow even wider. 'You mean I wouldn't have met my darling, darling girl without you? I do hope you're coming to the wedding. It's going to be a complete corker.'

'Of courrrse Annah come,' Svetlana purred, before Annie even had time to wonder whether or not she would be receiving an invitation, 'I need her there to make sure dress just so and bridesmaids vonderful. Of courrrse she come.'

In the warmth of Svetlana's beam, Annie felt a wave of gratitude. She may have inadvertently hooked Svetlana up with her next husband, but Svetlana was the one who had inadvertently landed her with the TV opportunity.

Would there have been a *Wonder Women* series without Svetlana? Annie doubted it very much.

When Finn's wife, Kelly-Anne, had come into the personal shopping suite she'd arrived as a friend of Svetlana's. And Svetlana was the one who'd taken dress-making shears to Kelly-Anne's hair and started the real transformation, which must have impressed Finn so much that he'd contacted first Svetlana and then Annie and offered them the chance to be auditioned for the show.

'You both look so happy together,' Annie told Svetlana and Harry generously.

'Ya. I suit a short, bald man, no?' Svetlana teased and landed a kiss on Harry's forehead. Then she unwound herself from his embrace and informed him: 'I need to go and say hello to some people. You stay, talk to Annah. You talk to Marlise yet?' Svetlana asked Annie. With a degree of disdain, she had not yet referred to Miss Marlise as anything other than Marlise.

'No, I'm trying to keep out of her way,' Annie confided. She had spotted Miss M once and walked quickly in the opposite direction. She did admire the girl's out-fit, though: black sequined trousers and a slinky tuxedo jacket. There wasn't anything about getting dressed that Annie needed to teach her.

'Ya. Marlise total bitch to Annah,' Svetlana explained to Harry. Then off she stalked on her four-inch Louboutins, prowling through the crowds like a panther.

'Well, Harry, it's very nice to finally meet you,' Annie said, hoping to bring his attention back to her, because he was finding it hard to tear his eyes from his fiancée.

'The pleasure is all mine.' He swivelled immediately back, then said, 'Isn't she marvellous? An absolutely capital girl. I still can't believe my luck! She's just so full of life. Grabs it by the . . . horns,' he settled on.

Though from what Annie had heard of Svetlana's vibrant sex tips, 'balls' might have been more appropriate.

'So is everything with Igor all sorted, then?' Annie felt she needed to ask. Svetlana's divorce from the gas baron had not exactly been smooth.

'Well,' Harry leaned in and dropped his voice: as a barrister he knew all there was to know about discreet behaviour. 'The house and the one-off settlement are hers and there's a monthly allowance for the boys. But there are still a lot of hideously vague terms and conditions that I'm not happy with.'

'Like what?' Annie ventured.

'Igor is a stinker and if he can oil his way out of anything, believe me, he will,' Harry confided. 'I don't want to say too much, obviously, but she's had to sign all sorts of "full disclosure" documents and should she ever do anything to bring the name of Wisneski into "disrepute" she stands to lose everything . . . which is why we're in a hurry to change her name to Roscoff as quickly as possible,' he added with a smile. 'No, she's had a rough old time and I'm delighted to be charged with taking great care of her in the future.'

'Lucky Svetlana,' Annie told him and she meant it.

When she'd first heard that Svetlana had set her sights on her divorce barrister, she'd been sure Svetlana had found herself another wealthy bastard. Especially as Svetlana had decided on Harry when she'd seen the first bill for his services. Obviously, he was much, much wealthier than she'd thought and suddenly he had 'fourth husband' written all over him.

It had not taken long for Harry to spot Svetlana's obvious attractions: about 2.5 seconds, to be precise. About as quickly as she'd first stepped into his office in one of her glamazon outfits, purring her rrrrrs like honey all over him.

He had not taken much longer to fall in love with her because she had simply carried out a careful seduction plan which had left him begging, gagging, divorcing for more.

But now, something more significant seemed to have taken place. Annie could sense a genuine warmth between them. This was not just the wealthy husband/trophy wife situation that Svetlana had put herself in so many times before.

'I think you're going to make each other very happy,' Annie told Harry.

'Oh my goodness, yes!' he gushed. 'She's brought me back to life! I wake up every morning excited to see her. I thought I was far too much of a withered old prune to feel like this about someone again. But there we go . . .'

For a moment, Annie felt just ever so slightly like asking him how his ex-wife and grown-up son were taking all this bubbling over of happiness and joy at the nubile new fiancée. But then she saw something that changed her mind.

There was Jody looking utterly sensational in the silky magenta dress and mini trilby hat they'd picked out together. Her head might have been tilted shyly downwards and her arm crossed just a little defensively

111

across her body, but there she was, looking gorgeous and smiling, talking, giggling with a cute and very arty-looking guy.

Result! Annie couldn't help thinking to herself and, saying goodbye to Harry, she went off in search of Bob. If he didn't already have a shot of Jody and her fan, he would have to sneak in there and get one.

No sooner had Bob been dispatched in the right direction than Annie began to scan the room for Cath.

There she was, beside the buffet table with her mask held up like a little invisibility cloak. She wasn't talking to anyone but her shoulders weren't hunched up, her arms weren't crossed, so maybe she was actually enjoying herself. With her mask still up and a champagne glass in one hand, she walked over to one of the sculptures for a closer look.

'Pretty impressive hey?' Annie asked Cath as she came up to her, 'and I'm not talking about this hunk of metal. I'm talking about you!'

When Cath smiled at this, Annie had to ask her, 'Are you having fun yet? I think you are! I don't think you're even ready to admit how much fun you are having. You're beautifully dressed, you're at an amazing event, you're a party girl in the making,' she added.

'I'm having fun,' Cath admitted. 'I don't recognize myself so I feel as if I'm in complete disguise.'

'Money is not so precious that you can never, ever spend a little on a treat for yourself.' Annie reminded her. 'Everyone needs a little, reasonable, perfectly within budget treat. Like this,' she held up a multi-coloured mock snakeskin clutch bag: 'Topshop, fourteen pounds and I'm loving it!' she gave Cath a wink.

Then she spotted Bob at a discreet distance, but probably on a long lens, filming them both.

One of the handsome young PRs for the event approached them. 'Hi,' he began, 'having fun? Getting all the footage you need?'

'Yes, it's fantastic,' Annie assured him, 'an amazing party.'

'I love your mask,' the PR told Cath, 'I wish I'd thought of wearing one. Then I'd be able to slink about and get into all sorts of trouble.'

Cath giggled in response, but Annie was sure the camera was whirring and in the all-important editing suite they were bound to make it look as if Cath was being chatted up and the Wonder Women had scored an all-round resounding dating success.

For a few more moments Annie, Cath and the PR made small talk, then Annie glanced around for Bob, hoping he would give them the thumbs-up that he'd got enough footage.

But he wasn't there. She looked again, wondering if he was shooting them from a different angle. No sign.

Then through a little break in the crowd Annie caught a glimpse of him. He had his back to her, because he was crouched down, busy filming Svetlana and Miss Marlise as they hugged up together and smiled for the camera.

There was something about this that made Annie feel a little uneasy. Shouldn't she be there? Shouldn't she be part of the group, hugging and congratulating themselves on the big party success?

'I'll be right back,' she promised Cath, then began to head in the direction of the others.

Just as she approached Bob, a hand shot out to catch

her shoulder. It was Finn's. 'One moment,' he instructed. 'Miss Marlise wanted a shot with Svetlana.'

'Shouldn't we all be in this together?' Annie couldn't stop herself from asking.

'Well . . . no,' Finn replied. 'This is what Miss Marlise wanted and we have to humour her a little. She's only twenty-five, she's going to be a big, big star. She's got her whole career ahead of her.'

Annie suddenly felt compared, judged and past it. All the fizz of success she'd felt watching Cath and Jody strut their stuff, seemed to instantly evaporate.

Chapter Thirteen

Paula does casual:

Grey leather jacket (Rick Owens, Store sale preview)
Pencil leg jeans (J Brand)
White T-shirt (Miss Selfridge)
Fuchsia pink cut-out shoe boots
(Givenchy, Store sale preview)
Orange nails (Mac)
Total est. cost: £630

'Rockin' the Chloé'

'I like the music . . . syncopated, very catchy,' came Ed's comment, as soon as the opening bars of the theme tune had begun.

'SHHHHHH!' Annie smacked his arm. She didn't want to see one moment of this, yet she didn't want to miss one single second. This was horrific. She was going to be sick.

But she'd organized a party! Well, no she hadn't. Not exactly. She'd told her family and just a few friends that the

Home Sweet Home channel was so excited about *Wonder Women*, it had begged Finn to put together a pilot episode which was screening at prime time, 7 p.m., tonight.

Her sister, Dinah, had insisted she come over to Annie's to watch it with her. Then so had her mother, Fern . . . and her Store best friend, Paula, plus Lana and Owen's friends, Greta and Milo.

This was why there were now nine people squeezed onto every available seat, chair, sofa and cushion in the sitting room of Annie's house with their eyes glued to the TV screen.

Annie, who had found to her dismay that she only had £65 in her bank account to last until *next month*, apparently, had had to drive to Costco and blow almost all of it on quiche, coleslaw, Coke, a wine box, monster bags of crisps and a bucket of popcorn.

Well, you couldn't have people round and not feed them.

Just maybe, for a few deluded moments, she'd thought it would be nice to have her nearest and dearest around as she watched herself on the small screen for the very first time. But now that the episode was about to begin, she was huddled up against Ed with a large sofa cushion in front of her. At the moment, she could only peek out over the cushion, ready to hide her face and stifle her screams if necessary. She couldn't remember when she had last felt so nervous.

In one hand she was holding her mobile phone, ready to take the call from Svetlana, in the other hand was her home phone and on the end of the line was Connor.

'Just hold me up to the TV,' he'd instructed. 'I won't be able to see it, but at least I'll be able to hear you.'

Annie stole a glimpse around the room. Every face was glued to the screen. No-one was looking at her, everyone was waiting expectantly to see if the woman they knew so well, the one sitting right in their midst, could manage to pull this off.

Except suddenly Annie's mother looked round and gave her a reassuring smile. 'Relax, sweetheart!' the comforting voice assured her, 'you're going to be fantastic. I know.'

'Shhhhhhh!' Lana shushed her gran.

The music had stopped and Miss Marlise was standing in front of Cath's house delivering her tirade.

'That's not very nice,' came Fern's comment.

'No,' Ed agreed.

'And she is exactly like that in real life,' Annie slipped in, 'a complete cow.'

Cath appeared on the screen looking beige, stern and extremely nervous.

'Oh boy!' Lana exclaimed, 'you had to get *her* all dressed up and off to the ball. No wonder you were worried!'

This time it was Owen's turn to demand quiet. But then any chance to tell his big sister off for anything and he was straight in there.

'Milo, I think you're a bit close to the . . .' Annie began but the words dried up in her throat because there she was on screen, being beamed into who knows how many houses up and down the country.

She could hear the intake of breath in the room.

'You look fantastic!' Ed whispered and squeezed her round the waist.

'Look at you, gorgeous!' Paula shrieked, 'Rockin' the Chloé!'

'I look huge!' Annie whined, watching as her on-screen self swung her rear end unflatteringly at the screen in an effort to get to the bottom of Cath's wardrobe, 'Oh no,' she wailed, 'I'm fatter than Sarah Beeny and she's almost always pregnant!'

'Be quiet! I want to hear what you're saying,' Dinah hissed.

Then there was total silence from the audience in the room; well, apart from chomping as Milo and Owen worked their way steadily through the popcorn bucket.

They all saw Cath in close-up and heard her words about not having anything nice to wear and her husband leaving her on her birthday.

'Awww, bless,' Paula sympathized at once.

'You're a natural,' Ed told Annie and landed a kiss on her ear. 'You're going to be a huge star. I can retire,' he joked.

Although this was very flattering, Annie wanted a professional opinion. 'Did you hear that?' she asked Connor.

'Brilliant!' he told her, 'and how do you look?'

'Like a whale,' she groaned.

'You do not, Mum!' Lana insisted. 'You look normal and real, not like her!'

Everyone's attention was now transfixed by Svetlana. There she was lounging on Cath's bed, flashing her legs and her cleavage this way and that.

'You look much, much better than her,' Ed assured her.

'She's so over-dressed,' Fern commented, 'and how old is she, Annie?'

'Thirty-six again,' came Annie's reply, 'but she looks

118

great, Mum. And she works so hard at it. I bought that dress with her; she's got the bod, she can totally carry it off.'

'Treat your man good,' Svetlana was panting into the camera, 'flatter him, never forget to every day massage his . . .' she paused with a saucy eyebrow quirk here, 'ego. If your man is happy,' Svetlana added, thrusting her cleavage at the camera, 'he will make you very, verrrrry happy.'

At this Dinah gave such a severe snort of laughter that a small crumb of popcorn shot out of her nose.

'I can't believe she just said that. Where is she from, Annie? The Dark Ages?'

'The Ukraine,' Annie replied.

'It's Mum again,' Owen pointed out.

'Are you at Bluewater?' Lana recognized the shopping centre.

'Yes, we have a bad moment in Wallis and a very good moment in Dorothy Perkins,' Annie rushed to explain, but now, scrunching the cushion hard against her stomach, she watched herself bustle about Cath and then, a few TV minutes and an ad break later, about Jody.

'The trilby is genius!' Paula told her, 'so like . . .' she began, and then Annie joined in with her, 'Marc by Marc Jacobs, this season!'

Both burst out laughing.

When Annie made a little speech to Jody about not needing to be blonde or wear short skirts but just to be yourself, Dinah, Fern and Lana all cheered.

Then Miss Marlise was on screen treating the women to her 'career advice'. It was peppered with the kind of tips that would suit Miss Marlise but not many others:

'Don't let anyone stand in your way. If you think you have a rival, take them on and take them out!'

'I think you've done a wonderful job on both of them, Annie,' Fern whispered. 'What Miss Bossy Boots and the Russian trophy wife have to do with it all I don't know, the programme should just be about you. What's Miss Bossy Boots just told that woman: demand a pay rise? That poor dear looks so embarrassed. Probably all she can think about is that her boss might be watching.'

'Shh, Mum! It's the ball,' Dinah broke in. 'Wow! What an amazing venue! Did you dress up too, Annie?'

The question was answered as the camera panned across the Tate Modern's vast ground floor and picked out Svetlana and Harry, Miss Marlise whispering instructions into Jody's ear and Annie in her classy red dress holding Cath by the arm.

Shots of Jody chatting to the arty guy and Cath giggling at the handsome PR followed. When the guy who'd been talking to Jody asked her to dance, there was another intake of breath in the room.

'Oh she looks so cute,' Dinah told them, 'he's definitely interested, isn't he?'

'Oh!' Greta, Lana's friend, pointed out, 'there's Cath on the dance floor, who's she—'

Before she could finish the question, Cath spun so that everyone could see her dancing partner. It was Annie.

'Go, girls!' Paula declared.

'She deserved some fun!' Annie defended herself.

The camera closed in on Annie's smiling face just as she shot Bob, the cameraman a wink.

Then the credits rolled.

Everyone dissolved into the rollicking laughter of relief and shouted out congratulations.

'Brilliant!' Ed kissed her on the cheek, 'I am so proud of you. You were brilliant!'

'Yeah Mum, you were great,' Lana added.

Annie watched the credits, reading each of the names of the team she now knew so well, in turn. Then she put the phone to her ear again.

'Did they close on you?' Connor asked in surprise. 'That's good, that's really good. You're a star, Annie Valentine! This is where it all begins.'

'Did it sound OK?' she asked anxiously. 'Did I sound OK?'

'You sounded just like yourself, which is great,' Connor gushed. 'That's all the camera wants, people to be just like themselves. So, I hope you're wearing nice knickers.'

'Why?!'

'Because that man of yours is going to be insatiable to-night . . . unstoppable,' Connor teased, 'the aphrodisiac of fame. I'm telling you, baby, better believe it. You are in for a long night.'

'I have to go,' Annie told him, as her mobile burst into life.

'Go,' Connor told her, 'your fans need you.'

This made them both snort with laughter.

'Svetlana!' Annie answered the phone, 'what did you think?'

'Vonderful!' came the gushing response, 'Ve all look fantastic. Ve do great job. Harry thinks best programme he's ever seen.'

'Yeah, well, no surprise there!' Annie laughed.

'My other line is calling . . . I see you tomorrow,' Svetlana explained before ringing off.

At this point Fern delved into her sturdy M&S shopper.

'Aw Mum,' Dinah joked, 'you've had it personalized.'

'Huh?' Fern looked at the outside of her shopper.

'A bag for life,' Dinah explained.

'Oh ha-ha, very funny,' Fern replied, then pulled out a bottle of champagne. 'C'mon everyone, time to celebrate. It's not every day that your daughter appears on national bloody television.'

'Er well . . . not sure that the Home Sweet Home channel is big enough to be national,' Annie began.

'Nonsense,' her mother insisted.

Glasses came out along with more crisps, more quiche and more Cokes for the children.

'Owen, is that your third?' Annie wondered at some point. 'You won't sleep a wink. That's far too much caffeine.'

'Mum, is that your third?' Owen pointed at her champagne glass.

'Was I OK?' she asked her son. She desperately wanted to hug him in under her arm and mess with his hair a bit, but she understood that with Milo present that would have been committing a motherly crime of embarrassment of monumental proportions.

'Yeah, you were fine,' came Owen's reply as he stretched his arm out once more for the crisp bowl.

She knew she couldn't expect much more gushing from her son. He was a man of few words. But if he thought it was 'fine', that was probably OK.

Greta and Lana were far more voluble in their praise.

They told Annie all about which outfits they'd liked best and where else she should go shopping on the high street, then disappeared upstairs to MSN all of Lana's friends who'd been told to watch tonight and make a full report.

Paula had to leave promptly too: 'I have an interesting meeting and that's all I'm saying.'

Once Fern was alone in the room with her two daughters and Ed, she surprised them by announcing: 'I've got a new medical condition: high blood pressure.'

'Really?' Annie felt a pang of worry. 'It's nothing serious though, is it?'

'I'm still only sixty-four,' Fern reminded her, 'not quite at the age where everything and anything is serious.'

'But still . . .' Dina joined in.

'Are you OK?' Ed was quick to express his concern.

Fern smiled warmly in his direction. She had a big soft spot for Ed: not just because he was so obviously good for her daughter but because he'd lost his own mother just a few years ago and he hadn't been shy about letting Fern fill at least a little of the gaping vacancy in his life.

'I'm going to be fine. I'm on this course of spanking new drugs and my doctor—'

'Which one is this?' Dinah broke in. 'Not the foxy Dr Bill? You're not making up ailments just so you can go and hang out with him?'

'No I am not, but he's been marvellous. A tower . . .'

'Of strength,' Dinah and Annie chimed in together.

'Mum!' Annie rolled her eyes and pretended to be stern, 'is this how it is dating in your sixties? You have to have an illness to get a bit of attention?' She was trying not to laugh.

'Annie, that's enough!' Fern picked up the champagne

bottle and topped up everyone's glasses. 'Now, what's up with you, Dinah? You look a bit puffy.' This was said kindly, Fern tilting her head understandingly at her youngest girl.

'Oh,' Dinah was caught off guard, 'I wasn't going to say anything yet . . .'

Annie could feel her stomach skip. This was one of her dearest, dearest people in the world. Say what? Why didn't Annie know? What was the matter with Dinah?

'We're back on the IVF treadmill,' Dinah admitted.

'No!!' Fern and Annie gasped in horror. Whereas Ed just gave a small smile meant to express both his understanding and his sympathy.

'But I thought Billie was going to be the one and only,' Annie said, referring to Dinah and Bryan's precious, cherished six-year-old daughter.

'You went through so much to have her,' Fern agreed; 'are you going to put the three of you through all that again?'

Dinah looked so taken aback at this reaction from them both that Annie immediately felt guilty. She and her mother had said the wrong thing, however well it was meant.

'I thought you'd be more supportive . . .' Dinah began.

'I'm sorry, babes,' Annie rushed over to Dinah's side of the sofa and put an arm round her, 'of course we should be more supportive. I'm sure you and Bryan have decided to do what's best for you. I'm sorry. We just saw how rough it was the first time.'

'But you can't say it wasn't worth it,' Dinah pointed out.

'Billie is fantastic,' Annie agreed.

'Ah Billie, there's only one Billie!' Fern was quick to add.

'Yes,' Dinah said, 'there's only one . . .'

She didn't need to say anything more.

Annie's mind was reeling: first Ed, then Connor, now Dinah . . . was there some sort of baby virus out there? Who was going to catch it next?

Chapter Fourteen

Post-bath Annie:

Blue silk slip (La Senza)
Clarins body lotion (eBay)
Sisley night cream, out of date
(The Store's staff-only bargains)
Total est. cost: £40

'Did you put the cats out?'

It was always close to midnight when things were finally calm and quiet in Annie's household.

She came out of the shower, dried and dressed for bed, then did a final tour of the house, checking that Owen's covers were on and Lana's lights were out.

When Annie pushed open the bedroom door, she understood at once that Ed was waiting for her . . . expectantly.

The light was low, provided by a small sidelight and the cluster of candles which had been lit in the room's long defunct fireplace. Music, the second love of Ed's life, was oozing from the iPod speakers right beside the bed, something soft and seductive that she didn't recognize. But then this was a man who delved for obscure CDs at charity shops and market stalls. Everything had been tidied away, so the room looked peaceful and calm, the idea being that she shouldn't be distracted, she should concentrate on her man already in bed, waiting for her.

He smiled and put down his book. He wasn't wearing a top but he was still wearing his glasses, a look which she found irresistibly sexy. She wasn't even sure why; it was like catching him half undressed. Or maybe it was the combination of intellectual glasses and big arm muscles which pressed all the right buttons for Annie.

'Did you put the cats out?' she asked him.

'Uh-huh,' he answered, with a little smile.

'Empty the dryer?'

'Oh yeah.'

'Wash out the packed-lunch boxes?'

'Ooooh, your sexy talk is turning me on . . .' he teased, 'Come over here!' He held out his arms to her.

'The aphrodisiac of fame . . . Connor's warned me, you know.'

She let her dressing gown fall open and walked towards him in the slinky ink-blue slip she'd put on after her shower, just for him.

As she reached the bed, she slid her hands over his arms and said, 'Last household chore of the day, huh?'

'Oh yeah,' he agreed, looking at her appreciatively, 'last household chore of the day. Come here,' he instructed.

She knelt over him and they began to kiss.

His tongue felt warm and minty against hers. She felt the soft silk of her slip sliding over her breasts.

127

'Under the covers,' Ed insisted, pulling her in beside his naked body; 'get your fantastic arse into bed beside me.'

His hands moved up over her buttocks, pushing the slip out of the way. 'Are you pleased?' he asked, pulling her in against his hairy chest.

'With you?' she asked, 'Always.'

'No! With *Wonder Women*. Are you happy with it?' he asked.

'I think so, I think it's fine. Can we keep the heavy stuff out of the bedroom, please?' she asked, feeling with her fingertips for his pleasingly smooth and springy erection.

He reached for the iPod control and changed the music. Something much more fruity began to fill the room: big, fat, sexy sax.

'Mmmmm,' she breathed against his neck, 'I want to slow dance with you.'

He slid the straps of her slip down from her shoulders, then teased the fabric over her breasts to expose them. Then he gave a lick to wet her nipples before blowing on them gently.

'I like that,' she heard herself murmur.

'I know,' he replied.

'Are you going to go down . . . and do that there?'

'Do you want me to?' he asked and blew on her nipple again.

She could feel her toes flex just at the thought of him doing that there.

'Uh-huh,' she agreed.

He moved down and she lay back and let him do all the things he did to make her feel so liquid, molten, so very incredibly hot and breathless and turned on right . . . yes, there.

He didn't just lick, he moved, he blew, he hummed and sometimes sang! Right there, right up against her, until her hands were wound into his hair and she was just about singing with pleasure herself.

She was just . . . just about, almost . . . nearly. Definitely. No, not, yes . . . about to . . . when he stopped. Abruptly.

'Don't!' she said urgently.

'Just a second.'

'No! Hello! You need to go back down there . . .' she insisted.

'Trust me.'

He leaned over, opened a drawer, took out a cable and attached it to the iPod.

'Close your eyes,' he instructed.

One moment later and Annie's eyes were wide open again and she sat bolt upright. Had he just . . . ?!!

'Ed!?' she exclaimed.

She was aware of a tingly buzz that wasn't coming from his lips. Wasn't coming from anything human.

'Shhhhhhhh,' he told her, 'it's in time with the music.

In Ed's hands she could see a small egg-shaped . . . vibrator.

'Are we at the sex toy stage?' she asked.

'You know I find it hard to resist a musical gadget,' he replied.

'What is it?'

A grin split Ed's face as he told her, 'This, baby, is the iPod-compatible *iGasm*.'

'The iGasm?!' she repeated. 'Are you joking?'

'Shhhhh,' he said, then reached over, turned out

the sidelight and put the iGasm back to work.

Now, he was good. But that . . . that was technologically advanced. It buzzed to the rhythm and she wanted to dance right along with it.

She was damp and clinging to him now. Desperate for him to push inside as she felt every nerve ending pulse and come alive. 'Baby,' she breathed against his ear, 'you are so hot.'

'Have you got your diaphragm in?' he murmured as his fingers slid against her.

'Oh yeah . . . I came prepared.'

'I wish you wouldn't.' He was moving inside her now, and she was so desperate to come, right, right, right now this very second, now.

'Oh Ohhhhh,' she heard herself exhale against his ear.

'Let's have a baby, Annie,' he said, holding her with every square inch of his body, pulling her right against him.

It wasn't fair. It was like the opposite of torture, lovemaking someone into a decision. Orgasming them into submission.

'Please, let's have a baby,' Ed repeated with the tension in his voice which told her he was going to come too.

Chapter Fifteen

Practical Bob:

Green army vest with pockets (military kit store)
Blue sweatshirt (M&S)
Comfy jeans (M&S)
Brown suede hiking boots (Timberland)
Digital watch (Casio)
Total est. cost: £230

'We'll get you right.'

Annie looked out of the window of Bob's car at the boring motorway scenery whizzing past. Today, the morning after the pilot screening, the Wonder Women were up early and on their way to Birmingham.

Bob had come to collect her just before 7 a.m. so they could get out of London before the worst of the morning traffic. To Annie's not so great surprise, Finn, Miss Marlise, Svetlana and Nikki were all travelling up together in Finn's car.

When Annie had first heard about the arrangements,

she had wondered if she should worry that yet again Finn was keeping Miss Marlise and Svetlana together while leaving her out. But then she'd reasoned with herself that Bob lived much closer to her than anyone else and then tried not to mind about the arrangements any more.

'So,' Bob had asked as soon as Annie had buckled herself into the front seat, 'did you enjoy seeing yourself on TV?'

She'd given a little laugh and had to think about that for a moment.

'I was a bit distracted by everything I did wrong and how I'd do it differently the next time,' she'd admitted. 'But for a minute or two, when it went right, when we got a good moment . . . yeah, I was chuffed,' was her honest reply.

'What did you think?' she'd asked him.

'Lots of things went well, a few things went tits up,' he answered. 'You're right to worry about how you did. That's exactly how you should be thinking. Yes, there were a few novice moments,' he hadn't been able to resist saying. 'Never point your big bum at the camera, for one! I can't believe they didn't edit that out. But we'll work on it. We'll get you right. I think you've got a real future ahead of you.'

She'd beamed at him. Beamed, because really deep down, in her heart of hearts, wouldn't she like that? A big future ahead of her in television?

'What's Finn said to you?' Bob had asked when they made the transition onto the motorway.

'Well . . .'

Finn had phoned her last night and she'd expected him to say something a bit more than, 'Did you watch it? Good stuff,' before moving on to talk about the travel arrangements to Birmingham.

'Not a lot,' she had to admit.

'Not to me either,' Bob told her. 'Hard to tell what he's thinking. The channel seems so keen, but he doesn't seem to be able to squeeze any more money out of them. He's asked me to lower my day rate for the last week.'

'Am I allowed to know what he's paying you?' Annie had to ask.

When she heard, she couldn't stop herself from spluttering: 'Bloody hell!!'

'I know, it's not good, is it?' Bob thought she was sympathizing.

Annie wanted to laugh out loud. She was going to earn in a month what Bob was picking up in three days! Just like crime, fame so obviously didn't pay.

The mobile in her handbag burst into life, and a glance at the screen told her it was Svetlana again.

'Annah! My phone not stop ringing since the show go on air! So many old friends contact me to say how much they love it. Finn, he's beside me in the carrrr, his phone ringing all the time too. People love the show, Annah! It is so exciting! Vhy you not in the car with us listening to all these good things?' she asked.

'I'm driving up with Bob,' Annie explained.

Svetlana gave that peculiar noise she used to express disapproval. *'Tcha!* It's not good. You not go home with Bob, you come in car with us. Nikki go with Bob,' she commanded.

'Now, vat I have to tell you . . .' Svetlana's voice sounded full of suppressed excitement, which was of immediate concern to Annie. There were only a few things that really excited the Ukrainian: and they were all related to mega-wealthy men and their mega money.

'Guess who phone me last night? At home on my personal number?'

'Igor?' Annie ventured, 'Igor Potato-face the Third?' she asked because if Svetlana was even thinking about a reunion, she needed to be reminded what a horror Igor had been.

'No! Igor. Tcha!' Svetlana made the disdainful noise again. 'No. A very interesting man. Also Ukrainian. He's called Uri and he has hedge fund, is vorth millions and he vants to take me to dinner!'

'Do you know him?' Annie asked.

'Yes, yes. He say we meet many times at parties when I am Igor's wife.'

'And he's never phoned you before?'

'No! And he get my home number! No-one has my home number. Everyone use my mobile. He loved the show.'

'He watches the Home Sweet Home channel?!' To Annie it didn't seem very likely.

'He hear from someone that I going to be on television, he find out about it and so . . . he is a very interesting man. He is going to take me out to celebrate my first appearance on television.'

'Erm . . .' Annie knew she was going to have to point out the obvious thing here: 'but darlin', does Harry know? Is Harry going along?' she ventured. 'You have told Mr Deep Pockets that you're getting married in a few weeks' time, haven't you?'

'Oh Annie!' Svetlana breathed an exasperated sigh, 'you not understand how it vorks. You never understand how it vorks.'

Chapter Sixteen

Tina pre-makeover

Grey turtle neck (Gap)
Black jeans (Gap)
Black ankle boots (Dolcis)
Total est. cost: £130

'I'm not good at clothes or make-up.'

'And that's everyone else arriving now.' Annie stood up and looked out of the window at the silver 4 × 4 pulling up in the street in front of Tina Balotti's flat.

She and Bob had arrived here half an hour earlier, so they'd had coffee with Tina and found out a little about her while trying to put her at ease. Tina was younger than Annie had expected. But then all Annie had been told was: 'Single mum, lives with her little girl, works full-time, contacted us herself.'

Then Finn had shown her a snapshot of a girl in a white duvet coat with long, wispy black hair and a sweetheart-shaped face.

'I think she's going to scrub up very, very well,' Finn had added. 'I think she'll be our knockout. She's got a good figure, a nice face, she just doesn't know how to make the most of herself. But by the time you three have finished with her . . .'

It turned out Tina was only 24, but she already had a 3-year-old daughter, her own flat and a full-time job. The flat was tiny but as it was only a few years old, it was bright, light and comfortable. Annie and Bob had squeezed onto the little sofa together as Tina served them mugs of coffee.

'Where's your gorgeous little girl?' Annie had asked, pointing at one of the many photos dotted all over the room.

'She's at my mum's today,' Tina replied. 'She does two days at nursery and three with her gran.'

'And you've got the day off. Lucky you!' Annie told her. 'You're going to have a fantastic time.'

The question 'So why did you get in touch with us?' had proved a little tricky for Tina to answer.

She'd shyly fumbled her way through an answer: 'Oh, I'm not good at clothes or make-up . . . I don't go out much . . . I mean, I'd like to go out more, but . . . since I've had Julia, I've been hidden away and I think I want to get out now . . . kind of.'

'Great!' Annie had encouraged. 'We're here to help you, give you all the good advice we can think of.'

Now that Finn and the others had arrived, Annie decided to go out and greet them.

Miss Marlise stepped down from the car, took one look around and declared, 'Oh my God, what a dump!'

Admittedly, Tina's block of flats was the only new one

on the street; the rest looked as if they could do with some care and attention. But still.

'It could be worse,' Annie reminded her. At this Finn handed her a holdall and said, 'Better not leave anything in the car round here.'

When Annie realized she was carrying Marlise's holdall, while Marlise marched towards the house empty handed, she felt like dumping the bag down there and then.

But then Svetlana was at her side, wrapped in another fur coat because her high heels and glamorous dresses really didn't stand up to the chilly weather.

'Vhat the makeover voman like?' she wondered.

'Shy . . . quite sweet.'

'Another saddo?' Marlise turned to ask, having over-heard Svetlana's question.

Annie wasn't sure how to reply to this because Cath, Jody and Tina hadn't struck her as 'saddos'. They were all just looking for the little push to take them to the next stage.

'She had a baby at twenty-one or something?' Miss Marlise snorted. 'Isn't that a bit sad?'

'Well . . .' Annie began, her hand gripping Miss Marlise's luggage, 'but she's got a flat, a job, her daughter's lovely. She just wants to get out more.'

'A mum at twenty-one. Talk about your life being over before it's begun,' Miss Marlise went on. 'What the hell am *I* going to be able to do for her?'

Leaving Annie open-mouthed in surprise, Miss Marlise marched ahead of them, her high-heeled patent boots rapping on the concrete path.

'I had my daughter at twenty-one!' Annie hissed at Svetlana, 'and I loved every moment of it.'

'Is very different if you have lovely man there with you. This girl single,' Svetlana pointed out. 'Verrrry different.'

By then they were at the doorway to Tina's home so there wasn't time for any more discussion.

Everyone was squeezed into the sitting room and introduced to Tina, who seemed to shrink a little with shyness.

After only a few moments of small talk, it was time for Finn to bring out his clipboard and get the shooting schedule started.

'If we do Tina with Svetlana and Miss Marlise first,' he began, making a quick check on his watch, 'the four of us will be able to check into the hotel and plan for our shoot tomorrow morning, which would be great, wouldn't it, girls?' He looked up at them for confirmation.

'Bob and Annie, if you do the shopping session afterwards you'll have all afternoon with Tina, you won't need to rush, and if it goes on past close of play, Bob,' Finn's voice dropped, 'obviously you bill me for the extra . . . How does that sound?' he asked cheerfully. 'Good? All happy? Wicked! Nikki, let's get Tina ready to roll.'

Svetlana's approach was quite interesting, Annie had to admit as she peeped out from the kitchen to see what was going on in the sitting room. Together, they were looking through Tina's photo albums, but flicking quickly past any cute baby and toddler shots of Julia and homing in on Tina's old boyfriends.

'This Julia's father?' Svetlana asked.

When Tina nodded in reply, Svetlana made her 'Tcha' sound.

'Big man,' Svetlana added. 'Can be frightening, no?'

Tina nodded again.

'Good you get rid of him – but you decide to keep baby?'

'My mum and dad helped me to make that decision,' Tina admitted.

'Ya. Verrry kind,' Svetlana said and Annie was surprised to hear the note of softness in her voice. She'd never asked Svetlana anything about her own mother and father, but she would try to do it the next time she got a chance.

'Are you going to look through Tina's wardrobe with her?' Finn wondered, when he was satisfied that he had all the footage he wanted of Tina with Svetlana and then Tina with Miss Marlise.

Annie's reply was simple: 'No. No need. I'm going to find all sorts of sensible work outfits and all kinds of practical mum outfits and we don't want any of that, do we Tina?' She shot Tina a smile. 'The girl wants to get out. She needs to get out. C'mon, grab your coat, I know just the place for you. Bob and I are whisking you off to Topshop.'

'How long has it been since you went shopping for yourself, sweetheart?' Annie asked as she watched Tina move around the brightly crammed rails, racks and shelves in one of Annie's favourite high street shops.

Tina really did look like a girl let loose in a sweetie shop. Her eyes were wide and she hardly dared to put out her hands to touch things, in case she was told that she wasn't allowed to have them.

Annie had once again been warned by Finn to keep the budget 'well below two hundred pounds if you can', but in this shop prices were low enough for that not to pose too much of a problem.

While Tina looked with confused curiosity all around her, Annie got on with the business of pulling out pieces for the changing rooms.

Looking at Tina's narrow hips and skinny legs, she guessed she was a 10 from the waist down, but a 12 on top. Annie's brief from Finn couldn't have been more clear: knockout dress or miniskirt and skimpy top, heels, big hair, full make-up. Ingredients to transform timid Tina into the bombshell Finn awaited.

Busily, she began to load up her arms with short dresses sprinkled with sequins, netted skater skirts, strapless tops, lots of shine, juicy colours and delicious textures.

Because the shop was busy, even on a weekday afternoon, the staff had obligingly cleared out the biggest style consultant's room for the filming session.

To Annie, each new outfit seemed to work better on Tina than the last. Underneath the baggy tops and scarves she'd been hiding a great figure, slim-hipped and long-legged but with boobs on top that she was clearly a little shy about.

'You need to learn to love those!' Annie insisted, hoicking her up into a corset top. 'That looks absolutely brilliant on you. I'm sorry, but you can't deny it.'

She stood back to admire Tina in the tight black top, teeny pink puffball skirt, black sheeny tights and high patent shoes. There was no doubt that Finn was going to love this look, but Annie could tell that the problem was going to be convincing Tina. She was scrutinizing herself in the mirror with something close to a scowl on her face.

'Let's ask Bob what he thinks,' Annie suggested. She pushed back the curtain and gestured for the cameraman to take a peek.

'Unbelievable!' was his appreciative comment. 'You look amazing, Tina! I can hardly recognize you.'

To Annie, he directed a thumbs-up and said, 'Finn is going to be very happy.'

Then he hoisted the camera up to his face and began to film.

But still Tina stood in front of the mirror on her long legs and scowled.

'What's the matter?' Annie wondered. 'Is it too much of a change? Too much of a surprise? But you are such a great-looking girl. I can't help feeling that the world should know! You've been hiding yourself away for too long.'

'It's just ... it's just so ... well, isn't it just a bit ... obvious?' Tina asked finally. 'I mean,' she went on, 'miniskirt and boob tube and long hair and high heels. I mean ... that's just too much.'

As soon as Tina said it, Annie knew it was true. Well, of course it was true. Would she let Lana go out like this? No. And even though Tina was eight years older than Lana, it was still too much. Finn might like it. Finn might want to see this kind of over the top transformation on screen, but as Tina said: it was too much.

Then came the kicker, which tugged at Annie's heartstrings and she knew she would have to respond to. 'It just isn't me,' Tina declared.

'Well, you have to be you,' Annie decided, certain that if she could make Tina look fabulous on Tina's terms, it would work for Finn. 'Is there anything about this outfit you like?' she asked.

Tina looked carefully. 'I like the top,' she said, surprising herself.

She was right. The black sweetheart-shaped corset looked stunning with her pale skin and strong shoulders.

'And I love the shoes.'

'Oh yeah, I love the shoes too,' Annie had to admit. They were a shiny, liquid black with high heels and satiny laces.

'Maybe, to tone it down, between the corset top and the shoes, maybe we should have slim satin trousers,' Annie suggested.

'Trousers, yeah. Black?' Tina suggested.

'Yeah, let's try black.'

Tina scraped her hair back off her face and held it up for a moment.

Annie admired Tina's pretty features and then spotted something she hadn't noticed before. An intricate tattoo of a rose at the nape of Tina's neck, the stem and the leaves curling out onto her shoulder.

'Oh, look at that!' she exclaimed, 'that's really pretty, we should have that on show. Tina,' she scolded, 'you've kept all the best things about yourself hidden.'

'Maybe that's the way I like it,' Tina said softly.

Annie stepped in behind her for a closer look. She wasn't really a tattoo aficionado, but this was very well done. It had been delicately shaded to complement Tina's slim neck and pale skin.

'Do you like it?' Tina asked.

'It's lovely,' Annie told her.

'I just had it done a month ago. The scabs have only just healed and . . .'

'You're almost ready to show it off,' Annie guessed.

'Yeah . . . my . . . friend designed it. And we took it to this tattoo artist.'

'Very talented friend,' Annie said and was surprised when a pink blush spread up from Tina's neck to her face.

'More than a friend?' Annie asked.

'Maybe,' Tina admitted, casting her eyes down. 'Maybe she's more than a friend.' Then a surprised look crossed her face, as if she'd said more than she'd meant to.

'Very interesting.' Annie gave her an encouraging smile; it wasn't the first time she'd heard someone's changing-room secrets. When you physically stripped people down, you seemed to get them to bare all sorts of truths about themselves.

'So there are lots of interesting things going on in your life at the moment,' Annie said.

'Yes . . . I suppose so.'

'So, new Tina. New look. Definitely!' Annie said, then caught hold of Tina's hair and pulled it back off her face again. 'Have you ever thought about cutting your hair off?' she asked. 'You've got such a pretty face and then the rose would be on display whenever you wanted it to be.'

'I'd love to cut my hair off!' Tina confirmed, 'I'm just not sure . . . where . . . or how . . .'

'To begin? Leave it to me,' Annie insisted. 'Right, let's sort out the satin trousers and then get ourselves down to the swankiest salon in town. Bob!'

There was a clunk as Bob, to Annie and Tina's surprise, pressed the pause button.

143

'You filmed all that?' Tina asked.

'Don't worry, they'll only use a bit of it,' he assured her. 'Annie, don't you think we should ask Finn about the haircut? I mean, he was wanting a very different look.'

Annie thought about the sketch Finn had shown her. He'd actually drawn a sketch of how he wanted Tina to look after the makeover: the long hair, the legs, the heels and the boobs. She glanced again at Tina, who was currently looking just as Finn wanted her to look but not liking it at all.

Annie knew just what Finn would say if she told him Tina was going to wear trousers and that they were taking her to a salon to have her hair cropped off. He would say NO.

Whereas, if he saw the end result – the sleek head with the rose on top of the tight corset and shiny trousers – he would realize what a knockout Tina was without having to be so obvious. And Tina would just glow with looking exactly as she wanted to look.

'It's going to be fine,' Annie told Bob, 'honestly. Tina will look amazing. We're going to knock Finn's socks off with this one. Remember Jody's hat? That wasn't in the schedule either and Finn loved it.'

'Yeah, but this is . . . this is big. This isn't a hat, this is irreversible.'

'Trust me,' Annie insisted.

'Yeah!' Tina agreed, totally won over by Annie now.

'Trust me,' Annie repeated.

Chapter Seventeen

Senior stylist Ben:

Comic printed zip-up hoodie (Topman)
White vest (Topman)
White board shorts (Rip Curl)
Flip-flops (Animal)
Total est. cost: £110

'Unbelievable!'

They'd had to wait over an hour for the haircut appointment. Then, because it was being filmed, senior stylist Ben fussed and tweaked and trimmed for a full three hours before he declared himself happy with the cut.

When the very first decisive slices were made and Tina could actually hear her heavy lengths of hair thwack against the ground, she'd had a sudden attack of nerves.

'Going for emergency supplies!' Annie had declared and run out of the salon.

She'd made it back fifteen minutes later with a half-bottle of champagne. Champagne was Annie's drug of choice, she applied it in most emergencies because it was comfortingly delicious, reassuringly expensive and, due to the bubbles, extremely fast acting.

She knew some people swore by herbal droplets of Bach Rescue Remedy, but in Annie's opinion a glass or two of fizz was guaranteed to make people see any disaster in a rosier light.

'Drink,' she'd ordered Tina, who was already down to an ear-length bob but once again looking excited, rather than terrified.

'I think I might need some of that too,' Bob had told her quietly, when the camera was on pause.

'Why?' Annie asked.

'Finn's been on the line. Wants to know what's taking us so long. He's at the hotel, desperate to see the footage. At the rate this guy's cutting, it's going to be a late one.'

By six o'clock, a full bottle of champagne had been downed in the salon and a party atmosphere was growing.

Just as Annie had predicted, the haircut was a triumph. Tina looked stunning, amazing. Like a young and luscious Demi Moore, her thick dark fringe falling just above her eyes. Everyone wanted to know where she'd had her tattoo done and Ben was busy taking more Polaroids of her haircut and asking her to come in at the weekend and do a proper photo shoot for the salon window.

Tina was laughing and crying with happiness. She insisted on phoning her mum to break the news – then got Julia on the phone so that she could tell her too.

'Mummy's cut her hair really short. Yes – really short! A bit like a boy's, but quite girlie too,' Tina explained.

And yes, it was a very wispy feminine cut, with Ben

busy waxing and tweaking tendrils so that they formed tiny curls against her neck.

'You have to get changed,' Annie urged Tina, 'show everyone the full look.' She pressed the Topshop bags into Tina's hands and ushered her into the salon's toilet.

When Tina strutted out in her heels, tight trousers and corset, the small crowd of hairdressers cheered her on.

'Unbelievable!' Ben told her, through the whoops and whistles of her new admirers.

Annie had only once been backstage after a fashion show and this was just what it felt like in the Taylor Salon right now. As if something amazingly creative and successful had just been pulled off by team effort. Maybe for a moment or two, they were all allowing themselves to feel that a star had been born.

Maybe she would only ever shine in her own little circle, but definitely, definitely Tina was suddenly star quality.

Shyly Tina approached Annie.

'Shoulders back,' Annie reminded her, 'head up, strut your stuff.'

Even Annie could hardly believe it was the same girl. The shy, baggy, self-contained person she'd met this morning, who'd forgotten how to dress up, who'd not been out for years – let alone come out . . .

She was being revealed. The layers and the hair had been stripped away and the new Tina was emerging from her cocoon.

Tina stretched out her arms and wrapped them round Annie.

Annie hugged her fiercely back. 'Way to go, girl!' she told her. 'You just show them. Knock 'em dead, ladykiller.'

147

This elicited a shriek of nervy excitement.

Bob busied himself capturing Tina from every angle. Finally he felt he'd done enough and that it was time to pack up, drop Tina back at home and get the footage over to Finn. Another text from the producer/director had come in asking what time he thought he might be at the hotel.

'I'm nervous,' Bob told Annie once again as they buckled themselves back into the estate car for the journey to the hotel.

'Don't be silly,' she assured him. 'Look at the reaction Tina got from everybody. Even her mum!'

'Yeah, but it's off the script, Annie,' Bob said heavily. 'And that is a dangerous place to be.'

Chapter Eighteen

Annie unwinds:

Unwrapped wrap dress (Diane von Furstenberg, via eBay)
Hold-ups on floor (Pretty Polly)
Undone eyes (Quickies eye make-up remover pads)
Undone hair (model's own)
Total est. cost: £360

'Cream-crackered, babes.'

Annie's room at the Novotel in Birmingham was cramped, to say the least. In fact, just opening her bag and taking out her make-up seemed to have caused major disarray.

Feeling, all of a sudden, very worn out by the busy day she'd had, Annie slid open her mobile, lay back on the bed and phoned home.

'Hey you,' Ed greeted her softly from the other end of the line, 'you've had a long day.'

'Yeah,' she admitted and she listened hard. As well as his voice, she could hear all the clatter and chatter of her home in the background and suddenly she wished she was there and not here in this strange little brown and beige box in the heart of an unfamiliar city.

'You sound tired,' Ed said once she'd given him an edited highlights version of her day.

'Cream-crackered, babes,' she replied, trying to stifle a yawn. 'What are you guys up to?'

'Busy, busy,' Ed assured her. 'We've had supper, we've tidied up and now we're moving on to cupboard clearing.'

'Huh? That's very unlike you!'

'Yeah well, Owen's got us all on a clearout for charity drive. All our old junk is being hunted out, rounded up and taken to the school for a big pick-up by our dedicated activist.'

'Very impressive,' Annie had to admit, 'but if anyone goes near anything of mine they will get their hands chopped off. Is that clear?'

'Yes my darling, we all know how very charitable you are with your prized possessions. Oh Annie,' he added, 'before I forget, please give your mum a call. I think she might need a bit of a word.'

There was an odd pause after this, which gave Annie a pang of anxiety. 'Is everything OK?' she asked quickly.

'Erm, I'm not sure,' Ed had to admit. 'She's phoned here three times this evening. And I get the feeling . . . well, I'm not sure that she fully realized she'd phoned before. Well, she sort of did, but not immediately. She just doesn't sound quite herself.'

'Oh no. Maybe you should go round,' Annie suggested, even though it was a full hour's drive and although Ed could drive, he didn't exactly like to do it and certainly not in her cumbersome Jeep.

'Well, I'll go if you want me to,' he said heroically. 'Look, why don't you phone her up and see what you think first?' he added.

'Maybe it's the new drugs she's taking, maybe they're causing her problems. Maybe she needs to come and stay with us for a bit; we can make sure she's OK,' Annie worried out loud.

'Well, if that's what you want. But we're both out of the house all day and you're going to be away on and off for the next few weeks,' Ed reminded her.

'Maybe Dinah could—' Annie began.

'Dinah has got a lot on her plate,' Ed broke in.

'Yes,' Annie remembered.

There was a distinct knocking at her door. 'Babes,' she said, 'I'm going to have to go. I'll try and speak to you later.'

'Oh right,' Ed sounded surprised. 'Yeah, phone me back, there's something I want to talk to you about.'

'What?' she asked straight away, wondering what he was going to come out with next.

'Let's talk later . . . and don't forget about your mum.'

'Right.'

Annie clicked off the call and got up to unlock the door, sure that it would be Bob. He was in the room two doors down from hers and had said he would come and get her when it was time to go out for supper. Nikki had made a reservation for them all at some Chinese restaurant not far from the hotel.

So it was a surprise to see Finn standing in front of her.

'Can I come in for a moment?' he asked, his face looking a little too serious for Annie's liking.

151

'Yes, of course,' she answered and ushered him into the room. Well, it was so small that really she just ushered him past the door, then closed it so that they stood awkwardly facing each other in the cramped space.

For just one fleeting moment, Annie wondered if he'd come to tell her how much he loved what he'd seen of the Tina footage so far. But another look at his face told her that something had gone wrong.

'I've just watched what Bob's spent his very expensive time filming today and I'm not happy,' Finn began.

'Oh,' Annie said.

The word seemed to hang in the silence between them for a few moments.

'Not happy at all,' Finn said and shook his head.

'No?'

'No. I thought I gave you clear instructions. Very clear instructions.' Finn's voice sounded tense and tight. 'Tina was going to be the knockout. We were going to end the series with Tina. She was to be your crowning achievement. Miss Marlise would help her land a better job, you would make her look absolutely jaw-dropping and Svetlana was going to get her the great guy. On the first night out. She was going to be my all-round 100 per cent success.

'Cath, Jody, whoever else we've got lined up for tomorrow, no-one has nearly as much potential as Tina did and now you've just completely, completely . . .' Momentarily he put his hands up to his forehead – 'completely fucked it up!'

Annie was in such deep astonishment now that she couldn't think of anything to say. She was just listening to Finn and to the pounding of blood in her ears.

'You've cut off all her hair!' Finn exclaimed, 'you've dressed her up in trousers and, as if that's not enough, you've got her talking about a girlfriend! I mean . . . that's all we need! Just all that we need!'

Annie suddenly found her voice. 'So what!' she began. 'She's found out she's gay? Or maybe slightly gay? Or maybe bi? So what? Hello? I think you'll find we're living in the twenty-first century now. I think you'll find there are laws against discriminating against her. And open your eyes, Finn! She looks absolutely stunning. Amazing! I've been making people over for almost ten years, and before that I styled actors for films, and I've hardly ever seen someone look so transformed.'

'You don't know what you're talking about,' Finn broke in. 'This is not BBC2! This is the Home Sweet Home channel. We're making TV strictly for the mainstream. There's an ethnic moment and there's no gay anything. This is plain white bread mainstream and you don't get to interfere – I should have been phoned about the hair!' he exclaimed, his voice starting to rise, 'I should have had a call about the hair!'

'You loved it when we cut your wife's hair, didn't you?' Annie asked, but now wondered if maybe he hadn't and this was why he was losing it.

For a moment Finn's eyes widened in surprise, as if he'd forgotten how Annie could possibly know anything about his wife.

'We've wasted a whole day of filming and you have to find a new person, just like Tina, to save the series,' Finn said, jabbing his forefinger in her direction.

With that he turned, walked out and shut the door in her face with a resounding slam.

Chapter Nineteen

Screen siren Svetlana:

Show-stopping day dress (Roberto Cavalli)
Show-stopping heels (Rupert Sanderson)
Sheer stockings (Wolford)
Pink nails (Chanel)
Diamond necklace (Harry Winston)
Total est. cost: £48,000

'Vat men vant is so simple.'

Annie next saw Finn at breakfast. He made only a slight nod in her direction, then went to sit by himself at a table for two where he promptly opened up a newspaper and hid behind it, making it clear that he wanted to be undisturbed.

Once he'd left last night, Annie had phoned her mother and reassured herself that she was OK. Then she'd gone to talk to Bob, who had recommended sending Finn at least a text of apology. So she'd done that, but there hadn't been any reply.

'I'm sure he'll get over it,' Bob had insisted. 'Maybe we could put Tina in a wig and a skirt?'

To Annie this idea seemed even worse than Finn's suggestion that she go out and somehow find a replacement for Tina.

'He must have some back-ups,' Bob had told her when he'd heard this, 'there's no way he doesn't have a few people in reserve. I think he just said that to give you the heebie-jeebies.'

The rest of the morning was awkward, to put it mildly. Bob and Annie travelled together to the home of Angela, the other woman they were in Birmingham to make over. When they got there, Svetlana and Miss Marlise were already rehearsing their pieces for the camera, to Finn's obvious approval.

Annie hung back out of the way and watched, trying to attract as little of Finn's attention as she could. Hopefully, if she gave him time, he would calm down. Maybe he would even come round to the Tina makeover.

'This "vat men vant" is so simple,' Svetlana began, standing beside the mousy mum who looked very nervous at having put herself in the hands of the Wonder Women.

Svetlana spread out one hand and with a long pink talon ticked off the requirements: 'Number one: men vant good-looking, young woman, beautifully dressed and groomed. Number two: men vant praise, attention and lots and lots of lovemaking. No disagreements, no telling what to do, no nag, nag, nag, this the death of every marriage and that all,' she beamed at the camera. 'There is no number three.'

Angela didn't crack a smile, in fact she looked sceptical

and turned to ask Svetlana, 'But what do women want?'

'Tcha!' Svetlana tsked disdainfully, 'Vomen vant rich man.'

At that the strident trill of a mobile began and Svetlana caused Finn and Bob considerable excitement by extracting a miniature phone from her cleavage.

'Hello Uri, no this not a bad time,' she purred into the phone, 'I always make time forrr you.'

'Great!' Finn said, although Svetlana wasn't listening to him now. 'You get set up, Bob and we'll try and do it just like that but this time with the camera running. And let's ring her, so we get that shot of her answering the mobile.'

Once Svetlana had done her piece to camera and offered Angela a few other choice nuggets of advice, Miss Marlise took over.

Although Angela declared herself 'very happy' with her job as a secretary, Miss Marlise wasn't impressed and launched into her strategy for sending Angela up the career ladder towards executive status.

Once the filming of this slot was over, Finn announced both 'Cut!' and 'Tea break, I think.'

Bob set the camera down, Angela went to put her kettle on and everyone prepared to relax for a few minutes. Annie knew she should take this opportunity to have another go at speaking to Finn. She never liked a situation to fester; much better to try and deal with it. He'd been really pleased with her work so far, she reminded herself as she walked over to him.

'Finn?' she began, 'could we have just a little word, if you've got a moment?'

'OK, Annie,' he replied and turned towards her.

'I'm really sorry about yesterday,' she said, 'really very, very sorry.'

She wished that somehow she could make Miss Marlise disappear. Instead, the presenter was looking over in their direction with an almost triumphant expression on her face.

'Well OK,' Finn said, 'but you've caused a lot of problems.'

'The afternoon with Tina,' Annie struck out again, needing to put her side of the story, 'it just took on a life of its own. I thought it was really interesting . . .' she faltered, ' and I thought it would be interesting for the viewers. I didn't mean to give you a big headache.'

'But you did. So . . . what I'm going to do with Angela here is take just a little more control. You can go out to town with her and bring back a selection of possible outfits. Then she's to be filmed trying them on here, with Miss Marlise and Svetlana giving her advice. I'll pick one that I'm happy with and then you can take the others back . . .' he gave her a tense smile. 'That's how we'll do it from now on. If that's OK with you.'

It seemed to Annie that Miss Marlise's words had come true. She was just going to be the wardrobe lady.

As Finn turned away from her and went to collect his mug of tea, Annie wanted to throw herself down on this sofa and sob. Instead, she picked her handbag up from the floor and reached inside for the trusty box of extra-strong chewing gum she kept in there. Many years ago she had learned that a sharp minty blast was just the thing to keep tears at bay.

Just as she popped the gum and crunched down on it, Svetlana put away her phone and hurried over. With a delighted smile on her face, she confided in a whisper, 'Uri offer to take me out again. He is young, handsome man, Annie. I decide there is only one thing to do: I need to see vhat he vant. So, I decide to press pause on the vedding plans.'

When she saw the horrified look on Annie's face, Svetlana added quickly, 'I not cancel. No. No. Not cancelled. Just pause, tell Harry I'm thinking if this best for me. I mean, a man like Uri . . .'

'. . . will never ever be as nice as a man like Harry,' Annie finished the sentence for her. 'Don't do this,' she urged her friend, 'please! You are making a big, big mistake.'

'But Uri,' Svetlana protested, 'he make so much money. He maybe make in day vat Harry make in a year.'

'You have your own money now,' Annie reminded her. 'You don't need another man to keep you.'

'I just interested. Verrry interested,' Svetlana told her.

'Here you go, girls.' Bob interrupted the conversation to hand them each a tea.

'Bob?' Annie kept her voice low because she didn't want Finn to hear.

'Has anyone told Tina what's happened?' Annie asked him with concern. 'I mean she thinks she's going to be on TV. She's told her family, her friends, her little girl . . . She was absolutely bubbling over with it all when we left her. How's she going to be told that it's all being dropped?' Annie had to know. 'She's not just going to get a letter or a cold call from Nikki, is she?'

Bob shrugged. 'I think you care just a little too much,' he said, 'you'll just have to let go of that one. Someone will take charge of that. Let it be.'

'Ya,' Svetlana agreed, 'you in enough trouble.'

'But she's going to be devastated,' Annie protested, 'completely devastated. And after all that effort, after we brought her along so brilliantly.'

'You,' Bob corrected her, 'you did that, I was just filming. I'm trying to pay you a compliment, Annie, stop looking so worried,' he added.

'Couldn't you put together some of the footage you took?' Annie asked. 'Especially when she was at the hairdresser's, all made up and looking gorgeous, couldn't you put that onto a little DVD for her? Then at least she would have something,' Annie pleaded, 'I can't bear the thought of her sitting at home with her little girl feeling that she's been dumped because she came out to us. That's what she's going to think, and let's be honest,' Annie hissed, 'that's the truth!'

'I'll see what I can do over the weekend,' Bob conceded, 'I'll take a look at what I've got and I'll run off a DVD for her. So you can give it to her. OK. Agony auntie Annie,' he added.

'Thanks. Thank you!' Annie squeezed his arm. 'I've got her mobile number, I'll let her know.'

'Be careful,' Bob warned. 'Make sure you've given Nikki time to tell her, otherwise you'll be breaking the news and you could land yourself in even more hot water.'

Looking past Bob's face, Annie was surprised to see Miss Marlise standing much closer to them that she'd expected. Much too close for comfort. She couldn't have heard, though . . . could she?

159

Chapter Twenty

Ed at home:

Blue cotton sweater (Gap sale)
White rugby shirt (school uniform sale)
Tattered jeans (Levi's, vintage)
Bare feet
Total est. cost: £55

'D'you want to take off your instruments of foot torture?'

It was late when Bob pulled up outside Annie's house to drop her off after the two days of filming in Birmingham. But there was still a light on in the sitting room because Ed had promised he would wait up for her.

Owen would already be asleep and Lana had gone to Greta's house overnight, but Ed would be there to welcome her home.

At the sound of the car engine in the street, Ed opened the front door and headed out to meet her. He said hello to Bob and unloaded Annie's bag from the back of the car.

'Nice to have you back,' he told her once they were back inside the house. 'Go and snuggle on the sofa and I'll make you tea and toast if you like.'

'Yes, I'd like that very much,' Annie told him.

'Yeah, but it's just the one slice, obviously, and I'll be spreading the butter very, very thinly because I know about the ongoing weight battle you celebrity types are always waging,' he couldn't resist teasing.

'Oh, don't worry, I'm not sure I'll ever be allowed on camera again. I've been demoted and at the moment I'm just the wardrobe lady.'

'Oh dear,' Ed sympathized as she lay down across the sofa, 'is it that bad?'

'At the moment, yes!'

'But it will blow over . . . won't it?'

'Maybe . . . I hope so . . . I hope things won't seem so bad once we've all had the weekend at home and chilled out a bit.'

'D'you want to take off your instruments of foot torture?' Ed pointed at her high-heeled shoes, 'and I could give you a little massage.'

'Yes, that would be very nice,' she had to admit, 'but could you just bring in the tea and the toast first? Pleeeese,' she wheedled, 'you're a very, very nice man.'

'I know,' he told her, 'and you've not even asked me how I've been.'

'No,' she had to admit. 'How have you been, sweetheart?'

'Someone has just failed their Grade Six violin and I have an uncomfortable meeting with two very disappointed St Vincent's parents waiting for me on Monday.'

'Ouch,' Annie sympathized, 'I thought pupils at St Vincent's never failed anything.'

'Well, that's the idea,' Ed replied. 'She's really good, too. I think she got too nervous.'

'That's a shame. Bring in my snack, babes, then I want to tell you all about Tina.'

When the story was over and Annie's feet were thoroughly massaged, Ed felt he could only offer her the advice to 'Wait and see how it plays out on Monday.' But he did agree that if Tina could be given a DVD of the event it would be a very kind, very Annie thing to do.

'You don't think Finn will mind if you and Bob organize that?' he wondered.

'No,' Annie assured him. 'How's he going to find out anyway?'

'Well . . . that's not quite the same,' he pointed out.

'I think that's the least of my worries.'

'Right, well . . . now that you're comfy and a bit more relaxed, there's something I want to talk to you about . . .' Ed began carefully.

'Oh no.' Annie sprang up so she was sitting bolt upright: 'not the baby talk again, I really can't handle the baby talk, Ed.'

'No, it wasn't that. I wasn't going to talk about that,' Ed protested, 'but now that you've brought it up – why shouldn't we keep talking about it?'

'I'm tired.' Annie ran her hands over her face.

'So am I, but the weekends are really busy for us and maybe I need to talk about this.' He looked so serious.

'Ed,' Annie mustered up as much kindness and understanding as she could, 'Ed, I really feel as if I've had my kids.'

'Yeah, with someone else,' he broke in. 'Am I not good enough to have children with? This is so unfair! I'm competing with someone who's dead, and I can never, ever win.'

Annie flinched at this mention of Roddy. She never, ever wanted Ed to compare himself to Roddy. As he said, it wasn't fair. Roddy was dead. Annie, her family and her friends all thought the very best of him. That's how it was when you died. Everyone remembered the really, really good things. The amazing bits, the ultra-romantic and the superdad moments. All the ordinary, everyday moans and gripes were totally forgotten. Did Annie ever think back to how untidy Roddy had been? Or how charmingly irresponsible? Or the fact that he was almost always the last man standing at the bar? No, she never wasted a moment thinking about all that.

'Ed, please don't,' Annie warned him, 'it's not just about you and it's definitely not about Roddy, it's about me. I don't want to have another baby. OK? I don't want another child enough to go through it all again. I don't want to be pregnant, I don't want to give birth, I don't want to be woken every three minutes every night and spend all my time puréeing and feeling dowdy and exhausted. I don't even want to be back on the benches at the play park talking about it with the other dowdy and exhausted people. I'm not going there,' she added vehemently, just in case he hadn't got the drift.

Ed sat at the end of the sofa with Annie's feet still in his hands. But he had forgotten all about them.

There was a very sad, hurt expression on his face as he told her: 'But I've never done any of that. I've never carried a baby around at night, I've never pushed my baby in a swing or round the park in a buggy . . .'

'Well, I'm sure Hannah would love you to spend a bit more time with her children,' Annie suggested. Ed's sister had two small children now.

'Annie!' Ed replied angrily, 'that's not the point. The point is that I want to have my own child. Is that so hard to understand?'

For a moment he didn't say anything else, then to Annie's astonishment, he added, 'I don't want this to break us up.'

'It can't!' she exclaimed. 'It can't break us up. I never said I would have another baby for you!'

'You never said you wouldn't,' Ed replied.

'But you never asked before!' Annie threw back at him, feeling uncomfortably angry. 'This is a new thing.'

'Did we ever even talk about it? Did we ever really talk about anything?' Ed asked. 'We just moved in, in a great big flurry. A lot of things went undiscussed and undecided.'

'Well, we're talking about it now.' Annie tried to level her voice and keep the anger at bay, 'and I'm telling you I'm not going to do it. I don't want to do it.'

'And I'm telling you this is the one thing I really, really want to do,' Ed replied. 'I can hardly think about anything else. I'm thirty-five . . .'

Annie snorted. 'Big deal! You've got at least another forty fertile years ahead of you!'

She was too tired. Why was he starting up with this again? It felt as if she'd only just come in the door and already they were in this deep, uncomfortable, irresolvable discussion.

'I can't do this right now,' she told him quietly, then picked herself up from the sofa and walked out of the room. Taking hold of her overnight bag on the way, she headed upstairs to the bedroom.

She would get undressed and she would run a bath. She would soak in it for a bit and calm down. There would be peace and quiet and Ed would calm down too. This would blow over. He was broody. It wasn't such a big deal. The feeling would pass. She knew this because she'd had broody feelings of her own in the past, and they passed.

Maybe he had too much time on his hands at the moment. Maybe he needed a new hobby or something. She'd been planning to get him helicopter flying lessons for his birthday. His dad had been a helicopter pilot and it was something Ed had said he'd always wanted to try. Maybe he'd get hooked and go out a few times a month. That would take his mind off all this baby stuff. Quite an expensive hobby though, surely? Helicopter flying . . .

Annie opened her overnight bag and began to unpack. Almost everything was grubby and would have to go into the laundry basket or the rack in her office for the clothes *en route* to the dry cleaner.

She picked up her beautiful blue silk blouse, shook it out gently, then headed to the office with it. As soon as she'd hung it up on the dry cleaning rack, she could tell that something wasn't right in here.

Where were her bags?

There was a slim wardrobe in the room where she kept her clothes overflow. In here were all the things not currently in use and it had got a little too full lately. So she had stored more overflow tops, skirts and even some shoes in big chequered zip-up laundry bags. There had been three of them, stuffed full, stacked against the side of the cupboards.

And they weren't here.

Annie made a cursory search of the room, but it was so small, there just wasn't anywhere else they could be. She opened the wardrobe but it was crammed full, there was no way the bags were in there. She went back to the bedroom and made a search. Not under the bed, not in the cupboards, not on top of the cupboards.

From the top of the stairs, she called down to Ed.

'Ed, where are my bags? From my office? The big laundry bags full of my spare clothes?'

There was a silence.

Oh this was so childish, was he going to do that whole sulking and not talking to her thing?

'ED!' she repeated, more loudly this time. 'Where are my laundry bags? From the office?'

Ed came out of the sitting room and stood at the bottom of the stairs.

'Laundry bags?' he asked, putting one hand on top of his head, as if this would somehow help him to think more clearly.

'Big blue and white chequered ones,' she explained.

'Owen had bags like that. He bought a whole load of them at the market to help him with his charity clearout.'

The words were falling from Ed's lips as both Annie and Ed realized what this could mean.

'He used laundry bags for the clearout?' Annie asked with horror. 'I'll have to wake him up!' she exclaimed. 'I've got to find out if he went into my office.'

'No,' Ed insisted, 'it can wait until the morning.'

Annie's head was reeling as she tried to make an inventory of all that could have been lost.

The charity clearout?!

'Where's everything been taken?' she asked Ed with a wail.

Chapter Twenty-one

Maria in service:

Blue cotton dress (Harveys workwear)
White apron (same)
Supportive white lace underwear
(Rigby & Peller via Svetlana)
White leather clogs (Ward Walker)
Support tights (Elbeo)
Total est. cost: £120

'Oh, Mr Harry!'

It was a bright, blue-skied morning in Mayfair. The housekeepers had already washed the windows, swept and mopped down the marble entrance halls and steps. Handymen had vacuumed lawns, trimmed topiary to millimetre perfection and watered the window-boxes and bay trees at the doors.

A black cab pulled up outside number 7 and Harry stepped out, dressed in a colourful brown and red tweed jacket and red cord trousers, bearing an enormous bunch of flowers. The bouquet was so laden with exquisite and luxurious blooms that Harry needed two hands to hold it up. When he got to the shiny door, he struggled for a moment to balance the flowers in one hand so that he could ring the bell.

He announced his name to the intercom and after several long, fraught minutes, during which he worried and paced back and forth across the top step, the door was opened by Svetlana's neatly turned out maid.

'Hello, Mr Harry,' the maid smiled. 'Miss Wisneski says to you, please to come in.'

'That is so very kind of you,' Harry told her.

'I take the flowers?' the maid offered.

'They are awfully heavy,' Harry warned, 'I think I should carry them to her myself.'

'If you like. Beautiful flowers!' she added.

'Maria, I will bring an even bigger bouquet for you the next time.'

'Oh, Mr Harry!' she laughed.

As she'd been instructed, Maria showed Harry into the downstairs sitting room where he paced the antique parquet floor – salvaged from a crumbling French château and imported at vast and astronomical cost to W1.

He breathed in the intoxicatingly spicy scent of Svetlana's home and wished he could be transported back in time to yesterday morning, when everything had been absolutely fine. When he'd been just weeks away from making this fascinating creature his wife.

He still had no idea what he'd done or what had gone wrong. He was still none the wiser as to why she had suddenly phoned him up on Friday morning to tell him that she needed to 'press pause' not just on the wedding but on their entire relationship. No use trying to talk her out of it, she'd insisted, she'd given this a lot of thought and she'd made her decision.

Because of an inescapable work commitment, he'd been unable to come here to try and change her mind last night, but that hadn't stopped him trying to call her every twenty minutes. Now that it was Saturday morning, he'd come as soon as he thought she'd be up.

He didn't care what he had to do, or how long it was going to take, there wasn't the slightest doubt in Harry's mind that he had to win Svetlana back.

In the vast mirror with the ornate golden frame above the mantelpiece, Harry looked at his reflection. There was a gleam of sweat on his large, white forehead, so balancing the bouquet awkwardly on his raised knee, he took a clean, ironed white handkerchief from his trouser pocket and wiped the dampness away.

Looking in the mirror again, he now caught the reflection of the painting hanging on the wall behind him.

Ye gods! he couldn't help thinking, *that's a Warhol! Maybe this woman is completely out of my league.*

'Bye-bye my darlings!'

He could hear that Svetlana was now downstairs in the hall kissing her two boys – Petrov, aged nine, and Michael, seven – goodbye.

Such well-behaved, solemn little boys, Svetlana thought as she ruffled Michael's dark hair and pinched his chubby cheek gently with her thumb and forefinger.

Maria immediately approached with a brush in her hand and smoothed the boy's hair back into place, shooting Svetlana a look.

'I miss you on Saturdays,' Svetlana told her children. 'Be good darlings and I see you at suppertime, ya? Maybe I come eat with you?'

Both boys smiled at this unusual prospect.

'OK, you go now,' Svetlana instructed and watched as they went down the steps and towards the back door of their father's car which the driver was already holding open.

As soon as the boys were in the car, Svetlana turned to the drawing-room door and burst into the room in a swirl of fragrance and fuchsia chiffon: 'Harrrrrrrrry!' she announced with one of her broadest smiles, 'vat vonderful flowers!'

She plucked the bouquet from him, placed it on the coffee table then threw herself into his arms instead.

'I've missed you!' she declared and pressed her lips against his, giving him a hit of Chanel lipstick.

'You've missed me?' he spluttered, when the welcome kiss was finally over, 'but I'm here, I've been here . . . I've been trying to phone you all night. You just needed to say and I would have rushed over!'

The surprise in his voice was obvious. He hadn't expected to be welcomed back so eagerly. Was this just some little game she'd been playing?

'I know,' Svetlana said, taking hold of his hand, 'I've been a verrry silly, silly girl.'

With these words, she led him out of the downstairs drawing room and towards the stairs, to her more cosy, less formal sitting room.

'We talk . . .' she told him, 'we make up . . .' she purred.

Harry trotted obediently in her wake, blissfully un-aware that it was Uri's unexplained, last-minute date cancellation which had helped Svetlana to change her mind.

As Svetlana and Harry made their way to the privacy of the upstairs sitting room, a second taxi was pulling up at the far end of the street. It wasn't a black cab this time, but a battered old minicab: a silver Nissan with rust spots and a dangerously low-slung exhaust. There was no fare to pay as the driver was doing the passenger a favour, because they had a mutual friend.

The side door opened and the passenger stepped out. Her red stiletto heel struck the tarmac with a crack. A very long, very slim leg tightly encased in skinny jeans followed. Finally narrow hips, a slim waist and willowy arms, showcased in a tight scoop-necked jumper. The long waterfall of blonde hair, the creamy face and glassy grey eyes, were stunning. But there was a determination to this girl. She was not just a pretty face. She looked as if she was a girl with a cause. A girl on a mission.

She'd popped the boot open and was hauling out her two substantial bags before the driver had even made it round to the back of the car to help her, but she assured him that she was fine. With strong arms and shoulders, she lifted the bags onto the pavement, then pulled out the handles so she could wheel them along.

With her head held high, she began to march pur-posefully towards number 7, heels rapping loudly on the pavement.

*   *   *

In the cosy upstairs sitting room, Svetlana was keeping Harry happy. Whether or not there was going to be anything on the cards with Uri, Svetlana had decided that she still needed Harry in the meantime, until it was a little more definite.

Harry was kissing her neck tenderly. 'What do you want me to do?' he asked as his hands untied the belt of her dress, loosening the fabric so it fell away from her body. 'What would you like?' he breathed against the skin at the nape of her neck as she slid down against the soft velvet of the sofa. He opened the front of her dress and stroked the pink satin of her bra in a way that made her nipples tingle with excitement.

Harry was without doubt the most considerate lover she had ever had. Well, for decades, anyway. Not since she was young and foolish had there been a man as kind as this in her life.

She was, even she had to admit it, going to make love to him for her sake. Not just for his. For her sake, because she really wanted to, because her body was now moving towards him and his touch.

Unlike any other lover she'd had before, nothing seemed to satisfy him as much as knowing she had come. Nothing made him happier than feeling her come strongly inside, right with him. Right against him. Pulsing with him. Whenever she'd faked it with him, in their early days, he'd shaken his head and told her lovingly, 'Please don't do that. I can tell nothing is happening down there. We'll just have to try something else until you come too.'

This had been a surprise to her. And she'd been so sure that she would be the one teaching him everything that she had learned.

Just as Harry had put his face against her navel and begun to bite lightly, just the way she wanted him to . . . Svetlana heard the strident blast of the doorbell.

'What now?' she snapped, moving Harry's head away and sitting upright.

She certainly wasn't expecting anyone to call. Her boys had gone to their Chinese lesson (their father's idea) this morning, then they were having lunch with Igor.

Svetlana heard the front door being opened and a brief conversation taking place. Then the door was closed and Maria began to walk up the stairs towards the door of the sitting room.

Svetlana adjusted her dress and tied the belt back on firmly. She smoothed down her hair and tucked the loose strands in behind her ears. Not that she cared what her maid thought . . . but maybe there was someone at the door who might have to be shown in.

Maria came into the room. 'Miss Wisneski, sorry I disturb. But there is a girl downstairs who say she need to talk with you.'

'Who is she?' Svetlana asked.

'I not know. She say only she need talk with you. Urgent.'

'What does she look like?'

'She young and foreign,' was all that Maria volunteered.

'Oh!' Svetlana put her feet back up on the sofa, 'she vant vork with me, huh? Tell her to leave her CV, I call her if I like the look of it. Maybe she see me on the television. Clever to get address and everything,' Svetlana had to admit.

It was slightly unsettling as well. Svetlana wondered

174

how many other people would now be able to work out how to find their way to her door and start begging for one favour or another.

Maria made a little bow, then closed the door and began to trot down the stairs again.

The front door opened as Harry and Svetlana resumed their excited embrace. But Svetlana could hear that the conversation down at the doorstep was taking longer than she had expected. The two voices were now becoming slightly more raised.

The front door closed once again and then came the sound of Maria beating a fresh path up the stairs.

Svetlana gently pushed Harry back as the knock at the door sounded.

'Yes!' she commanded, a little irritated now.

'Miss Wisneski,' the maid looked anxious, 'she not go away! She say she stay on doorstep all night – all next day if have to. She has bags,' the maid added nervously, 'I think she camp here. You must tell her to go. She not listen to me. She very angry-looking girl,' the maid added.

'Tcha!' Svetlana swung her feet down from the sofa and checked the belt of her dress again. She strode determinedly to the door, more than a little curious to find out what this was all about.

Secretly, she quite admired a girl who wouldn't take no for an answer. Was that not how she had been all her life?

'Stay here!' she barked at Harry, who was anxiously intent on following her.

'I vant to deal with this, stay!' she commanded and held out her hand like the traffic police.

'I'm right here if you need me,' he assured her and

made for the window, planning to at least look down on the scene.

Even in her heeled mules, Svetlana took the stairs at a speedy pace. Rounding the corner into the hall, she caught her first view of this prickly visitor. The girl was tall, very thin, a spectacularly striking blonde with a pale and angry face.

Now Svetlana's curiosity was roused. This girl was far too pretty to be a domestic: maybe she had come to London to be a model. Immediately, Svetlana hoped the girl was clever enough to stay away from all those creeps who promised modelling careers and lured girls like this into lap-dancing and much, much worse.

'Hello,' Svetlana's voice rang out as she approached the threshold of her house, 'I'm Svetlana Wisneski, why are you bothering me?'

The girl began to speak in Ukrainian.

She didn't say many words, but a passer-by would have been shocked by the effect they had on the stunning woman in the pink taffeta dress. She visibly paled, then slumped slightly to the side and had to lean against the door frame for support.

If the passer-by had also, by chance, been able to speak Ukrainian, he'd have understood the devastating words spoken by the girl.

'Hello, I'm Elena, I'm twenty-two years old and you are my mother.'

Chapter Twenty-two

The Oxfam lady:

Orange suede pinafore (Oxfam, Camden)
Blue blouse (Oxfam, Highgate)
Blue tights (M&S)
Brown cowboy boots (Camden market)
Total est. cost: £74

'Would you like to take a leaflet about us?'

So far, Annie had spent almost four hours of her precious Saturday morning trying to locate her missing clothes.

Ed had made numerous phone calls to teachers, to the school building, even to the school janitor in search of the precious items that had accidentally been swept up in the great charity clearout.

Hundreds of bags of unwanted clothes, bedding, books and toys had been collected by the St Vincent's pupils. Everything had been gathered into the school gym and was now being sorted out and moved on to the relevant charities.

'Most of the clothes are going to Oxfam,' Ed had been able to tell Annie. 'The north London branch has had a delivery of stuff from the school, so that might be a good place to start. I'll keep phoning and let you know if I hear anything else that's useful.'

No sooner had Annie heard these words than she'd jumped into her Jeep and headed at speed for the shop before the early-bird, eagle-eyed shoppers started walking out of the place with some of her choicest belongings.

Unfortunately the woman behind the counter at the shop couldn't answer any of her questions, but when she saw Annie's agitation, she decided to phone someone who'd been on duty the day before, to see if they knew more.

Looking round the shop, Annie had started at the sight of one of her flowered Paul Smith skirts dangling on a rail.

She rushed over and checked the size. Yes! This was hers. Definitely.

She'd rushed to put it on the counter.

'This is mine!' she'd told the assistant.

Finding the skirt had given her hope, but her relentless rake through the other racks hadn't turned up anything else.

'Would you like to see if your bags are still in the back?' the woman had suggested.

So Annie had been led through to the back shop, where she could see at once that there was no life-saving stack of bulging laundry bags containing all her treasured belongings.

Pointing to the huge mountain of old clothes, the woman said helpfully, 'Well, if the bags have been unpacked, the things will have been put in there, ready to be sorted out. Sorry, we're a bit behind at the moment, we've been short-staffed.'

Annie had looked at the mountain. It would take all of the morning to search through this. This was where clothes came to die. Surely nothing of hers could have ended up in this rubbish dump?

'OK,' she'd agreed hesitantly, but just as she put her hand onto the first shrunken, bobbly and stained top from Zara, the shop's phone had rung.

The assistant came back in and informed her: 'Good news! Janice, who was in yesterday, says only your skirt was unpacked here. When they saw how nice everything was, they took the bags down to Oxfam Style – that's our sort of premium store in Camden.'

Snatching her skirt from the counter, Annie had headed at speed for the door.

'But you'll need to pay for that!' the woman's voice had rung out behind her.

So that was that. She'd had to pay £45 to get her own skirt back. *Good grief!* What if all her other belongings were already hanging out on the racks at Oxfam Style with price tags attached?

'Can you phone ahead for me?' she managed to ask as she was leaving the shop. 'Stop them from putting out anything they haven't already?'

But when she'd finally made it to Camden she'd only been able to find two summer tops. 'Almost' everything else had been set out, according to the assistant.

Now it looked as if almost everything else had gone.

'But I had Prada sandals in there! You sold my Prada sandals in Oxfam Style?'

'Erm, yes.' The assistant looked a little nervous, 'I think they went for thirty pounds.'

Annie hadn't been able to say anything, she'd been so astonished.

Thirty pounds! Those shoes had only been worn three times! Someone had scored themselves the bargain of the year!

'You've made us lots of money, even if you didn't mean to,' the earnest young girl behind the counter went on. 'Would you like to take a leaflet about us? At least you can find out where the money's going to. It might make you feel a bit better.'

The girl had given her sweetest smile and said, 'They're only clothes – it's not a matter of life and death.'

She really didn't understand.

'I used to work at The Store,' Annie tried to explain, 'I used to have a fantastic staff discount and there were so many lovely things I was able to buy. But I don't work there any more, so I won't be able to go out and replace all of those things . . . replace *any* of those things! They were treasures, all unique, one of a kind, very special . . . and they were all in my size,' she said, her voice almost breaking with these words.

'Why don't I phone our other branch in Notting Hill?' the girl offered kindly. 'Maybe one of the bags went on to them? And there's always eBay,' she added, a little hesitantly, 'good things from our shops are always popping up on eBay with people trying to sell them for more than they bought them.'

'Yes,' Annie said a little snappily now, 'I know about eBay, I will keep an eye on eBay, but the problem is I don't have an inventory, a list, I don't really know what's gone. I won't know until I'm getting dressed and wonder where's my . . . and it's all going to dawn on me slowly, bit by bit, just like when people are burgled,' she said, with emphasis, glaring at the girl.

That was just what it felt like: a burglary.

Only her own son was to blame. If he was standing in front of her right now, she would find it very, very hard to be nice to him, no matter how much she really did love him.

Annie's phone began to bleep. Taking it out, she saw that she had a new text from Ed.

'Urgent. Phone me.'

Chapter Twenty-three

Elena arrives:

Tightest jeans (Primark)
Black and white scoop jumper (market stall)
Stilettos (market stall)
Lucky gold letter necklace (ex-boyfriend)
Total est. cost: £35

'You certainly have plenty, don't you?'

Svetlana spent several long, shaken moments just looking at the girl. She searched her face thoroughly; saw the
shape of the nose, the determined set of the mouth and
the glassy clearness of the eyes and knew that what the
girl said was true.

Not all of the features were hers; some were unmistak-
ably those of Elena's father.

'You need to come back later,' was the first thing
Svetlana asked of her daughter, in her native Ukrainian.

'No,' Elena replied coolly and crossed thin arms over her
chest, 'you'll have called a guard by then, or the police.'

'No,' Svetlana began. 'There's someone here in the house now. A visitor. I need to see you alone.'

'Then I'll wait on your doorstep,' Elena replied fiercely.

'No!' Svetlana felt panic rising in her chest. Harry was not to see this girl. Harry was not to know anything about her. Nothing. And not Igor. Never Igor!

At the thought of the documents she'd had to sign to get her divorce, her boys, her house and her allowance, Svetlana felt sick. She'd promised no future scandals and no past secrets. She had promised! She had to get Harry out of the house and Elena as far away from her as possible. Before there was a terrible, terrible disaster.

'Maria will show you to the kitchen,' Svetlana said, making a snap decision. 'Please go quietly downstairs and wait there for me.'

An unexpected smile broke out across Elena's face and, grabbing her two bags, she bundled them in through the front door then followed Maria down to the basement.

'What was that all about?' Harry wanted to know as soon as Svetlana came back into the sitting room.

'Very determined Ukrainian girl look for job,' Svetlana breezed as casually as she could. 'I decide Maria can give her cup of coffee and take her details.'

'Are all Ukrainian girls very determined?' Harry asked.

'All the ones who've made it over here, yes,' Svetlana confirmed with a throaty laugh.

'My darling, darling girl . . .' Harry began, 'please say we going to get married?' It was the question he'd been burning to ask ever since he'd arrived at the house.

He put his arms around her and she looked into his kind eyes. With Harry she felt safe.

Svetlana's life had been one long struggle with powerful, overbearing personalities and when Harry looked at her like this, she remembered why she'd been so determined to marry him in the first place. When Igor had tried to take everything away from her, including her children, Harry was the one who had come to her rescue. He had fought for her in the courts.

'Fair and square,' was how he'd described the victory.

And when he'd fallen in love with her, he'd been the first man to ever, ever think about what she wanted.

'Yes,' she told him confidently, 've get married, Harry.'

Immediately her mind turned back to Elena. There was a time bomb down in the kitchen just waiting to go off. How would Harry ever forgive her for keeping such a dark secret when so much was at risk?

'Maybe ve bring wedding forward?' Svetlana asked with her most charming, winning smile.

'Well, well,' he laughed, 'that might prove to be a bit tricky. People have invitations, the venue has to be booked in advance. I'm not sure we can just move the whole show forward.'

'You try for me, Harry,' Svetlana wheedled. 'I must be your vife as soon as possible.'

He planted a long and loving kiss on her mouth, hoping they would be able to pick up from where they left off earlier. But Svetlana pulled away telling him, 'You need to go now, my love.' She glanced at her watch and effortlessly lied, 'I have hairdresser in fifteen minutes.'

Harry just smiled and shook his head as if to tell her that there was absolutely not one hair out of place on her lovely head and why should she need a hairdresser now?

'We go out for dinner later?' Svetlana asked, 'then you come back and stay night with me.' The request was accompanied by a hand which slid between Harry's legs and gave a playful squeeze.

Once she'd seen Harry to the front door, Svetlana shut it firmly behind him, then, taking a deep, steadying breath, she braced herself and began to walk downstairs to the basement kitchen.

In the large, well-equipped room she saw Elena at the table with a cup of coffee in front of her, while Maria stood at the cooker stirring at food she was preparing for the children.

The women were in silence, although Svetlana could not believe that Elena didn't speak English. Everyone in Eastern Europe spoke some English. It was not possible to even think of travelling abroad without at least a basic knowledge.

'Do you speak English?' Svetlana asked her in English.

'Yes,' came the reply; then, in Ukrainian, 'but I prefer to speak to you in private.'

'OK,' Svetlana agreed, also in her native tongue, 'follow me, we'll go to my office.'

This small room was also down on the basement level. Svetlana had no real use for an office. She had dabbled with thoughts of a business venture, but had never followed any idea through. Still, in this neat room she had a desk, a computer, space to answer letters and a table with two chairs. She directed Elena to sit down.

As soon as Elena had pulled up a chair, Svetlana's mind raced with all the questions she wanted to ask this girl: *How had she found her? How had she got her address? Where had she been living for the past four years? What did she want?*

And perhaps most importantly: *How much money would it take to make her go away?*

But before Svetlana could say a word, Elena looked up and began her story.

'I live in Kiev now, I'm studying engineering at the university,' she said, still in Ukrainian. Maria was well out of earshot, but maybe she just wanted to tell her story fluently.

'How do you have money to study?' Svetlana asked immediately.

'I'm clever,' Elena replied, 'I got a scholarship. I have a little job too. I work at the records office and help people find out more about their families.'

She let this piece of information settle on Svetlana.

This is how she had found the mother who thought she had carefully covered her tracks, the mother who thought she would never hear from this girl unless she chose to initiate contact.

'I found all my original documents and I managed to make contact with other relatives who weren't so scared to tell me who my parents are, and why they don't want to have anything to do with me.'

Elena paused and turned her clear grey eyes directly towards her mother's clear grey eyes.

'The famous ex-Mrs Igor Wisneski began to fascinate important men from an early age, huh?' Elena asked.

'I paid for you to be well looked after until you were eighteen,' Svetlana said, in a low voice: 'your father paid nothing and it was hard to get the money to your carers without anyone else finding out.'

Elena just laughed at this. 'Fifty pounds a month! You think that's a lot of money? You probably spend that on . . . on . . . your fingernails!' she exclaimed.

Now that was frightening. Svetlana had indeed always accounted the fifty pounds per month as 'manicure services' and very privately looked after her nails herself. It would be a lie to say that she hadn't thought about this girl. Whenever she'd wired the money, Svetlana had wondered how the girl was doing. Whenever she met girls of the same age, she'd also wondered. Elena's birthday was painfully engraved on Svetlana's heart and every year when the date came round, she had privately acknowledged that her unknown child had become another year older.

Svetlana looked closely and couldn't deny that there was something of a thrill in finally meeting this person. Scanning Elena's face, Svetlana could read the story of her past mistake in the features there.

'Why have you come to London?' she asked. 'What do you want from me? Is this just about money?'

'Well you certainly have plenty, don't you?' Elena glanced disdainfully around the room.

'I've worked hard for it,' Svetlana defended herself.

Elena just laughed before exclaiming, 'Organizing weddings to rich men?'

Svetlana replied with a tight smile. Elena obviously had no idea what was involved in being married to a rich man. 'Believe me, I worked very, very hard for all this.'

'Ha!' was the disgusted comment, 'and how much plastic surgery have you had to look like this at the age of forty-five?'

'Ah!' Svetlana gasped as sharply as if she'd been plunged into icy water, and almost automatically began her usual defence: 'I'm only . . .' But then she remembered that there was no point lying to this girl. Elena knew. Elena had seen her own birth certificate, Elena had probably seen Svetlana's.

She had to go. She had to be got out of this house. Elena and all the best-kept secrets of Svetlana's past had to be dealt with as soon as possible.

'What do you want from me!?' Svetlana cried. 'I'll get my chequebook and we can come to an arrangement,' but she said these words with a heavy heart: she knew this was blackmail, and it would only get worse.

'Keep the money you earned in the bedroom,' was Elena's contemptuous reply, 'I only wanted to get to know you. Don't I deserve to get to know my own mother?'

There was silence in the room. Svetlana sat very still and looked into eyes as serious, as intelligent and as defiant as her own.

Elena wanted to get to know her. Of course, this was so much, much better than money. Elena wanted someone to welcome her with open arms, someone to take her in, someone to help her make all the right connections, someone to take her into their hearts, where she would be for ever, right in the bosom of her new-found family.

If Svetlana said no, where would Elena go?

Maybe to the press . . . maybe to Harry? Or to Igor?!

If Elena knew so much about her, she must already know about Svetlana's husbands, past and future.

Svetlana would have to agree . . . but carefully, in stages, keeping Elena at a distance from herself and from everyone else until she had time to break the news, tell the story in her own way.

Elena would have to be kept safely away until she was Mrs Roscoff. There was no doubt about that.

'I need somewhere to stay,' Elena said.

She looked up at Svetlana, and for a moment the older woman thought she saw a glimpse of vulnerability. Maybe Elena wasn't nearly as scary and ballsy as she was trying to make out.

'You can't stay here,' Svetlana informed her. She had her sons, Harry and all of Igor's terms and conditions to think of.

'You must know somewhere I can stay,' Elena insisted. 'I have no money to pay for somewhere myself. I've spent all my money travelling to find you!'

Svetlana may have been wealthy, but she didn't want to start bankrolling a daughter she barely knew in a hotel or a nice flat. She needed temporary accommodation, she needed a friend who would do her this favour.

The problem was, women like Svetlana didn't really have friends. There was no-one in her circle of glamorous wives and divorcees that Svetlana could really count on. A nugget of information like this – Svetlana Wisneski's secret love child – would whip round the circle like an angry wasp and before she knew it, it would have buzzed into the ears of her future husband and the past husband who currently feathered her nest so well.

For a moment, Svetlana's mind raced but could come up with no answer, no possible solution.

Then she thought all of a sudden about the one woman who already knew some of her secrets.

'I make a call,' she told Elena and with that she stepped out of the office and went in search of her mobile.

As soon as it was in her hand, she pressed speed dial.

'Yes?!' came an exasperated voice from the other end of the line.

'Annah,' Svetlana began, 'something terrible has happened.'

Chapter Twenty-four

Lana's weekend wear:

Grey and white print tunic (Fat Face)
Jeans (Miss Selfridge)
Brown suede boots (Greta's)
Total est. cost: £80

'Wow!'

'What's so urgent then?' Annie demanded once her phone call with Svetlana had ended and she had Ed on the other end of the line.

'Where are you?' Ed asked.

'In the car . . .'

'On hands-free?' Ed interrupted.

'Yes, on hands-free, d'you think I want to mow down a cyclist? I've been to Oxfam in Highgate, Oxfam Style in Camden and now I'm heading to their branch in Notting Hill. So far I've only been able to rescue one skirt, Ed! And they charged me forty-five pounds for it!' she told him, sounding just as heated as she felt.

'OK, try and calm down,' he soothed, 'Owen and I are walking up to the school right now. We've got hold of the janitor, he's says there are still lots of bags up here and he's going to let us in to take a look.'

'Right.'

Annie let out an exasperated sigh. She didn't hold out much hope. She was going to check out the other branch of Oxfam Style, then she would have to return home, to meet their guest. Ah yes . . . the guest. That was something she would have to mention to Ed.

For a moment, she was almost grateful for the lost clothes. Because of that trauma, Ed was not going to be able to feel as if he could say no to the guest.

'Someone's going to come and stay with us for a week or two,' Annie began.

'Really?' was Ed's surprised reply, 'who?'

'Well, this is really very top secret. I can tell you, but you can't tell anyone else and you can't tell the children.'

'What?' Ed sounded baffled. 'Who? In fact, should you tell me the gritty details if this is such a big secret? I might tell someone by mistake.'

'True. It's something to do with Svetlana . . .'

'Oh good grief,' was Ed's reaction, 'it's always something to do with Svetlana.'

'A relative of hers has to come and stay for a bit.'

'Why?' Ed demanded. 'She's richer than anyone we know, why can't she put them up in a hotel?'

'This is a top secret relative,' Annie said darkly.

'It's the Russian mafia, isn't it? We're going to have some drug lord hiding out in our house. I think you should just say no, Annie. Just nip this in the bud now before we have to change our names and go on the run.'

'Ed!' Annie told him off with a giggle, 'it's nothing like that. Nothing at all.'

When the conversation was over, Annie's mind turned back to Svetlana.

'*What do you mean, your daughter?!*' was the question she must have asked Svetlana four or five times at least.

It just did not compute. A daughter? Svetlana had two boys. She didn't talk about them much, but she was devoted to them. Her greatest fear had been that Igor would take them away from her during the divorce. But a daughter? There had never, ever been mention of a daughter. And Annie had a teenage daughter, not so different in age from Svetlana's surely? So would that not have sparked some sort of hint from Svetlana?

'You had her adopted as a baby?' Annie had asked her friend in astonishment.

'No. She went to distant relatives,' Svetlana explained. 'I was a model, I had money to pay them. I didn't want to give her avay completely. I thought this vay I could come back to her one day. But . . .' Svetlana had hesitated, before guiltily admitting, 'there was never good time.'

Of course Annie would take the girl in, but she was bewildered as to why Svetlana wouldn't take her in. Svetlana was the one with the Mayfair mansion.

'No-one can know about her until I'm married to Harry!' Svetlana had hissed. 'Otherwise Igor say I bring scandal to his name. I'm not supposed to have any secrets, Annah! This part of my contract . . . and Harry asked me before I sign, is there anything, anything Igor should know? Is there anything which he could use to spoil this deal? And I not tell him about Elena!'

'Harry loves you,' Annie had assured her, 'he knows

you've been married three times, he knows you've been left penniless twice, he knows your sons will inherit one of the world's biggest gas fields, he knows you were Miss Ukraine . . . he knows everything that you've told him so far and he still loves you. So, tell him about your daughter!' Annie urged. 'He'll still love you and he'll help you.'

'No. I think, this . . . this too much,' Svetlana had insisted. 'She stay with you until I ready to tell him.'

Annie had only just arrived back home and broken the news of a house guest to Lana when they heard the rumble of a black cab's diesel engine in the street.

'That must be her!' Annie jumped up. 'C'mon, let's go and welcome her in.'

'Where's she going to sleep?' Lana wondered as they headed for the front door.

'Down in one of the basement rooms, maybe,' Annie suggested. 'It's about time we cleared them out.'

But she knew that was going to be a big job, not exactly the work of an afternoon. This was the problem with living in a big house, the spaces seemed to fill up without anyone even trying to fill them.

Annie opened the front door and set her most welcoming smile in place.

Then with their jaws dropping lower and lower, she and Lana watched Elena emerge from the taxi, stalk over to the driver's window, wiggle a wallet from the back pocket of her skinny jeans to pay him and then sashay towards the garden gate with her bags in tow, like two obedient puppies.

She's at least twenty! was the first thought to cross Annie's mind, followed by: *she's absolutely gorgeous, but she looks like trouble.*

Lana's polite smile had widened into something much more genuinely excited.

Ohmigod! Here she is! Lana was telling herself, *My. New. Best. Friend!*

Elena paused at the garden gate to look up at Annie and Lana perched on the front door steps.

'Hello, I am Elena,' she said cheerily in an accent just like her mother's. 'Thank you for inviting me to stay.'

'Come in!' Annie said, heading down the steps to help her with her bags, 'it's lovely to meet you. It's a surprise, but it's a very nice surprise. You're much more grown up than I expected.'

'Yes, I'm twenty-two,' Elena confirmed, 'my mother not tell you that because she alvays lying about her age, no?'

'How old is she?'

It was sneaky, but Annie felt she had to ask. This girl must know and it might be Annie's one and only chance to find out. In another day or so, Svetlana might have bribed Elena never to tell.

'Forty-five,' Elena confirmed.

Annie gave a little gasp. This wasn't much older than she'd expected, but boy, Svetlana must be on first name terms with a team of cosmetologists.

'She have me vhen she twenty-three.'

'She's never told me about you,' Annie said, her voice still full of surprise.

'Today first day I meet her,' Elena said. She was at the front door now, and held out her hand for Lana to shake.

'Hi there,' Lana managed shyly before adding in a burst,

195

'Elena can share my room . . . really it's not a problem. There's plenty of space. She doesn't have to go down to the basement. It's cold down there and kind of dark.'

'No, I'm sure Elena . . .' Annie began her protest, absolutely sure that Elena and Lana should not share a room. This twenty-two-year-old looked altogether too slinky and calculating to inflict on a 16-year-old teenager with exams ahead of her.

'That vould be very kind,' Elena smiled, accepting Lana's offer straight away, 'sharing room no problem for me. I always share room, vhen growing up and at university.'

'You're at university?' Lana asked, ushering her into the hallway. 'What do you study?'

'Engineering at Kiev University,' Elena replied. 'I get scholarship.'

'Wow!' came Lana's impressed response.

'Do you like tea or coffee?' Annie asked as soon as Elena had been shown round the house and set her bags down in Lana's room.

'Coffee, please. Your house is so big and so beautiful!' she marvelled. 'No-one has money for such a big house in Ukraine.'

'No-one has the money here either,' Annie had to confide, 'but we just borrow more.'

'Ah yes. Crrredit crrrunch,' Elena said, settling down at the kitchen table, 've have in my country too. Is hard to get good job as engineer, but I hope maybe I can come back to London vhen I finished and get good job here. Maybe my mother help me to stay here.'

Annie marvelled at how easily Elena used the term 'mother' although she'd only met Svetlana for the very first time today.

'You must have thought about your mother a lot? Did anyone tell you anything about her?'

Elena gave a shrug of her slim shoulders.

'Only that she very beautiful and she leave country once I am born,' Elena replied.

'So she had you when she was twenty-three and then . . .' Annie had her back to Elena and was busying herself with the cafetière and the coffee grounds, partly so that Elena couldn't tell how very, very interested she was in this story.

'. . . you were brought up by relatives of hers?'

'Ya,' came Elena's reply, a little too short for Annie's liking.

'Do you know much about your father?' she prompted.

After giving a contemptuous snort, Elena replied, 'My father is politician. He was forty-eight vhen I was born, married, three sons, a very important man. This is vhy I am secret.'

'Oh . . .'

Annie brought the coffee over.

'Are you having some, Lanie?' she asked her daughter, trying for a moment to imagine not even setting eyes on her beloved girl for twenty-two whole years.

'Yes please,' Lana confirmed, eyes fixed on Elena. She didn't want to miss a word. Elena was definitely the most interesting thing to have happened in this house for some time.

'Were the people who looked after you kind?' Annie asked.

'Ya, but I alvays feel angry about this. I alvays want to know: who my mother? Vhy she leave me?' Elena said,

197

managing in her halting English to convey some of her feeling.

'Maybe it was hard for her . . .' Annie began but Elena just snorted again.

'I think my father pay her big, big money to hide baby and go away. Problem solved. So,' Elena took a sip of coffee, 'she is on television now? And my father is big, important politician in Ukraine. I could make lots of trouble.' She gave a mischievous little smile.

Now Annie understood why she had been handed the Elena-bomb. Because it could go off at any moment, and Svetlana had immediately understood that Elena had to be housed with someone of diplomatic skill.

If you could tactfully advise long-haired polonecked women who had been doing long hair and polo necks for thirty-odd years when the last things on earth which truly suited them were long hair and polo necks, then really what was a 22-year-old with a devastating, international pressworthy family secret?

'Svetlana told me today that your father never paid any money for you,' Annie ventured carefully. Instinctively she wanted to bridge the gap between Elena and her mother, 'she was the one who paid for your care. She had three rich and important husbands . . . maybe she would have liked to meet you, but she didn't want these important men to find out about you.'

'Ha!' Elena gave another shrug and snort.

'So, engineering . . .' Annie decided to change the subject to something less controversial, 'I don't know anything about engineering, unless you're talking about bras and corsets.'

'Mum!' Lana shrieked, embarrassed by her mother as usual.

'Yes! Bra!' Elena pointed at her own, to indicate that she'd understood this properly, 'much engineering in good bra. Especially big one,' she cupped her hands under her dainty little bosom to demonstrate.

As Annie and Lana laughed at this, there came the sound of the front door opening, then Owen's voice rang out into the hallway.

'Mu-uuuum!' he yelled, 'We've got *two* bags! We've got two of your bags and they've not been touched. Nobody's even looked inside them. Everything's folded and even smells just like the inside of your cupboard!'

He was in the kitchen doorway now, beaming at her happily.

Then he caught sight of Elena and dropped his gaze with shyness.

'Really?' Annie jumped up from her chair and ran over to her son, who had one of the bags clutched triumphantly in his hand. Ed was close behind him with the second. Owen set the bag down on the kitchen floor and undid the zip.

'Da-nah!' he declared, a little mutedly as there was a stranger present.

Annie's heart leapt to see three pale cardigans neatly folded on top of a stack of other, cleaned, folded and cherished items. Just as Owen had said, nothing inside the bag had been touched.

'Oh hello there,' Ed noticed Elena at the table, 'I'm Ed,' he said and gave her a wave. His gaze travelled to Annie's face and they exchanged raised eyebrows.

So OK, the contents of almost one whole bag were

missing, scattered across Oxfams all over London and maybe even on eBay already – but it was still a huge relief to get two bags back. Annie felt as if she could almost cope with the one missing bag. But three would have been a disaster.

'Owen, thank you!' she declared and put her arms around him. Owen tucked his chin down so that she could hug him, but woe betide if she moved in for a kiss in front of That Girl.

'If you ever, ever take any of my clothes to Oxfam again,' Annie began in a voice which was jokily threatening, 'I will *kill* you! I will personally kill you and kick you out of my house.'

'What? Once I'm dead?' came Owen's practical reply, followed by, 'Mum, can I smell bacon?'

'No,' Annie told him, 'but is that a hint?'

'Mmmm, bacon!' he closed his eyes and rubbed his stomach.

'OK, go sit,' Annie instructed him.

She followed Ed, who had a bag in each hand, out into the hall.

'What do you think?' she asked him.

He understood the question at once.

'Oh. My . . . Word,' he settled on finally, 'she's terrifying,' he added in a whisper, 'she's Svetlana twenty-odd years ago. No man stands a chance!'

'I know,' Annie replied. 'I'm going to Glasgow on Monday and I'm scared to leave you here alone with her.'

'Me too,' Ed replied.

Chapter Twenty-five

Elena in the changing room:

Pink and black backless, sideless, strapless dress
(River Island)
Black peep-toe, ankle-strap heels (River Island)
Armful of bangles (same)
Black clutch bag (same)
Total est. cost: £95

'Vhat I not have is clothes for fun.'

'I think maybe you should go away and shop on your own!' came Lana's angry response to her mother's comment about the outfit she'd just strutted from the changing room in.

It was almost four o'clock on a Sunday afternoon in the shopping centre closest to Annie's home. Although she had only spent fifty minutes touring the shops here with Lana and Elena, she was already convinced that it was fifty minutes too long.

'But don't you need me for the bit at the till?' Annie

reminded her daughter, glaring at the skimpy vest and skin-tight PVC trousers she was wearing . . . perhaps because Elena had selected exactly the same ones from the racks.

Elena's taste in clothing was . . . well, 'breathtaking' might be the word. Nothing was too tight or too skimpy or too strappy for Svetlana Junior.

'Weren't you thinking about job interviews?' Annie couldn't help asking when Elena stepped out of the changing room in a dress that seemed to be backless as well as sideless.

'They have some very smart suits here,' Annie added, without much hope.

'I have suit,' Elena had airily waved away the advice, 'I have clothes to be warm, I have clothes to work. But my mother give me money and what I not have is clothes for fun.'

Oh boy . . . just how much fun was the supermodel lookalike planning to have while she was under Annie's roof?

One look at the growing pile of club wear in the changing room would suggest: a lot.

It was when Elena started giving Lana advice about what to buy that Annie began to get worried.

'You have good legs,' Elena had told Lana. 'You must have very short skirt!'

'No,' Lana answered Annie huffily now, 'I don't need you at the till, I've got my pocket money!'

Although Annie felt offended, she relaxed at this news. She only gave Lana £5 a week, so how much bad fashion could she buy on her savings?

'Fine,' she'd huffed back, 'I'll leave you both to it. I'll go

and shop for myself and I'll meet you both for coffee at
. . .' she looked at her watch, 'five p.m.'

'Good!' Lana agreed.

That was how Annie had found herself wandering
through several clothes shops with no-one else's wardrobe on her mind but her own.

Working in The Store had spoiled her, there was no
doubt about it. The clothes were all so cheap in here.
Look at the hems, so small and tight. And the material
was not nearly as nice as she was used to. The jackets
all seemed to be made of wool blended with a touch of
sandpaper and the blouses were thin and insubstantial
cotton, bulked up with fillers which would disappear in
the first wash.

Still . . . oooh! Her hand went to the rail. Now that was
a very, very lovely pink silk shirt. She pulled it out and
examined the label. Only £45!

This season, she was in love with every single one of the
new colours: the pinks, the oranges, the yellows and the
moody greens. She wanted something in every shade.

If she added just a few new scarves or cotton tops in the
right colours, she would be refreshing everything in her
wardrobe.

Mmmm . . . the jewellery here was absolutely delicious
too. That glossy fat bangle in pinky-purple? That was
just exactly what she wanted. And the magenta batwing
jumper?

She took it down for a closer look. It was so strange
when things you had worn in the past, loved, then got
over and finally loathed, came back around again. Look
at this. She'd had one almost exactly the same in cobalt
blue when she was 17.

Her blue one had had the same slashed neck but longer sleeves. Clearly, the designers had gone back to the drawing board with the batwing and accepted that the only way it worked was with elbow-length sleeves. That way, you could put your arms down and not flap about like an actual bat.

Looking at this jumper Annie decided she had to try it on, at least for old times' sake. She even remembered the confusion with the old cobalt one: what with the slash neck and the draping sleeves, it was almost impossible to tell which way up the thing went.

In the changing room with an armful of stuff, Annie went about her shopping professionally, assessing everything mindful of how it looked on her, rather than the hanger, and making a mental list of what it would go with back at home, in the master wardrobe.

The one thing she didn't really give much thought to was price. There was about £3.26 left in her bank account, so technically she couldn't afford anything. But, she was reasoning with herself, this was chain-store shopping. If she bought a few things here with her overdraft, the damage wouldn't be so bad. And, she narrowed her eyes to think about this, weren't there a few things she could sell lurking about in her cupboards? A few faded gems which could be unearthed and put up on her eBay site to unlock just a couple of hundred quid?

The jumper and the silk shirt were lovely. As she stared in the mirror at herself, it wasn't the clothes she was having a problem with, or her figure. She knew exactly how to dress this buxom, apple-shaped body which she managed to keep just on the right side of a size 12.

No, the thing that suddenly attracted her attention was

her hair. There was nothing unusual or out of place with the hair today. The golden and ash blonde highlights were totally up-to-date for the TV cameras. The hair was combed back and tightly fastened into a high ponytail the way she always wore it.

She'd worn her hair like this for years because it totally suited her. She had small features: a pointy chin, a little nose and lips that needed vibrant lipstick to make the most of them. The flippy, bobbing ponytail also suited her quick movements and high energy. Plus it gave her skin a definite tug back. Usually she loved the ponytail and never questioned it.

In fact, at bedtime when she let her hair down, she looked unusual. 'The Annie only I get to see,' was Ed's frequent comment.

But now, all of a sudden, the hairstyle bugged her. Just a touch . . . just a moment of doubt.

She'd worn it like this for years . . . she was struggling to think how long. Could it honestly have been since Owen was born? Twelve years ago?! Was she going to wear her hair like this for ever?!

Maybe she should change to a chignon? A slightly more formal up-do? That would look the same at the front but be a little more grown up and *soigné* at the back. Maybe.

Maybe a short, blonde crop?!

She terrified herself with the thought. But didn't you have to be tiny and skinny as a rake to get away with really short hair?

A short, blonde . . . c-rrrrr-o-p.

Just the word crop scared her. She thought of Tina's haircut and tried to imagine all of her own golden tresses thudding onto the white tiles of the hairdresser's floor.

205

No! She gave an involuntary shudder. It was too brutal. Every single time in her teens and early twenties when she'd had her hair cut short, it had taken less than a week for her to regret it completely and a long, long year for the mistake to grow out.

Still, short hair was meant to be liberating and whacked years off your face. Hadn't she seen it with so many clients? From frumpy bob to knockout crop. Maybe she'd talk about a little change with her hairdresser ... just *talk*, just consider the options.

By the time she got to the till, she'd netted a sizeable haul. There was the batwing sweater, two cotton tops in fuchsia and cobalt blue, the pink bangle, a filmy lime green scarf which she couldn't refuse, and the pink silk shirt so extravagantly ruffled at the front.

Ker-ching, ker-ching, ker-ching.

'That's one hundred and eighty-four pounds and eighty-five pence,' the assistant informed her.

Bringing her overdraft to £181.59. But so many things, all for the price of just one top or so at The Store. It was a bargain here, really.

In fact, she picked up her bags and headed for the coffee shop feeling very pleased at all the money she'd 'saved'.

She even took out her phone and sent a text to Bob, who was always complaining about his wife's spending habits.

'Tell yr wife to shop at Mango. Cheap and fabulous. See you Mon. Annie x'

After a few minutes the reply beeped in: 'OK. U on 10.15 train Mon?'

'Yup,' she texted back.

'Bring gd book. It takes 6.5 hrs,' came Bob's reply.

'What!' she responded, 'Hw will Svet n Miss cope?'

She had looked on Owen's map and told herself that Glasgow was not so far away really. It certainly hadn't occurred to her that she would be spending almost all of Monday on the train.

They were filming up there for two days, just like in Birmingham, so did that mean she'd be spending all of Thursday on the train too? Plus Saturday was Ed's birthday and she still hadn't got him anything.

That was when the pang of guilt about the bags in her hands struck for the very first time. She should have been extending her overdraft for Ed . . .

Her phone buzzed with another text from Bob.

'Svet and Miss go on plane,' it read.

What?!

That was so UNFAIR!

Chapter Twenty-six

Nikki on the train:

Floral blouse (Mango)
Jeans (Evisu)
Black ankle boots (Hobbs)
Total est. cost: £230

'I'm on the slow train to nowhere.'

It was 4.30 p.m. when the slow train finally pulled up in Glasgow Central station. There had been other much faster trains which had whizzed past them, shooting passengers up to Glasgow in under five hours in brand new tilting carriages. But Annie, Bob and Nikki with their £45 budget tickets had chuntered slowly up towards Scotland, stopping at every little station on the way.

Annie felt rumpled, bored, toxic, dehydrated and horrible.

'I'm on the slow train to nowhere,' she'd heard Nikki complain on the phone, 'along with my career.' If she'd spent six and a half hours on a plane, she'd be in New York by now! Instead, she was piling out along with Nikki, Bob and all his camera equipment into a cavernous Victorian monster of a station.

And Finn, Svetlana and Miss Marlise had flown! She still felt outraged about this. They had touched down in Glasgow hours and hours ago.

'I'm going to do a bit of location scouting with the girls,' Finn had apparently explained to Bob. 'I'll take my camera and if we find some good spots I'll record a few to-camera pieces just to save time.'

Annie had had to choke back the lump of wounded pride in her throat when she'd heard that.

It was more proof, as if she needed it, that Finn didn't like her. Never mind all the good work she'd done with Cath and Jody, Finn hadn't forgiven her for Tina and maybe he wouldn't. Maybe she was going to be shunted down to wardrobe lady status for the rest of the filming. Maybe she would just be filmed in the background? Dressing the women, but not saying a word on camera.

The thought of this had brought the lump of wounded pride bobbing up into her throat again.

'Finally in Scotland!' she'd texted Ed as the train had pulled into the station . . . because she wanted to keep in touch without making him feel she was obsessing.

Even though she was obsessing.

Annie's main concern was: what would Elena do to her family while she was away? Would she lure Lana away from her studies and off into London's swirly nightlife?

And what about Ed? He was completely immune to the giggly charms of sixth-form girls but Annie didn't like the way Elena smiled at him, seemed to study him when he wasn't looking . . .

'She's trouble,' Annie had whispered to him. 'Please don't go falling in love with her while I'm away, will you?'

'Annie! You're away for three nights,' Ed had laughed. 'I think I can handle Miss Slinky Trousers while you're gone. But how long is she staying with us anyway? Did Svetlana give you any sort of clue at all?'

'No, but no vorrrrry, I ask when I see herrrrr,' Annie had told him.

When she arrived with Nikki and Bob at the Novotel all Annie wanted to do was get to her room and get under the shower before the first briefing meeting. She felt grubby and grungy. Even if grunge did make a comeback, which surely it was bound to do if right now was the tail end of the eighties revival, she wouldn't be going there.

Her look was grown up: chic, polished and pulled together.

'Annie Valentine,' she told the receptionist, as she watched Bob and Nikki picking up their keys. The receptionist tapped at the computer keyboard but then looked at it with a puzzled expression.

'I'm with the film crew, same booking as them,' Annie added, trying to be helpful.

'Yes.' The receptionist tappity-tapped again but didn't seem to find anything useful. 'Who made the booking?' she asked.

'Donnie Finnigan' Annie said, assuming this would be right.

'I'll contact him for you,' she said with a smile, then picked up a phone and dialled the number on the screen in front of her.

'Hello, is that Mr Finnigan?' she asked. 'This is Novotel reception. I have an Annie Valentine here who's looking for a room . . . right . . . right then . . . OK thank you Mr Finnigan.'

When she'd replaced the phone, the receptionist looked up at Annie and told her, 'He's just coming down.'

'He's coming down?' Annie repeated. That didn't seem right. 'Can't you sort this on the phone?' she asked.

'Well, we could, but I think he wants to speak to you,' came the receptionist's reply.

Why hadn't he queried the room not being booked, anyway? Annie wondered. Had he known it wasn't booked?

Oh no.

Maybe she wasn't staying here.

Maybe there was an ever cheaper hotel round the corner that poor old Annie Valentine would have to stay in because, guess what? There just weren't quite enough rooms available at the Novotel.

Annie began to walk in a circle round the reception area. She caught a glimpse of herself in a shiny glass partition. She wanted a shower! She needed that shower! Even her sharp black mac collars seemed to have wilted during their time on the train.

Once again she found herself querying the ponytail. Was it the right thing? It had been the right thing for so long, but was it still the right thing?

'Annie!' Finn interrupted her thoughts. He was wearing his leather jacket, carrying his trusty clipboard and had his Bluetooth in one ear. These were all meant to signal that he was Extremely Busy making Important Decisions.

'Grab your bag, I'm taking you across the road,' he instructed.

She knew it. This bloody hotel was bloody full and she was going somewhere crap! Unfortunately, she wasn't allowed to express any sort of anger or disapproval because right then Finn began to talk at speed and she guessed that it wasn't to himself but in response to a voice in the earpiece.

Maybe Finn was controlled by the earpiece, Annie speculated as she followed him out of the hotel door, across the road and into a small bar. It was a nice bar; usually she would have enjoyed being taken to a bar like this with its traditional wooden floor and wooden, leather and brass fittings. It looked cosy and quiet. But the thought of a sit-down chat with Finn about her crap hotel and her new position as wardrobe lady was not exactly appealing, no matter how nice the setting.

'Sorry, I'm going to have to shoot,' Finn told his caller and immediately turned to Annie with a tense smile. 'So what's your poison?' he asked.

'I don't really need a drink. I think I'd prefer a shower,' she replied.

'No, no, I want to buy you a drink. Glass of wine?' he suggested.

'Well . . . OK,' she agreed hesitantly.

What the bloody hell was going on? Maybe he was about to apologize? Maybe he'd looked at the Tina footage again and realized how brilliant it was? Maybe she too would be on the plane . . .

With two glasses of wine now in his hands, Finn steered Annie and her bags to a booth at the back of the bar.

As soon as her bottom hit the seat, Finn began his spiel. He certainly didn't want to hang about.

'Annie, I'm really very sorry,' he began, 'but we're going to have to let you go.'

Let.

You.

Go.

Go? Her mind repeated the question.

Go where? she wondered frantically.

Let you?

But she didn't want to. Certainly hadn't asked to.

Let.

You.

Go.

What was this?

Things seemed to go into slow motion. Even Finn's words seemed to be coming out one by one, too slowly, with very long pauses in between, giving Annie's mind time to race.

Was he sacking her? Was the TV show about to be pulled away from under her feet? Was this all over now?

'Let me go?' she repeated, her voice full of confusion.

'I am so sorry,' Finn repeated, 'but the budget is just being squeezed and squeezed. Every day I'm working with less money than I was the day before.'

'But you're hardly saving any money getting rid of me . . . I have a contract . . .' she blundered on.

Surely she would still be entitled to all of the £3,600, wouldn't she? They were two-thirds of the way through the filming schedule, plus she'd schlepped all the way up to Glasgow.

'Of course, we'll pay you for all the work you've done,'

Finn said carefully, 'but I think you'll find that . . . er . . . under the terms and conditions, we don't need to pay for anything else.'

Silence hung between them for a moment or two.

Despite the horrible sinking feeling in the pit of her stomach, Annie heard herself ask, 'But won't it look a bit strange? You know – you have me shopping and sorting out everyone's outfits in the first episode and then I just disappear?'

'Well, yes, we are going to have to address that . . .' Finn fudged. He reached for his glass and took a gulp of wine.

'You're going to edit me out!' Annie exclaimed. 'You're going to use all the clever outfits I chose, but you're going to edit me out. Aren't you!?'

Suddenly Finn came over all sympathetic and best-friend-ish – the rat.

'It's awful, it's just absolutely awful,' he agreed, 'I am so, so sorry. If I'd had any idea how tight the margins were going to be, I wouldn't have dreamed of having three presenters. I can barely afford one. Miss Marlise has a watertight contract and thank goodness Svetlana has agreed to waive her fee. I need to keep her on for all the useful publicity she's going to generate for us . . .'

As Finn went on with his pleading and excuses, Annie could only think: Marlise has a watertight contract and Svetlana has agreed to work for free! *Annie Valentine, you are the weakest link: goodbye!*

'Well, I signed the contract you gave me,' Annie pointed out, 'I trusted you.'

There was a pause, which Finn didn't offer to fill.

'I can't afford to work for free,' Annie told him, holding

her head up high and trying to retain a scrap of dignity although she felt as if she'd been hit in the stomach and she was sure this was obvious from her flushed face.

'No, that's what I thought . . .' Finn took another sip from his glass. He looked uncomfortable; his eyes kept travelling towards the door as if he was desperate to make a bolt for it.

'You were good on TV,' he added, but Annie could really have done with less of the 'were'. Clearly her TV career was over, before it had even begun.

'It's not just the budget,' Finn added finally. 'Tina's been given a video diary of her makeover and Marlise informed me that it was your idea.'

'Oh.'

She hoped she hadn't got Bob into trouble as well.

'I twisted Bob's arm,' she added, hoping to get the cameraman off the hook. 'I was just trying to be nice to Tina,' she said softly, not that anything was going to save her now. She was just another necessary budget cut.

Watching Finn take another gulp from his glass, Annie thought of another question:

'Couldn't you have told me this in London?'

'I always like to tell people face to face, like a grown-up,' the *rat* replied.

'So . . . have you arranged for me to get home?' Annie asked. The more she tried not to cry, the more fierce and icy she seemed to sound.

'Ah . . .'

Maybe he hadn't. Maybe Finn was enough of an idiot to imagine that he could summon someone up on a six-and-a-half-hour train journey before firing them and making them disappear into the ether.

'I'm sure there's a plane. Easyjet . . . they go up and down all the time. Cheap, too . . . because we obviously won't be able to pay . . . erm . . .' he coughed, 'you understand.'

No. She definitely did not understand. Not any of it. She did not understand why she was being sacked, when she was the presenter who did the most work and for so little money! She did not understand why Finn couldn't have phoned her this morning and spared her the humiliation, not to mention the expense, of finding her own way back to London.

'I thought I was doing a good job,' were the words she chose carefully to argue her case one last time. 'The women looked great when I'd styled them, I was always bang on budget and they opened up to me.'

Finn tweaked at his earlobe and had the decency to look slightly embarrassed.

'I'm sorry, Annie. I'm just in a difficult situation. I've no money.'

'Well,' was all Annie could manage for a moment, 'this has all been very interesting.'

She thought about slipping on her coat, picking up her very nice handbag and walking out. But then she thought of a better plan.

'Right well, you can go now, Finn,' she said firmly, 'I'll be fine.'

She watched Finn scrambling for his jacket, clipboard and other bits and pieces while she sat calmly. Now he was issuing guilty bits of apology: 'So sorry about this . . . you will be OK, won't you? You will get back to town OK? Obviously, I hope we might be able to work on something else in the future.'

Annie wanted to laugh out loud at that one. Work with

this weak, deceitful, conniving nincompoop again? Don't think so.

He stumbled out of the bar as she sat and looked on with total composure. Yes, this was much, much better. This way she got to fall apart in the quiet comfort of the booth, whereas if she'd walked out, she'd have fallen apart in the confusion of the street.

Annie put her hands up to her face and decided that for a few minutes at least, it would be OK to have a little cry.

'Now, now, hen . . . the wine's no that bad, is it?'

She looked up to see the barman, a broad shaven-headed bloke in a black polo shirt, beside her table.

She raised a smile, despite herself.

'Nah,' she said, 'I think I'll have another glass.'

'Another wee tot of Charrrrdonnay for the lady, coming right up. I take it he's nae coming back?' the barman asked. Taking the two empty glasses from the table, he gave a wink. 'Ah, you're well shot of him. Plenty mair fish in the sea.'

'Exactly,' was all Annie said, not really ready to have a great big heart to heart with the barman just yet.

The phone in her bag beeped.

'See,' the barman winked again, 'a fine-looking woman like yersel will hae another one already lined up!'

She took the phone out and saw the text: 'Where u?' from Bob.

'In bar opp hotel been fired,' she texted back, sure that would get a good response.

It was just seconds before, 'coming' appeared on her screen.

Ah well, the phone calls to Ed and to Connor would have to wait just a little bit longer.

Bob arrived minutes later with, to Annie's surprise, Svetlana in tow.

'Annah! This is terrible!' Svetlana gushed as soon as she set eyes on her. 'Terrible! Terrible! I go to tell Finn right now that I don't vork on this stupid show unless you vork on it too!'

Which was very touching. It really was very kind.

'I don't think it will help,' Annie told her. 'He's got no money. He's just trying to save it in every direction.'

'He's slashed my daily rate,' Bob added gloomily.

'It's terrible,' Svetlana repeated.

'He's not even booked me into the hotel, I'll have to get back onto the train, if they let me use my ticket.'

'It's an APEX, you'll have to pay extra,' Bob warned her.

'No, no, Annah,' Svetlana shook her head decisively. 'I buy you hotel room. Now you have drink with us, then you rest and take train home tomorrow.'

For a moment, Annie laid her head gratefully on Svetlana's Yves Saint Laurent clad shoulder.

'Poor Annah,' Svetlana soothed, then she clicked open her python clutch and brought out a platinum Amex card.

Waving the card in the air, she summoned the barman.

'Champagne on ice,' she instructed.

Annie was more than a little the worse for wear when she finally made it to her room and thought to call home.

'Hello babesh,' she slurred when she heard Ed's voice on the other end of the line.

218

'Hello? Is that you?' he asked, then added, 'Been living it up in TV land, have we?'

'No, not at all, been fired,' she said baldly.

'Fired?' he replied. 'Fired?' he repeated. Then to her surprise he said, 'Annie, just give me a minute,' and he seemed to step away from the phone.

'Ed?' Annie asked. 'ED! I've been fired!' she said much more loudly now.

Then she listened. Was that barking she could hear in the background?

'Hi!' Ed was back on the phone.

'What's that barking?' she asked.

'Erm . . . yes. Some dog outside,' came his reply. 'Fired?' he repeated, 'are you serious? You're not joking me here. You've been fired?'

'I am no longer a Vonder Voman,' Annie said, making herself giggle.

'But don't you have a contract?' Ed asked.

'Yes, but apparently it's not a good one. Not watertight like Miss Marlise's. Apparently.'

'Good grief . . .' Ed began, but then she was sure she heard him hiss: 'Down!'

'Down?' she asked.

But he ignored this and asked anxiously, 'Are you OK? Where are you staying? Is there someone with you?'

'I'm in a hotel, I'm fine. I love you,' she told him, deciding right there and then that she would take everything back to Mango and buy him helicopter flying lessons for his birthday.

'Yes, yes, I love you too,' he replied, 'but why I am now babysitting a teenager who only wants to go clubbing with a twenty-two-year-old supermodel, I do not know.'

'Oh God! Is Lana all right? I have to come home!' Annie exclaimed.

'She's fine, she's in her bedroom studying. Elena went out on her own . . . looking terrifying,' Ed added.

'Are you sure Lana's there?' Annie almost screeched, remembering how often she'd stuffed her bed with pillows and crept out of the back door.

'I will go and double-check,' Ed assured her. 'Please go to bed,' he added, 'We'll talk this all through in the morning.'

'Night-night, babes, I love you,' she repeated.

'Me too,' Ed added.

Then came another sharp bark before Ed hung up abruptly. Annie looked at her phone in surprise, as if it had barked by itself.

It was 11.45 p.m. . . . possibly a good time to make a little transatlantic phone call to the other adorable man in her life.

'Hello doll face,' were the words Annie used to greet Connor.

'Hello baby,' he replied, 'I'm still on my bike.'

'Guess what? I got fired,' Annie told him, then suddenly had to laugh at everything that had happened that day.

'No!' Connor protested, 'You didn't!'

After the surprise had registered, Connor listened to the whole story. Then took a deep breath and began to issue rapid instructions.

'OK baby, here's what you do,' he began. 'You need damage limitation and to enhance that reputation. With my help, you are going to approach this totally LA style. Now, first thing tomorrow, you will phone this number. Write it down, babes, write it down.

220

'Got it? OK, that's the number of the TV gossip columnist on *Screentalk*. You tell her hello from Connor, and you're his friend Annie Valentine. You've been shooting *Wonder Women* and . . . let me think . . . let me think . . . what's the most positive spin we can put on this . . . you've decided to leave the show because . . . ?'

Chapter Twenty-seven

Fern does smart casual:

Beige wool trousers (Paul Costello)
Oyster silk blouse (M&S)
Salmon cashmere sweater (M&S)
Comfortable loafers (Ecco)
Total est. cost: £270

'Come and see me!'

It was nearly 5 p.m. when Annie finally arrived at her front door. She'd spent much of the train journey from Glasgow asleep, trying to escape from the throbbing headache and dry scratchy eyes and throat which were proof – as if she needed it – that she'd drunk too much and cried too much the night before.

Slotting her key into the lock, she was astonished by a volley of short, yappy barks. She thought she must be hearing things and looked out across the garden and back to the pavement to see if she could spot the dog. Nothing. No dog.

She pushed open her front door, stepped over the threshold, called out her usual, 'Helloooo! I'm home,' and was hit full on the legs by a whirling, springy ball of yapping fur.

'Aaaargh!' she exclaimed in fright.

What was this thing?

'Annie darling!'

That was her mother's voice.

'Why on earth have you got a dog, Mum?' Annie shouted from the hallway, trying to detach the ball of fluff from her legs.

'Down!' Annie ordered the dog, but it didn't pay any attention, it kept jumping, barking and trying to nip at her fingers.

Owen was now bounding down the stairs towards her. 'Isn't he great?' Owen enthused with a beaming smile.

'Lovely,' Annie said and bundled Owen up in a hug before he wriggled out and turned his attention to the dog.

'He's from a dogs' home and he's deaf so you have to communicate in doggy sign language.' Owen proceeded to hold out his hand, palm flat to the floor.

'This is the sign for sit,' he told his mum.

The dog kept bouncing up and down and yapping.

'I don't think anyone's told him,' Annie pointed out.

'Dave, Dave!' Owen called, clapping as he said the dog's name.

'Dave?' Annie asked, 'is that his name?'

'It's a nice name,' Owen insisted, crouching right down in front of the dog. As soon as it saw him on his knees, the hairy little mutt bounced right into his lap, knocking him onto his back. Then, while Owen giggled hilariously, the dog began to lick all over his face and mouth.

'Eeeeeugh! Owen, not on your face! No, Owen!' was Annie's horrified reaction, though she still had to smile at the obvious enthusiasm dog and boy had for each other.

'Annie.' Ed was in the hallway now, 'hello!'

He held out his arms and folded her up in them.

'I have a headache,' she said, resting her forehead on his woolly shoulder.

'Yeah,' he said, patting her gently on the head. 'So you've met Dave then?' he asked.

'Yes.'

'So, what do you think about him?'

'He's totally disgusting, but Owen seems to like him,' was her reply.

Ed put his hands on her shoulders and pulled her gently back so he could look her in the face. With concern, he began: 'Are you really OK about it? I thought you'd be much more . . .'

'Am I OK about it?' she repeated with surprise. 'I've been sacked, I'm completely hungover, I've been on a train living off salt and vinegar crisps for six hours. I'm not in the mood to be OK about anything!' she exclaimed. 'But I'm trying to get used to the idea.'

'Oh, poor Annie,' he sympathized, pulling her in to his shoulder again, 'I think it's going to be fine . . . I think it's all going to work out somehow.'

'Annie!' Fern called out from the sitting room, 'come and see me!'

'I didn't know Mum was coming to visit us,' Annie whispered to Ed.

'She arrived an hour ago. She thought it was my birthday today and she said that she wanted to give us all a surprise.'

224

'Really? She just turned up without phoning or anything?' Annie asked. This was unusual. Fern wasn't really a surprise kind of person, she liked to plan and organize in advance.

'Yes,' Ed confirmed.

'Well, that is a bit strange. Can she stay the night? So we can keep an eye on her.'

'Yes, I think she'll be fine with that. She's OK, Annie,' Ed added, 'she just seems a bit forgetful.'

'Annie!' Fern shouted again.

'I'm coming, Mum!'

'Where are the girls?' Annie asked Ed, assuming that Lana and Elena were out.

'They've gone to the shops together to get some things.'

'Together?'

'Well, I've let Lana go out and meet Elena in a café, but she's promised to be home by seven for supper,' Ed said with a sigh. 'Lana is besotted. There is no other word.'

'Oh boy.'

Annie set her bag down in the hall and went into the sitting room to see her mum.

'Hey you!' she said, greeting her with a big hug, 'what's up, then? Ed says you've gone round the bend.'

'I have, darlin', there's no other word for it,' Fern replied but with a smile.

'You look all right,' Annie told her and this was true. Fern had dressed smartly for the surprise visit in a pastel pink skirt suit with her hair freshly blow-dried and her make-up carefully applied.

'I look fine,' Fern assured her.

'What's the matter then?' Annie asked, sitting down beside her on the sofa.

'There are just these blanks in my day when I know I've been somewhere, or done something, or I know I should have done something . . . but I have absolutely no idea what it was,' Fern explained, her brow creasing with concern.

'Isn't that normal, Mum?' Annie asked, patting her reassuringly on the arm. 'Aren't those just senior moments? They're coming to us all. I'm always running up the stairs to get something and by the time I'm at the top, I've completely forgotten what the hell it was.'

'I don't know . . .' Fern began.

'Have you told your doctor?' Annie wondered. 'Have you talked it over with him? Maybe it's something to do with the pills you're taking for the high blood pressure.'

'He's away,' Fern said thoughtfully. 'I thought I'd better go and see him when he gets back next week.'

'Yeah,' Annie agreed, 'I can come with you, if you like. Or maybe Dinah.'

'Is Dinah going to come over tonight?' Fern asked brightly.

'I don't know. I'm seeing her tomorrow, so why don't we get her to come round then if she can't make it tonight. You'll stay, won't you? Stay for a few days? Just so that we can keep an eye on you, make sure you're OK.'

'Yes,' Fern smiled, 'I'll stay.'

Just then Ed came into the room with a glass of orange juice in one hand and a gin and tonic in the other.

'I presumed you'd be detoxing,' he said to Annie with a smile as he handed Fern the gin and tonic.

'You know me so well,' she smiled back, gratefully accepting the orange juice.

Owen followed Ed in, carrying the little dog. It had calmed down now and seemed to be accepting the lift quite peacefully. Annie looked at it with distaste again. It was one of those wiry-coated, fuzzy brown things. A border terrier? But its legs seemed too long. Well, what had Owen said? It was a rescue dog, it was probably some cross of several different breeds. A right little mutt.

When had her mum *ever* said anything about wanting a dog? And why would she want a scrubby little dog like that?

'What on earth made you get the dog, Mum?' Annie asked, with a roll of her eyes. 'Now that really was flipping madness!'

'What dog?' Fern asked, looking at her with round eyes.

Annie nearly gasped with shock. Her mum had forgotten the dog? She must be bad! Really bad. What was the term? Dementing?

'The dog,' Annie repeated, then pointed at the little mutt in Owen's arms, 'What made you decide to get him?'

Now everyone in the room was looking astonished. Owen's mouth made a little O of surprise.

'That is a dog, isn't it?' Annie asked, 'I'm not seeing things?'

'Dave isn't Granny's. He's ours!' Owen said, his arms fiercely protective around the creature.

For a long moment there was silence. Annie was too shocked to even form the word *What*?!

'Dave's our dog,' Owen repeated, 'Aren't cha, boy?' he

rubbed the dog's head vigorously and the dog responded by licking his hand.

'Ed!' Annie exclaimed, glaring over at him, 'why didn't you? . . . Why didn't we? . . . You've not said one, single word . . .'

'I thought you just said you were OK with it,' Ed said in his defence.

'OK with it?!' Annie repeated, 'I thought he was Mum's!'

'I've been trying to mention the idea . . .' Ed began.

'Well you can't have tried very hard,' she hissed, desperately wanting to shout but feeling restrained by the presence of both her mum and her clearly dog-devoted son. 'An ugly, deaf, rescue dog?' she exclaimed. 'Is this your idea of a joke? Or maybe this is your idea of a substitute? Your substitute for a you-know-what?'

'Oh dear,' Owen said into the expectant pause that followed this remark.

'I'm sorry . . . sorry. I shouldn't be saying any of this in front of you,' Annie muttered.

'No. Oh dear – I've just stood in a puddle,' Owen admitted and held out his wet, dog-wee-soaked sock for everyone to see.

Chapter Twenty-eight

Dinah's wine bar look:

Brown and blue long-sleeved minidress
(T-Bags, via Annie)
Brown belt (Topshop)
Blue beads (jewellery box)
Bright blue tights (Topshop)
Funky brown boots (Camper sale)
Total est. cost: £90

'Stay away from the hairdresser's until
you're feeling better.'

'And so, to recap,' Dinah began as she snuggled in a little closer to her sister, happy that they'd managed to snag their favourite booth seat in their favourite wine bar, 'you've been unceremoniously sacked from your TV star job. You're going to be edited out of the programme. You've got no money. You've got to drum up your own business from scratch all over again. Your partner is in a baby frenzy and you're not going there. Our mum is possibly beginning to lose it. Your daughter's hanging out with a Russian supermodel/hooker in waiting—'

'Ten p.m.!' Annie broke in, 'They finally came home at ten o'clock last night, only after we phoned them four times. And they smelled of smoke. If Elena starts Lana smoking, I will kill her. I'll kill both of them!'

'Then we have your son,' Dinah went on, 'who is totally in love with a hideous dog you'd like to destroy.' Dinah raised her eyebrows, rolled her eyes and couldn't resist a smile. 'Hey, I'm only doing IVF. And I am feeling so much better about it, already,' she added.

At least this made Annie laugh briefly.

'And I hate my hair,' Annie added.

'Your hair?' Dinah turned to take a look at the offending ponytail. 'The colour looks fine. What's to hate about it?'

Annie ran her hands grumpily over the ponytail: 'This!' she said, 'Do you know how many years I've been wearing my hair like this?'

'No,' Dinah had to admit.

'Twelve years!'

'Well, it's a trademark hairstyle. Everyone knows you're the one with the bouncy blonde ponytail.'

'Trademark? No, I think you mean rut.'

'Well some people just have trademark hair: Anna Wintour's bob, Jerry Hall's blonde mane, Annie Valentine's ponytail.'

'Do you know what I would do to a client who'd been wearing the same hairstyle for twelve years? I would take her by the arm and frog-march her to a new hairdresser.'

'Well . . .' Dinah sipped at the glass of sparkling mineral water in front of her. Obviously she wasn't drinking, she was in the state of pre-pregnancy purity recommended by the clinic. 'Could it be that with so much going on and so much to stress about you're transferring all that angst onto your hair?'

'Oooooh,' Annie elbowed her gently in the ribs, 'get you, Dr Dinah. Yeah, you're probably right.'

'I would stay away from the hairdresser's until you're feeling better. Remember when you got that mullet, when we were still at school?'

Both of them snorted at the memory.

'And it took sooo long to grow out,' Annie lamented.

'Seriously,' Dinah picked up her water as Annie drank another mouthful of wine, 'Mum first. Is she OK?'

'Well, you saw her. Tonight she seemed totally fine, yesterday she seemed fine. Well, apart from turning up out of the blue. I said I'd go to the doctor's with her when he gets back from his Caribbean cruise or whatever.'

'I can go if you can't,' Dinah added.

'Yeah, I know. Maybe we should both go. See what he thinks.'

'So what are you going to do for cash?' was Dinah's next question.

'Same old, same old,' came Annie's reply: 'phone up all my trusty old girls, tell them to take me shopping with them for a "seasonal refresh", phone up my friend Mr Timi Woo, see if he'll sell me some of his fancy shoes to flog on eBay – all that kind of thing. Been there, done that, scraped by on it before . . .'

Despite Annie's best attempt at enthusiasm, Dinah could tell that this time her heart wasn't really in it.

'Bummer about the TV,' she commiserated.

'I know,' Annie admitted, 'I thought there was

something really new, really exciting starting there. I didn't like Finn and I wasn't wild about the Wonder Women idea . . . but something about it was great, fired me all up. Now it's over before it even began.'

'Is it worth going to some TV agents?' Dinah ventured, 'talking it through with them?'

'I don't even have a showreel!' Annie wailed, 'but maybe I could ask Bob . . . oh I don't know,' she grumbled, 'all that knocking on doors and begging for a chance. Don't you think there are twenty-five younger, blonder, showier Miss Marlise wannabees for every saggy old Annie?'

'Oh cheer up.' It was Dinah's turn to prod Annie in the ribs now: 'you're really good at your personal shopper job, just work your clients, work your eBay shop and something good will come up. Do you want to go back to The Store?' she ventured.

'Go back again? For the second time, with my tail well and truly between my legs?' Annie took a swig at her wine, 'I don't know,' she admitted.

'The staff discount,' Dinah reminded her.

'I know . . . without that staff discount, I'll be shopping in chain stores for ever.'

'What does Ed think?' Dinah asked.

'Well, as you can flipping imagine, last night's pillow talk was mainly about the dog,' Annie told her. 'We didn't get round to what I was going to do next, because I think Ed still imagines I'm going to be on maternity leave any moment now, having succumbed to his persuasive charms.'

When Dinah made something of a grimace at this, Annie had to apologize: 'I'm sorry, I feel like such a cow talking about how much I don't want a baby, when here you are shoving drugs up your nose and into your bum cheeks desperate to have one.'

'Ah well . . . each to their own,' Dinah said heroically.

'How was Nic when you saw her?' Annie remembered to ask about their older sister, who was now in charge of a four-month-old baby.

'Very happy,' Dinah reported. 'She was really very, very happy. You should do it,' Dinah added, surprising herself, 'do it for Ed. He absolutely loves kids, he's obviously going to make the best hands-on Dad ever. Give him his baby, Annie. Let him be the house husband, then you get out there and start working on that handbag empire you were desperate to set up last year.'

Annie looked at her sister in surprise. She had not expected this. She only ever got totally loyal and unwavering support for everything from Dinah.

'I don't want you and Ed to break up,' Dinah added, trying to explain her outburst. 'People break up over babies. All the time.'

'Oh no – are you and Bryan?' Annie asked, suddenly concerned.

'No,' Dinah shook her head, 'we're fine. We've been through all this before to get Billie. Our eyes are wide open. But Ed . . . he deserves a baby, Annie, and there are plenty of other women out there who would trample you in the rush to get their hands on a caring, sharing, broody man like him.'

'Yeah, now that I've made him over,' Annie grumbled, 'now that I've bought him new clothes and tidied his hair and his eyebrows and domesticated him. Now they come. Now they see the dream man. So much for the sisterhood!'

233

'Annie Valentine!' Dinah scolded, 'the man was dating gold dust even before you got your hands on him.'

'Dating gold dust,' Annie smiled.

The phone in her bag began to ring and when she pulled it out she was delighted to see Connor's number on the screen.

'It's Connor,' she told Dinah, 'he must know we're having a girls' night out without him.'

'Babes!' she said into the receiver enthusiastically.

'Mzzzzzzz Valentine, this is your agent speaking,' he schmoozed back down the line, 'how are you coping? Are you detoxing, exercising and grooming yourself for your next role?'

'Yes, my love, I am in the pub with Dinah on my second large red and I may even stop for a kebab on the way home, just for you,' Annie told him.

'No Annie, no!!' he moaned theatrically. 'She is so hard to keep on the rails this one, she tortures me . . . after all I've done for you. Right, listen, girlfriend. This is what *Screentalk*'s Gossip Roundup will be printing about you *mañana*, thanks to your friend Connor. Yes, I phoned *Screentalk* myself, because I knew you were far too wussy to do it.'

'No!' Annie shrieked, genuinely horrified, 'no, you shouldn't have, I didn't want to stir up any trouble.'

'Donnie Finnigan's star find,' Connor began to read, 'Annie Valentine, former personal shopper at The Store has walked off the set claiming the show is trite and demeaning.'

All Annie could do was scream.

'Shut up,' Connor instructed. 'Ms Valentine . . .' he read on, 'who has years of hands-on makeover experience, a client list and a wardrobe to die for, was described by set insiders as "an absolute natural on television" and, according to long-standing friend, *Manor* star, Connor McCabe: "She won't wait long for another plum job".'

Connor paused for a moment before he delivered the last line of the story: 'Ms Valentine's late husband was the well-known stage and television actor, Roddy Valentine.'

'Oh,' Annie felt sobered by that. 'You told them about Roddy?'

'Well . . . me phoning up, the name Valentine, she put two and two together. But it will help – something to talk about when you do press.'

'What?' Annie swallowed hard. 'If I did an interview I'd have to talk about Roddy?'

'Well yes. Personal tragedy . . . the mags love all that stuff. Nothing worse for them than being a happily married mother of two. But, let's not worry about that. We're not exactly there yet,' he blustered on. 'I've told Emma if anyone phones *Screentalk* to find out about you, she's to give them my agent's number.'

'Rafie boy?!' Annie had to laugh at this. Connor couldn't stand his agent – real name Ralph Frampton-Dwight, nickname Rafie Frightful-Twit.

'He's a good agent . . .' Connor defended himself. 'I've not actually told him about you yet, but I don't think he'll mind too much.'

'You're very nice,' Annie said, 'very, very nice to me. I wish I could do something as helpful for you.'

'Well you can't, especially now that you can't get me cheap things from The Store.' Connor sounded almost huffy.

'Cheap things! I think movie stars can afford to pay

full price, can't they? Maybe you'll start getting things for free now that you're so famous.'

'Oh ha, bloody ha.'

'How's work going for you anyway?'

'I am as brown as a bunny and twice as buff . . . in other words, no work, bored shitless,' Connor confessed with a sigh.

'Really? What's happened?'

'Oh don't go feeling sorry for me. *The Manor* starts shooting in a few weeks. I'll be back in Britain with my pockets full of wodge.'

'Ooh, when are you back?' Annie wanted to know. 'I need to clear my diary.' She snorted, because really there was absolutely nothing in her diary now. 'Just make sure I get to see you first.'

'I will,' Connor promised her.

'And how's Hector?' Annie asked.

'Good. Still on about a baby. How's Ed?'

'Good. Still on about a baby.'

'How's Dinah?'

'Good . . . trying for another baby.'

'We're all mad, aren't we? Must be a mid-life crisis or something,' Connor said, unusually serious for a moment, before reverting to type. 'Send her my hot and sticky man-love.'

When the call was over, Dinah told Annie with a smile, 'I know what we have to do. I have a plan. You have to have twins, Annie, give one baby to Ed and one to me. Then you go out and found the twenty-first-century's Louis Vuitton and we all live happily and fabulously wealthily ever after.'

'Oh yeah,' Annie agreed, jauntily raising her wineglass, 'of course! Why didn't I think of that? Twins and a handbag empire. No problem.'

'Annie!' Dinah exclaimed, putting her glass down with a jolt, 'I nearly forgot!' She rummaged vigorously in her handbag: 'for Ed's birthday . . .'

Annie watched as she pulled out a chunky white envelope.

'I've booked the two of you into the luxury Lullworth Hotel in the Cotswolds for two nights. Friday and Saturday,' Dinah announced.

'This Friday and Saturday?' Annie asked in astonishment.

'Yeah! All paid. Mates' rates because Bryan did work for them. I'll babysit. You're going on a minibreak!'

Annie's mouth hung open with surprise.

'You'll look after Lana and Owen?' she repeated, 'and possibly Elena? Dinah, do you have any idea what kind of a saint you are?' Anne reached over and gave her sister a big hug.

Dinah hugged her back. 'And you two will drive off into the countryside and be pampered and reconnect and make love in front of a roaring fire . . .'

'Yeah: me, Ed and my two diaphragms.'

Chapter Twenty-nine

Bettina at home:

Wide-legged jeans (Notify)
Short-sleeved blouse (Paul & Joe)
Flat brown sandals (Jimmy Choo)
Gold watch (Gucci)
Total est. cost: £760

'My husband has slashed my budget.'

Annie looked at Dave.

Dave looked at Annie.

Then the dog cocked his head ever slightly to the side and winked.

It winked? Did dogs do that? Did they mean to do it, or was it just a reflex action? It must be another one of their stupid strategies for trying to get you to like them. Like leaving warm puddles of pee in unexpected places, hiding under the duvet just before you got into bed and snuggling up with the cashmere in your hand-washing basket.

'What?' she asked the dog. 'You've just been out. You can't need to go out again.'

She was talking to a dog. She couldn't believe this. *I'm talking to a dog, ED! I'm talking to your stupid dog!*

Dave just sat on the floor of her office and continued to stare at her.

Ed, Lana and Owen had all gone to school, as this was a Thursday morning. Elena had gone out to meet a Ukrainian friend who'd just arrived in London. And now Annie – the Dave hater – was home alone, with Dave.

She had expected Dave to have the sense to go and curl up in his basket in the kitchen and leave her alone. But no, he was evidently lonely and had come into the office to see what she was doing.

What was she doing? she asked herself, looking across her desk at her laptop, her telephone, the pot of pencils and stack of magazines.

What she was trying to do was brace herself for the rest of her life. She might as well face it, unless Frightful-Twit suddenly phoned completely out of the blue with an unbelievable offer (and quite frankly what were the chances of that) then she was Annie Valentine, personal shopper and eBay entrepreneur, starting up all over again.

With a deep sigh, she switched on her computer and opened up her file of contacts. Then she logged onto her eBay account and clicked through to her little shop front.

AnnieV's Trading Station had been completely neglected of late. For the first time in years, there was nothing for sale. Just her eBay name and beside it the blue star of a power seller and the number of items she'd sold in brackets (14,521).

Selling off her unwanted wardrobe items, plus discount buys from The Store, plus all the things her clients parted with every season, had been a lucrative sideline for Annie for many years. Last year, she'd flirted with the idea of going into business full time and had begun something interesting, importing Chinese shoes and Italian bags. There had even been a meeting with the shoe buyer from Fraser's. If the TV offer hadn't come up, she would probably be running her own small shoe business by now.

She could begin again, she told herself. She would get all fired up again.

It was just today . . . She gave a deep, tired sigh and sank her head down into her hands. Today felt a bit hard. Today felt as if everything she had done so far had brought her all the way to precisely nowhere and she was standing just where she'd stood so many times before. At the beginning.

'Oh, stop with the gloom!' she told herself fiercely, 'you're going to be fine.'

Annie looked up. Dave was still sitting there, his head cocked to the side now as if in surprise. Wasn't he deaf? Maybe he picked up the vibrations of sound or something.

She *was* going to be fine, she thought again. If there was one thing she could do, it was to pick herself up, brush herself down and start all over again. It was her unique talent.

She glanced up for inspiration at the small card she'd pinned to her noticeboard this morning. She didn't have to read it again, she knew what it said: 'Annie Valentine, how can I ever thank you enough? You've changed my life! Love Tina.' It had arrived in the post yesterday, with two of the Polaroids which Bob had taken and given to Tina: the 'before' and the knockout 'after'.

'C'mon!' Annie told herself, when looking at the card didn't work, 'let's have just a teeny, weeny look at handbags on eBay and cheer ourselves up, ha Dave? You don't look like much of a handbag kind of guy but bear with me . . .'

She started tapping at the keyboard. Handbags . . . Mulberry . . . used . . . (there was no point buying new Mulberry bags on eBay because they were bound to be fakes.) Up came 168 results. Annie scanned expertly.

Then almost without thinking about it she began dialling the relevant contact from her list.

'Angela! How are you, sweetheart? It's your favourite personal shopper, Annie V.'

'Annie!' Angela shrieked in response, 'how are you? How's it going on TV?'

'Pants!' came the pithy reply, borrowed from Owen.

But Annie set a smile in place and made the story of her own personal Armageddon as funny as she could. Then she breezed on with: 'So I'm checking out some Roger Saul Mulberry originals on eBay this morning and of course, I'm thinking of you.'

'Ooooh, what have you seen?' Angela asked.

'A square tote, leopardskin effect leather, tortoiseshell handles. Absolutely gorgeous. Starting bid forty-five pounds.'

'Mmmm. I am seriously tempted. Usual conditions?'

Annie took 15 per cent for everything she bought and sold for clients on eBay.

'Uh-huh. How's your wardrobe looking, my darlin',

241

want to go on a shopping trip with me? Make my week?'

'Annie, you know I would have loved to . . .'

Uh-oh.

'But I thought you were off. Away, out of it all. So I've gone and spent my wardrobe allowance without you. I didn't make too much of a mess of it either,' Angela added proudly.

'Glad to hear it,' Annie said, which wasn't exactly true.

'Bettina! It's Annie Valentine . . . yes . . . lovely to hear you too. How's it going?'

Annie was soon on to her sixth client cold call and she still hadn't drummed up one single job. Everyone had been shopping without her, or worse still claimed they weren't shopping this year at all.

The credit crunch.

If she heard those words one more time, she would scream.

'But we don't have to go to The Store,' she'd tried convincing one former client, 'there is so much fantastic stuff out there on the high street at giveaway prices, you just need to know where to look.'

'The high street?' had come the uncertain question. 'I think I'll just wear the lovely things I already have for another season instead of getting anything new and a bit . . . cheap.'

'Cheap is clever,' Annie had tried to persuade her. 'I mean have you seen the bangles in Topshop? They look just like the ones in Theo Fennell. We're all doing recession chic now . . .'

But to no avail.

Bettina wasn't in the mood for spending big money with her personal shopper either.

'My husband has slashed my budget,' she complained, making Annie wonder for a moment why Bettina didn't just get up off her pampered behind and make some money so she could set a budget of her own.

'I don't think I'm even going to be able to afford my make-up – not even my special face creams!' Bettina wailed.

'I'll take you to the Rimmel concession,' Annie wheedled, 'it's fabulous, Kate Moss doesn't use anything else. And you have got to try the new Olay moisturizers. They are giving them away at Superdrug. Seriously!'

'Really?' Bettina's interest was a little pricked.

'They're the business,' Annie enthused, 'my face has looked like a baby's bottom ever since I started using them and you know what a wrinkled old bag I used to be.'

With those words, Annie glanced over at her reflection. The Botox was still holding firm. She liked it. But a little tiny top-up just there over her eyebrows wouldn't go amiss. Once she had some money coming in!

'Bets, I've got an idea,' Annie began. 'Why don't we have a wardrobe play date? I come over, I look through everything you've already got and we work out how to make it fresh. How to tweak it for the months ahead. We dig through the scarves, belts and necklaces. We move some hemlines up or down. We work with what's there, babes, and for just a few pounds, we reinvent your clothes for the new season. Plus . . . we'll have a laugh! Go on . . . just say yes,' Annie wheedled. 'I could come tomorrow . . . you know what, I could even come today.'

'The usual rate?' Bettina asked. Now Annie knew the bait was taken, she just had to close the deal.

'Mates' rates,' she assured her, 'I'll charge you by the hour and you just stop me when you've had enough fun.'

'Well, I think tomorrow would be good,' Bettina said.

Annie wanted to dance about the room.

'Say lunchtime?' Bettina added.

Annie ran the plan quickly through her mind. Tomorrow was Friday, minibreak day. There were bags to pack, meals to organize . . . they'd hoped to leave London at four-ish, before the Friday rush hour kicked in properly. If she was at Bettina's at 11.30 and stayed for three hours or so, that would leave just enough time to get home, get organized. Well, it would be a rush, but three hours at Bettina's would at least be something in her wallet for the weekend.

She had to do it.

'Does 11.30 suit?' she offered.

'Yes. And bring a bottle of the Olay. I'll give it a try.'

As soon as Annie had hung up, she opened her diary and wrote on Friday's page: 'Bettina, wardrobe play-date 11.30' in bold letters with a red felt-tip pen.

It wasn't that Annie was in any danger of forgetting, it was just so encouraging to see it written down there. To know that she was back and she really could drum money up out of nothing with her skills. She felt a little burst of her energy return. Just enough to make the next round of calls. As soon as there was a whole week in the diary packed with appointments, she would feel like her old self again.

Turning her head quickly back to the clients' contact

page, she saw the flick of her ponytail in the mirror again. It was under serious review, that ponytail.

Before Annie could punch in the numbers of her next target, her mobile began to trill.

It was Ed. She glanced at her watch: 12.45 already, so he was on his lunch break.

'How's Dave?' was his first question.

'Oh, so that's how it is now? No more, hello darlin' how are you? It's the dog first?' she teased.

Looking round the small room, she couldn't see Dave. He must have wandered out while she was on the phone. She would have to go and check on him, make sure he wasn't peeing on the rugs or looking for another one of Owen's *Dr Who* figures to chew. There had been a temporary suspension last night of the fond dog/boy relations when a small platoon of plastic alien Judoon had been discovered in a state of total annihilation.

'He's part terrier,' Ed had tried to explain: 'terriers love to dig and chew.'

'And yap and wee,' Annie had added.

'I just want to make sure that you and Dave are getting on,' Ed told her now.

'I still hate you for Dave,' Annie replied, 'I really do not need a Dave in my life. I mean it's such a stupid name for a start. If he's deaf, why can't we rename him?'

'Well . . .' she had a point, Ed had to admit, 'I think you'll have to speak to Owen about that. He's the one who wanted a dog so badly, he's the one who chose him.'

'Why did I not know anything about this? *Before* it was done?'

'You'd have said no,' Ed admitted. 'Anyway, how

many times have you gone and done something without telling me because you knew perfectly well I'd have said no?'

Annie couldn't answer.

'How's your mum?' he asked, to move away from the dog debate.

'I've sent her to the shops. If she's not back in half an hour, I'll have to send out a search party. But I think she'll be fine.'

'I'm really, really looking forward to going away with you,' Ed told her.

'Yeah . . . wait till Saturday, when you find out what I've got you for your birthday.'

'You need a little break after everything you've been through.' He cleared his throat hesitantly, before adding, 'But . . . I think we'll have to take Dave.'

'WHAT!?'

'Well, it's a lot for Dinah to deal with as well as the kids and Elena. She'll have to keep some sort of tabs on Elena for us.'

Annie's call waiting began to beep.

'Another call, babes,' she told Ed, determined that somehow she would not be taking Dave on their mini-break, 'gotta go.'

'Annah!'

There was no mistaking Svetlana's voice on the other end of the line.

'Hey, how are you doing?'

'Terrible! I am missing you completely on the set. It is fraught. Marlise go shopping with the fat women and make them cry.'

Annie couldn't help giving a satisfied smile at this piece

of news. Ha! It wasn't as easy as Finn had thought to just erase her and replace her.

'Are you phoning to ask how Elena is?' Annie asked pointedly. It was nearly a week since Elena had landed and Svetlana had still not even come to see her.

'This is all such a bad time Annah! Terrible!' Svetlana complained. 'Igor is making me nervous. He lose so much money on the stock market, I think he somehow try to get my house back.'

'I thought the house was yours?' Annie asked, 'I thought you got it in the divorce settlement.'

'Oh yes, but so many conditions. This not good time for trouble. Not for any trouble at all. And Elena is trouble. I can see it. Harry alvays fight for me, but Igor he has more lawyers, more money and anyway, Harry honest man. Igor: crook!'

'Have you spoken to Harry about it?'

'Ya, about Igor of courrrrse. But he keeps asking me: are you being totally honest with me? Is there anything else I should know?'

'You've told Harry about Elena, though?' Annie asked.

There was a pause before Svetlana confided: 'No Annah. Not yet. Is not a good time.'

'But Harry needs to know,' Annie tried to persuade her. 'What if Igor finds out and Harry doesn't know?'

'You know, I vorry that Igor already find out about Elena. Maybe this is how he is going to convince me to give up the house.' There was real anxiety in Svetlana's voice now. 'Maybe Igor bring Elena over in the first place. He is doing something secret. There is going to be a surprise, I know it, I vill be cheated.'

Annie understood Svetlana's fear. When Igor had first

moved for divorce, he had tried to take his sons and leave his wife with nothing. This had been her third divorce and with the kind of wealthy men she was up against, Svetlana knew you had to fight for every penny. They did not take kindly to the women they'd finished with demanding a slice of their fortune.

'Have you heard from Uri again?' Annie asked, hoping that Svetlana had at least let this other source of trouble alone.

'Ah yes, but I put him off. Is good for me though to have another man in the background, if ever there is problem with Harry, I can click my fingers, call on Uri, make Harry jealous. Simple.'

'So we keep Elena for a bit longer?'

'Yes please, my darlink friend. I thank you so much for this.'

Annie could hear the call waiting beep so she finished up with Svetlana and clicked over to this new caller.

'Hello Annie? Hello . . . this is Cath – you remember, you came round with the TV . . .'

'Cath! Yes, of course I remember, how are you?' Annie asked.

'I'm fine,' Cath told her.

'Did you cope with being on TV?'

'Nearly . . .' came the reply, but it sounded as if it came with a smile.

'Have you been wearing your foxy black dress?' Annie asked.

'Yes, it's lovely.'

'Glad to hear it.'

'That's why I was phoning. You know you gave me your card and said if I ever wanted to go shopping with you . . . I mean, if you're still offering the service . . . I mean now that you're on television, you might not have the time and you might have put your prices up . . .'

'No, no, no,' Annie interrupted, feeling a surge of enthusiasm, 'if you're ready for the Annie Valentine personal shopping service, then I am more than ready for you, babes!'

As Annie listened to Cath talking about what she wanted to buy and when she'd be available, she was sure she could hear a strange scratching sound. A bit of scrabbling, then a definite scratching. She stood up, phone at her ear, and began to look around the room. No . . . nothing.

It seemed to be coming from her bedroom. Walking quickly in there, she found Dave growling and vigorously shaking something that flashed grey and silver in his mouth. His teeth had a firm grasp on the object and one paw was holding it down and determinedly scratching it into submission. The dog had its prey, it was gripping and chewing, certain that the Miu Miu handbag wasn't going to make a break for it and get away.

'No!' Annie shrieked and began to run towards the filthy little animal, 'NO! Put that down. DOWN!'

Chapter Thirty

Ed scrubbed up:

New jeans (Gap)
New white T-shirt (same)
Navy cashmere V-neck (Annie)
Blue and white trainers (Puma)
Total est. cost: £170

'I'm a generous man.'

'Pls be hm soon. Packing. Have new gadgts just for you.'

Annie had just finished up at Bettina's and climbed into her Jeep when she got Ed's text.

It made her smile.

Now all she wanted was to be back with him. They would load up the car and drive off into the countryside for peace and quiet. With sex toys.

She giggled. Sex toys . . . and contraception? She ran the thought over in her mind several times. Then she heard Dinah's urgent words about having a baby and felt a rush of love for Ed. He was a lovely man. He'd been so willing to take on the responsibility of caring deeply for Owen and Lana – even Elena and bloody Dave. Who else would bring the ugly, deaf dog home from the animal shelter? He was a kind, grounded person, who wanted children of his own. Hadn't Dinah warned her that people break up over children all the time?

What would Annie do without him?

Well, she knew. She had been alone before him. Life would be OK, but it would be quiet, lonelier, more child-obsessed, not nearly so much fun . . . and definitely not nearly so fruity.

This made her think of the gadgets again, with a smile. Apparently they were to keep her very happy.

A baby. That was what would make Ed very happy.

A baby? Would she really be able to give Ed a baby? Do this just for his sake?

She tried for a moment to imagine Ed's baby and pictured a gurgling thing with wild hair, little glasses and a tweedy jacket. That was ridiculous.

Then she imagined Ed holding a baby and that was much clearer. She saw his face so full of love he could barely tear his eyes from the little person in his arms.

Maybe she could begin to think about doing this for him.

Maybe?

Annie had barely made it through the front door when she was hit by a volley of complaints.

Her mother's voice rang out from the sitting room: 'Is that you, Annie? When are we going to Dinah's? For heaven's sake, will someone at least tell me when we're

251

going, so that I can be prepared? I just want to know when we're going.'

Before Annie could drop her bags and head in her mum's direction, Owen bounded up to her.

'Why do *you* get to have Dave for the weekend?' he asked angrily. 'It's *so* unfair. Dinah won't have to do anything, I'll look after him. I'll look after him all the time. I'll take him out and feed him and he won't be any trouble at all. He's just settling in, he shouldn't be moved again . . . pleeeeeeeease, Mum,' Owen protested, looking up into her face with the most earnest, most pleading, most mother-heart-melting expression he could possibly muster.

'Hello to you too, Owen, nice to see you,' Annie responded grumpily, 'Look, I'll have to ask Ed.'

Personally, she couldn't think of anything she'd like better than for Dave not to come with them. But she had to think about what would be best for Dinah.

Owen wasn't happy with this answer: 'It's not fair! Well, if you're going to take him all the way to some boring hotel in the car, then I'm going to the shop to get him some chews!'

And with that, he clipped the lead to the dog's collar, grabbed his anorak and made for the front door, giving it a good, hard slam on the way out.

'That's a bit of an over-reaction, Owen!' Annie shouted after him.

'We're taking the dog and that's final!' Ed called from the upstairs bedroom, sounding unusually harassed himself.

'When are we leaving for Dinah's?' her mother's voice rang out again.

'All right, keep your hair on!' Annie headed for the sitting room where she found her mother standing by the window, peering out with anxiety.

'What's the matter, Mum?' she asked her. 'There's no need to get your knickers in a twist. You're not going to Dinah's. Dinah is coming here. She's leaving Billie with Bryan and she's going to stay here for two nights and look after everyone. You can stay on here if you like, but didn't you say you wanted to go back home tomorrow?'

'Oh yes,' Fern replied, as if she'd just remembered.

'Is our Ukrainian friend in?' Annie asked.

'She left with a big bag under her arms . . . that's why I thought we were all going to Dinah's,' Fern replied, 'and Lana, she's packed up to go to Dinah's too. I saw her leaving with a bulging schoolbag this morning.'

'No, no!' Annie assured her, 'Lana's got a study date after school and Elena . . . maybe she has friends to see or something, I'll give her a call.'

'So Dinah's coming here?' Fern asked again, still looking out of the window, as if she was waiting for someone.

'Yes,' Annie answered trying to control her exasperation. 'Please sit down and let me get you a cup of tea. Are you looking for Owen?'

'Owen?' her mother turned to her in some confusion.

'He's just gone out of the house with Dave to get some dog treats from the corner shop . . . I didn't even know they sold that kind of thing,' she added, 'Now sit down,' she ordered her mother, 'I'll bring tea.'

'Dog treats,' Fern began, 'that dog doesn't deserve treats. I found him eating one of my shoes. Got it off him just in time.'

'No!' Annie was horrified, she'd already lost one Miu

253

Miu bag . . . what if Dave decided to attack her shoes? She'd have to move them to a safe cupboard, maybe start keeping them under lock and key.

'I'll get the tea,' Annie said again, but first she took the stairs two at a time to see how Ed was getting on with the packing.

'I don't want the dog to come,' she whined as soon as she set foot in the bedroom.

Ed turned his attention from the overnight bag on the bed to her. 'Not even a hello?'

She went up and kissed him on the lips. Felt his arms close in round her back.

'No . . . still don't want the dog to come,' she said afterwards, but with a smile now.

'I'm sorry, he has to come. Dinah shouldn't have to mop up dog pee as well as everything else this weekend.'

'Why didn't you get a house-trained dog?' Annie complained.

'He is! He's just not on familiar territory yet.'

Annie decided to stop talking and start packing. She examined the things lying on the bed in front of Ed's bag.

'Is that a present?' She picked up a package carefully wrapped in colourful paper and tied with a ribbon.

'Uh-huh,' he added with a little wiggle of his eyebrows.

'For me?' She smiled at Ed.

'Hey, for all you know that might be a bone to keep the dog happy.'

'A bone? A bone, huh?' She read the playful look on his face. 'I'm looking forward to the bone.'

'Me too.'

'But it's your birthday,' she protested, 'you're the one who should be getting presents.'

'What can I say?' He put his arms around her again. 'I'm a generous man.'

She might have turned to kiss him, but then the doorbell rang.

'Must be Dinah, I'll go,' Annie offered and headed out of the room.

'When's Lana back?' Ed called after her.

'She's going to Andrei's for a study date,' Annie informed him, 'promised to be home by ten and I've given her money for a taxi.'

'Andrei's?' Ed repeated. He followed her out of the bedroom and stood in the hall at the top of the stairs with a concerned look on his face.

'Yeah,' Annie shouted back.

'Andrei's not home tonight,' Ed called down to her.

Annie could see Dinah's outline in the glass panes of the front door, but this information stopped her in her tracks.

'What d'you mean?' she asked, turning to look at Ed.

'At 7 p.m. tonight, Andrei's at Dulwich High School, opening up for the St Vincent's debating team.'

For a moment, Annie and Ed looked at each other in silence.

Then Dinah's second ring at the doorbell punctuated their anxious thoughts. Annie flung open the door.

'Hi. You're a star. Mum's in the sitting room. Help yourself to tea, biscuits – anything! Slight Lana crisis, babes. We've got to get her back home before we go.' Dinah crossed the threshold into apparent chaos.

Annie was already dialling Lana's mobile number. But to her frustration, the call went through to voicemail.

'Lana, it's your mum, whatever your plans are for this evening, I need to know about them. Call me,' she ordered, and hung up.

Annie then went through the list of numbers she had for Lana's friends and Lana's friends' mothers. She would phone them all. She would ring everyone until she knew where her daughter was. At the forefront of her mind was the thought that Lana had recently been so trouble-free, so studious and so honest . . . but things had changed as soon as Elena had come along.

Now Lana had bought scary clothes, spent a school night out too late in a café, smelled of cigarette smoke, and there obviously wasn't as much studying going on as there had been before.

She dialled Elena's mobile.

Voicemail.

'It's Annie, call me as soon as you get this message. Straight away,' she barked.

When the two friends and three mothers she'd been able to reach had been unable to give her any further information, Annie decided to go up to Lana's room to see if she could find any clues there.

A quick look around told her that her daughter's latest shoes and dress were missing along with her make-up bag. It was enough to make the tears well up.

'Elena!' Annie whispered to herself feeling anxious, angry and hurt, 'this is all about Elena!'

Last night, Elena had come back after midnight. Annie had heard a car pull up in the street and wait until Elena had let herself in the front door. It hadn't bothered Annie particularly. Elena was 22. She'd got herself all the way from Kiev to London, it was obvious she had friends in town and she could look after herself. Annie hadn't considered that maybe next time, Elena would want Lana to tag along with her.

Back down in the sitting room she found Ed, with Dinah and her mother, texting with his phone.

'Is there someone you can call?' Annie asked him.

'Just wondered about getting a message to Andrei,' Ed replied. 'I've got a number for the teacher going to the debate with him. Maybe he can pass on a message.'

'I can't think of anyone else to phone . . . maybe someone will call back,' Annie said. She looked down at her phone and tried first Lana's and then Elena's number again. She couldn't sit down . . . she walked round the room, fussing at things: straightening magazine piles, re-arranging the framed photos on the mantelpiece . . .

'Try not to worry,' Ed soothed, 'she's a sensible girl. She's maybe gone out with Elena, but I bet you anything you like she'll be home in a taxi at 10 p.m. on the dot.'

Ed's mobile began to ring, and everyone turned towards it hopefully.

'Hi,' he answered it, 'hi, Andrei. Thanks for calling. Sorry to bother you. We're looking for Lana . . .'

Ed was listening with concentration.

'Right . . .' he said, 'did she? . . . Yeah . . . that's right . . .' Ed listened for several minutes, before asking: 'D'you think you could? That would be really helpful. Brilliant. OK, speak then . . . cheers.'

He folded up his phone, stood up and told Annie: 'She's over in the East End with Elena. I don't know where exactly, but Andrei's going to try and find out. She's texted him already to ask him to come. I'll head over there,' Ed added.

'What are they doing? Why does Lana need Andrei?' Annie asked frantically.

'Apparently Elena's meeting someone about a job and she wanted Lana to come with her.'

'What kind of job?'

'I don't know. Look, I'm going to take the car and head over there. Andrei will tell me more just as soon as he can. We'll find her,' he added as reassuringly as he could.

'I'm going to come,' Annie said.

'No, I'll be fine, stay here and man the phones,' he told her. 'Keep calling everyone who might know where she is and you might find something out sooner than me. Please Annie, you know it makes sense.'

'All right . . .' she agreed reluctantly.

Ed had decided that telling Annie what Lana's text to Andrei had said wouldn't be helpful just now. She'd told him she didn't like the place and could he please come as soon as possible. Andrei had just been wondering how he could make it to the East End and be back in time to catch the minibus to Dulwich High School when he'd got the message to phone Ed from his English teacher.

Ed took Annie's car keys and headed out of the door, promising to call as soon as he had any more news at all.

'How are you doing?' Annie asked her sister, once she'd accepted a fresh cup of tea and finally been persuaded to sit down. Dinah, leaning back on the sofa beside their mother, looked pale and tired. Now that Annie had put down her phone she noticed this for the first time.

'Oh OK,' Dinah replied, 'the embryos are in but no

point counting that as pregnant yet,' came the frank revelation.

'Oh Dinah!' Fern turned sympathetically and patted her hand, 'I'm so sorry you have to go through all this. It always seemed easy . . . a little too easy for me to get pregnant.' This must have caused Fern to think fleetingly of her ex-husband because a particularly dark expression crossed her face. Her husband had lost contact with his family years ago. He was a cargo ship captain who'd specialized in trans-global relationships of the wrong kind, and Fern had been glad to get rid of him; now, quite honestly, she and her girls had no idea whether he was dead or alive, it was so long since they'd heard anything from him at all.

'Dinah, I don't think we should go away this weekend,' Annie announced. 'It's not fair on you. It's you and Bryan who should be going on a minibreak, not us.'

'We will. We have it planned,' Dinah said, 'we'll take a proper holiday in a couple of months, either way: up the duff or not. Why do you think I'm here?' she asked with a smile. 'I'm building up Brownie points for when I need you or, even better, Ed to babysit.'

'Well, you're definitely not here for fun, are you? I mean, what a blooming disaster!' Annie exclaimed. 'How could Lana do this?! And today!'

'Because she's a teenage girl?!' Fern chipped in. 'When I think of all the things the three of you used to get up to – and especially you, Annie.'

At this, Annie had to lean back in her chair and consider for a moment. Looking back, it all seemed innocent enough because nothing really terrible had happened to her. But would she want her daughter to do the things

259

she'd done? Be in the risky situations she'd put herself in?

Annie had been out almost every weekend, aged 17 onwards, always taking the night bus home and walking the final stretch, in heels and miniskirts, with her house keys poking out from between her fingers as if that was going to protect her from an attacker.

'But it was different back then!' she protested.

'Aha!' Fern chuckled. 'How many mothers have heard themselves saying that? You know that isn't true. It's Lana's job to get out and have some adventures. It's your job to rein her in and keep her safe. That's just how it should be, love.'

Annie smiled at her mum. This was all true. But mainly she was smiling because whatever fog had been clouding Fern's head lately, it seemed to be clearing.

'Annie?' Dinah began, 'I've not seen your dog yet. Has Owen . . .'

'OWEN!' Annie shrieked, jumping up from her chair and flipping her cup of tea straight onto the floor. He'd been away for far too long.

Chapter Thirty-one

Lana goes out:

Yellow boob tube (New Look)
Black miniskirt (same)
Black leggings (Topshop)
Long black boots (Greta's)
Lashings of mascara (Rimmel)
Total est. cost: £45

'I feel sick.'

Ed glanced anxiously at his watch. It was already 7.45, dark outside and now the rain had started. He was parked on a busy road near Old Street watching the Friday evening hustle around him.

Workers had finished for the day and the streets were busy with people hurrying home or hurrying to go out for the night. There were pubs, clubs, bars and cafés on every street, on every corner. It was no use knowing that Lana was around here because he would never be able to find her: he had to sit still and wait.

Lana was ignoring his and Annie's phone calls, but she had already texted Andrei and if they were all patient, she would phone or text Andrei again. She'd wanted Andrei to come and get her, so surely she would let him know exactly where she was some time soon.

But what if something had happened? Ed's thoughts whirled round to this again. What if she'd lost her phone? Or the signal? What if something had happened to her? Ed chewed at the skin beside his fingernail and tried not to think like this. He looked at his watch again. It had been over fifty minutes since Lana had told Andrei to come and get her. In another fifteen minutes, Andrei would be on stage, debating; then, even if Lana did phone him, he wouldn't be able to pick up the call for an hour.

Ed let out a sigh of irritation and began to drum his fingers against the steering wheel. He just hoped that Lana was safe. He tried to keep telling himself that in two hours she would almost certainly arrive home in a taxi and wonder what all the fuss was about.

His phone began to ring and he answered it immediately. 'Yes?'

'I've had another text,' Andrei's voice informed him, 'Club Z Old Street.'

'Is she OK? Did she say anything else?' Ed asked urgently.

'No, and I think this one's taken a while to come through because it says it was sent just after the last one. I'm sorry. Maybe it's the reception here.'

'No worries, that's great. Good luck,' Ed remembered to add.

'Yeah, you too. Will you let me know she's OK?'

'Of course,' Ed said, then closed up the phone and hurried to get out of the car.

Walking quickly along the pavements, looking left and right all around him, he called Directory Enquiries, hoping to get a phone number, an address, anything that would help him find this place more quickly.

'No, I'm sorry,' the voice on the other end of the line was telling him, 'we don't have a listing under that name. You're sure it's E3?'

'Well, no, it's this area . . . could it be E something else?' Ed asked impatiently.

'No . . . no, I haven't got anything coming up for that name.'

Ed ended the call and began to look for people to ask. Young couples, people who looked as if they were dressed up for a night out . . . he asked four or five, to no avail.

Then he passed a kebab shop: 'Open late' read the neon letters in the window. Maybe someone there would know?

Within minutes, Ed had a street name and clear directions for Club Z.

'It's not open yet, mate!' the guy behind the counter called after him.

But if Elena had been there for a job interview . . .

He hurried out into the street, then began to run. Past the traffic lights, second left, along this road right to the very bottom . . . there on the corner was a shabby looking awning with the letters 'Club Z' spelled out in faded silver paint.

Ed went straight to the door, pulled at it and found that it was open. Immediately he was in strange, timeless nightclub land. The wide corridor, then stairs, lit with a dim halogen glow and carpeted in deep red. No-one was around. No-one challenged him as he walked up the steps, then through the double doors at the top towards the loud throb of music.

Now he was in a large, dark bar with a dance floor. At the tables on the far side, he could see people were drinking and talking.

The club wasn't busy yet, but it was obviously already open. Slowly he walked towards the table nearest to him. It was dim, but he could make out the faces and quickly realized that none of them was Lana's or Elena's.

Heads turned in his direction and although he couldn't understand the language, he got the feeling that these guys were either talking about him or talking at him. But then he wasn't exactly dressed to fit in here.

He carried on steadily past a second table, then a third. There weren't many people here and they all seemed to be taking a bit too much interest in him.

Then in the far corner, he saw a flash of blonde hair. Elena's? He began to walk quickly in that direction when suddenly he felt a pair of hands on his shoulders.

'Private club,' a deeply accented male voice behind him said firmly.

Ed turned and found himself face to face with a very broad man in a very broad black suit.

'My daughter is here and I've come to take her home,' Ed said, equally firmly.

'Daughter? No,' the man insisted. 'Private club,' he repeated.

'She's here,' Ed insisted. 'Let me find her, then I'll go. Immediately.'

He stood up as squarely to this man as he would stand up to any cheeky, meat-headed, rugby player from the sixth form. For a moment, neither seemed sure what would happen next. Both suspected it wasn't going to be very pleasant.

Then a door opened, just to Ed's left and Lana stumbled out.

'Lana!' Ed gasped with surprise and relief.

'Wha...?' Lana began. She stood still, swaying slightly, before stepping forward and tumbling into his arms.

'You OK?' Ed asked, holding her tightly against his side. Her bare arms felt cool and clammy to his touch and he tried not to notice that her tight boob tube had slid down much lower than it should have and was revealing glaringly white cleavage and the top of a girlish white bra.

'I feel sick,' Lana told him and swayed again, unsteady on her tottery high heels.

She smelled of sick as well. And that would explain the damp look to her face and its unusual pallor against the darkly made up eyes and lips.

'What have you had?' Ed asked anxiously, ignoring the threatening looks the bouncer was giving them both.

'A cigarette,' Lana confessed, 'and a drink. They've made me sick ... I think I'm going to be sick ...'

She seemed to flop down in his arms but to his relief, she didn't throw up.

'Ed?'

He recognized Elena's voice and turned to see her striding towards them.

'Come on,' he ordered her sharply, 'get your things. Get Lana's bag, we're leaving.'

'No,' she insisted, 'I get job here.' She turned towards a table where two sullen men were sitting.

'If you don't come out of here with us right now, you'll have nowhere to live,' Ed informed her calmly. 'Now get your things.'

The bouncer called out something in a foreign language and the men at the table Elena was walking towards called back. Ed didn't like the sound of this. It sounded angry and threatening.

The two men got up from the table. Surely they weren't going to try to stop them from leaving? Ed tightened his grip on Lana and began to walk towards the dance floor. He wanted them to know he wasn't looking for trouble, he just wanted to leave.

Elena was talking back in the same language. Ukrainian? he wondered. Or maybe she spoke Russian as well? He could feel his heart thump in his chest. This was a little too threatening for his liking.

Glancing back, he saw Elena thump her fist on the table. He turned, knowing that somehow he was going to have to help her out.

But then the men sat down again and handed her two bags. Taking hold of them, she began to walk towards Ed.

He didn't turn to look at her again until they'd gone out through the double doors, down the stairs, along the corridor and out of the door back. Safely out on the street again, he wheeled round, despite Lana's groans at the abrupt movement.

'What on earth do you think you're doing?!' Ed asked, barely able to control his voice he was so furious.

Elena, clutching Lana's schoolbag against her because

her flimsy dress didn't offer much protection against the cold, held her head up defiantly.

'I look for job,' she said.

'As what?' Ed asked.

'Dancer,' she said casually.

'You're studying to be an engineer,' Ed couldn't stop himself from reminding her. 'What's Lana had to drink?' He would save the furious lecture he was bursting to give Elena, until he'd established that Lana was safe and hadn't been drugged.

'Vodka with lemonade.'

'Did you have one?' Ed asked.

'Two,' Elena admitted.

'Were they OK? Nothing else in them?'

Elena shook her head and had the decency to look concerned now that she understood Ed's meaning.

'I think the cigarette make her sick,' Elena offered.

'Yes,' Ed hissed.

He walked the girls to the Jeep without another word, clicked open the locks and helped Lana into the back seat. Elena buckled herself into the seat beside her.

Then Ed started up the engine. Only when the car was on the road, did he glance in the rear-view mirror and catch Elena's eye.

'Lana is sixteen,' he said angrily, 'she doesn't drink and she certainly doesn't smoke. What on earth made you think she should go to a nightclub with you and hang out with monkeys like that? Anything could have happened! To both of you.'

Elena shrugged her shoulders and raised her eyebrows. She'd been her own boss for several years now and she certainly didn't expect to be lectured on her behaviour.

'I told you on Wednesday not to take Lana out with you,' Ed reminded her. 'You'll have to leave our house. You'll need to speak to your mother and arrange somewhere else to stay. As soon as possible.'

'Take me there now,' Elena replied.

'Well, you'll need to speak to her . . . get your things together.'

'Take me there,' Elena repeated, 'she has huge house. I can stay there.'

This struck Ed as an excellent idea.

Lana's teenage years were, so far, going smoothly. Nothing really terrible or really out of the ordinary had happened . . . so far. Both he and Annie wanted to keep it like that. Plus, she had exams soon and they wanted her to do well. Not ruin all her hard work by hanging out with some glamorous, 22-year-old liability who was living in their house because Annie found it impossible to say no when she'd been asked to do someone a favour.

'Fine,' Ed said. 'What's the address?'

Elena was delighted to tell Ed. Although she'd now been living with her mother's friend for more than a week, somehow Svetlana had not even managed to find the time to have more than one little phone conversation with her daughter. Even that had been vague and non-committal.

If Ed were to be honest with himself, he would know that he wasn't just angry about Elena taking Lana to a place like that. He was also angry with Svetlana.

The pampered princess was always allowed to get away with childish, bad behaviour just because she was rich, just because she was someone. Bad enough that she'd dumped her baby on relatives and never gone back to see her once in all these years. But now that Elena was here, Svetlana was trying to fob her off again. That just wasn't how you treated children, in Ed's book. If he were ever allowed to become a parent . . . He felt a fresh surge of anger now, made up of so many different ingredients . . . not least the frustration that maybe he would never persuade Annie to let him be a father.

Ed followed the City Road west and thought that, like it or not, this was going to have to be a good time for Svetlana to receive a visitor.

Chapter Thirty-two

Lady behind the counter:

Maroon and gold sari (her sister's)
Fluffy pink slippers (eBay)
Cashmere cardi (M&S)
Total est. cost: £85

'I'm not sure . . . I was watching Strictly Come Dancing.'

Annie ran through the rain. She ran without stopping all the way to the corner shop. There, she established that a boy had been in about half an hour ago and bought a packet of dog chews.

'Did he say anything, anything else at all . . . did he look upset?' she asked wildly.

But the lady behind the counter couldn't add anything to her recollection: 'I'm not sure . . . I was watching *Strictly Come Dancing*.'

Annie ran back out into the rain. She ran along both sides of all the obvious streets, looking up and down any side streets or narrow alleys. She called Owen's name out in the dark and asked every passer-by if they'd seen a boy with a dog. People couldn't remember. Or they could sort of remember. They might have . . . but they weren't sure where or when, or heading in which direction. Annie continued in her wild, crazed hunt of the wet, dark streets. She wondered what she had done to turn today into the worst day for a very long time. If she could just have Owen and Lana safely back at home, she'd do anything, give anything . . .

It was raining and Owen would want to keep Dave dry. This was the only idea in Annie's mind. Where would he go to keep a dog dry?

A café? Would he have had enough money to go to a café?

She was on the main road now, looking frantically left and right. A big double-decker bus was hurtling down the hill on the other side of the road. Annie glanced over at the bus stop. She stopped and stared, opening her eyes wide with the effort of looking clearly.

There was a boy in an anorak with the hood pulled tightly round his face. And a dog? Yes, she thought she could see a dog.

'OWEN!' she yelled across the street. But the bus whizzed down towards the stop and blocked the bus shelter, the boy and the dog from her view.

She ran out into the road, but had to wait halfway across to let two speeding cars past. To her horror, the bus pulled off and she uselessly shouted: 'Stop!' in its wake, frightened that Owen was on board. Running across the last part of the road, she reached the bus stop and through the rain-soaked glass she saw that Owen, his anorak and his dog, were still there.

'Owen!' she cried out, running towards him, 'Owen! I'm sorry!' She felt a rush of mixed feelings as she sped round the glass and threw her arms round his shoulders. 'I'm so sorry!' she repeated, feeling a wave of relief wash over her, 'Please, please tell me you weren't going to go anywhere? You weren't going to go away?'

'Nah!' he answered, almost cheerfully, 'they won't let Dave on the bus.'

'What are you doing here?' she asked, trying to keep any note of anger from her voice.

Owen shrugged. 'Staying dry.'

'I'm sorry,' she repeated and hugged him once again. 'You've got to come home now. I've been so worried.'

'Can Dave stay with me?' Owen asked, hoping that his cold, damp protest hadn't been in vain.

'What, so that every time you don't like what I tell you, you can disappear off down the road, have me running round the whole of Highgate like a lunatic, then give in when I've found you? NO,' she said firmly, 'Dave's coming to live with us 365 days a year. I'm putting up with that, even though I don't like it. So for two tiny little days, you'll have to let him out of your sight and put up with it, even though *you* don't like it.'

'Aw!' Owen began to make a half-hearted attempt at protest.

'If you're going to argue or pull another stunt like that, then it's straight back to the bloomin' dog home he goes,' she threatened.

When Owen remained silent, Annie told him: 'You know that I love you really.'

'Yeah.' A shrug of the shoulders.

Annie heard her phone beep. Desperate for news from Ed, she pulled it out and read: 'Have Lana, taking E to Svets.'

Chapter Thirty-three

Svetlana at the door:

Cashmere robe (Harrods)
Beige sheepskin boots (Ugg)
Unbelievable underwear (Myla)
Pearls (Tokyo)
Perfume (Givenchy)
Total est. cost: £1,800

'Vhy you here?'

'Ohhhh, you are a bad, bad, girl. Bad . . . tooooo bad,' Harry groaned in genuine pain. He pressed his face back down into the black sheet and breathed in Svetlana's richly exotic perfume.

Meanwhile Svetlana sat on top of him in one of her favourite lingerie ensembles: knickers made of pale pink silk and black stretch lace with a matching quarter-cup bra. Just one look at her heaving, voluminous white breasts barely constrained within these structural masterpieces was usually enough to make Harry promise to do . . . well, whatever she wanted. But then he tended to do that anyway, which was sweet. She just thought she should keep up the nice bedroom outfits, to make sure he continued to behave as well.

Silky black stockings and very high black heels completed her look, along with the rope of pearls at her neck. She liked to make use of the pearls now and then: running them along his stomach, twisting and moving them around his wet, firm erection. And he liked that. He liked that very much.

'Nooo!' he protested with a gasp, 'No! No!'

But still she sank her fingers in deeper.

'It's too much,' he groaned.

'No!' she insisted, 'Is good. Is very, very good!' She leaned further into him, feeling for the most hidden, most tender places.

'Aaaaaaargh!' he complained when her fingers found and manipulated them mercilessly.

'Is good,' she insisted, moving into the muscle fibres at the very base of his neck.

In Svetlana's opinion, as well as regular sex, every man of Harry's age needed a vigorous bi-weekly dose of Swedish massage to stay healthy.

Ed parked the Jeep in the street.

'Right then, here we are,' he announced and reached over to open the driver's door.

'Coming, Elena?' he asked. Elena nodded in reply and stepped out.

Lana looked up sleepily at Ed. 'Are we home?' she asked.

'No. Not yet, just stay put, I'm dropping off Elena.'

Lana didn't argue with this, just nodded and closed her eyes once again.

Ed walked with Elena to the door and rang the bell long and loud. Within moments, Maria was opening the door. Her eyes widened in surprise when she recognized Elena.

'Hello,' Ed began, 'I'd like to see Svetlana. I'm dropping off Elena.'

Now the maid's eyes were as wide as an owl's.

'I see . . .' she said and closed the door in their faces.

Elena looked at Ed as they waited. 'She not vant me,' Elena told him with more than a hint of sadness.

'She needs to get to know you,' Ed told her. 'I want to give her the chance.'

'She von't like it,' Elena pointed out.

'Well, sometimes the things you don't like turn out to be good for you,' was all Ed could think of saying.

The door opened and Maria was standing in front of them once again. In a whisper, she said, 'Now is very bad time, can you please visit tomorrow?'

'No,' Ed replied, 'tomorrow is not convenient. I need to speak to Svetlana now. Elena is coming to stay here.'

Closing the door, the maid scurried off again.

'Now what?' Ed wondered out loud.

His question was answered when the door opened and Svetlana herself appeared on the threshold, hair ruffled and wearing only long sheepskin boots and a belted cashmere robe. Maybe she'd been in bed. More likely she was lounging about having some minion do her nails or something, Ed guessed.

She looked put out, to say the least.

'Vy you here?' she'd demanded urgently, looking from

Elena to Ed, then back again. 'Not now! Not here!' she insisted.

'Yes,' Ed insisted: 'now and here.'

Keeping his voice low and controlled, he explained briefly: 'Elena can't stay with us. Elena doesn't even want to stay with us. We have a sixteen-year old girl. I've just found her drunk and sick in a bar with your daughter and a crowd of seedy men.'

When Svetlana said nothing to this, Ed went on. 'Your daughter Elena, who's thinking about becoming a dancer, by the way. A nightclub dancer. Don't you care at all what happens to her?' he asked. 'Aren't you interested? Don't you want to help her at all?

'She's not my problem,' Ed went on, flinching inside as he said this, because it wasn't in his nature to turn away from young people who needed help, but somehow, he had to get Svetlana involved, 'she's your problem. You deal with her.'

Svetlana had never been spoken to like this by anyone. Everyone else always told her exactly what she wanted to hear. And if they had something to say that she wouldn't like to hear, they got their lawyer to fax it to her.

She gasped with shock and ran through a list of threats she could throw at Ed. But there was nothing she could use. He didn't work for her. He didn't need anything from her. He couldn't benefit from her in any way. He and Annie had been keeping her daughter as a favour! She had no control over them.

She gasped again – this time, because she could hear the door at the top of the stairs opening, and footsteps descending rapidly.

Now Harry was coming into the hall behind them in a hastily assembled outfit.

'What the dickens is going on?' he demanded.

First of all he saw Ed at the doorstep, then his eyes fell on Elena. With her pale skin, blonde hair, proud upright posture and light grey, defiant eyes, she almost didn't need to say the words that tumbled from her lips.

'Hello, I am Elena. I am Svetlana's daughter.'

Chapter Thirty-four

Annie dressed to go:

Pink silk skirt (Oscar de la Renta, Store sale)
White shirt (Gap)
Beige fishnet hold-ups (Pretty Polly)
Beige suede boots (Jimmy Choo, via eBay)
Beige mac (Valentino, via eBay)
Total est. cost: £420

'You're old enough to know.'

'You did not! She did not! What happened then?'

The news of Elena's dispatch was so exciting, Annie had to put the long lecture she'd prepared to give Lana on hold. In fact, one look at Lana's pale and contrite face as she'd sidled in the front door had told Annie that the whole lecture might not be necessary.

'I'm going to my room to change,' Lana had told her meekly, leaving Ed to finish the Svetlana story.

'Harry stormed off!' Ed went on, 'without another word . . . without even tying up his shoelaces! Then Elena went in and that's all I can tell you. She slammed the door in my face!'

'Oh blimey, I have to phone her.' Annie reached for her mobile, but Ed put a hand on her arm.

'No you do not,' he said: 'why don't you just let her be? Let her sort out her own mess for once. Owen!' Ed's attention had moved to the puddle close to the dog basket. 'You've not let Dave out! Now he's peed and you're clearing up, mate.' Ed added: 'Some lessons have to be learned the hard way.'

'Shhh,' Annie told Ed, 'Owen's had a bit of a time of it himself.'

Owen groaned, but got up from the sofa.

'Dog ownership comes with responsibilities, buddy,' Ed told him, patting him on the shoulder as he passed.

Annie's eyes met her partner's. He'd tracked down her daughter and brought her home in the face of tough-guy opposition, he'd gone to one of the wealthiest women in Mayfair and told her how it was; he'd even delegated dog wee duty to Owen.

She was impressed.

Annie could have done all these things herself. Easily. But it was the fact that he was here and he did them too that was impressive. He was her equal. Maybe even, right now, he was slightly more powerful and slightly more in charge.

And the fact that they held the balance of power like this between them, constantly making tiny shifts and adjustments, like two tightrope walkers with poles, was impressive. And very, very sexy.

Annie quite liked the fact that to other people, Ed might appear too nice, too cuddly and too much of a pushover, but really, there was a core of strength running through him. He was upright. One hundred per cent. He would never let you down.

'Thanks,' Annie told him, moving to put her arms round Ed's waist and pull him in, 'I don't think we should go tonight,' she said.

'No,' he agreed.

'I need to go up and see Lana now.'

'Yeah.'

Annie could see, as soon as she stepped into Lana's bedroom, that her daughter was very sorry.

She was sitting on her bed. She hadn't changed out of her boob tube and leggings, but she'd pulled a blanket across her shoulders and was looking scared and sad.

So there was no need for Annie to lecture. She just needed to put an arm round Lana and remind her of all the rules about staying safe. And she did, gently.

Tears were squeezing from the corners of Lana's eyes as she told Annie, 'I'm sorry, OK? I won't do anything like that again, ever.'

'Yes, you will' – Annie squeezed her and couldn't help giving a little laugh – 'and we'll be right here for you. To pick you up and help you out again. But you better not ever, ever pick up a cigarette again or I'll cut off your hands,' she warned.

'Thank you,' Lana sniffed and pushed her face into Annie's shoulder: 'I don't know what would have happened if Dad hadn't shown up . . .'

Just as Annie sucked in a breath of astonishment at the mistake Lana had made, Lana corrected herself. 'I mean

Ed,' she said quickly and there was a sob in her voice; 'of course I mean Ed.'

Annie rubbed her hand across her daughter's blanketed back and felt a lump rising up in her throat.

'You're old enough to know, baby . . .' she began, swallowing hard, 'you're old enough to know that you had a wonderful dad who would have loved you to bits and who would have taken on anyone for your sake . . . but it's really OK to think of Ed as your dad now. He deserves it. And it doesn't take anything away from your real dad. Not one thing.'

Annie could feel tears at the back of her own eyes. She felt as if she was falling forward into commitments she hadn't yet decided to make. Someone, somewhere had taken off her mental brakes without even telling her.

All of a sudden, she felt certain that she was going to marry Ed and sign the legal papers that would make him the children's real stepdad. Maybe even from tonight she would throw her diaphragm in the bin, make love without a safety net and get pregnant with him. Then he would finally be the one thing he still longed to be – a real dad.

'Call Ed "Dad",' Annie whispered into her daughter's hair, 'he'll absolutely love it.'

Just then there was a tap at the door and Ed looked into the room. 'Everything OK?' he asked with concern.

'Fine,' Annie told him. 'Get over here,' she instructed him gently.

Ed sat down on the edge of Lana's bed and put his arm around her shoulder just like Annie was doing. 'You feeling better?' he asked.

To his surprise, Lana used both arms to hug him back

and resting her head on his shoulder, she sobbed against it. 'I'm so sorry . . . thank you . . . *Dad*,' she whispered the word tentatively, as if she were trying it out. As if she wanted to make sure it was OK.

Ed hugged her protectively and kissed the top of her head. When he looked up at Annie, she could see that his eyes were swimming.

'DINAH! ED! HELP!'

Their tender family moment was broken by loud shrieks from the landing below.

'It's Mum!' Annie said, springing up and rushing across the room.

By the time she'd made it down from the attic, Ed and Lana hot on her heels, Dinah and Owen had also rushed up from downstairs.

'He's taken my shoe!' Fern pointed with agitation in the direction of Ed and Annie's bedroom, 'I saw him running in there with it!'

'The dog?' Annie asked. 'If that dog has become a shoe eater, he is . . .' a glance at Owen told her she'd better not utter the threat she had in mind, 'in serious, serious trouble.'

'No!' Owen assured them, 'it'll be his chew, not a shoe. I bought him a whole box. He loves them, carries them around.'

'He does,' Lana confirmed, on Owen and Dave's side.

'No. It's my shoe!' Fern insisted. She hurried towards the open bedroom door and everyone else fell in behind her.

'It did look too big for a chew . . .' Dinah added.

Dave had jumped on top of her bed! Annie thought with outrage. The disgusting little mongrel was growling, chewing frantically and digging his filthy little claws into the silk velvet bedspread in a frenzy of excitement.

'Down!' Annie blurted out.

'Now Dave,' Ed said, much more kindly, as if he was going to begin a long explanation about why you shouldn't bring Granny's shoes or your chew toys into the bedroom.

Annie looked more closely at the bed: it was scattered with paper.

'What is that?' Owen asked, coming in for a closer look at the dog just as Annie was registering that the scattered paper was a pattern she'd seen before. It was . . . wrapping paper. In fact, it was the paper Ed had used to wrap his gift to her!

Oh . . . good . . . GRIEF!

She looked at Ed.

Ed was looking at Dave.

Fern, Dinah, Lana, Owen: everyone was looking at Dave, moving in on him, fascinated to see what he was working away at with his jaws.

With a flash of horror, Annie realized, but it was too late to do anything to hide it. Everyone was going to see. She flicked a glance at Ed and saw the colour rising in his face. So he'd realized too.

Dave's strong teeth had already raised bumps on the rubber surface but they hadn't done much to disguise the exaggerated, but obvious, shape of the object. The stupid mutt then managed to bite down on the switch so that all of a sudden it sprang to life, whirring and twisting in his mouth. He growled and tried to shake it vigorously into submission.

'Put that down, Dave!' Ed commanded, making a lunge

at the dog, desperate to be the first to get hold of him. But Dave ducked out of his grasp and now Owen had the dog's head in his hands and was prising his jaws apart.

Annie watched in slow motion as her 12-year-old son picked up a large pink and purple, nubbly rubber vibrating vibrator and held it up in front of his family.

'What is this?' he asked.

'Oh. My!' was Dinah's surprised response.

'Oh . . . my word!' Fern managed with a gasp.

'Is that a . . .' Lana began, her face wrinkled with disgust.

Before she could utter the dreaded word, Ed, redder than a beetroot on fire, snatched the battery-operated boner from Owen's hand muttering, 'Right, OK, we'll take that away from him and . . .'

But Ed seemed to hang there, vibrator vibrating in his hand, at a loss for words. He didn't even have the presence of mind to switch the thing off. So it continued to buzz and twist.

Annie didn't mean to catch Dinah's eye, she just happened to turn her head as Dinah turned hers, and somehow their glances caught in the middle.

Then there was no return, as both sisters began to rock and shake with their suppressed hysterics.

'That looks like a giant, Barbie willy,' Owen declared.

Chapter Thirty-five

The wedding guest:

Tight white skirt (Debenhams)
Black and white bustier (same)
White feathered fascinator hat (same)
White shoes (Next)
Total est. cost: £160

Dinah had tried to persuade them. Fern had joined in. Even Owen had agreed, but it was Lana who had finally convinced Annie and Ed to pack up their bags and leave.

'If you don't go on your special weekend away just because of me, I'm going to feel so bad,' Lana had insisted. 'Go! I'm fine. I'm absolutely fine and I'll do every single thing Dinah says – and just go or I'll never forgive myself!'

'But it's nearly 9 p.m.!' Annie had argued.

'You'll miss dinner but you'll wake up to breakfast in bed,' Dinah had wheedled.

So finally Annie and Ed had agreed and were now crawling along an M25 still clogged with Friday night traffic. In the back of the Jeep was their luggage plus Dave, chewing on a dog chew, for a change.

Annie was behind the wheel, driving with charm but restless determination to forge a precious few feet ahead at all times. Ed was in the passenger seat, selecting songs from the choice of thousands on his iPod.

Now that they were on the road, they were properly excited about this trip. In the two and a half years they'd been together, this was the first time they'd managed to get away just the two of them. And it so nearly hadn't happened.

As Annie put her hand down to change gear, Ed brushed his against it. 'I love you,' he told her casually, 'even though your driving terrifies me.'

'I love you too,' she said, glancing momentarily from the road, 'even though your taste in music is weird.'

'No it is not!' he defended himself, 'I'm just trying to educate a disco queen!'

This was his favourite insult when it came to Annie's musical preferences. She was the first to admit that her tastes in music were similar to a very camp male diva's.

'Blame Connor,' she said, 'I spent too much time with him in Heaven. You know, the gay nightclub,' she added in explanation.

'What did you get out of it?' Ed had to wonder.

'Oh, I was just looking,' she told him, raising an eyebrow. 'I was in recovery, I didn't need to touch, or be touched.'

'But that's all changed now,' he said, and moved his fingers against the inside of her wrist.

'Yeah,' she said, as if he needed to be told.

The Jeep was finally free of the M25, Annie moved it down the slip road towards the M40. The motorway ahead was much freer, the wide lanes inviting her to move up the gears and put her foot down.

She pulled into the fast lane and heard the throaty rumble of the engine as they began to gather speed.

Ed changed the music accordingly, so as the speedometer began to rise towards 70 m.p.h., very earthy boy rock 'n' roll thumped out from the speakers.

'This is great!' she shouted over the music.

She looked over and saw a flash of surprise cross Ed's face.

'What is it?' she called out, eyes back on the road ahead of her. What had he seen that she hadn't? Instinctively, she touched the brakes.

'Annie, slow down! Change lanes!' he said urgently, pointing ahead of him.

She braked and swerved for the middle lane, feeling worried: 'What?' she repeated.

Then she saw it.

Spreading like a huge spider web from Ed's corner of the Jeep windscreen was a network of silvery cracks. They were moving furiously fast, threatening to engulf the whole window. In just a second or two she wouldn't be able to see out and after that, the whole windscreen might cave in on them.

'SHIT!' she exclaimed with real fear in her voice.

'Get to the hard shoulder! The inside lane's clear,' Ed instructed, craning his head towards the rear window to make sure she didn't swerve into another car.

Annie pressed on her hazard lights, hit the brake and changed down then moved into the slow lane. She made it onto the hard shoulder, jamming on the brakes, just as the spider web appeared before her eyes, throwing silver sparkles and slivers into her vision and totally obscuring the road.

By the time she'd brought the car to a standstill, the windscreen was a mosaic of tiny opaque pieces of glass and nothing could be seen beyond it apart from the glare of passing lights.

For a moment, they sat in stunned silence, feeling their hearts beat hard.

'Blimey,' Annie exclaimed finally, 'that was close.'

They looked at each other, relief loosening the tight pressure on their chests.

Annie wasn't quite sure whether to laugh or cry.

'Well done,' Ed told her quietly, 'you were great.'

She leaned over and they hugged each other across the handbrake.

'I take it you never got round to fixing the chip in the windscreen, then?' Ed said next.

'No, I didn't.'

Cuddled together, they laughed with relief.

'Did you renew the AA cover?' was Annie's next question.

'Oh shoot,' Ed hissed.

After a long wait and many phone calls, a man in a yellow van arrived. He explained that because it was so late and they had such a heavy car, all he could do was tow them to the nearest town with a windscreen repair service.

'They'll sort you out in the morning,' he'd told them.

'The morning?' Annie had gasped, 'we can't wait

until the morning! We've got a hotel booked . . . in the Cotswolds.'

The driver had laughed. He'd actually laughed at her.

Annie had only just come to terms with the fact that they'd missed their five-course dinner at the Lullworth, but the idea of missing the whole night . . . She'd been on the hotel's website, she'd even seen the view from the balcony of their room! Whatever Dinah's husband, Bryan, had done for the hotel, he was being handsomely repaid. There was a white four-poster bed in their room, emperor size . . . and a white marble wet room with a steam shower!

In less than an hour's time it would be Ed's birthday and they were still on the hard shoulder miles and miles from the Lullworth Hotel about to be towed to Reading by the AA van.

It was nearly midnight when they pulled up in the car park of the King's Head. Annie had a feeling this was going to be a lot less luxurious than the Lullworth. It was a rowdy, charmless bar with rooms above. A crowd of women in tight dresses and feathery fascinators were huddled in the car park, smoking.

Ed put his bag over his shoulder, picked Annie's up in his left hand then took a tight hold of her hand and Dave's lead with his other.

'C'mon,' he shot her a grin as they began to walk towards reception, 'where's your sense of adventure? Pretend we've run away together,' he added in a whisper, 'we're having an affair and neither of our partners knows anything about it.'

'But you've had to bring your dog. Right,' Annie grumped.

The door swung open to reveal a lobby with embossed, glossy yellowed walls and a brown and yellow carpet of the most hideous variety.

Once they'd signed in and been given a key, they were directed up brown and yellow stairs towards their room.

Opening the door, Ed felt for the light switch and cracked it on to reveal the most ghastly hotel room Annie had ever seen. It had the same brown and yellow patterned carpet as the hallway, the walls had been papered years ago with a cream and brown floral pattern and the small, rickety-looking double bed was draped in an orange candlewick bedspread.

The room smelled smoky and sweaty.

'Oh no,' she groaned, just imagining the horrible clammy polyester sheets that would be under the bedspread, 'I can't! I can't sleep here, babes. I think I'd rather sleep in the Jeep.'

'Annie – ' Ed put an arm around her waist – 'it's going to be fine!'

He went over and turned on the bedside light: a small, fringed orange lamp. He came back and turned off the overhead light so at least the room wasn't so glaringly lit.

Although she was still standing at the door, completely unconvinced, Ed sprawled out across the bed – causing it to bounce and creak alarmingly – and told her, with a grin, 'I've got a bottle of cold champagne in my bag. I'm here with the woman I love.'

'And your dog.'

'This is very sexy,' he purred at her.

Finally, she moved across the room towards him, the white four-poster, the beautiful windows with the billowing white curtains, the marble steam shower all still at the front of her mind.

This was just so, so disappointing.

Ed held out his hand and reached for her, pulling her down onto the bed beside him. It dipped, creaked and wobbled so much, she thought it really would collapse.

She pulled back the bedspread and had to ask, 'Are the sheets clean?'

'Not for long,' he replied cheekily.

Ed wrapped his arms around her and moved his mouth over hers.

Minibreak, she told herself, tasting him, *I'm on a minibreak and I'm going to enjoy it . . . going to enjoy him. Going to enjoy having him all to myself.*

Her eyes flickered open and she saw Dave, paws up on the bedspread looking at them with his head cocked to one side.

'Ed!'

It took a long time for Annie to wake the next morning. She lay, eyes shut, as the very first moments of consciousness filtered through, and registered that she was naked in bed. She was on her side with Ed's heavy arm across her, his fuzzy chest close to her naked back and their legs tangled together.

She felt warm and sticky. When she opened her eyes, the lids were heavy and her eyeballs felt dry.

The brown and white flowers swimming before her eyes made her to feel a jolt of panic until she reorientated herself.

They were in that room. Oh, they were in *that* room. With a rush of arousal, she remembered last night.

Oh! Last night.

Oh. My. God. Last night!

There had been champagne. Poured into tumblers. Then poured over naked bodies. Over breasts and into navels to be licked and sucked off. Cool mouthfuls of bubbles which had tingled, fizzed and popped against all the most tender and most swollen of places. They had noisily used and abused this bed, banging the headboard recklessly against the wall in a frantic hurry to enjoy themselves to the full.

Annie ran her hand slowly over her breast and wriggled backwards until she was pressed tightly against Ed. She'd wake him up, she thought, moving her fingers down between her legs and strumming there until she was tingling to be touched by him again.

Her diaphragm was in place, she could just roll over, roll against him and they could start up all over again.

Her diaphragm? The white disc of rubber which kept her from where Ed wanted her to be?

She sat bolt upright now and opened her eyes wide.

Now she saw the hideous room properly. Her clothes were tumbled into a heap on the floor and over there was her overnight bag. Inside was her wash-bag, inside her wash-bag was her diaphragm case, and inside her diaphragm case was . . . the diaphragm.

He'd persuaded her. Maybe she'd persuaded herself. Anyway . . . here in the cold light of day, she could see it was madness. And they certainly weren't going to do it again.

The dog! Where was the bloody dog?

Her eyes scanned the carpet and she spotted Dave curled up in the cashmere sweater she'd given Ed for

Christmas. Before she could order him out of it, she saw an unmistakable little pile, close to the door. It was a heap of Dave's small, chipolata-shaped turds.

This was just too much. She could not cope with this stupid little furry fuck-wit. There was no other word for this stupid dog. It was ugly, deaf and incontinent! And she didn't want to be dealing with any more *shit*. There was quite enough metaphorical shit going on in her life. She refused to get her hands dirty dealing with the real stuff!

'Ed!' she urged, shaking him awake, 'Dave has crapped on the carpet. Ed!!' she hissed, 'Wake up! I'm not dealing with this!' With that she pulled the covers off both of them and got up to go to the bathroom.

As she peed, she considered the contraception situation. It was two days since her last period, so totally safe. So safe that in the back of her mind last night had been the thought: I can still revise this decision.

But now she had decided, thanks to Dave's early morning dump, that no way was she going back to nappies and fingernails full of poo and getting up at all hours. Now, she wondered whether she shouldn't just pop a morning-after pill, just to be on the ultra safe side.

But then what if Ed found out? It was one thing to not get pregnant; it was another thing entirely to say that you were trying while actually popping preventatives.

She stood in front of the mirror and brushed her teeth. She was safe. Good grief, she was in her late thirties. She tried to crinkle up her eyes. The Botox was wearing off so quickly, she'd soon be just as crumpled as she had been when she walked into Dr Yaz's. And what was up with her hair? No matter how many conditioning lotions and potions she smeared over it, it seemed to get bushier and wirier by the day.

No. Approaching-40-year-olds were totally safe from getting pregnant on one attempt two days after their period. With a wave of sympathy, she thought of Dinah . . . maybe she should have a baby for poor Dinah.

Ed knocked on the bathroom door. Then came in holding a suspicious package wrapped in toilet paper.

'I'm just going to flush this away,' he said.

Annie spat her toothpaste into the sink as Ed plopped dog poo into the hideous grey toilet bowl.

'Happy birthday,' she said.

Chapter Thirty-six

Cath's fifth new outfit:

Charcoal knee-length skirt (Hobbs)
Jade green and black knitted jacket (MaxMara)
Long black patent boots (Russell & Bromley)
Black mini-fishnet tights (Pretty Polly)
Total est. cost: £380

'I've spent over £1,000!'

'Oh yes . . . we went to the Lullworth Hotel for Ed's birthday. It was absolutely gorgeous,' Annie chirped on the hands-free to one of her former shopping suite clients.

This was actually true. When they'd finally made it to the Lullworth, their night there had been wonderful and memorable. But then, Annie had to admit, the night in Reading had definitely been memorable too.

She was in the Jeep, which was all repaired now, on the road, trying to make her personal shopping and eBay businesses from home work again. Well, she couldn't go back to The Store. Not just yet anyway. And there were possibly going to be other opportunities to consider. She'd let assistants she knew at both Harvey Nichols and Selfridge's spread the word that she *might* be open to offers. If they were the right sort of offers.

Sometimes, when her phone rang and she didn't immediately recognize the number, the thought crossed her mind that maybe it would be Ralph, Connor's agent, phoning with some amazing new opportunity that had just come out of the blue.

But really, she kept telling herself off for hoping. When did amazing opportunities *ever* just come at you right out of the blue? Everything Annie and those closest to her had ever achieved had always been the fruit of endless hard work.

So she was keeping herself very busy now. Phoning, visiting, cajoling all the women she'd ever helped to dress in the past to use her again. She also kept a sharp eye out for new clients. The day of shopping with Cath had gone very well and Cath had promised to pass on a few members from the gardening club.

'Any handsome strangers been in touch since your TV appearance?' Annie had asked.

'Not a stranger, exactly,' Cath had replied shyly. But she wouldn't be pressed to reveal anything else.

'The next time we meet,' Annie had teased, 'I'll get it all out of you.'

'The next time? I've spent over £1,000!'

'Yeah, you are starting to get the hang of it,' Annie had told her.

Annie's eBay shop had also been revived and stocked up with whatever she could find. Clothes, shoes and bags from her own wardrobe, from charity shops and clients' wardrobes and most importantly, she was in the process of reviving her contact with the Hong Kong shoemaker, Timi Woo.

Last year, she'd imported his shoes and sold them really successfully on eBay. Maybe she should try and see the woman who bought shoes for House of Fraser again.

She would get over her TV disaster. She had to. Ed's savings were spent. The mortgage had to be paid this month, the household bills, the school fees. There was absolutely no point sitting at home fretting about it, it was best to just get into the Jeep, get on the phone and get the show right back on the road again. And put absolutely all thoughts of taking a little preview peep at the new Vivienne Westwood collection right out of her head. Right to the furthest reaches of her mental outer Siberia.

Casting a glance at her watch, Annie saw that it was just after one o'clock and she thought of Bob. He'd always liked to have his lunch break at 1 p.m. on the dot, otherwise he went in a huff and started his little rants about 'this Mickey Mouse operation'.

Maybe it was worth giving him a call, just to see what the on-set gossip was, now that she had gone. Annie was also hoping to find out what she could about Svetlana this way. There had not been a word from her since Ed had dumped Elena on her doorstep. Annie was more than a little concerned that this might be the end of her friendship with the glamazon.

Had it really been a friendship? Maybe Svetlana's use for Annie was over. She didn't need Annie to shop for her any more: no doubt she used The Store's new personal shopper. She didn't work with Annie on the show and Annie was no longer putting up her secret daughter. So possibly Annie was about to feel the Mayfair ex-wife's famously chilly cold shoulder.

Still, she would like to hear from Bob how they were all getting on without her. She hoped she'd been able to hear that the clients' new outfits weren't nearly as good as the ones she would have found for them.

At the next red light she called his number, then, eyes back on the road, waited for the sound of his voice.

'Annie Valentine!' he greeted her warmly.

'Hey you! Missing me?'

'Of course!' he said, then with his voice lowered, he went on: 'Wait till you see how the next victims look, there will be rolling in the aisles. The programme's utter crap, you are well out of it. I'd leave too,' he added, 'but I have a contract for the whole thing, so they have to pay me.'

'That may be where I went wrong,' Annie observed. 'How are Marlise and Svetlana?' she asked.

'Miss Marlise, nothing to report, just as much of a cow as ever,' came Bob's reply. 'Svetlana, on the other hand, well she seems to have a lot on her mind. I think her fancy barrister has well and truly called the wedding off. He's told her he can't trust her and that she's put her whole divorce settlement in doubt. Apparently she's got a secret grown-up daughter or something? She's not given me the full story. To be honest, I've picked up most of it from the phone calls she keeps taking all day long. She's doing Finn's nut . . .'

'The wedding's really off?' Annie asked. She couldn't believe it.

'Oh yeah,' Bob confirmed.

'No!' Annie hadn't seriously considered this. Harry had

299

finished with her because of Elena? Annie had taken for granted that he was so besotted with Svetlana he would take any revelation in his stride.

But then he was a barrister, he had a reputation to maintain and maybe Svetlana was proving too much of a liability. Maybe he was seriously going to backtrack.

'Bloody hell,' Annie exclaimed, 'never a dull moment with her. How is she? Is she OK? Does she think it will blow over?'

'I dunno, matey,' Bob answered, 'you're the one who knows her best. You ask her.'

'Yeah . . .' Annie replied, but she wasn't so sure. She'd be right in the firing line if she did that. Maybe she would wait a few more days. Let Elena and the air turbulence that followed her wherever she went calm down a little.

'What are you up to anyway?' Bob asked.

Annie had prepared for this question. She was going to have to handle it. An awful lot of people knew she was supposed to be forging a new career in television and were going to ask about it, so she'd practised her answer.

'Well, as my TV career hasn't quite got off the ground yet, I'm busy doing what I do best: selling clothes and making people look fabulous! I've got some new irons in the fire to consider,' she chirped. It sounded a little false, even she had to admit. Never mind, she'd practise more.

'OK,' Bob sounded unconvinced, 'does that mean you're bricking it? And desperate to find something else?'

'Erm . . . a bit,' she felt relieved to confide in him. 'But I'm still breathing, babes. I get up in the morning, I hustle. Something will turn up.'

'Good girl,' he agreed. 'Still want to do telly?'

'It's not been great fun so far,' she had to admit.

300

'You've had the bullshit end of it. And you've been pooped on from a very great height.'

'Babes, I'm being pooped on from every direction,' she told him, thinking of Dave.

'You're good,' Bob added, 'in fact you're better than good. You're a natural. I'm going to keep my ear to the ground for you. OK?'

'Thanks,' she said, 'that's very sweet of you. Now if you're needing any advice about the cut of your jeans, or where to get a new leather jacket cheap, you just let me know, doll.'

'Hey, I took your advice and sent my wife to Mango. She said to tell you that you've made her very happy. When I saw the bill, I wasn't quite so happy myself, but . . .'

'Skinflint!' Annie teased.

Chapter Thirty-seven

Uri dresses to impress:

Off-the-peg suit (Gieves & Hawkes sale)
Silk shirt (same)
Black shoes (Prada sale)
Steel Rolex watch (eBay)
Total est. cost: £700

'You are a once in a lifetime find.'

'Madame, pour votre plaisir aujourd'hui nous avons . . .'

Svetlana listened to the French waiter describe the complex and wonderful choice of dishes on the menu today. Her French was good enough to understand that everything would be unforgettably unique and delicious.

But then she was at the Maison Beaumonde, one of the most famous and most celebrated restaurants in the north of France.

'Let's go somewhere fabulous for lunch, where you've never eaten before,' Uri had told her. Then, to her astonishment, he'd driven her to the west London helipad, and flown her himself ('I've had to let my pilot go, crredit crrrunch') in his personal helicopter, across the Channel to Normandy where they'd landed in the grounds of the restaurant.

The staff had treated this with much more nonchalance than Svetlana had expected, but this may have been because several helicopters landed here every weekend, despite the economic downturn.

Svetlana acknowledged the waiter with a smile, then looked back down at the beautifully handwritten pages of the menu. She should really make some new choices. Here of all places, she should be adventurous and try something different. But really, what was the point of lunching with a man like Uri if you didn't drink the premium champagne, order an indecent amount of caviare and then have lobster to follow?

These were of course all the costliest items on the menu and at Maison Beaumonde the prices were even more astronomical than she had ever seen.

So she placed her order and Uri chuckled.

'Same again,' he teased, reaching over to hold her hand.

'Seafood is so good for the complexion,' she replied, 'and the figure.'

'So I can see,' he purred.

Svetlana allowed the hand-holding to continue as she looked at Uri long and appraisingly.

He was still young. Younger than Igor, younger than Harry . . . even, possibly, younger than her. This was the surprising thing. She had not expected now to have a rich suitor under the age of 60. Rich men invariably

303

liked much younger woman. Trophy wives. She'd always liked the description: she'd enjoyed being the shiny, cherished trophy in the cabinet, often taken out purely for display.

But Uri had told her he wasn't interested in another 'identikit woman'. He was interested in her. What was it he'd told her on the helicopter? *'You are like a unique and flawless diamond, Svetlana. Your age and the fact that you've been enjoyed by others makes you no less valuable. You are a once in a lifetime find.'*

Cute, no?

Uri wasn't especially, though. He was young, he still had his dark hair and he looked fit, but his face reminded her of a dog's. He was thin-lipped with hungry eyes.

'enjoyed by others . . .' She wondered, as he held her hand in his, just how unusual might his tastes in the bedroom be. She should really try and track down an ex-lover to find out. But he was worth . . . she'd Googled him and no-one seemed to know exactly. Harry was wealthy but Uri was rich. Super-rich.

Just this one lone thought of Harry was making Svetlana feel strange. He'd called it off! This had never happened to her before. Yes, in the past men had called off their marriage to her. But no-one had ever called off a wedding!

After he'd stormed out of her house, when Elena had been returned, there followed a series of fraught phone calls over several days. She had phoned Harry. Harry had phoned her. She had called him back. And again. And once again just to make sure. But, as far as Harry was concerned, it was over and she was not going to lure him back, no matter what she did.

'You lied to me!' he'd repeated so many times, 'you lied to me as your barrister. If Igor ever finds out about this girl, he has grounds to have you back in court. He could take it all away.' – This was the bit that devastated Svetlana.

'You lied to me as the person you were supposed to be in love with, as the person you are about to marry!' – This was the bit that devastated Harry.

They hadn't spoken for five whole days now.

Svetlana still couldn't get used to it. She'd accepted Uri's invitation because she wanted to have something to do today, while the boys were with their father.

And Elena! Elena was still in her house, using her phones, eating her food, instructing her maid! Even worse, threatening to go to the press or to Igor if Svetlana didn't allow her to stay. Svetlana was furious with her. Seething. More than once it had crossed her mind to dig up some of her deepest, darkest Ukrainian contacts and have the Elena problem 'solved'.

'*Encore du champagne, madame?*' The wine waiter was hovering at her elbow. Svetlana knew this was her third glass and the caviare hadn't even arrived yet . . . but, 'Yes, thank you,' she agreed.

If she was going to put Harry right out of her mind and throw herself on Uri, she would need another glass or two.

Harry pulled up in Svetlana's street just before eleven on Saturday morning. After another sleepless night and several hours spent pacing his Kensington flat, he'd decided to come in person to Mayfair, to apologize and to beg that she take him back.

He'd made a terrible, hideous mistake.

What madness had possessed him?

He had to win her back and marry her. He only hoped he hadn't left it too long. Five days had gone past, and hadn't he noticed so many times before how men circled Svetlana like wolves, ravenous for an opportunity?

Of course she hadn't told him anything about this girl from the Ukraine! The girl might turn out to be a fraud. Svetlana was volatile, insecure and totally stressed out, Harry had convinced himself. The girl had no doubt turned up looking for money and if Igor found out, he would use this as an excuse to try and take everything away from his ex-wife.

How could Harry have been so unsympathetic? How could he have run from her, instead of running to help her?

And he could help her. He was her divorce lawyer. He was the one who should be reinforcing the rules he'd helped to draw up. He was the one who could have an injunction taken out banning Elena from contacting her mother or speaking to any member of the press about it.

Harry pulled in to the kerb behind a vast black limousine that was parked outside Svetlana's house. The driver was holding open the passenger's door and as the front door of the house was open, Harry expected to see the love of his life walking out any moment now.

Where was she going? Whose car was this? Then he remembered: it was Saturday. It was the day the boys were with their father, who often sent his car, although his house was only a few streets away. Here they came now: Petrov and Michael, the younger boy following his older brother. Harry couldn't help smiling at them. They were so small and so serious in their blue blazers with their thick black hair in heavily fringed pageboy cuts. They reminded Harry of his boy, Robin. All grown up now, of course.

'Hello!' he called over to them and both serious little faces turned in his direction, 'off to the old man's for a jolly afternoon?'

'We're going on holiday!' Petrov said with a flash of smile, 'he's taking us skiing!'

'Well, well! How marvellous! Have a wonderful time, won't you?'

Petrov gave him the thumbs-up.

'Is Mummy at home?' Harry asked.

'No,' Petrov said. He disappeared into the car and Michael followed.

The driver closed the door and because the tinted windows were so dark, the boys were immediately hidden. The driver then moved round to his door, stepped into the car and started up the smooth Rolls-Royce engine.

Harry stood on the pavement to watch them leave, giving a cheery wave. He was caught up in memories of when Robin was a boy, heading off for school on the other side of town in his taxi every morning, looking just as small and as serious as these two . . .

It was only as the car rounded the corner of the street and disappeared from sight that it struck him as strange that the boys weren't taking any bags if they were going on holiday.

And if they were going away, wouldn't their mother be here to wave them off? She was very protective of her sons. In fact, she had never given Igor permission to take them away before. If this was their first holiday, why was she not here?

Growing more and more uneasy, he felt in his jacket pocket for his phone.

Then Maria poked her head from the front door of the house. 'You come in, Mr Harry?' she asked.

'Just one minute, my girl . . . where's Svetlana?' he asked.

'She meeting *man* for lunch' – this came with as much of a disapproving roll of the eyes as Maria thought she could get away with. 'Boys go to see father like every weekend,' she added.

'But they said they were going on holiday, skiing?'

'No, no, no.' The maid shook her head.

Agitated now, Harry speed-dialled Svetlana by pressing '1' on his phone. It rang and rang, with an infuriatingly long pause between the rings. There was no voicemail because Svetlana didn't do messages. Harry looked at his phone in frustration. He'd have to send a text. He was going to be 56 in two weeks' time and texts were not exactly his forte.

He fumbled for the buttons and began the agonizing process.

'Bows.'

No.

'Cows'

NO! Goddam the stupid bloody predictive text setting, but he had no idea how to turn it off.

'Boys hone.'

DRAT!!

'Boys gone ball me.'

Well that was going to give her entirely the wrong message.

'Boys snatched,' he managed at last.

That was enough, that would do.

He pressed send. Then waited, out there on the pavement with Maria still standing at the front door looking at him in confusion, for Svetlana to reply.

What if she didn't? What if Igor was busy sneaking the boys out of the country while Svetlana was being wined and dined by . . . another suitor? Already? But he didn't doubt it, women like Svetlana were never left alone for any length of time. That was a plain and simple fact.

Once children were out of the country, Harry knew just how hard it was to get them back. It was a lengthy, expensive legal process and Igor had enough funds to keep it going for years.

He began to pace the pavement.

'Where is she?' he asked Maria. 'Do you know which restaurant?'

The maid shrugged. 'Come in,' she urged.

But then Harry's phone began to ring.

'Harry? What is this?!' Svetlana sounded angry. 'Why are you joking with me? I'm busy.'

There were many niceties to be sorted out between them – *Sorry I walked out on you, do you want me back? I'm desperate to have you back. Who the hell are you lunching with?* – but there was no time.

'I've just seen the boys leave in Igor's car,' Harry fired out. 'They said he was taking them on holiday, skiing. Is this right?'

'Vat?' came the stunned response.

309

'Could Petrov have been joking?' Harry asked, 'Could he have misunderstood something?'

'No! He's very smart boy. Oh Harry!'

There was unmistakable fear in Svetlana's voice. 'He's going to take them away to get my house! HARRY!'

'Phone him, right now, then phone me back,' Harry instructed her then ended the call abruptly because he now had urgent phone calls of his own to make.

Mobile clamped to his ear, he headed into the house, and into Svetlana's downstairs sitting room because he would need a table, papers, pens. He had to do everything he possibly could to help her.

Anyone listening in to the round of calls he began now would have heard terse, clipped instructions as Harry Roscoff, barrister, got down to serious business.

'Ronald, hello, how are you old chap, yes . . . 'fraid I need a favour . . . mmm . . . and on a Saturday too . . .'

'Hello, yes, I have an emergency protection order. Fax it to Gatwick, fax it to Heathrow . . .'

'Good afternoon, can you tell me which airports in Greater London are used by private jets? Who clears them for take-off?'

'So it's BAA head office I need . . . that is so incredibly helpful of you.'

Only briefly did he talk to Svetlana. She confirmed that Igor was already in St Petersburg and gave Harry as many details as she could remember about his private plane.

'Come back,' he'd urged her, 'where are you?'

'In France,' she'd wailed.

'France? What the devil . . . Just come home,' he'd instructed. There was no time for questions now.

'Hello, police please, this is a genuine emergency . . .'

'I'm waiting for the necessary legal papers. They'll be ready within fifteen minutes or so . . . but someone will have to serve them at Luton airport . . .'

Would they be in time, he wondered?

Chapter Thirty-eight

Connor returns:

Green and white polo shirt (Gant)
White jeans (Ralph Lauren)
Brown belt (same)
Tennis shoes (Dunlop)
Total est. cost: £280

'He will bend you till you scream.'

'There's no need to be jealous, Annie and I go way back.'
With these words, Connor moved his hand onto Annie's
left breast and squeezed.

Annie smacked him, but Ed just laughed. He was sitting
on the sofa opposite the two of them and found it funny
and more than a little bit sexy that his lover was draped
across a famous TV star.

But as Connor had mentioned, he and Annie went way
back, 'but not back to before I was gay', he had added
pointedly, earlier in the evening.

Evening! Ha! Ed flicked a look at his watch. It was only

4.15 p.m. and he was already hammered. Thank God it was Saturday.

This was the Connor effect.

Connor had returned in a triumphant blaze to London, demanding immediate partying and celebrating with lashings and lashings of booze. He had touched down in Gatwick at eleven yesterday morning, dumped his bags, had a shower, and rung round all his agents, producers and directors to arrange a series of meetings and lunches. Then he'd re-established contact with his personal trainers and masseuse, and finally, bearing two bags of duty free, turned up this afternoon at Annie and Ed's, where he'd installed himself in the kitchen.

Not to cook, but to busy himself with limes, crushed ice and a blender making sensational margaritas.

'I know, so nineties,' he'd told them, 'but just the thing for a wet Saturday afternoon.'

So they'd moved into the sitting room with an entire jugful of margarita and begun a great long chat session, punctuated only by the comings and goings of Owen and Milo, plus Dave's joyful yip-yapping if anyone so much as walked past the house.

'You have a dog!' Connor had gushed as soon as he'd set eyes on Dave, 'how come you've never even told me you have a dog?'

Annie had rolled her eyes before insisting, 'The dog is nothing to do with me.'

Meanwhile Connor had got down on his knees and started fussing over Dave with the whole tummy rubbing and 'hello boy', 'good boy', 'you like that doncha' routine

313

which separated the dog people from the non-dog people.

The margarita afternoon was allowing them to catch up on all sorts of news. Hector was still in California, sorting out the handing over of the lease, the return of the gym equipment and the hire car. All the 'star management' stuff he seemed to enjoy doing for the man in his life.

'No little American baby come home with you then?' Annie asked, teasing but also curiously concerned to know what had happened to those plans.

'Don't think it was going to be quite as easy as we'd hoped. Turns out you can't just jet in and say "I'm a star" and snatch up a bambina,' Connor drawled, making light of it as he made light of every single thing in his life.

'Although that does seem to work in Cambodia,' Ed couldn't help observing.

'I think it's easier for the lady stars over there,' Connor pointed out. 'Not sure how keen they are on single-sex adopters. They'd probably chop our hands off . . . or worse.'

'So, are you back?' Annie asked, resting her head on Connor's large, comfortable chest, delighted to have him in close proximity once again. 'You're not going to live in LA any more? You're going to be a proper British movie and telly star . . . like . . .'

'. . . Dame Judi Dench,' he joked: 'you know, never say never. I'm back for now. There's something new in the pipeline . . .' he waggled an eyebrow at them.

'Tell!' Annie instructed.

'No way. This is secret. Top, top secret.' He put his hands over his lips.

'Pour him another drink, babes,' Annie instructed Ed, 'we'll get it out of him.'

'No!' Connor insisted. 'Over there, I barely had one glass of wine a week – for five months! I'm already schlosched,' he added, slightly for effect, but already seriously in danger of slurring.

'And to think you used to be AA,' Annie pointed out.

'Oh, that was just for the showbiz contacts,' Connor confessed, 'everyone who's anyone goes, you know.'

'That is so shallow,' Ed pointed out.

'I know, but shallow is my middle name,' Connor said with a lazy grin.

'At least you look good,' Annie told him.

And he did too. He was bronzed, but the real stuff, not the whiffy orangey glow from a bottle. And he was so buff, his teeny waist leading straight down to snaky dancer hips. And the buttocks! Well, Annie had spotted them and they were magnificent. *Girls, this is such a shocking shame!* was the thought which had popped straight into her head.

'Ed should go to the gym, maybe you could give him a few tips,' Annie volunteered, hopefully, as Ed snorted tequila from his nose.

'Hey, I run . . . a bit. I referee rugby,' Ed said in his own defence.

'You're all right,' Annie assured him with a smile.

'Ed, my place, Saturday mornings, 11 a.m. Just wait till you meet Ben. He will bend you till you scream.'

'We *are* talking about exercise here?' Annie just wanted to be sure.

'So, your career,' Connor began, putting an arm protectively around his girl, 'we need to talk about your career.

I saw the DVD you sent me of the pilot episode. You were wasted! They threw you, the gem of the entire show, away. Your producer was a tit.'

'Aw sweet, you're just saying that cos you're my friend.'

'No. I'm saying that cos you're my rival. You've got the magical X factor, girl.'

'Oh yeah,' Ed agreed from his sofa.

'You got charisma.' Connor chucked her under the chin. 'Has Rafie been in touch?'

'Has he hell,' Annie couldn't help saying, 'I think he has slightly more important things to do, like making your next top-secret mega deal. You're not going to be the new James Bond or something, are you?' she asked excitedly.

'Oh please, I think Daniel Craig is wearing those Speedos very well . . . for the moment. Where's it all going for you?' Connor asked, focusing on Annie's career again, 'what doors have you knocked on? And what is that buzzing noise?'

Annie sat up and looked around the room. 'It might be my phone,' she said, spotting the mobile on one of the side tables. She picked it up: 'Three missed calls and a message.'

Usually, she might feel a flicker of worry at this . . . that it was something to do with the children. But right now she knew Owen was upstairs with Milo and an enormous bowl of salted popcorn watching *Dr Who* reruns, and Lana was at Greta's house. Greta's mother had even phoned to say she'd arrived.

'Talk amongst yourselves,' she instructed Ed and Connor, then dialled up her voicemail.

What she heard surprised her. To say the least.

'Hi Annie, Bob here, trying to get you urgently. Phone me. Been speaking to Tamsin Hinkley. She produces two great cookery shows for Channel 4. She's thinking about the makeover format, but is wondering how to make it fresh and modern. I mentioned you, she's interested in having a chat, so you should speak to her as soon as possible. Phone me.'

Annie's eyes widened in excitement. Channel 4? Channel 4! *She's thinking about the makeover format . . . she's interested in having a chat!*

'Oh boy,' Connor said to Ed, pointing in Annie's direction, 'looks as if she's just heard something . . .'

'Uh-huh,' Ed had to agree.

Annie wanted to call Bob back straight away, but Connor wasn't going to have that.

'Tell!' he instructed.

'It's just a thought . . . just an idea . . . but there's someone who wants me to give her a call . . .'

'Who?' Connor asked immediately.

'Tamsin Hinkley?' Annie said, not sure if she'd got the name right.

'Tamsin Hinkley . . .' Connor's brow creased, which made Annie think two things: Tamsin is bad news and Connor hasn't had Botox yet.

'I've not heard of her,' he said finally.

'Oh.'

Annie couldn't deny that this was disappointing. Tamsin was bound to be another Finn-type, scraping about for a slot on digital TV. Maybe she'd already heard that Annie would work for £1,000 a month.

'What kind of programme is it?' Connor asked.

'She's thinking of doing a makeover show, but apparently she wants to make it different.'

'It's got to be you,' Connor chipped in, 'Annie's Wardrobe on a Budget. Annie's Recession Chic.'

'Why Costco is cool,' Ed added.

'How to buy Prada on eBay,' Connor went on.

'How to make do with Mango when you really want Miu Miu,' Ed couldn't resist, then: 'Annie Valentine, the Nigella of budgeting,' he announced.

'Ooh, I like that!' Connor was grinning.

'Will you both shut up?' Annie was beginning to feel nervous, despite the four or – good grief – *five* margaritas she'd had.

'I'm going to phone Bob and talk to him about it. Then I'll . . . I'll try and get hold of Tamsin.'

Both Connor and Ed could hear the anxiety in her voice.

'Let me help,' Connor offered, 'I could speak to her first. I could introduce you.'

'No, babes,' she insisted, turning on her way out of the room, 'I think I have to do this for myself.'

'Doncha just love her?' Ed asked Dave, as he scratched the dog's head.

Chapter Thirty-nine

Svetlana rushes home:

White fur coat (boutique in Moscow)
Green, pink and white silk day dress (Celine)
Green ankle-strap sandals (Manolo)
Diamond jewellery (various ex-husbands)
Total est. cost: £140,300

'I have to phone!'

Harry took another exasperated look at his wristwatch: 4.26 p.m. His mobile was in his hand but he had to wait. There was no point calling anyone else right now, he had done everything he could. Now he just had to wait and see if he was going to be in time.

He walked up and down the drawing room, tugging at his cuffs and chewing his fingernails. Then lacing his fingers together, he cracked his knuckles. If Harry's secretary had been in the room, she'd have assumed he was waiting for the judge's verdict after a particularly long and difficult case.

There was the rumble of a black cab's engine in the street, and Harry hurried to the window. In the back of the cab he could see Svetlana, her beautiful face peering from a white fur collar. Even from here, he could see how pale and anxious she looked, her hands clasped tightly in front of her lips as if she was praying.

Maria must have heard the taxi too, because Harry could hear her rushing to open the front door. As soon as Svetlana approached the steps, Maria cried out, 'Oh Miss Wisneski, I not know! If I know anything, I tell you! I not let boys go with him! I never want to let boys go with him on Saturdays!'

When Harry came out into the hall, he found the two women on the doorstep, tears streaming down their faces. Svetlana was bending over to put her arms round the shoulders of the tiny maid. Maria was reaching up both for support and to try and bring comfort.

'Harry . . .' Svetlana began, looking across at him, but she was too upset to say anything else. She reached one arm out for him, and before he knew it Harry found himself in an embrace with both Svetlana and the maid.

'Everything's in place at the airport,' he tried to reassure them. 'If that's where they're flying from, it won't happen.'

But he could hear the dreaded 'if' in that sentence and he knew it would be all that Svetlana and Maria would focus on.

'We just have to wait for news now. Try to stay calm,' he said soothingly.

Maria was the first to pull out of the embrace. She lifted her white apron and patted it against her face before telling them that she would go and make tea.

'I come to the kitchen with you,' Svetlana insisted, 'you not cry on your own.'

Maria immediately burst into tears at this unexpected kindness.

'I make the tea,' Svetlana told her, putting an arm round her shoulder, 'strong, Russian Caravan tea. We must be strong now too, for . . .' but her voice cracked before she could say her children's names.

A tense and anxious hour passed during which Svetlana and Maria ran through the full range of emotions. The boys were lost. The boys were saved. The boys would never be seen again. The boys would come back. Today. Tomorrow. Some time very soon. Just as soon as extradition proceedings began.

Svetlana did know she would fight for them for the rest of her life if she had to, using every penny in her bank account if necessary.

She began to question Harry at length about extradition hearings. How did they work? Did he know any cases? Could he tell her what had happened?

Harry tried to make it sound as simple and hopeful as he could, without blatantly lying.

Finally, Svetlana couldn't stand it any longer.

'I have to phone! Someone! Somewhere!' she screamed at Harry and he handed over his mobile and called the direct line for the inspector at Luton police station.

'Hello, Inspector Thompson speaking,' came the reply.

'This is Svetlana Wisneski, I need to know vat happening with my boys at Luton airport. Petrov and Michael Wisneski. Is there any news from the airport? Have they been there? Have they been seen? Have they been taken out of the country yet?'

'Hello, Mrs Wisneski,' the woman responded, calm and friendly, 'I've got two constables down there right now. I've been told the operation's under way. I'm expecting the briefing shortly.'

'Vat this mean?!' Svetlana demanded in exasperation. *Operation under way? Expecting briefing?* 'You have boys?' she asked, furious with fear, 'Ya? Or no?'

'The constables are on the scene along with a child protection officer and I believe a protection order has been served. As I explained, I am awaiting a full briefing on this,' the inspector tried to explain.

'Speak to her!' Svetlana commanded and passed the phone to Harry.

Only when Svetlana at last saw Harry smile and utter the words, 'That's marvellous, thank you so, so much', did she calm a little.

'Vonderful! Vonderful!' she repeated, over and over. She hugged Harry, kissed him, told him he was 'vonderful' too. Before he could put his arms around her and make up with her properly, she darted out of the room to go and tell Maria.

Never mind, Harry told himself, there was the drive to Luton police station ahead of them. Plenty of time to talk about getting the wedding plans back on track.

His mobile rang again.

When he answered he wasn't surprised to hear the voice of one of the most expensive lawyers in London on the other end of the line.

'Mr Roscoff?'

'Speaking,' he confirmed.

'I don't imagine for one moment that Ms Wisneski will

be pressing charges,' Humphrey Twistleton began. 'She obviously only stands to lose . . .'

'Now, listen here,' Harry broke in, 'charges will most certainly be filed today unless we reach clear agreement that certain restrictive clauses in the divorce settlement are removed immediately. Table an emergency meeting for Monday morning. Then my client can begin to *think* about withdrawing charges.'

As Harry hung up, he couldn't help feeling he'd learned a lot from Svetlana.

Chapter Forty

Amelia's workwear:

Silky grey off-the-shoulder dress (Milly)
Pale blue strappy heels (Topshop)
Multi-coloured beads (Accessorize)
Bluetooth hands-free headset (Nokia)
Total est. cost: £385

'Annie Valentine?'

Annie stared at the page in her A–Z map of London, then looked around for a street sign.

Perry Street! There it was! That's where she was headed. Soho was a blooming labyrinth. Even with a map, she'd been looking for this street for ten minutes now, but a quick glance at her watch told her that it was OK, she was still going to make it for her 10.30 a.m. appointment with Tamsin Hinkley.

She strode briskly along the pavement, paying close attention to the door numbers so that she wouldn't miss 117. The street was one of the narrow ones which lead down towards the grand, open space of Soho Square. On Perry Street the buildings were narrow and old, but smartly renovated, converted into computer, graphics and special FX offices, teeny cafés and boutique hairdressers.

This was a busy, bustling slice of London, every square foot of space pressed into action. Every one of the two or three floors of each building was an expensive office or luxury flat.

89 . . . 93 . . . The closer she got, the more Annie's heart began to thud with fear. She still hadn't spoken to Tamsin in person. When she'd finally found the courage to make the call on Monday morning, a chirpy secretary had informed her that Tamsin was 'interested in meeting' and would 10.30 a.m. on Tuesday be convenient?

Bob had told her that Tamsin was responsible for two cookery series on Channel 4 and Connor had promised to do some research, but possibly due to relaunching himself on the London social scene, he hadn't come back with anything yet.

Number 113 . . . Annie's phone began to ring.

She fished it from her pocket and saw it was Dinah.

'Hi – are you OK?' Annie asked.

'I'm fine. Are you there yet?'

'Nearly,' Annie said and paused for a minute so she could take the call.

'I just wanted to wish you luck,' Dinah told her, 'knock 'em dead and all that, but be cool. If it's not for you, tell 'em to swivel.'

'Swivel?' Annie had to ask. 'Have you been watching too many gangster films? Are you OK?' she asked again.

'Six-week scan today, I'm so nervous I have actually been sick.'

'Maybe it's the other kind of sick. Maybe it's a very good sign.'

'Maybe . . .' Dinah agreed doubtfully. 'What are you wearing?' she asked, wanting to change the subject.

Annie was desperate to tell her, because it was a very, very good outfit. It had taken hours to assemble but it definitely did not look as if it was trying too hard. Getting perfectly dressed was, in a way, all the interview preparation Annie had done. Well, OK, Connor had sat her down for a 'how to talk TV corporate bollocks' chat. That's what he'd called it anyway.

'Talk about building yourself as a brand, they love all that . . .' She couldn't remember much more of his advice.

'It's a great outfit,' she told Dinah, 'coat, dress, great boots, great bag, scarf. I'm rocking. But I have to go now.'

'Loads of luck.'

'You too.'

Just as Annie folded away her phone, a woman stepped from a door several feet ahead of her. Annie only caught a glimpse of her profile before she turned and began to walk briskly in the other direction. But the hair, the high-heeled boots and the tight trousers – it was absolutely, without doubt, Miss Marlise!

Annie began to walk forward again. For several seconds she tried to tell herself that this was just a coincidence, but then she was there. At the door from which Miss Marlise had just emerged. It was number 117.

So this was how Bob had found out about Tamsin Hinkley's interest in a makeover show . . . good grief!

Annie extended a finger with a manicured, palest pink

326

nail and pressed the buzzer.

She let her breath out slowly and set a pleasant, welcoming smile on her face, but her stomach was churning with nerves. Miss Marlise! Bloody Miss Bloody Marlise! She would get the job. She was the famous one. She was the name!

Annie wanted to turn and run away down the street. But she thought of Dinah, and Ed, and Connor. What would they want her to do? If Lana was standing here right now ringing the doorbell, wouldn't Annie tell her to hold her head high and do her best?

What was the worst that could happen here? Nothing. So she wouldn't be any worse off than she was before she rang the doorbell. The best that could happen was that Tamsin would love her and would make her the star of her very own series . . . and even if it was on Channel 1026, it was a start. Another start . . .

Annie widened her smile as a voice crackled over the intercom: 'Can I help you?'

'It's Annie Valentine,' she said. The buzzer sounded and the door lock was released.

She followed the sign pointing up a flight of narrow, rickety stairs and found herself in a small, bright white office where a girl with a short, funky blond haircut was seated on a high stool with castors, at a desk which tilted upwards like an artist's drawing board. A set of white earphones were attached to her head.

'Annie Valentine?' The girl stood up and came forward to shake her hand. 'Hi. I'm Amelia. Tamsin will be through in just one second . . . oh here she is now.' Annie didn't even have time to take another breath and let out her rising anxiety.

'Annie, hi,' a warm, resonant voice announced from the doorway of the office.

Annie turned to face one of the most striking-looking forty-somethings she'd seen in a long time walking towards her with her hand already extended. Tamsin had very long caramel-coloured hair, straight at the top, but curling into soft ringlets which fell down past her elbows. She was fit and athletic looking, so could easily carry off the pink silk miniskirt and black thigh-high boots she was wearing, especially as she'd toned down the body-con look with a loosely draped violet sweater

On the elegant wrist of the elegant hand being offered to her, Annie saw the pink and purple bangle she'd bought last week from Topshop. Suddenly her nerves seemed to lift, her smile broadened and for the first time since she'd seen Miss Marlise, she began to feel hopeful.

'Hi Tamsin, lovely to meet you,' she enthused. 'I have that bangle!'

'Do you? Isn't Topshop great? I buy so many things there.'

'This season's little skirts are perfect . . .' Annie jumped in.

Tamsin nodded: 'I have two already. OK, follow me,' she added, 'we'll go chat. Amelia, if you could hold my calls, that would be fantastic.'

On the short walk along the corridor Annie glanced at the framed photographs, award certificates and publicity pages and felt in awe once again. There was Tamsin being cuddled, kissed and congratulated by a host of famous TV faces. There was a front page story about one of Tamsin's new programmes . . . oh my goodness she was the producer of that?

Tamsin cast a glance round at her.

'Oh, sorry,' she said, 'it's my willy-waving wall, don't let it put you off. I'm not really like that.'

'No . . . erm . . . it's impressive,' Annie managed.

'Nice boots,' Tamsin said as she opened her office door and waved Annie in. 'I don't think they came from Tosho.'

'No,' Annie confirmed.

'Don't tell me,' Tamsin instructed her. 'I'll just want to go there and splurge.'

Tamsin had a very pretty office with a white-painted wooden floor, dusty pink walls, a white sofa, a white desk and two of those high end perspex dining chairs. One wall was filled with a white bookcase crammed with DVDs, labelled boxes and white box files. Such a girlie space, Annie couldn't help thinking. It even smelled perfumed. If Annie had been able to breathe in and out normally, she'd have identified the scent as gardenia and jasmine, but she was feeling another burst of nervousness now.

'Bob was kind enough to send me a showreel of clips from the series you were doing with Donnie Finnigan,' Tamsin began once she'd offered Annie one of the 'ghost' chairs and settled down in the other one herself. 'You were good;' Tamsin went on, 'very good with the women, making them feel at home on screen. You looked as if you were really enjoying yourself.'

'Yes,' Annie agreed.

'I love the girl with the short hair who comes out to you! Tina? That's fantastic TV!' Tamsin said eagerly.

'Do you? Yes!' Annie agreed. 'She sent me a thank-you card and said I'd changed her life.'

329

'But you're not working on the series any more?' Tamsin's head tilted. She fixed cool grey eyes on Annie and clearly awaited further explanation.

Annie racked her mind for Connor's advice here. Something about artistic differences, creative strengths, differing ethoses, or should that be ethes?

'Finn *hated* that Tina makeover: he pulled it. Plus he had no money and I was the presenter who didn't have a proper contract, so that was handy for him.' From what she'd seen of Tamsin so far, Annie decided she was the kind of person who could stand the truth; who would, in fact, appreciate the truth.

'How was the show working out?' Tamsin asked next.

Here was another kicker. If Annie hadn't known Miss Marlise had been sitting in this very same chair being asked this very same question just ten minutes or so ago, she might have said, diplomatically, 'I thought the first episode looked pretty good,' and left it at that.

Instead, she was going to have to say more.

'I don't think it was working at all,' Annie began, 'the whole idea was just . . .' she paused, with remnants of Connor's lecture in her mind. She was supposed to be positive about everything, at all times.

'Stupid?' Tamsin suggested.

'Yes,' Annie agreed with relief, 'we were supposed to turn these women into completely different people in half an hour. Life isn't like that. Not even on TV! And when I did completely transform someone, they couldn't handle it and as for bossy Miss Marlise – you know, from *The Apprentice* – she was always making everyone cry.'

Now that was bitchy and unnecessary, but Annie

hadn't been able to stop herself. She'd suddenly felt a burst of fury at Finn and his ridiculous Wonder Women. She'd quit her very well paid job of nine years for that show. They'd given her the least money and they'd fired her for no reason. And as for Miss Marlise, she had done everything to undermine Annie at every turn and been delighted to see her go . . . Well, now it was Annie's turn to kick her in the pants.

More than anything, Annie suspected it would be fantastic to work with Tamsin and she was damned if she was going to let the conniving Miss Marlise get in there first.

Tamsin looked at her in surprise.

Oh no. She'd blown it. This obviously wasn't what you were supposed to do in TV land. You were supposed to say that everyone was 'wonderful', 'a joy to work with' and insist that you were best friends for ever and couldn't wait to work with them again.

'Bossy Miss Marlise?' Tamsin repeated.

'Sorry, that was a bit rude,' Annie apologized.

'She seems very ambitious, Miss Marlise,' Tamsin said.

'Yes. To put it mildly,' Annie managed.

'Right, well let me tell you what I'm looking for and what I liked about your showreel.'

So Tamsin began her pitch.

She had been offered a half-hour show on Channel 4. *Channel 4!* Annie told herself. Bob had been right. It really was proper TV this time! Tamsin wanted a pithy, speedy, buzzy half-hour.

'A woman's magazine show,' she explained, waving her hands animatedly, 'full of tips, but fun! Not that sort of po-faced, we can improve you kind of crap. This is cheeky, where to get the amazing Topshop bangle and party dress, which face creams are as good at a tenner as the ones at a hundred pounds, what to buy at—'

'The Pound Stores,' Annie cut in, 'and what to steer well clear of.'

'Exactly! Which supermarket shoes—'

'Are decent and which ones are total mingers,' Annie broke in again. Because she understood, she understood totally.

'Yes! There's nothing quite like that on TV right now. Yes, there will be a makeover element, you'll pick someone from the street, take them to a shop and help them create a great new outfit, but not for a date.' Tamsin pulled a face: 'How sexist and patronizing is that? If anyone needs to learn about what to wear on a date—'

'It's the bloody man,' Annie finished her sentence.

'Exactly.'

'This sounds perfect!' Annie was smiling. 'So it's what to wear for your job interview, for meeting your mother-in-law . . .'

'Yes!' Tamsin broke in, 'dressing to meet your cancer surgeon, what to wear . . .'

'In labour?' Annie suggested.

'Brilliant! When I had Myrtel, all I wore for six hours was big pants and a TENS machine, I looked like something from backstage at MTV.' Tamsin spun the small framed photo on her desk in Annie's direction. It was a recent snap, picturing Tamsin with three children as strikingly attractive as her. A teenage daughter with the same long hair, a boy of Owen's age and on her lap a golden-haired baby of about eight months old.

'You've got a baby?' Annie asked in surprise.

332

'Yeah. I got broody at forty-two . . . and lucky,' she added, 'it's great this time round. Mind you, I'm a third-time mum. I wouldn't be a new mum again for all the Baftas in Britain! Was that not worse than being a . . .'

'Teenager?' Annie offered.

'Exactly, thank God for getting older. How old are your children?'

'Sixteen and eleven,' Annie told her.

'Going to have another? It's OK, you can tell me,' Tamsin added, 'pregnant presenters do not fill me with the Fear, unlike some male producers I could mention. In fact Botoxed, permanently youthful presenters fill me with the Fear.'

'I don't think so,' Annie said in answer to the baby question, but then felt compelled to confide, 'My partner's desperate, though. But I don't think I can go through it all again.'

'Which bit? Pregnancy? Birth? Babyhood? Sleeplessness? It's all awful, but worth it.'

Annie thought for a moment. It wasn't any of those things. It was . . . it was hard to understand what her reluctance was . . . even harder to express.

'I've never felt so frightened,' Annie began, thoughtful now, 'as in the weeks after Lana and then Owen were born. They were so tiny, I was so responsible and it wasn't just that . . . going to the registry office and putting their births down on paper, in that official red book. I felt as if I'd set something in motion that I didn't even understand.' She swallowed, but Tamsin gave a tiny nod to indicate that she should carry on. 'Once their births were recorded, with the time and the dates and the details, all I could think about was how one day they'd be in the black book the registrar keeps on her desk too.' Annie's memories of going to register her husband's death briefly swam before her eyes.

'You're so vulnerable when you've just had a baby,' Tamsin agreed, 'I did some crazy things that I wouldn't have dreamed of doing if I wasn't in the post-birth state. It's as if you've been peeled, you're exposed to the world in a way you weren't before.'

'Yeah, but I felt just like that when my husband died . . . I spent two and a half grand on a black Valentino dress for the funeral,' Annie heard herself confessing. And there were only two other people in the world who knew about that. 'I still have no idea what I was thinking. I just had this idea that it had to cost more than my wedding dress and I had to look amazing, just for him.'

'Oh, I'm so sorry, yes . . . I read that bit about you in *Screentalk*. Roddy Valentine.' Tamsin looked straight at her and Annie could see the startled sympathy in her eyes. 'How awful . . .' she added.

'It's OK,' Annie said with a smile, 'life's moved on. We've all made peace with it.'

'Obviously from a telly point of view, we insensitively love it,' Tamsin said softly, 'Annie Valentine, the Nigella of budgeting.'

Annie smiled and thought of Ed.

'I can't tell you how many stupid girls I meet every day who are desperate to be TV presenters,' Tamsin went on, 'but meeting someone who wants to really connect with people – connect with the people on the show and with the viewers – that is rare. And it's a find.'

Annie's nervousness seemed to have been replaced with a dizzy, breathless giddiness.

Channel 4? Nigella? Women's magazine show? Fun, funky? Tamsin was saying all the right things and seemed to have in mind exactly what Annie longed to do, just what she'd hoped the Finn show would be all about.

'How did you and *woohoo* Finn get together?' Tamsin wanted to know.

'Ah well, I did a personal shopping session with his wife at The Store,' Annie replied.

'The haircut?' Tamsin broke in. 'Were you responsible for the haircut?'

Annie flashed back to the day Kelly-Anne had come into her personal shopping suite with her long black, lacquered locks and Connor had appeared and interfered and got his blazer buttons all tangled up in the hair, and Svetlana had cut the locks right off. Kelly-Anne had just about died of shock.

Annie looked at Tamsin's mane and wondered if being responsible for a long hair massacre was a good thing. 'Not exactly,' she fudged, 'but I thought it did look good.'

'It's fantastic, I'd get one too but . . .' she flicked her long hair over her shoulder, 'maybe not just quite yet.'

'Your hair's beautiful,' Annie complimented her, 'but I think I'm going to go short.' She tugged at her ponytail.

'Great!' Tamsin enthused, 'but do it on the show, please. We'll start you off with the ponytail and then third episode in or so, we'll hand you over to Nicky Clarke or someone like that for the chop.'

'Wow!' Annie could feel her cheeks glowing. Was she going to get this job? Was Tamsin really going to make her dreams come true?

'OK, running away with myself here,' Tamsin said.

'We have to talk about money. Women must talk about money. Even though we're conditioned not to. Are you the biggest earner in your family?'

Annie nodded. Well, it had been true in the past.

'Yeah, me too. It's so common, but bloody men in this industry always assume you've got some wealthy husband propping everything up at home and your wages are a lovely "extra" for everybody. Anyway, it's going to be about eight thousand pounds an episode.'

Before Annie could gasp with astonishment, Tamsin went on: 'We'll talk again in detail about the whole idea and make sure we're both really happy to go forward together. It will be a six-episode contract, then if it does well, we'll renegotiate and all make more money. If it really takes off, then you'll be loaded. For as long as it lasts . . .' came the warning. 'Who's your agent?'

'Well . . . I think Ralph Frampton-Dwight, or maybe someone in his office is possibly going to handle the contract side of things for me . . .' Annie stumbled. This is what Connor had told her to say, but as she hadn't spoken to Ralph or any of his underlings, she was hesitant to nominate them.

Tamsin pulled a face. 'Well, that's very generous of you. But he didn't set this deal up. Anyway, I think Ralph's a twit,' she said bluntly. 'If you're not signed up with him, will you please phone this woman?' she opened up the orange Filofax on her desk and extracted a business card. 'I'm not saying this because I'll get you cheaper this way. In fact Jenny will probably cost me extra. But she's the business. Anyway, we girls have to stick together.' Tamsin shot her a wink.

'Now, before I wind this up – ' she looked up at the

clock on the wall behind Annie's head – 'because I have to get to a lunch on the other side of town for more willy-waving,' she confided, 'I'm sure a very stylish girl like you will want to know about the presenter's clothing allowance. Not that we're frivolous,' Tamsin winked, 'not that we let clothes rule our lives or anything. It's just an interest.'

'Yeah,' Annie agreed, 'men have football and we have fashion.'

Chapter Forty-one

Fern goes to the doctor's:

Camel skirt suit (Paul Costello)
Patent bag (Annie's Chloé cast-off)
Silk scarf (Accessorize)
Comfy loafers (Ecco)

'I'm fine! I'm fine!'

'So you're going to be on Channel 4? Presenting your own show? And it starts filming in two months' time?' Dinah, sitting in the passenger's seat of the Jeep, asked her sister once again. She just wanted to be sure she'd got the details right.

'I know,' Annie confirmed, more than a little amazed herself, 'it's going to be called *How Not to Shop.*'

'I still can't believe it,' Dinah laughed.

'Neither can I, but my . . . a-agent,' Annie stumbled over the word because it was just so new and so exotic.

'Your agent?' Dinah had to chip in, 'get you!'

'I know, my agent and Tamsin are talking. I've not

signed yet because they're still agreeing details and . . . the fee. But we're due to sign later this week.'

'Oh. My. God. You're going to be rich and famous!'

'I think it's more like I'll be earning a good wage and people might start giving me those "do I know you?" looks on the street. Let's not get carried away.'

'It's absolutely amazing . . . but I always knew something amazing was going to happen to you.'

'Did you?' Annie asked, surprised.

'Yeah,' Dinah assured her, 'you're just such a trier. What's that phrase? "God loves a trier".'

'And you are going to have another baby,' Annie told her with complete confidence, 'didn't I tell you that long before Billie arrived, and I was right, wasn't I?'

'I'm much older now,' Dinah pointed out.

'Oh forget age. Age is just a number,' Annie said, trying to sound convincing.

'Yeah right, I'll remind you of that on your birthday, Botox babe.'

'Tamsin says I'm to stop fudging my age and injecting my face. She thinks it's sexist and she's very down on sexist behaviour, especially by women,' Annie said.

'That's very interesting . . .' Dinah said thoughtfully, 'I still can't believe you froze your face.'

'Yeah and no-one, not one person, noticed!'

It was 9.45 a.m., the worst of the weekday rush hour traffic was over and they were heading out of London and into the Essex countryside to accompany their mother to an important doctor's appointment.

Fern was only 64 but she was going to be assessed for early senile dementia. Annie and Dinah were chatting so lightly and jokily because they both felt filled with anxiety about what lay ahead this morning.

Annie had already imagined their mother's file being stamped with the irreversible word 'dementia' from which there would only be decline. When the sisters had gone with Fern to visit her doctor the last time, he had offered hope that perhaps the medication for the high blood pressure was making her confused. But even when the dosage had been reduced, she was still saying and doing things that suggested all was not well. There had even been a phone call from a neighbour who had wanted to know if there was any reason why Fern should be gardening at 11.30 at night with an anglepoise lamp rigged up to an extension cable.

Annie switched on the windscreen wipers to deal with the light drizzle on the glass. When the rubber blades smeared across her vision, she squirted a jet of cleaning fluid over the windscreen.

'Oh good grief!' she turned to Dinah with a pained expression on her face as the vapours drifted into the car, 'what's wrong with that stuff? It stinks! Maybe I didn't dilute it properly.'

'What?' Dinah wondered.

'The window cleaning fluid. It's making the whole car stink,' Annie complained.

'Well, open a window if you like, but I can hardly smell a thing,' Dinah told her.

The test took some time.

Fern sat nervously in her chair opposite Dr Bill, her small patent handbag in her lap. Annie and Dinah sat in the chairs pushed to the side of the room, looking on even more nervously than their mother.

'Just relax everybody, it really isn't so serious.' The doctor attempted to jolly them along. 'We do this test several times because everyone can have an off day, so really, take a deep breath and let's try not to worry.'

Annie looked at her mother, all neat as a pin today, her hair brushed and sprayed down into its bulky brownish-grey bob. A silk scarf was tied at her neck and she'd put on her most comfortable lace-ups. Fern had been a podiatrist before she retired, so she didn't hold with any kind of foot-deforming heel.

Dr Bill began slowly, but soon the questions were rattling along and Fern was doing fine. She was cheered by how well it was going and how much she was remembering.

'When did the Second World War end?' the doctor asked.

'1945,' Fern answered quickly and confidently.

'Who's the current prime minister?'

'Gordon Brown.'

After current affairs, came more personal questions: 'What's your full name? What are your children called?'

It was all going so smoothly that Annie risked a glance at Dinah and a confident smile.

'Nearly there,' the doctor said reassuringly. 'Now, can you tell me what day it is today?'

'Erm . . .' All of a sudden, Fern looked totally unsure of herself, 'it's erm . . . oh for goodness sake . . .' she looked round at her daughters, but they weren't allowed to help, 'Tues . . . Friday . . . no, Wednesday,' she decided finally.

It was Monday morning.

'OK and finally,' the doctor began with a smile, 'what's my name?'

Again Fern looked completely thrown.

Annie and Dinah stared at her with surprise. How had she managed to forget the doctor's name? She loved him! Ever since they'd arrived at her house to take her to the surgery, she'd been talking about him, convinced that if anyone could help her, it was Dr Bill.

Fern looked deeply uncomfortable. 'I can't believe I've forgotten this!' she exclaimed. 'Apart from anything else, it's so rude of me.'

'OK, well not to worry,' Dr Bill said and made a few notes on the papers in front of him.

In the conversation that followed, Dr Bill offered advice and what he hoped was reassurance. He spoke about the possible need for a home help and wondered how often Fern's daughters could phone and visit to check up on her. Then there was the matter of more appointments to track the 'progress' of the 'dementia'.

Annie could feel nervous sweat pricking in her armpits. This was her mum. Fern wasn't even 65 yet. She was in good health, Annie had assumed she would have at least another twenty years ahead of her. The thought that she might spend those years in a confused and foggy place, unable to recognize the people around her, her family and friends, was just terrible. She could see the shock registering on her mother's face as well.

'So it's bad news then, doctor?' Fern asked at the end of his talk.

'No, no. Please don't think of it like that,' he said with a smile. 'Your short-term memory is a little weak. It might stay just as it is for years, but we need to keep an eye on you, because if there's a sudden decline, we need to know and be able to get help or treatment for you. The treatment in this area is improving all the time. I don't want you to worry about a thing.'

Annie and Dinah smiled at him, pretending to be upbeat, but really both of them could feel their hearts sinking. *Mum will have to come and live with us* – both daughters were thinking. *Well, that wouldn't be so bad, would it? Much better than worrying if she'd made it to bed or if she was spending the night gardening in her pyjamas.*

With these thoughts still uppermost in their minds, the two sisters were quiet on the drive home in the afternoon.

Fern had shooed them away after a quick lunch: 'I'm fine! I'm fine! Get back to your busy lives and stop worrying about me. I'm not the first person to get old, you know, these things happen. Look at Aunty Hilda,' she'd reminded them, 'still living on her own, soldiering on with her bionic hip and she's nearly ninety! Losing your marbles is probably the best way to go,' she'd joked darkly, 'otherwise you just get older and older and more depressed about what lies ahead. I've looked after some very depressed old feet in my time and it doesn't look like fun.'

'I'm going to have to stop for petrol,' Annie announced as a service station was flagged up ahead.

'Great, I can buy peanuts,' said Dinah.

'Who buys *peanuts* in a crisis?' Annie scoffed. 'I'm going in there for a bar of Galaxy the length of my arm and I don't want to hear any objections.'

But as she stepped out of the Jeep and onto the garage forecourt, Annie reeled with dizziness and had to grab at the car door for support.

'What on earth's the matter?' Dinah asked urgently.

'I don't know, I feel dizzy . . . it's the smell out here, eurgh!' she said, then retched slightly.

'Get back in the car,' Dinah ordered her. 'Maybe you've got a virus or something, there's some kind of ear infection that makes you dizzy whenever you stand up.'

'Maybe,' Annie replied and slowly lowered herself back onto the seat.

'I'll fill up,' Dinah volunteered, opening the passenger's door and stepping out.

But as she did so, with horror, Annie registered the dark stain on her sister's skirt.

'Dinah!' she exclaimed and reached her hand out to stop her sister, 'Dinah!' she repeated, hating that she was going to have to deliver this bad news, 'you're bleeding. You have to phone your doctor. Now.'

Chapter Forty-two

Billie in school uniform:

Blue sweatshirt (school uniform)
Grey skirt (school uniform)
Black patent shoes (Start-rite)
Pink head-girl badge (gift shop)
Hair grips (Hello Kitty)
Total est. cost: £45

'No, I'll be fine.'

'So you're going to wait for us right here, noodle,' Dinah instructed her six-year-old daughter. 'This nice lady is going to keep an eye on you,' she motioned to the waiting area's receptionist, 'and there are plenty of toys to play with and we won't be long. OK?'

Billie, tearing her eyes from the bedraggled Barbie she'd found in the stack of toy boxes, nodded solemnly.

'You don't need the loo or anything, do you, because I could just take you if you needed to go?'

'No,' Billie assured her anxious mum, 'I'll be fine.'

From the garage, with Dinah making urgent calls on her mobile, they'd driven straight to Billie's school. Billie had to be picked up before Dinah could go to the clinic because Bryan was in Ireland on a work trip and both of the Mummy-friends who might have stepped in to collect Billie were at work today.

Then there were more discussions to be had as Annie point blank refused to stay outside and insisted, in fierce whispers, that of course Billie would be fine in the waiting room and of course Dinah should have someone's hand to hold.

Aside from being anxious about all the practical arrangements, Dinah had kept calm about the bleeding. They had bought sanitary towels at the garage and Dinah had swivelled her skirt round so that she could hide the bloodstain with her handbag.

Apart from once turning to Annie and exclaiming, 'God it's hard, isn't it? Having children . . . well for me anyway,' she'd said nothing else about the situation. She was being incredibly brave, Annie couldn't help thinking as they followed the nurse into the scanning room.

This was private health care for you. No waiting for appointments, no coming back in the morning . . . Dinah had spoken to her doctor in person and been told to come in just as soon as she could.

But Annie knew the private IFV came at a cost to Dinah and Bryan. There would be no summer holiday this year, a frugal Christmas and all sorts of other savings to pay for another go at baby roulette.

The sisters were ushered into a small room with an examination couch, an ultrasound machine and an adjoining bathroom.

'OK, up you go, try and make yourself comfortable,' the nurse said with a reassuring smile.

As the lights were dimmed so that the image could be seen better on the screen, Dinah reached her hand out for Annie's.

Annie took hold of it in both of hers and felt how cool Dinah was to the touch. She instinctively began to rub a little, to impart some warmth. 'I'm sorry I'm not Bryan,' she told her sister.

'Oh, it's OK,' Dinah said in a whisper, 'you're the next best.'

Annie fought back the lump in her throat.

The gel went onto Dinah's stomach and the nurse began to move the scanner back and forth, causing grainy black and white images to appear on the screen. Both sisters had had enough scans in their past to be able to interpret the pictures almost immediately. There was a small white embryo sac visible on the screen in front of them and what was immediately obvious to Dinah and Annie was that it was still. It hung before them and did not pulse with the mysterious and magical heartbeat of life.

There was nothing but tense silence in the room until the nurse said gently, 'This is the embryo here and, I'm sorry, but at eight weeks we would expect to see a heartbeat.'

Dinah just nodded.

Annie couldn't say anything either; instead she squeezed at Dinah's hand.

'OK, I'm going to leave you to get sorted out,' the nurse said, 'then we'll go to the consultation room and talk about what's going to happen next.'

As the nurse went out of the door, she turned the light

back on. Now Annie could see Dinah's face properly. She looked incredibly calm.

'I'm so sorry,' Annie told her, not letting go of her hand.

'I didn't get my hopes up,' Dinah replied, 'we went through this four times before we got Billie.'

'I know . . . but wouldn't it have been wonderful if it had just worked first time this time?' Annie couldn't stop herself from asking. 'You were owed a really lucky break.'

'Billie was our lucky break,' Dinah reminded her gently.

To Annie, the room suddenly felt very small and far too warm. She stood up and felt beads of sweat spring up on her upper lip.

'I think I need a splash of cold water,' she told Dinah, 'I'll just go to the loo.'

She hurried to the adjoining bathroom, shut the door and ran the cold tap over her hands, then patted water onto her face. But it wasn't any use, there was a hard ball of nausea in her stomach. Turning to the toilet, to her astonishment, she threw up violently in the bowl.

'What the bloody hell is wrong with me?' she whispered weakly to herself afterwards. With a wet paper towel she wiped her hands and face and tried to pull herself together again, so she could go out and be with Dinah.

Now that she'd been sick, she felt better and mentally she began to go over all the things she'd eaten in the last twenty-four hours that might have caused a problem. Nothing obvious came to mind, but she would ask Ed what he thought. Maybe it was just worry . . . about her mother and now about Dinah.

Never mind. Never mind feeling sick, the important

348

thing was to get back to Dinah's side. Opening the bath-room door slowly, hoping Dinah hadn't heard anything of what had just gone on in there, Annie stepped back out into the scanning room.

Dinah had moved from the couch onto a chair and sat with her head tucked into her chest. Despite her earlier calm, a low, desperate wailing was breaking out from the very heart of her now.

'Oh Dinah,' Annie cried, hurrying over to her side, 'Dinah,' she soothed putting an arm tightly around her. 'It's going to be fine. I promise you, it is going to be OK. They got you pregnant, that's the main thing. It means it can happen for you.'

The wail only stopped for the second or two it took Dinah to draw breath, then it carried on again. So low and so raw, it made Annie want to cry too.

Four times! they were thinking. Dinah had gone through four miscarriages before Billie was born. Annie shuddered to think of her sister going through the same ordeal again.

'Come and stay with us tonight,' she said, rubbing Dinah's back, 'we'll distract Billie and I don't want you to be on your own.'

'Have a baby, Annie,' Dinah blurted out, 'please have a baby for all of us.'

The house seemed unusually quiet when Annie, Dinah and Billie arrived back. There was no barking from Dave, no Ed and no Owen. Just one of Ed's cats curled up in a ball on the sofa.

'Dog walk maybe,' was Annie's guess. 'Lana!' she shouted up the stairwell. 'She might know where

349

everyone is. Come in,' she urged her guests, 'take off your coats, dump your bags, get into the kitchen. We'll make some supper, but maybe have a few biscuits first, Billie. Let me just go and tell Lana we're all here.'

Annie set off up the stairs, calling out her daughter's name. By the time she made it up to the attic level, she could see light coming out from under the door. Maybe Lana had her iPod on and couldn't hear Annie calling her. She rapped on the door and when there was still no reply, she opened it gingerly: 'Lana? It's Mum, are you OK?'

There on the bed, was Lana, curled into a ball, iPod in her ears, face wet with tears, sobbing as if she'd just heard the most terrible news ever.

'Lana?'

Annie rushed forwards.

Chapter Forty-three

Lana's revision wear:

Big grey cardigan (Ed's)
T-shirt (can't remember)
Jeans (Gap)
Slippers (Christmas)
Pencil in hair (school stationery cupboard)
Total est. cost: £70

'Don't talk to me . . .'

'So what is going on in there?' Connor pointed at the open sitting-room door as he followed Annie into the kitchen.

He'd spotted Lana at a big table set out in the middle of the room. She had her head bent over and was writing so furiously, a heap of school books in front of her, she hadn't even noticed Connor at first. But then had hissed: 'Don't talk to me, Mum will get mad.'

Annie scowled and when she'd closed the kitchen door she hissed, 'She is in so much trouble! She's not going back to school until the exams. I've signed her off sick.'

Annie ushered Connor to a seat.

'She is studying in the sitting room with old-fashioned books, pens and papers. She's banned from going anywhere near a computer. All those hours and hours and hours I thought she was studying away upstairs . . . all the things I thought she was busy researching on the internet. All the essays I thought she was writing. Ha!'

'And? What was she really doing?' Connor was desperate to know. He handed Annie the bottle of wine he'd brought with him, 'Open,' he instructed, 'So . . . running an internet porn empire? Surely at least a dating agency?'

'Shut up!' Annie told him off, 'she was running some whole little set-up on eBay! Selling all her friends' old clothes for them, buying cheap make-up and flogging it at school, trading CDs and DVDs – who knows what else. Pointless! All that time wasted! Then she realizes how little work she's done and has a total meltdown,' Annie ranted.

'On eBay . . . hmmm . . .' Connor couldn't resist smiling, 'remind you of anyone we know? Anyone at all? Anyone who also had a business selling Chinese shoes and second-hand bags and unwanted glad rags? She's following in her trader mum's footsteps!'

'Shut up,' Annie repeated, 'those days are all behind me now.'

'Yes, yes, we'll come on to that,' Connor said, accepting the glass of wine Annie had poured out for him, 'but how has Lana been sorted?'

'No computer,' Annie told him. 'No internet, no eBay, no pocket money and she has to cram. Good, old-fashioned

352

cramming. Nine hours a day with meal breaks for the next fortnight, and I'm supervising.'

'Meal breaks? That's very thoughtful of you,' Connor teased.

'Well, it's too bad. This is how I passed my exams.'

'This is how I failed mine. I couldn't do it. Who can be bothered to have their heads stuck inside boring old books for *nine* hours a day.'

'Shhh!' Annie warned him, 'I don't want her to hear you. You are a totally bad influence.'

She looked at the glass of wine in front of her. It was one of those heavy, treacly, Australian reds that Connor was so fond of. Just thinking about taking a sip was making Annie's stomach feel acidic. She poured herself a glass of water without saying anything to Connor.

'OK, now tell me all about the fabulous you, you, you,' Connor said. He sat back in his kitchen chair. 'So you've snubbed Rafie boy . . .'

'But I have Jenny Belmont!' Annie announced, all wide-eyed with enthusiasm, 'Tamsin told me to try her and she's brilliant. Honestly, she is so tough and so cool and so sussed, I love her. Connor . . .' Annie's voice dropped almost to a whisper, 'I think this really could be it. Jenny and Tamsin are talking about the Big Time. One day in the not so distant future, people really might know about Trinny and Susannah, Gok Wan and . . . me!'

'You better believe it, baby,' was Connor's delighted response. 'So have you signed the big C?'

'This morning. That's why we're celebrating.'

'Is this a party?' he looked round the kitchen sceptically.

'It will be soon,' Annie assured him. 'Ed's picking Owen

353

up from orchestra, which is why I'm meant to start the cooking . . .' she remembered, and headed to the fridge for the onions, 'Dinah and Bryan will be here in about an hour with Billie.'

'How are they doing?' Connor asked.

'OK-ish,' Annie told him carefully, setting up the chopping board and peeling an onion, 'they're having a big think about whether they really want to go through this all again. They have Billie, maybe Billie is going to be enough . . . we'll see. What about you?' she asked next. 'Are you and Hector still thinking about . . .'

'Might get a dog instead,' Connor told her with a wink as Dave padded into the kitchen. 'So how much are you getting then? It better not be more than me.'

'Ha-ha,' Annie responded, but then looked up from her onions with a grin and squealed, 'Jenny's upped it to ten thousand per episode!'

Connor whistled. 'Not bad!'

'And they're making six this year!' Annie added gleefully. 'And if there's another series . . .'

'You and Jenny hold out and haggle hard,' Connor finished her sentence, 'Congratulations. I am very, very proud of you. You are going to be terrific. I just know it.'

'Thank you,' she said.

'Now I must make dinner!' she reminded herself, after a long, happy moment of smiling delightedly at Connor. She took the packets of chicken legs from the fridge. She was to fry them briefly with the onions then put them in a big casserole dish with chopped tomatoes. By then Ed was supposed to be home to finish the dish off – dabble with herbs and stock and all that stuff she couldn't be bothered with.

354

As she took the pale pink legs out of the packet and heaped them up on the chopping board, she suddenly felt a lurch of sickness, the unexplained, low-level sickness which had been bothering her for some time now. There had been no vomiting since the scanning room but now she wasn't so sure.

She turned back to the table and groped for her glass of water.

'Whoa, what's the matter?' Connor asked with concern.

'Some kind of bug,' Annie mumbled. She gulped thankfully at the cool water. Phew, that was better. She ran a hand over her forehead . . . she was going to be fine.

Dave padded over to her and without any warning lay down right on top of her feet.

'Oh for goodness sake!' she exclaimed, bending over to move him out of the way, which was a mistake: right then, with a violent hiccup, she puked the whole glass of water and the watery remains of her lunch right out onto the floor, splattering Dave in the process.

'Annie!' Connor was at her side, catching hold of her arms and holding her up just as she thought she was going to crumple, 'I know you don't like the dog, but . . .

'Sit tight,' he instructed, moving her onto a chair. 'Dave!' he called sharply to the dog which was shooting across the kitchen floor bound for the sitting room where he was no doubt intending to roll on a sofa and dry off his wet, vomit-soaked fur. Amazingly, Dave spun round and looked at Connor. 'Sit!' Connor commanded.

Dave looked at Connor, then turned and looked at the kitchen door, as if weighing the pros and cons of staying or running. 'Biscuit?' Connor wheedled. At this Dave stuck out his pink tongue and lowered his back haunches into the sitting position. 'Good boy,' Connor praised him as he caught hold of his collar and made sure he couldn't get away.

'Kitchen roll's over there,' Annie said in a muffled voice because she was holding her hands over her face.

Once the dog had been rubbed dry and turfed out into the garden to air, and the floor wiped, Connor turned his attention to Annie.

'If you're not feeling well, you need to go to bed,' he instructed. 'Ed and I can handle dinner, or maybe I should call Dinah and we'll do the celebrating another night. Hey,' he put a hand on her shoulder, 'are you OK?'

Annie, her head still in her hands, shook her head.

'How long has this been going on for?'

There were tears in her voice. 'About two weeks.'

'Two weeks? That's ridiculous! You have to get to the doctor,' Connor urged, 'I can phone up right now, book you an out-of-hours appointment.'

Annie just shook her head, but then wished she hadn't because it was making her feel dizzy.

'Why not?' Connor asked.

'Because . . .' she began, tears squeezing from the corners of her eyes, 'because I know what the doctor will say.'

'What?' Connor wondered what on earth she was talking about. Then his eye fell on the big glass of wine standing on the table in front of Annie. Now there was something he'd never seen before. Annie leaving a glass of wine untouched.

Oh.

Oh!

'Annie, are you . . . um . . . ?' he paused, wondering how to phrase this question.

'Yes,' came the response, again muffled, because her arms were laid across the table now, with her face pressed into them.

'Yes, what?' Connor was suddenly unsure about what he'd asked. Or what she'd thought he'd asked.

'You know,' came the stubborn response.

'Annie,' he took a breath, 'are you up the duff?'

He thought that the bobbing of her ponytail probably meant yes. He had enough sense not to say anything else just yet. Clearly, as far as Annie was concerned, this was not exactly great news. Well, for a start, she had just signed a contract to present six episodes of a brand new TV show.

'What will Dinah say?' came the tearful question from under the arms, 'Poor, poor Dinah. And Owen and Lana? What will they think? And what about Tamsin and the show? Will she really not mind, the way she said she wouldn't? And my mum, she might have to come and live with us, you know.'

'What does Ed think?' Connor asked.

'Ed?' Annie squawked. 'This is all Ed's fault!'

Which was kind of stating the obvious, Connor thought, but maybe he wouldn't point that out right now.

'We only had sex once without my diaphragm – no twice – no, maybe three times. But that is nothing! Three times in one month! I'm in my late thirties, you know,' Annie blurted out, an outraged note in her voice.

'Well . . . what does Ed think? Connor asked again gently.

'He doesn't know,' came the confession.

'Connor?' Annie finally raised her red face from the table and fixed her tearful eyes on her friend's. 'Please don't tell him. I don't know anything yet . . . no,' she corrected herself, 'I do know that I don't want to do this.'

She thought immediately of a dream she'd had the night before of being pulled underwater, deep, deep down, past the point of no return because tied to her ankle was a baby made of lead.

There was a heavy silence in the kitchen before Connor answered, 'I won't tell him Annie, but you have to. There's no option here. You have to tell him.'

It was ten the next morning when Annie went upstairs to her bedroom and took out the card she'd tucked into the back pocket of her wallet. For several long moments, she stared at it, not sure whether to go ahead or not. What if Ed found out about this? And what would Tamsin think? But still, she dialled the number on her mobile phone.

The briskly efficient secretary picked up and answered cheerfully, 'Hello, this is the Yarwood Clinic, how can I help you?'

'Hello . . . yes . . .' Annie began uncertainly, 'erm . . . I'm hoping you'll be able to give me some advice. Yes, because, well . . . I seem to be pregnant . . .'

Chapter Forty-four

Bridesmaid Elena:

Cappuccino-coloured strapless column dress
(Oscar de la Renta)
Nude suede shoes (Manolo)
Jewels (borrowed from Mama)
Total est. cost: £22,800

'Pretty good, ha?'

'It's time to go in if we want to get a good seat!' Annie glanced at her watch and chivvied Ed, Lana and Owen – all decked out in wedding finery – towards the entrance of the cool grey chapel.

'You look great! Have I told you how fantastic you look?' Ed slipped his arm round Annie's waist and smiled at her.

'I know!' she winked at him.

'Look at your boobs!' he couldn't help himself, 'they are magnificent.'

Glancing down at the cleavage straining her dress at

the seams, she felt a rush of guilt. This wasn't just about a new bra . . .

She was in a tried and trusted wedding outfit because it had been a frantically busy morning and there had been no time for experimentation in the twenty-five-minute slot she'd left herself for getting ready. But she did look good in the teal empire-line silk, lace matador jacket on top. Fantastic hat, fantastic green heels, and the vibrant glow which followed the morning she'd had. She'd been so busy, she'd been so needed and she'd been so excellent at her job.

Since seven this morning, Annie had been at Svetlana's Mayfair home, styling and perfecting the outfits of everyone in the bridal party.

Ever since Svetlana had been reconciled with Harry, the Svetlana and Annie friendship had been back on track. Perhaps not so surprisingly, Svetlana had also begun to make friends with the daughter she'd not had for all these years.

'She have hard time in Ukraine. Is hard there. And she very clever girl. Very clever, very beautiful with big ambition. She just like her mama,' Svetlana had told Annie, proudly. As if Annie hadn't already spotted the family resemblance.

Annie had personally laced Svetlana into her elaborate couture wedding gown, transforming her into a picture of grown-up bridal perfection. Then she'd helped Elena into her tall, cappuccino-coloured column dress, noting all the physical as well as mental features that the mother and daughter shared.

'Pretty good, ha?' Elena had asked when she'd seen herself in the mirror.

Petrov and Michael wore matching pageboy outfits which might have looked ridiculous on most other little boys, but these two were dark-haired and serious enough to carry off cream knickerbockers, pale tights and buckled shoes.

Many other female friends of Svetlana's had arrived for Annie's expert finishing touches, and final decisions on which hat, which shoes and where to pin the flower corsage.

'How does Igor feel about your wedding?' Annie had asked her friend.

'It does not matter,' Svetlana had told her with a smile, 'the divorce deal now vatertight. No changes permissible or I press abduction charges, plus, he lose so much money with bad investments. Plus his new girlfriend run off with the tennis teacher . . .' At this Svetlana had given a great roar of laughter which had threatened to unravel the magnificent up-do perched on top of her beautiful head. 'Silly, silly Igor,' she'd added with an almost soft and nostalgic look.

'I think you're going to be much, much happier with Harry.'

Svetlana had turned from gazing critically at her reflection in the mirror to look at Annie directly.

'Yes,' she answered, 'I think you right, I'm going to be happy with Harry. Not super-rich any more, but happy. Something new for me, ha? My good friend Annah,' and at this she'd wrapped Annie in an unexpected embrace.

Now, Annie ushered her family into the Victorian splendour of the chapel. Set on an emerald lawn, it was surrounded by a peaceful quadrangle of equally Gothic style buildings, where the lavish reception was to be held afterwards.

She couldn't help taking long, curious looks around the church at the assembled crowd. There was such an intriguing variety of people. On Harry's side it was very posh and old-school English: lots of morning suits, feathered hats and sensible frocks with matching coats.

On the bride's side, things were much more unusual. Heavy-set, shaven-headed men sported gangsterish pinstripes and blatant gold jewellery. The girls – each one more gorgeous and more beautifully dressed than the next – were tall, thin, blonde, elegant and Eastern European, draped in Gucci, Valentino and all the luxuries money could buy.

Harry was already in the front pew, tugging nervously at his cuffs. Annie wondered if he still had any doubts . . . if he was worrying whether this much called off wedding was actually going to happen now or not.

Then came the stir at the back of the chapel, which suggested the bridal party had arrived. Annie looked behind her and saw that Svetlana's boys and Elena were entering the vestibule.

Then the phone in her handbag began to buzz. She'd turned it to vibrate just in case there was some last-minute dress smoothing to be done.

'Annah!' Svetlana's voice hissed at the other end of the line, 'I'm in the church!'

Annie looked back at the vestibule again, but couldn't see any sign of the bride.

'Uri just courier me huge diamond ring. Huge!' she repeated, 'he say I should be his vife, not Harry's. Now I'm not so sure. Uri very rich man. He vant to invest all my money in his fund, make me multimillionaire. With Harry . . . ve just comfortable.'

'WHAT?!' Annie exclaimed prompting curious looks from the people around her. Then in a fierce whisper she told Svetlana, 'but Harry's going to make you happy! It's time to forget about the whole multimillionaire thing, it's over, babes. It's credit-crunched. If you ask me, Uri sounds like a fraud! And anyway, bling is finished. Real is in. The noughties are over and it's time to grow up.' With a final attempt at persuasion, she burst out, 'You can't even flog off gold snakeskin bags on eBay! No-one is bidding!'

Annie looked helplessly at Ed, who was sitting beside her looking confused.

'Svetlana?' he guessed, 'Crisis?'

'Just a moment,' Annie said into the phone.

'No! I have no moment,' Svetlana replied, but Annie had already removed the phone from her ear.

'It's the kind of crisis only Svetlana could have,' Annie whispered urgently to Ed: 'another supposed millionaire has just proposed to her. Now, she doesn't know what to do.'

An amused look settled on Ed's face and he shook his head slightly. 'Could it get more colourful?' he asked with an eyebrow raised. 'Pass me the phone.'

Now Annie's eyebrows shot up: 'The phone? *You* want to talk to her? Are you sure . . . I don't know if that's such a good idea.'

Guest's heads were turning, and Harry was beginning to turn a shade of pink which Annie knew would only get deeper, the longer this delay went on. The organist was still trilling away with the treadmill music and had obviously not yet been given the signal to begin the Wedding March.

'Hello Svetlana, this is Ed, Annie's Ed,' he began, 'there was something I wanted to say . . .'

'Ed?' Svetlana asked with surprise. This was the man who'd brought Elena back. The man who'd spoken so sternly to her on her own doorstep!

'If you marry for money,' Ed began, 'there will always be someone richer. If you marry for beauty, there will always be someone more beautiful, but if you marry for love . . .'

He looked up and his eyes found Annie's as he went on in his calm, teacher's voice, 'you'll never find anyone else who can compare.'

With that he folded up the phone and took hold of Annie's hand.

'What did she say?' Annie was desperate to know.

'I dunno,' Ed gave a little shrug, 'she's a big girl. It's up to her.' He still didn't take his eyes from her. 'I love you,' he whispered, 'let's get married.'

Suddenly, Annie wrapped both arms around him very tightly and whispered her confession in tiny words, right against his ear. 'Ed, you got me pregnant.'

To her astonishment, he turned his head and whispered straight back, 'I know.'

'You know?' She pulled away: 'what do you mean you know?'

Aware the rows of guests both behind and in front were now really taking an interest, Ed leaned to whisper in her ear as quietly as he could, 'Annie, you look pregnant, you act pregnant . . . how could I not know?'

'Why didn't you say?' she asked, but realized as the

words left her lips that he was just waiting for her to say . . . he was giving her time. 'Thank you,' she said, moving in to him again.

With a tight hold around her waist, whispering to keep this as private as he possibly could, he had to ask the question now. He would burst if he kept it in for any longer.

'I answered your phone and someone wanted to confirm an appointment with . . .' he faltered for a moment, 'a clinic?'

'Oh no, no! It's not what you think, oh Ed,' she held him tightly, 'I had Botox and I'm allowed to get a tiny top-up as soon as I pass week twelve.'

Whatever Ed might have said in response to this was lost as the great booming sound of a 24-pipe organ filled the chapel and reverberated off the walls. Mendelssohn's Wedding March: it was a classic. Svetlana had used it for all her ceremonies.

As she came magnificently down the aisle, she managed to spot Annie and Ed in the sea of guests and she actually paused for a moment, just long enough to mouth a few words at them.

Because Annie had tears in her eyes, she couldn't quite be sure, but she thought Svetlana said, 'Love, ha? OK, ve try love.'

Chapter Forty-five

Annie's early pregnancy look:

Red ruffled wrap dress (Picchu maternity)
Black support tights (Elbeo)
Black suede boots with mid-heels (Hobbs)
Total est. cost: £220

'Oh my God.'

This was strange. This was definitely a little bit too strange, Annie couldn't help thinking as she watched the nurse slide the ultrasound scanner over her lower stomach. Just four weeks ago, Annie had been holding Dinah's hand in a scanning room. Now, here she was on the couch.

Ed had a tight grip on her left hand and from the corner of her eye, she saw the images begin to flicker to life on the screen. She closed her eyes and took a deep breath. For a moment, thinking of Dinah, she wasn't sure if she wanted to look.

She still wasn't totally sure if this was where she wanted to be. Part of her wished that it was Dinah lying here in her place on the couch with a twelve-week-old pregnancy happily in progress inside her.

But it was her. For whatever reason, this had happened to her instead.

Ed was so frantic with excitement, with the strange newness. He was so bursting with gratitude, how could she not go along with it?

Somehow, she was sure, he would carry her through. So she would do this for him. And when the baby was born, she knew she was going to fall in love, all over again. Because that's what mothers do.

She had once loved Lana so intensely that she worried she'd never feel quite the same about her second baby. But oh, the rush of instant love she'd felt for that bright red baby Owen, with his sticky fuzz of black hair. Some magical cell division had happened in her heart and suddenly there was more than enough love for two children.

So she was staying calm, accepting the pregnancy, letting this embryo grow, take over and move into all the areas of her life that she knew it would soon inhabit.

'There we go,' the nurse's voice broke into her thoughts, 'a nice steady heartbeat over here . . . and . . .'

Annie looked and saw the pulsing white shape, already more defined than the blob she'd seen on Dinah's screen. Over and over, the rhythm of life already beating strongly.

'Amazing,' Ed murmured, his eyes fixed to the screen.

The scanner slid over her stomach and they saw the shape again.

'OK, let's just move over here again,' the nurse said, pushing the scanner towards Annie's hip bone and pressing in firmly. 'I thought I just saw . . .' she began, looking closely at the screen.

Annie felt a flicker of anxiety. Was something wrong? All of a sudden, her uncertainty about this baby seemed to evaporate. Now she only wanted to know that everything was OK. Annie looked at the screen again.

This time there was no mistaking what the nurse had seen . . . This mysterious process had been set in motion weeks and weeks ago and now she was going to have to face it. Try to get used to it. Make sense of it.

'Is that . . . ? Ed began in astonishment.

The nurse nodded her head and smiled at them.

'Is that *really* . . . ? Ed still couldn't finish a sentence, he was so surprised.

Annie just stared. Stared and stared at the screen. She didn't move, she didn't even blink as she tried to let this register in her scrambled mind.

'Are there any twins in the family?' the nurse asked, still not wanting to confirm what they could both see so plainly before them.

Annie felt as if she couldn't keep up. Within seconds, it seemed, she was supposed to pass from not being sure about a baby, to being anxious about the baby, to being the prospective mother of *two* babies. Now she was unsure all over again, yet all she wanted was for the nurse to say that yes there were two babies and both looked absolutely fine.

'Are there two?' Annie found her voice.

'Yes, there are two embryos here,' the nurse confirmed.

'And they look OK?'

'Everything looks fine. I'm just going to take some photos and take a few measurements.'

As she pressed buttons and examined the stills on the screen, Ed turned to Annie.

She didn't think she'd ever seen him look so happy. He seemed to be keeping his smile tight and small so that the happiness couldn't burst out of him.

'Two babies,' he whispered, gripping her hand, 'you are so clever!'

Annie's eyes turned back to the screen. Every other anxiety could wait, she just needed to know from the nurse that everything was OK with the . . . two . . . babies. Two. Babies.

'Everything looks normal,' the nurse said finally, 'I think we'll book you in for a sixteen-week scan, just to take another look because of your age, but at this stage, there doesn't seem to be anything to worry about. Congratulations.'

Ed moved Annie's hand up to his face and kissed her fingers.

'What about Owen and Lana?' Annie asked him.

'They're going to love it! They get a baby each!'

'What about Dinah? And Connor?' she asked, almost tearful now.

'You are surrounded by people who will love these babies,' he said calmly.

'What about Dave?' she asked, with a small sob.

'Connor has offered to adopt Dave,' Ed replied.

'Oh no,' Annie shook her head, 'Owen will never forgive us. He loves that dog!'

'Well, then I suppose Dave will have to get used to the babies.'

'Two teenagers . . . a dog . . . a live-in mother . . . and twin babies.'

'And a TV career,' Ed reminded her. 'Congratulations,' he repeated, 'clever, clever girl. Two babies,' he repeated, sounding a little bewildered. Then he uttered the phrase she really had been trying to avoid all day. 'Happy birthday, Annie!'

She was going to have twins and she'd found out today, on her dreaded birthday.

'Oh my God,' she began and then, as if it was a mantra, found she couldn't stop repeating it.

Epilogue

Tamsin Hinkley opened the studio door as quietly as she could and tiptoed into the darkness. In her hand was the printout, still warm from the printer, which revealed *How Not to Shop*'s latest audience figures.

The last episode had been watched by 1.4 million viewers and was taking a major share of the Wednesday night audience. Channel 4 executives were delighted and there was no question that there would be a second series. Tamsin hoped she might even convince them to sign up for another two.

Good producer that she was, she'd been unable to wait to share the news with Annie and the film crew. Plus, she liked to come down and catch the tail end of the recordings whenever she could find the time. She prided herself on being totally hands on, and perhaps even interfered just a little too much with the shooting and the editing. But that was the only way to stay on top of your output and make sure it was the best.

In front of her, studio lights blazed onto the vibrant black and white set, but keeping herself tucked away in the darkness at the back of the studio, she made for the chair she'd spotted and noiselessly sat down.

Annie was talking solo, direct to the camera.

She was talking with such lively interest and conviction that, along with everyone else on set, Tamsin couldn't help but be drawn in.

Holding up several items of jewellery, Annie insisted: 'Look at this colour, it's an absolutely gorgeous blue and it's only two ninety-nine! No-one shouldn't have one! It's a crime not to buy this cuff. But you don't have to go to the high street, we found this beautiful brooch in a second-hand shop for just fifty pence.'

This was why lorry-loads of clothes, accessories and beauty products were now rolling up at the office every day. The industry was paying attention to the show. If Annie mentioned something, sales rocketed. Chains were demanding to know in advance what she was going to pick out, to ensure they had enough on the shelves.

It was almost frightening.

Annie had already been offered several advertising contracts but interestingly, she'd so far turned them all down, claiming that if she was paid to promote something, no-one would believe in her independence any more.

'That's what people like about me,' Annie had understood about her appeal straight away, 'I'm their honest, best friend on the TV. I'm on their side.'

The studio lights were twinkling on Annie's glossy lipstick and her baby blonde, softly shaggy, short hair. Just as Tamsin had predicted, last week's programme, which had featured Annie's much-trailed haircut, had pulled in the biggest viewing figures to date. This new TV star was six months pregnant, but that seemed to make her predominantly female audience love her even more. Viewers were already sending in babygros, bootees and name suggestions.

Annie liked to joke on air about her enormous twin baby tummy: 'Darlins, I can't even wipe my own bum. The situation is out of control, I should have police tape, or an alarm, you know like lorries: caution, this vehicle is reversing. Caution: this vehicle may tread on your toes and demolish your furniture.' Both pregnancy and stardom suited Annie. She had blossomed before everyone's eyes.

'So, that's all we have time for this evening. I know! I'm sorry too! It's flown by,' Annie was telling the camera with great sincerity, 'but it's OK, if you're missing me, you can log on and check out the website. There's the blog, there are tons of fashion tips and pointers . . . honestly, girls, it will get you through a whole seven days without me!

'Next time,' she continued, 'we'll talk about what you can and can't give to charity shops. Owen Valentine, you'd better be listening! And we are going to have my very, very special guest Svetlana Roscoff here to give you her Girls' Guide to Sensible Investing. Yes, just because your fund manager has a helicopter doesn't mean your stocks will fly . . . apparently!' She tilted her face and gave the camera a wink.

Look at her! Tamsin couldn't help smiling. She was blonde and beautiful and absolutely in the prime of life, buoyed up with the confidence of so many challenges met, so much potential fulfilled, and vibrantly looking forward to the future ahead. This very interesting life with all its highs and lows still to come. In the bright fuchsia velvet dress she'd chosen for today's session ('it's a pregnancy craving: I have fuchsia fever, babes') there was only one word for her. Resplendent.

Half an hour of Annie made you feel better. Made you feel glad to be alive. Made you think, *I will give a damn about the shoes I put on and the lipstick I choose,* because as Annie constantly warned, 'something amazing might happen today, so you'd better be dressed for it!'

Bob Barrett held the camera in position on Annie's smile for just one moment longer, then the director stood up, checked her monitor, held up her hand and announced,

'Cut!'

THE END

Acknowledgements

Time for the big luvvy-huggy thank you speech moment . . .

I know just how lucky I am to have the support and advice of my fantastic agent, Darley Anderson, and his terrifically talented team: Becky, Camilla, Ella, Kasia, Maddie, Rosanna and Zoe, take a bow, and thank you so much for all your hard work on my behalf.

Huge thanks to my editor Sarah Turner, a champion for Annie Valentine, who also makes story nip-tucking almost painless! I hope Sarah and copy gurus Judith Welsh and Beth Humphries appreciate how much I admire and rely on their story polishing skills. (Diana Beaumont, fear not, your great advice is still very much in my mind when I write.)

I have a genius team behind Annie V at Transworld: the covers, the sales and marketing, the website, the PR – all utterly brilliant! Thank you hugely for all your support, I am truly grateful. (Tragically!) some fashion research has to be done for the books (thank you Vogue and Net-A-Porter), also I can't get enough of Lisa Armstrong's fashion columns in *The Times* and Brenda Kinsel's utterly Californian advice books and website.

To my vital home support system: very, very special thanks to T, S and C, who know just how much I love them. Love also to all the fabulous friends and family who make sure I am dragged from my desk regularly. Huge hugs to the writer buddies. OK, yes, I understand. You can drag me in my ballgown off the stage now . . .

DIP INTO CARMEN REID'S
FABULOUS FIRST NOVEL

THREE IN A BED

HERE'S THE FIRST CHAPTER . . .

Chapter One

It was 6.29 a.m. The digital alarm clock beside the bed was about to go off. Just as it started up with its nasty little beeping, the bedside phone began to ring too.

Bella leaned over to click off the alarm and answer the phone.

'Hello?'

She heard a distant 'Hello!' far from the other end of a crackling line, followed by singing.

'Happy birthday to you, happy birthday to you . . .'

'*Don!*' she shouted and heard it echo back at her.

'Hello Bella, wake up, I love you, I want phone sex now.'

'I love you too,' she said laughing.

'What? It's a terrible line.'

'I love you too!' she shouted. 'When are you allowed to come home?'

'Ah ha . . . well I'm phoning you from Grozny airport. By the time you get back from work, I'll be there.'

'Yeah?! I can't believe it! That's bloody brilliant!'

'My job here is done,' he said in mock superhero voice. 'Seriously, it's been a nightmare and it's getting dangerous now, so they're pulling me out. Plus I told them it was

379

your birthday and I had to get home, or else a fate worse than a rebel gunman awaited.'

'Are you OK?' she asked.

'I'm very tired, it's been three weeks from hell. Oh bugger, hon, I have to go now, I'll see you tonight and I am so looking forward to it.'

'Me too. Take care.'

'Missing you already,' he joked, then the line went dead.

She was smiling hard, was going to be smiling all day long, she thought, as she got out of bed and started on Operation Bella. The difference between Bella and other women whose looks were somewhere between moderate to good on the scale was that she tried harder. In fact, 'tries hard' was a description that had peppered her report cards since she was tiny.

At the very start of her career, she'd spent a long summer on assignment in New York and it was there that she had found her spiritual sisters, the immaculate New York women who jogged, gym-ed, power manicured and treated sex as just another way to business network. Her eyes had been opened and she always joked that she'd checked all her insecurities in at JFK airport and never bothered to check them out again. This wasn't exactly true, the insecurities were still there, she'd just learned to hide them well.

She pulled on her running clothes and trainers now, because Monday to Friday, she jogged for twenty-five minutes every morning with NO EXCEPTIONS. She loathed almost every second, but it was the only way to shake off any remaining booze from the night before, stay on the slim side of curvaceous and guarantee that she got some exercise crammed into her day.

After the run, she showered, shaved, dried off and moisturized. Then, with her hair wrapped up in a big white towel, she stood in front of the bathroom mirror.

She stared hard at her face. Twenty-eight years old today. Pulling a smile, she looked at the tiny crinkles radiating out from her eyes and the very first hint of bagginess on her eyelids. It was obviously all downhill from here.

She sponged a generous squeeze of foundation from collarbone to hairline and loaded up a powder brush to dredge over her face. She thanked God every morning for make-up. Then she shook her hair out of the towel and blasted it dry, before bundling it up into the loose chignon which she thought made her look older and more serious for work.

Back in the bedroom, she pulled open her underwear drawer and rifled through it. Don was coming home! He'd been away so long, he'd find her a turn-on in greying pants and a jogging bra, but hell he deserved a treat. She took out her newest pink and black underwired lace bra and matching G-string, then opened the wardrobe. She slipped into a crisp shirt and hold-up stockings then buttoned on a black suit with tightly fitted jacket and a narrow skirt which fell to the knee.

She checked herself over in the long bedroom mirror and approved. Of course, since New York, nothing about Bella's workwear was left to chance. She'd taken the hair and make-up lessons, been colour-consulted and image madeover. Her perfectly appropriate outfit, about to be perfectly accessorized, was supposed to scream 'woman headed for the top'.

She fished about in her jewellery drawer for small chic

earrings and the tiny platinum pendant Don had given her, fiddled to put them on then grabbed high-heeled leather pumps from the shoe rack and hurried into the kitchen.

Two oranges were blitzed in the small electric squeezer. She put the glass of juice and a pot of yoghurt onto the tiny marble-topped table in the kitchen, then went to the front door of the flat to bring in the newspapers. She sat down and studied the *Financial Times* carefully as she had breakfast, then flicked through Don's tabloid until she found his latest report, and read every word.

At 7.45 it was time to go, so she collected raincoat, briefcase, laptop and keys and headed out to work. As her left hand pushed shut the heavy wooden and glass front door of the mansion block, her eyes fell on the thin platinum band, sparkling with tiny diamonds on her fourth finger, and she couldn't help smiling. God! Marriage was still such a novelty.

Just one birthday ago, she'd woken up in yet another unfamiliar 'loft-style' bedroom, with makeup caked deep into her pores and the roots of a truly monumental hangover taking hold in her skull. Her nostrils had burned suspiciously and she'd been repulsed to see a fleshy, snoring equities trader, whose name she couldn't recall, fast asleep beside her.

She had retrieved her underwear, pulled on a dress stiff with sweat from the night before, picked up her bag and shoes and crept out of the flat. Three heart-attack-inducing espressos later in an Italian café on the corner, she'd come to the realization that it was time to put as much effort into her personal life as she'd put into her career. And about a month after that, all psyched up to stay away from men and sex and one-night stands until she'd got her head together, she'd bumped smack bang straight into The One. After a thirteen-week romance, the longest she'd had for years, they got hitched. Fear of commitment, ha!

She had crossed that line, made the jump, taken the plunge. Well, actually, Don had seen straight through the tough City-girl-shagger defence to the person underneath, the one who hadn't dared to fall in love since Big Romance Number One had gone all horribly wrong. Don had taken her hand and convinced her this was the real thing. He'd urged her to make the leap with him and when he'd slid the slim ring onto her finger, she'd felt a surprising solemnity. She'd felt terrified of it too. But there was so much love just radiating out of him, she had committed, signed on the line, sealed the deal.

She turned away from the front door into the lukewarm May sunshine. In the distance she could hear the gentle roar of traffic: another day in the capital was already under way. She unlocked the door of her low, cream-coloured classic Mercedes 280/SL soft-top, threw her coat and bags onto the passenger seat and climbed in, smudging her right calf with oil on the door frame.

'Damn,' she said out loud, then leaned over to the tiny glove compartment and popped the button, causing half a dozen packets of black hold-ups to slide out onto the floor. She held her leg out of the car door, whipped off the smudged stocking, rolled on a new one then, tossing the spoiled one into the back, she fired up the engine and set off for the office.

At 8.25 a.m., juggling coat, briefcase and laptop with the packet of twenty Marlboro Lights and large bottle of Evian from the shop round the corner, Bella arrived at Prentice and Partners, one of the City's smallest, but sharpest, firms of management consultants.

'Morning, Kitty,' she said as she walked in.

'Hi, Bella.' Kitty looked up from her desk in the large reception area.

'Is Susan in?'

'Of course,'

'Girls first. Are the boys in to play today?'

'Yup, Hector's due in any time and – ' Kitty checked her screen – 'Chris will be in for the afternoon meeting but he might be earlier.'

'OK. I'll just go through my diary and put the coffee on then I'll be ready for you,' Bella said with a smile.

She went into her little office and settled in, hanging up her coat and filling the coffee machine before she took out her laptop, checked through her e-mails and clicked open her schedule.

MAY 8

Tuesday

* Happy Birthday – just in case you've forgotten. Old Bag.

* Put in follow-up call to Petersham's office to answer/reassure on queries/nerves/cold feet.

* Prepare for meet with Merris.

* BOLLOCK Hector.

* Chris and Susan meet 2 pm – Petersham's and Merris details.

* Get pregnant?

What???! She re-read that last bit. God, why had she put that in there? It was on her mind, but that didn't mean it had to be in her diary. She hit delete. It was off the screen, but not out of her head. She knew she wanted a baby: really, really wanted one. Something that had begun as a vague interest several months ago had now grown into a fully-fledged desire. It was weird.

Why did she want one so much? She'd tried to analyse her reasons endlessly: maybe because her own parents had made such a mess of things and she wanted to do better, maybe because she worried a lot about what the future held for her and Don without kids. He was thirteen years older than her and she couldn't help imagining herself growing ancient, all alone with deranged, incontinent cats for company instead of children and grandchildren.

Bella also worried that it might take a very long time to have a baby. Her own mother had given birth to her at 29, then spent eight years enduring miscarriage after miscarriage before finally giving up hope of a second child. She remembered the little cradle and the boxes of baby clothes, all carefully labelled, in the upstairs loft room and how sometimes as a small girl she would find her mother up there, weeping furiously.

But Bella's biggest problem right now was that when she married Don seven months ago, he didn't want children – said he was too old, too independent, too set in his ways – and she'd agreed 'no kids' with him. But now she knew she hadn't meant it, hadn't really thought it through.

The idea was beginning to form in her mind that if a pregnancy were to happen 'accidentally', Don would of course be shocked, but she was sure he would come round to it. Anyway, her mother's experience had left

Bella with the belief that conception was a million miles away from actually having a baby. So, would it be so bad to get pregnant and see what happened?

There was a knock on the door and Bella was interrupted from her thoughts by Kitty.

Bella poured them both coffee and, as usual, teased Kitty about her latest office outfit, in between briefing her for the day.

Kitty, small, spiky red-haired and generously curved, was crammed into silver hipster trousers, a tiny purple T-shirt and a silver padded waistcoat. Platform-soled trainers with flashing lights completed the look.

'When is the mother ship due to land?' Bella asked with raised eyebrows.

Kitty looked at her blankly.

'You do not speak the language of earthlings?' Bella added.

'Shut up, Bella.' A grin split Kitty's face. 'Just because you like looking like an airline hostess, you twentieth-century throwback.' She ignored Bella's exaggerated gasps of horror and added: 'Silver is so *now*.'

'But are you dressed for success, Kitty? I think not,' Bella answered.

'You are such a corporate clone! Power dressing does not equal power,' Kitty snapped back. 'Where are you headed Bella? Straight for the glass ceiling.'

'Oh God,' Bella groaned. 'It is way too early for a radical feminist rant, *please*.' She cracked open her pack of cigarettes and lit up, closing her eyes with pleasure for the first drag of the day.

As it headed towards 9 a.m., Bella shooed Kitty out of her office and started on her calls. She was in a gap between two big contracts and restless to drum up new business. After she'd made the first call, the phone on her desk buzzed.

'Hello. Bella Browning,' she answered.

'Bella, it's Kitty, I've got a very angry caller for you. Do you want me to say you're busy?'

'No, they'll just ring back. I might as well face the music. Who is it?'

'Tom Proctor at AMP.'

'OK, give me just thirty secs then put him through.'

She closed her eyes and took a deep breath, willing herself to stay calm as she slowly put her finger over the flashing extension button to connect him.

'Hello Tom, how are you?' she said.

'Don't call me Tom, you bitch,' he shot back at her. 'You know perfectly well how I am. I'm fucking sacked. Sacked after seventeen years of working my arse off for this company only to have you come in here for eight weeks and pull the entire thing apart.'

This was the worst part of her job, the part that racked her with guilt. Tom was 53 with three kids in full-time education and a very expensive lifestyle to maintain. He did not have a great track record and was going to find it hard to get another job as good as the one she'd had him fired from.

'Have you any idea how much damage you've done here?' he raged. 'My colleagues, men with families and young children to look after, are packing their things into bin liners and leaving in tears.'

She swallowed hard, really not wanting to hear this.

'Just who do you think you are?' he screamed down the phone. 'I'll tell you – you're some cocky little graduate with a bollocks business degree whose only idea of cost-efficiency is sacking people and you probably only got your ludicrously overpaid position by sucking every cock in the city.'

Christ, that was way too much.

She answered coolly: 'Mr Proctor, I have a starred first in Economics from the London School of Economics, where I was top of my MA year. I spent four years working for the biggest consultants in the country before I joined Prentice and Partners. And Susan Prentice is a woman, so I certainly didn't need to suck her cock.'

Undeterred, he shouted back: 'We didn't fucking well need you lot of bloodsuckers in here. You've destroyed us. I'm going to make sure you never get another contract in the City again, you smug cunt.'

She couldn't believe she was hearing this. She stood up at her desk and her voice began to rise: 'If you were even half as good at your job as I am at mine, AMP would never have needed to call consultants in. Without my help that firm would have gone to the wall in two years max and everyone would have been laid off without the kind of generous redundancy payout you've received.'

Just for good measure she added: 'How dare you phone up to insult me? You kept telling me one day you'd move to the country and restore antique furniture, so why don't you sod off and do it?'

Damn, she instantly regretted that, but *cunt*! Cunt? How dare he?

At that moment, she glanced over to the door and saw Chris grinning at her and giving her the thumbs up. That was all she needed, Susan's number two listening in on this. Quickly she added: 'Mr Proctor, I'm very busy, you'll have to excuse me. Thank you for your call.'

She heard an astonished gasp, but put the phone down before he could say anything else.

'Phew, you tell them Bella,' Chris grinned at her. 'Just sod off to the country and restore antique furniture. I must remember that the next time someone calls me a cocksucker.'

'Chris, you heartless shit,' she said, relieved he was treating this lightly. 'I'm really embarrassed you heard that. Are you going to fire me now?' She asked with a little arch of her eyebrows.

'No,' he paused for effect, 'but I may have to get very firm with you, Ms Browning.' Then he added: 'Just try not to make too many enemies for life. Anyway, how was your weekend?'

'Good,' she replied. 'Don wasn't around so I did girlie things, you know, drank ten pints of lager, did three lines of coke, shagged a complete stranger in the toilets.'

He gave her an intrigued look.

'I'm joking, Chris.' Then the penny dropped. 'Oh!! You actually did that. Well you're a lucky boy, but at your age you have to think of your health, you know.'

'I'm only 34!'

'Mmm, but you have the added stress of being a senior partner,' she teased.

'A job you would probably kill me to get. Which is why I never send you out for sandwiches.'

'I'd never go!'

'Bella—' he reached for the door handle. 'It's been a pleasure as always, but we have lots of work to put together before this afternoon's meeting. Merris, Petersham, any queries, I'm next door, watching you through my spyhole.'

'See you later,' she said and he was gone, leaving her with a slightly too flirtatious smile on her face.

There was another knock on the door.

'Come in.' She knew it was Hector. Hector, the fresh out of university new boy who seemed never to tire of telling them about his heroic Highland pedigree. And that was just one of his many annoying qualities.

'You wanted to see me?' He poked a tousled head round the door.

'Yes,' she said.

He came in, looking arrogantly crumpled, as usual. He still bought into that boho tweedy suit, pashmina, I'm not going to conform or try too hard kind of look. He was a very brilliant guy: why else would he be working here? But he really was going to have to get it together.

He sat down on the chair opposite her desk.

'So, what is this piece of crap?' She tossed a thick, spiral-bound report onto the desk.

'Ah, I was wondering if a few inaccuracies might have crept in.'

'A few inaccuracies!!' She picked the report up again. 'Let me just open it at random . . . 32 per cent of £586,000? That is . . .' she barely paused, '£187,520. Yet unbelievably, you've got £28,500 down here. Totally, utterly out of the ball park.'

'Well, I suppose I'm not a mathematical genius like you, Bella,' he had the nerve to reply.

'What does that have to do with it? Why don't you buy yourself a sodding calculator?' she snapped. 'In fact go and buy a proper sodding suit while you're at it. It's about time you sharpened up.'

He looked up at her rather surprised, but she continued: 'You've been here for four months now and you don't seem to have learned anything. This report is about a major company, you were working out their profits, their losses, their expenses. Your mistakes could have cost hundreds of thousands of pounds, could have cost people their jobs. This is not a game, Hector, this is not a theoretical problem you discuss in a tutorial. Christ. It's all very well having potential if you're 10. There comes a time when you have to prove it.'

There was a long pause.

Hector wondered why Bella was holding the report right in front of her face and shaking slightly.

'Are you OK?' he asked.

He was surprised to hear a snort of laughter emerge from behind the pages.

'Oh God,' she put the report down on the table. 'You really deserve a strip torn off you, but I can't do this with a straight face.'

'Er . . . I'm sorry. Do you want me to do it again?' he asked.

'No, I've already sorted it. Will you just try and concentrate hard on the next thing you get from me?'

'Yeah, sorry.'

When Bella was on her own in her office again, she laughed at herself. 'Potential is all very well if you're 10' – she suspected she'd read that on a billboard somewhere.

She lit up another cigarette, took a deep drag and massaged her temples. This was turning into one hell of a day.

There was another knock and Kitty came in with an enormous bouquet of flowers.

'You thought we'd all forgotten, didn't you?'

'Forgotten what?' Bella asked.

'Your birthday, you idiot.'

'Oh God . . . thanks.' She went over to take the flowers, reading the note signed by all four of them.

'Thanks,' she said again, looking round her room and wondering where to put them.

'There's a vase at reception, shall I keep them out there till the end of play?' Kitty asked.

'Yeah, you're a star, Kitty. I bet everyone else would have forgotten.'

Nine hours later, after hundreds of calls, calculations and a gruelling meeting with Chris and Susan, Bella was finally tapping in her last memo and tidying her desk for the day. It was 7.15 p.m. when Chris appeared at the door to ask if she was coming for a drink over the road.

She declined because, at last, it was time to get home to Don. The traffic was infuriatingly slow all the way back across town, so she redid her make-up, sprayed on perfume and flipped through her CDs before giving up in disgust and enduring the radio. She couldn't wait to see Don again. Three whole weeks: it was the longest they'd ever been apart.

When she finally made it back to the block she swung open the front door, ran to the lift and impatiently jabbed on the button over and over again until the doors pinged open.

In the flat everything was still and for a heart-crushing moment she thought Don hadn't been able to make it back. Then she saw his bag and his battered oilskin coat in the hall. Quietly she walked through to the bedroom. The curtains were closed and Don was lying in bed fast asleep.

She was so happy to see him she felt her stomach flip. She moved closer to take a long look at him. His face was brown against the white pillow, but tired and drawn. His thick steely-grey hair was rumpled and still wet from the shower he must have taken. His glasses were on the bedside table and he looked deliriously clean and freshly shaven.

She was sure he was naked under the duvet and she couldn't help herself, she longed to feel his body against hers. She put down her bags and coat, took off her shoes and undressed, then slid into the bed beside him, curling her naked body up against her husband's warm, naked back. Wrapping her arms round him, she put her nose to the nape of his neck, breathing in the smell of the sandal-wood soap she'd been using too because she missed him so much: 'Hello Don,' she whispered.

He stirred a little and answered with a 'hmm' so she moved closer. She ran her hands down his warm, fuzzy chest and stomach until she reached his sleeping cock.

A longer, throatier 'mmmm' came from him now as she held his cock in her hands.

'Hello,' she said. 'Aren't you going to wake up and say hi?'

'Oh yes,' he answered, surfacing from sleep now. He rolled round to face her and kissed her on the lips.

Then he smiled, creasing the skin round his eyes and looking at her with so much love and longing she felt a lump in her throat.

'Hon, I'm so glad to be back, you have no idea,' he said in a voice still thick with sleep.

'I've missed you too.' She kissed him back, winding her legs round his, pulling him so close their pubic hair brushed together and she could feel his cock stir against her as he moved his hands down from her waist to her buttocks.

'I still can't believe I'm married to you . . .' he said, in between small hungry kisses, 'and you're naked!'

He kissed her properly now, squeezing her into him and parting her lips with his tongue. She tasted his hot, minty mouth.

As he pulled her up against his hard erection, she wound her fingers into his hair and placed teasing kisses on his neck and round his ear.

'I have missed you so much,' she whispered.

'I've missed you too, especially your breasts,' he said with a smile, gently stroking and licking at her nipples and the soft white skin around them.

They felt and touched and kissed and licked until she rolled over and pulled him on top of her. Watching her face, he pushed inside and slowly moved in and out all the way along the length of his penis.

'You tease,' she murmured, holding her hands on his hips and moving him faster until they were gasping together in a fast and frantic fuck.

When they fell apart, they were slightly sweaty and breathing heavily.

'God you're good,' she said with a smile. 'I still can't believe you're my husband. I mean husbands are meant to wear slippers and wash the car, not give a girl multiple orgasms.'

'All in a day's work!' he answered.

'Hey!' she sat up, loving the fact that he couldn't take his eyes off her breasts. 'You better not have forgotten it's my birthday today.'

'I phoned you first thing, remember.'

'Yeah, you phoned, but where is my large, expensive present?'

'Bella, I've just come back from a war zone, there wasn't much to buy . . . give me a chance.'

She didn't know what to say. Maybe she was being unfair. What could Chechen Duty Free have had to offer?

'But . . .' he leaned over to fish about under the bed, 'I did get you this.' He handed her a big, khaki green furry hat with earflaps. 'Genuine Russian Army issue,' he said with a mischievous smile.

'Oh! Thanks.' She tried to look appreciative, then added, 'My first ever birthday present from you. Next year, remind me to get a different husband.'

'And –' he reached under the bed – 'I can't tell you how hard I had to barter on the black market to get this.' He turned round and presented her with a glossy pink box tied with ribbon.

'Happy birthday.'

She untied the ribbon and lifted the lid. Inside was an extravagant set of lilac and black silk underwear. A lace-trimmed bra and G-string, a camisole top and French knickers. She picked the bra up and looked at the label – correct size. She was impressed. Black market ha, ha.

'Is this a present for me or for you?' she asked, but before he could answer, said: 'Thank you very much. You're very sweet,' and kissed him on the mouth.

'Oh good, I'm glad you like them, because I *really* like

them. Now stay there,' he said, getting out of bed and putting his dressing gown on.

'I'm opening the wine, ordering Chinese, and I'm going to try and persuade you to spend the whole evening in bed with me.'

'Well, OK then, since I now have the outfit for it,' she said, lifting the camisole out of the box.

They ate the food in bed and made each other laugh, Bella talking about work and Don telling war stories.

'God, I do wonder if I'm getting a bit old for it, though,' he said, serious for a moment.

'Will you stop it?' she told him. 'You are not old, you're 41, you're very fit,' she leaned over, letting her dressing gown fall open and kissing him on the forehead.

'In many ways, you're like a man half your age,' she teased.

He pulled her across so she was sitting in his lap. 'Thank you for your vote of confidence darling,' he kissed her on the mouth.

'Yeuuck, black bean sauce.' She screwed up her face in mock horror.

'I'm going to kiss you somewhere else then.' He dropped her down onto her back and began to kiss her breasts and her stomach. Then he moved down to her pubic hair and blew on it gently. She drew one foot up, bending her knee . . . as she thought about how she would not be taking her pill tonight, because she wanted to get pregnant.

Read the novel – available from Corgi Books

The Personal Shopper

Carmen Reid

There's just one accessory Annie Valentine can't find . . .
the perfect man!

As a personal shopper in a swanky London fashion emporium,
Annie can re-style and re-invent her clients from head to toe.
In fact, this super-skilled dresser can be relied on to solve
everyone's problems . . . except her own.

Although she's busy being a single mum to stroppy teen Lana
and painfully shy Owen, there's a gap in Annie's wardrobe, sorry,
life, for a new man. But finding the perfect partner is turning
out to be so much trickier than finding the perfect pair of shoes.

Can she source a genuine classic? A lifelong investment?
Will she end up with someone from the sale rail, who'll have
to be returned? Or maybe, just maybe, there'll be someone
new in this season who could be the one . . .

'More heart-warming than an expensive round of retail therapy'
Daily Mail

A fabulous read. A sexy read.
A Carmen Reid

Order your copy now at **www.rbooks.co.uk**

9780552154819

Late Night Shopping

Carmen Reid

A little retail therapy goes a long way . . .

There are some things the man in your life doesn't need to know:
- The price of your delicious new handbag (. . . and shoes)
- The fact that you've reached the limit on all your credit cards
- You're planning to start a retail business of your own

(and there are 500 imported accessories in the spare room)

Then there are a few things you may have to mention:
- You've booked a 'surprise!' romantic holiday to Italy

(but your relatives are coming too)
- You seem to have put the house up for sale
- A gorgeous Italian has fallen madly in love with you

Could this be one challenge too many for Annie and Ed?

A fabulous read. A sexy read.
A Carmen Reid

And for teenage readers:

Secrets at St Jude's

New Girl

By Carmen Reid

Ohmigod! Gina's mum has finally flipped and is sending her to Scotland to some crusty old *boarding school* called St Jude's – just because Gina spent all her money on clothes and got a few bad grades! It's so *unfair!*

Now the Californian mall-rat has to swap her sophisticated life of pool parties and well-groomed boys for . . . hockey *in the rain*, school dinners and stuffy housemistresses. And what's with her three kooky dorm-buddies . . . could they ever be her *friends?* And just how does a St Jude's girl get out to meet the gorgeous guys invited to the school's summer ball?

978 0 552 55706 1

www.rbooks.co.uk

Take the fabulous

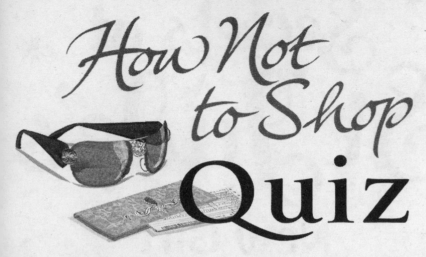

How Not to Shop

Quiz

Are you a Prada Princess, Topshop Tiger
or an Oxfam Opportunist?

Find out when you take the hilariously
funny **How Not to Shop** quiz at

www.carmenreid.com

Then reward yourself with
a recession-busting voucher for

35% OFF

other books by Carmen Reid!